Also by Amulya Malladi

Serving Crazy with Curry

The Mango Season

A Breath of Fresh Air

Song of the
Cuckoo Bird

Song of the Cuckoo Bird

A NOVEL

AMULYA MALLADI

BALLANTINE BOOKS

NEW YORK

Song of the Cuckoo Bird is a work of fiction. Names, characters, places, and incidents are the products of the author's imagination or are used fictitiously. Any resemblance to actual events, locales, or persons, living or dead, is entirely coincidental.

A Ballantine Books Trade Paperback Original

Copyright © 2006 by Amulya Malladi
Reading group guide copyright © 2006 by Random House, Inc.

Published in the United States by Ballantine Books, an imprint of The Random House Publishing Group, a division of Random House, Inc., New York.

LIBRARY OF CONGRESS CATALOGING-IN-PUBLICATION DATA
Malladi, Amulya.
Song of the cuckoo bird : a novel / Amulya Malladi.
p.   cm.
ISBN 0-345-48315-4
1. India—Fiction. 2. Ashrams—Fiction. 3. Spiritual life—Fiction.
4. Women—India—Fiction. I. Title.
PS3613.A45S66   2006
813'.6—dc22   2005048099

Printed in the United States of America

www.thereaderscircle.com

9 8 7 6 5 4 3 2 1

Book design by Nicola Ferguson

For Isaiah and Tobias

ACKNOWLEDGMENTS AND AUTHOR'S NOTE

The first time I thought about writing this story I was fifteen years old and not skilled enough to write it or old enough to imagine its broad scope. It has taken me a decade and a half to finally write this story and I needed the help of many, many people to get here.

Thanks are due to:

My husband, Søren, who read all the drafts, listened to all the versions, plots, and subplots, and never let me give up, even during the darkest of times, which there were plenty of.

My mother, Lakshmi Malladi, who told me the stories that inspired this one; without her this book would never have been written.

My editor at Ballantine Books, Allison Dickens, who gave my book (and me) a chance and loved it as much as I do; without her faith in me I would be completely lost. I owe her more than I will ever be able to repay.

My agent and strongest supporter, Matt Bialer, who stood by me through some difficult decisions; I write better because of how well he does his job.

Special thanks to Arjun Karavadi for support via telephone; to Stanley Hainsworth and Jody Pryor for support via e-mail; and to my sons, Tobias and Isaiah, for support via laughter—I wouldn't have remained sane without them.

I would like to add that even though this story presents several historical facts about India, it is still just a story and mostly a product of my imagination. I have made an attempt not to distort the facts, but this book is not a documentary about India, her history, or an average *ashram*. This story is my perception of how things were for the set of people I created and wrote about.

Amulya Malladi
January 1, 2005

Song of the
Cuckoo Bird

1961-64

17 December 1961. Provocative action against Indian nationals in the vicinity of Anjadip Island and Portugal's belligerent attitude toward the problems of its colonial possessions in India resulted in the government of India's decision to liberate Goa, Daman, and Diu. Operations were launched at night and the Portuguese were driven out of India.

3 May 1962. Hundreds of Muslims were killed in clashes with Hindus in West Bengal.

Tella Meda, the House with the White Roof

*T*hey took strips of coconut leaves and made dolls with them. The supple leaves could be twisted and turned without breaking. They would use red *tilakam* to make the eyes, nose, and mouth of the dolls. A small swatch of white cloth would sometimes become a *sari* or a shirt. Then the dolls would be forgotten, left to dry in the sun when the call for lunch or dinner came from downstairs.

Kokila's earliest memories of living in Tella Meda, the house with the white roof, were of making those dolls with Vidura and Chetana. Closest in age to her, they were her best friends in the *ashram,* and together they got into a lot of mischief. They tied leftover crackers from *deepavali* to the tail of the cat, Brahma; they tortured those who sat in meditation by making noises and faces; and they ran around the courtyard, squealing and screeching in the afternoon after lunch, while everyone was trying to take a nap.

Those were the happy times, Kokila would think later on when she looked back. Those were, alas, only happy memories.

Kokila came to Tella Meda an orphan, a month after her marriage. She had just turned eleven.

In those days girls were married before they reached puberty, but they couldn't go to their husband's home until after they menstruated. For Kokila the three years before she menstruated were spent at Tella Meda, the home of her late father's friend Ramanandam Sastri.

Built right by the Bay of Bengal in the small coastal town of Bheemunipatnam in southern India, the house with the white roof was not a conventional home. Tella Meda was a home for the weary, a safe harbor for lost souls, the last refuge for some and the only home for others.

Tella Meda was an *ashram*, a religious dwelling where a *guru* led her folk to the right path through prayer and the reading of scripture. But it was not a conventional *ashram*. The *guru*, Charvi, refused to be called *"guru"* or "Amma," as the norm was for those as enlightened as she. Charvi went by just Charvi and would not call her home an *ashram* but just a home, hers, which she willingly and openly shared with those who were in need.

Tella Meda was a beautiful house, the most beautiful house Kokila had ever seen and definitely the most beautiful house she would ever live in. On a full moon night the house glittered as if diamonds were studded all over it and its outer walls shimmered from the reflection of the waters of the Bay of Bengal.

The foundation of the house was first laid in 1947 but every time construction began the hurricane season arrived with a vengeance, destroying whatever had been built. Finally in 1955 a man named Srikant Somayajula succeeded in building a house on that foundation. It was a house unrivaled in Bheemunipatnam for its size and opulence.

As soon as Kokila walked past the gate with Ramanandam Sastri and stepped into the big front yard and garden of Tella Meda she was struck with awe. A large verandah covered with stone tiles was sprawled in front, separated from the garden by an ornate knee-high cement balcony. Big decorative flowers molded out of cement and sand adorned the short white balcony. Opening into the verandah were doors from four rooms, one left of the main entrance and three on the right.

The left door led into Charvi's room and the three on the right led into guest rooms, which housed the devotees of Charvi. Many came to Tella Meda to give their respects to Charvi and to find some peace and quiet in the house with the white roof by the Bay of Bengal.

"This is the *puja* room," Ramanandam Sastri told her as he led her into Tella Meda through the main entrance, "and the music room."

A beautiful mahogany temple was the platform for a large golden Venkateshwara Swami and his consort, Lakshmi. Several other idols of gods and goddesses—Ganesha, the god of obstacles; Saraswati, the goddess of education—and a large marble Shivaling were arranged on mahogany platforms within the temple.

The temple had obviously been cared for; everything was polished and shone. Fresh flowers from the front garden—red and white roses, red hibiscus, and small white jasmines—lay at the feet of the gods and goddesses and the smell of sandalwood incense pervaded the room.

Between the temple area and the music area a bright yellow and red coconut straw mat was laid down as a divider. It spanned from the front door to the door into the interior of the house. The music area of the room was covered with a brown cotton rug; a *veena*, a pair of *tablas*, a *tanpoora*, a harmonium, and small and large cymbals lay on the rug, leaning against each other.

Kokila wondered who kept the large house clean. Ramanandam Sastri had warned her that she would have some chores, as did everyone else who lived in the *ashram*. Kokila hoped her task would not be to clean the house because the size of it was intimidating.

Past the temple room, Kokila stepped into another verandah and gawked as she saw how big the house really was. Coming from a small house that was more hut than real house, she felt as if she were stepping into a palace.

Beyond the verandah was a huge courtyard covered in the same stone tile as the front and inside verandahs. Ten rooms surrounded the courtyard, where clothes of different sizes and in different colors hung on clotheslines that crisscrossed the courtyard. *Tulasi* had been planted in a cement pot in the center of the courtyard. The pot was painted red and yellow, auspicious colors that signified *kumkum* and turmeric and were the colors of a married woman.

The bathrooms were on the right side; they seemed to have been built with less care than the house. The doors were made out of cheap wood, not like the doors and windows elsewhere, and the walls were uneven, not smooth as in the *puja* room.

There was one bathroom and three toilets. This was a luxury, Kokila knew, and she was now convinced she had fallen into a basket of *ladoos*. When her father had died and the question of where she would live until she could go to her husband arose, Ramanandam Sastri arrived like a hero to arrange the funeral and take her away with him.

She couldn't believe she was going to live in a house with a bathroom and toilets. There no longer would be the need to take a steel mug with water and find a discreet place to go in the mornings. And she could take a bath in a real bathroom, not a makeshift one covered with bedsheets.

One room adjoined the bath area but Ramanandam Sastri didn't show her the room, nor did he tell her what it was for.

A staircase from the courtyard led up to the open terrace where Ramanandam Sastri said some of the kids slept on warm summer nights. The Bay of Bengal lay ahead, an unbelievable blue, shimmering like a silk *sari*, and Kokila truly fell in love with the house when she saw the bay.

Ramanandam Sastri had then taken her to the kitchen to meet Subhadra, who lived in the *ashram* and took care of all the cooking. Subhadra was a portly woman, her skin dark as coal, her hair slick with coconut oil and tied in a neat bun. She wore small gold earrings, a thin gold chain, and two thin gold bangles, one on each hand.

Subhadra had a soft voice that Kokila would soon learn turned gruff when she became angry.

"This house used to be grander," Subhadra told Kokila as she gave her a tiffin of *idlis* left over from breakfast and some coconut chutney. "Out in the verandah and courtyard you can still see the tiles, brought from Mysore, especially made for Tella Meda. Srikant Somayajula, a contractor from Hyderabad, built this house. But during the *gruhapravesham* itself his wife died. He never lived here; no one from his family did. Imagine that! Some people have terrible luck."

Kokila ate the slightly hardened *idli* with the spicy coconut chutney and listened to Subhadra talk about the house, the people, Charvi, and everyone else.

Even though the kitchen was massive and could easily seat thirty people, meals were served outside in the verandah, Subhadra told Kokila, where a long knee-high table stood between thin strips of coconut straw mats used for seating.

The kitchen had been built to feed an army. The stove had six burners instead of four and there were several large cupboards for storage. On the stone-tiled floor there was a wooden floor knife with its blade laid down, like a ship that had lost its mast. A large stone mortar stood on one side with an equally large pestle. It was used to make the *idli* and *dosa* batter from soaked *urad dal* and rice every Saturday and Sunday, Subhadra said, and she explained to Kokila that grinding the *dal* and rice was the worst thing she had to do every week.

"When the house was built all the rooms had ceiling fans. Not anymore, though," Subhadra said as she fanned herself with a straw fan.

"What happened?" Kokila asked as she finished eating and washed her hands in the plate with the remaining water in her glass.

"Somayajula-garu was so distraught after his wife's death that he left the house to looters and the like. When we came here the house was all but ruined," Subhadra said. "We had to clean it all up, whitewash the walls. We set up the bathrooms; just had to, couldn't have Charvi taking a *chambu* of water and going out, now, could we? But it has been all worth it—we live here rent free."

"Rent free?" Kokila's eyes widened.

"Hmm," Subhadra said, and smiled. "Everyone should be so lucky to have a saint like Charvi live in their house. So, of course, Somayajula-garu doesn't charge us a *paisa*."

Charvi was Ramanandam Sastri's daughter. There were different stories as to how Charvi became a *guru* and a representative of God itself and Kokila wasn't sure what to believe. According to Subhadra, Charvi was goddess, *guru*, and saint all rolled into one.

"We found the house because Dr. Vishnu Mohan—he lives three houses down the road—and Sastri-garu are friends. So when Sastri-garu was looking for a house to rent, Doctor-garu suggested Tella Meda," Subhadra said. "Did you know that it was Sastri-garu who first saw the light of knowledge in Charvi?"

Ramanandam Sastri had been living in Tenali when the alteration of his soul began and he saw the light of God in his daughter.

He hadn't started out believing in God and Hinduism. He'd started out an atheist, always ridiculing his wife, Bhanumati, for her religious beliefs. Manikyam, his eldest daughter, with her fat pockmarked face, also turned to God; Ramanandam Sastri, who never learned to mince his words, told her that praying to God wouldn't change the fact that she was ugly. But his second daughter, Lavanya, came out looking like a movie star. Her skin was light in color, her eyes light brown, almost catlike; she was beautiful. She grew up to be vain, stubborn, and shallow, and ultimately amounted to nothing.

And then Bhanumati had a third child. Ramanandam's third daughter was ethereal and he named her Charvi, which means "beautiful." When Charvi was but a week old, Ramanandam saw the light of God in her and deemed her a Devi, an Amma, a goddess. His sudden transformation from nonbeliever to believer was viewed with some skepticism by Bhanumati but she knew it was not her place to question her husband and she didn't.

For years after Charvi was born Bhanumati did not get pregnant again and quietly endured the role of wife, mother, and particularly mother to an Amma. She was quiet and complacent and she fulfilled the duties prescribed to her.

Eight years after Charvi's birth, the much-desired son was born. It had been a time of great joy, as both Bhanumati and her eldest daughter, Manikyam, were pregnant at the same time. And they each, by the grace of Lord Venkateshwara Swami, had a son.

Ramanandam named his son Vidura, for the great wise man from *The Mahabharata* who narrated the entire battle between the Pandavas and Kauravas to the blind king, Dhritrastra. Bhanumati died just a month after giving birth to her son because of a blood clot in her uterus, but not before she extracted a promise from eight-year-old Charvi that she would watch over her baby brother. It was a promise Charvi was unable to keep and until the day she died she felt the burden of that broken vow.

People who flocked to Ramanandam for his words, his books, and his writing didn't question his ability to see a Devi, a goddess, in his daughter. The number of people who came to stay with Ramanandam increased dramatically. In the beginning it was students who came to discuss his work and pay their respects. Of course, everyone stayed for free.

Ramanandam could barely pay his bills on his meager schoolteacher's salary and his book sales didn't bring in much money even though he was quite a well-known writer among the intellectual elite. It was, after all, only the elite who could pretend to believe in Ramanandam's theories that a woman had the right to independent living beyond the men in her life. Ramanandam wrote about a woman being a woman first and then being a daughter, sister, wife, or mother. He wrote about how man and woman were equal in nature and how he believed that a woman's ability to give birth actually made her superior to man. Through his writings he encouraged women and men to break the traditional trappings in their life and be freethinkers and live a life unfettered with the customs and mores of an ancient culture.

But not everyone believed he was the champion of women that he claimed to be. His own daughter Lavanya did not respect her father and felt that he did not live up to what he wrote about. Her father, the great defender of women's rights, would complain if she was seen talking to a boy; he would complain when she talked about a woman's freedom to marry anyone from any caste; he would turn his nose up when she would talk about living with a man without the benefit of marriage. For all his writing about the rights of women and gender equality, when it came to his own daughters Ramanandam was quite traditional. He even had his eldest daughter, Manikyam, married to a doctor, Nageshwar Rao, the arranged way.

It was after Manikyam married and left the family home that the scandal happened. And what a scandal it was. The news was fanned with grotesque imagery and plenty of gossip.

Ramanandam's sister Taruna, who was almost twenty years younger than he, had been married at the tender age of twelve to an aging Brahmin. Her husband died six months after the marriage. Her husband's family wanted their twelve-year-old daughter-in-law to shave her hair off, wear white, and live in a corner of their house, as was traditional.

Ramanandam refused to let his young sister be subjected to such anachronistic and demeaning rituals, so he brought her to his house. He helped her go to medical college and become a doctor. She set up a small clinic, open to women only. She dealt particularly with "woman troubles"—one of which was unwanted pregnancies.

It didn't take long for everyone in Tenali to find out that Taruna Sastri was performing abortions. Everyone talked about it. Taruna's clinic was broken into, people threatened her, and one night someone even put a knife to her throat, warning her to either leave Tenali or stop the abortions. Finally Taruna left for Bombay, where an old classmate offered her a job in his clinic as a general practitioner. She stopped performing abortions. Ramanandam accused her of abandoning her principles and she responded by cutting him out of her life.

The backlash against Taruna's radical ways struck Ramanandam harshly too. He lost his job as a schoolteacher. He took his family and moved to Tirupati, to the famed Bhagwan Hariharan *ashram*. They stayed there for almost a year before Ramanandam decided that he needed to find his own home. Already devotees were coming to Bhagwan's *ashram* to see Charvi, causing some tension between Ramanandam and Bhagwan Hariharan. It was time to find Charvi an *ashram* of her own.

Ramanandam wanted a large place with minimal rent. When he

lost his job, he was allowed to keep his pension, and that would have to suffice as income. As luck would have it, he found Tella Meda.

"The owner, Somayajula-garu, didn't want to rent the house to anyone. After all, his wife died here, you know," Subhadra told Kokila. "But when he heard about Charvi he just handed it over, free of charge. That was four years ago. Charvi was just fifteen then, but you know how it is with saints—age is not material."

Subhadra was awestruck by Charvi, convinced she was an incarnation of a goddess.

"You can see it in her eyes," Subhadra claimed. "Do you know she named this house? Before her the house had no name but then when we did the *gruhapravesham* and the boiled milk spilled on the floor, Charvi just looked at the house and said, 'This is Tella Meda.' And this became our *ashram*."

But when Kokila met her, Charvi clearly said, "This is not an *ashram* and I'm not a *guru* or your religious leader or your god. Others call this an *ashram*, but Tella Meda is a home, and this is now your home for as long as you want and need it."

Kokila should have been in awe of Charvi, but she was suspicious of such disarming modesty from a *guru*.

The Cuckoo
Bird Girl

*I*n the beginning, Kokila was afraid, unsure of her new surroundings and the people in them, but soon her shyness dissolved in the good company of her two new friends, Vidura Sastri and Chetana, another young girl who stayed at Tella Meda.

Ramanandam Sastri believed in freedom. He believed that children should be allowed to run as they like and do as they please. If they didn't want to go to school, they didn't have to go; if they wanted to eat only *chakli* for dinner, they could; and if they wanted to stay up until midnight watching the stars, that was allowed as well.

Coming from a conservative Brahmin home, where rules and regulations had shaped her childhood, Kokila dove into her new, unfettered life with unmatched eagerness. The *ashram* to her was a grandiose house where food was always available and no one ever scolded her. Later on Kokila realized that the food was actually meager, and that it would have been better if someone had scolded her and taught her to live a more disciplined life. But at the time she thought she had fallen into heaven.

Kokila sat with Charvi while she performed the morning *puja,* making long garlands with jasmine flowers. They prayed in the room that was the music and temple room. Only Charvi was allowed to touch the mahogany temple, which she cared for every day with love and respect and plenty of wood oil.

In those days not too many people lived in Tella Meda, and several rooms were empty. Guests would come and stay in those empty rooms. They would come to visit Ramanandam Sastri and then they would be mesmerized by the goddess they could see in Charvi's face. And before they left they would leave some money behind as they paid their respects to the *guru* of Tella Meda.

"Are you a goddess?" Kokila asked Charvi once, and Charvi became sad. She was twenty-one years old then, but she seemed much older than her years.

"No," she replied softly.

"But everyone says they see Amma in your face," Kokila prodded.

Charvi closed her eyes then and sighed. "I can't control what they see."

Kokila wanted to ask her what she saw when she looked at herself in the mirror but didn't. Charvi's eyes were already closed in meditation and Kokila didn't have the courage to question the *guru's* godliness.

Kokila and Chetana, her closest friend in Tella Meda, had discussed Charvi several times. The daughter of a prostitute who had all but abandoned her, Chetana was devoted to Charvi, who had given her a home when so many would have cringed at the idea of a prostitute's daughter living with them. But even Chetana agreed that she couldn't quite see the light of knowledge burning brightly in Charvi's eyes.

Every evening Charvi would go for a walk on the beach and many of the residents of the *ashram* would join her, among them Vidura, Charvi's young brother. Chetana hated getting sand on her feet, so she would stay back in the *ashram* to help Subhadra in the kitchen. Ever since Subhadra had come to Ramanandam Sastri's house eleven years ago, it was she who had played the role of mother to Chetana.

But it wasn't Subhadra's attention that Kokila wanted, it was Vidura's. So she joined Charvi on her walks in order to be alone with Vidura, away from Chetana.

Kokila was thirteen years old when her body started burgeoning, making her a woman. Desires that had been unknown were unraveling within her and each time Vidura smiled at Kokila, touched her, she felt a tingle that ran through her entire body. Except for Charvi, who once when she saw Kokila hold Vidura's hand mentioned to her that she should be careful with her dreams, no one objected to the time Kokila spent with Vidura.

Kokila, Chetana, and Vidura had been playing together since they were children and no one noticed their transition to adulthood. No one noticed Kokila's shy smiles, Vidura's knowing eyes, and Chetana's full breasts. On the beach no one cared that Vidura and Kokila would wrestle in the sand like children, even though their bodies could feel the sensations of adults. No one seemed to mind that Vidura would openly stare at Kokila after she had been drenched in the sea.

This was just another aspect of Ramanandam Sastri's faith in freedom. He didn't believe in dictating how people lived and children, although small, were still human and had rights.

Kokila dreamed that Ramanandam's openness and acceptance toward her meant he liked her and would accept her marriage to Vidura. The only problem with Kokila's dreams was that she was already married to a boy named Vamsi Krishna from Visakhapatnam. But she couldn't even remember Vamsi's face anymore, wouldn't be able to recognize him in a crowd, so she didn't feel pressure from the validity of that union.

"No matter what you say, you are still married," Chetana reminded her when Kokila confessed her growing feelings for Vidura. She pointed to the *mangalsutra* Kokila wore around her neck. The thin gold chain holding two small gold coins that looked like little gold breasts symbolized her marriage, but it had lost its meaning for Kokila. How could this symbolize marriage? And if it did, wouldn't it be powerful, so powerful that her heart would not be tempted?

"No, I'm not," Kokila said adamantly. "I haven't set up household with anyone."

"You're going to menstruate soon," Chetana warned her. "And then they'll come, your husband's family, to take you away. You'll have to go, you're their daughter-in-law."

To Kokila that was a potent threat.

"Maybe I'll stay," Kokila said, not knowing how she could. But the idea of leaving Vidura, and especially of leaving him to Chetana, was intolerable. The idea of leaving what had become her only true home for a stranger's house was intimidating.

"No, you won't stay," Chetana said confidently, and added slyly, "You're a married woman. You should not let your eye wander so."

After that Kokila waited in dread to see blood in between her legs. How would it gush out, where would it happen? Maybe if she was careful no one would know her menses had begun and she could continue to stay in Tella Meda. If there were no celebrations confirming her arrival at puberty, her husband's family would not know and would not come to take her away. Yes, she decided, she would hide it.

Chetana had already started having bleeding. It began three months earlier and since then, for five days every month she would sit in the room by the bathrooms where all the other women in the *ashram* who had bleeding congregated. The women having their monthly were not allowed to cook or touch anything in the rest of the house, except for the things in the room assigned to them. Subhadra would place their food outside the "menses room" and would not touch the utensils until they had been washed by the woman or women having their monthlies. Those utensils were not mixed with the other plates and glasses in the kitchen. They were stored in the menses room, away from everything, and were used only while the women "sat out."

Chetana hated to sit out but would pretend as if the menses room were a palace. Kokila had never been inside the room. With so many women in the house, the room almost always had an occupant. And in any case it was an impure room and if Kokila went in she would have to be doused with water drawn from the well in the backyard to be cleansed.

But Kokila had been fascinated by the mysterious room where women sat out from the first day when Ramanandam had avoided the room on their tour of the ashram. The first menstruation was a bona fide rite of passage, and Kokila couldn't imagine how it would be to bleed from between the legs.

"Oh, it hurts and hurts," Chetana warned her. "But Subhadra gives me this rice medicine and all the pain goes away. Maybe she'll give it to you . . . or, maybe your mother-in-law will. Because once you start you'll have to leave."

At the mention of leaving Tella Meda, the fascination Kokila had for the menses room turned into fear.

The only woman who didn't sit out with the other women was Charvi. No one even knew if she had monthlies. According to Chetana, a goddess didn't have monthlies. It was true that Charvi never missed the morning *puja* and everyone knew a woman having her period was a soiled woman and shouldn't be allowed in the presence of God.

"Do you have monthlies?" Kokila asked Charvi once after the morning *puja*.

Subhadra, who was hovering around the music room, snapped at her, "What stupid questions you ask, Kokila! Go and sweep the courtyard. It's your turn this week."

"I just . . . ," Kokila began, but fell silent when Subhadra sent her another fierce glare. She left the *puja* room and went to sweep.

Everyone had chores in the *ashram*. Subhadra was responsible for all the cooking. Each person had to wash his or her own plates and glasses, but Subhadra cleaned all the pots and pans.

Chetana and Kokila shared the sweeping of the courtyard and the inside verandah. One week Kokila did it and the next Chetana had a period, so Kokila did it again. It wasn't fair but Kokila didn't want to complain about something so silly, especially since the Mysore tiles were so easy to sweep.

Kokila had gone to school until the fourth class, but when she got married that stopped. Chetana still went to school, though she stayed home more often than she caught the school bus. Ramanandam Sastri had asked Kokila if she wanted to study in a school or stay home and study in Tella Meda. The decision was an easy one: the *ashram* it was. Who wanted to wake up early in the morning and run to the school bus and go to school? In school there would be exams, strict teachers, and punishment, but at Tella Meda there was none of that. In addition, Vidura was home-schooled and the lure of being with him all day was too much for Kokila to resist.

Every evening before dinner, from 4 to 6 PM, Ramanandam Sastri would teach the children. Vidura, Chetana, and Kokila sat next to each other with black slates on their laps and thin chalk in their hands. They had no books. Occasionally, Ramanandam Sastri would give a book to them, asking them to read it, but they never did.

Ramanandam believed in imparting what he called a "real-world" education. He didn't want the children to just learn math; he wanted them to learn the applications of it. He didn't want them to just know the capitals of all the states; he wanted them to know what every state's political affiliation was and how each state was part of India as a whole. But the children didn't have any basics, not in math or geography or social studies, so Ramanandam's lengthy lectures about social models made little sense. They learned little about the applications of the knowledge they didn't have.

Ramanandam was not consistent either. He would tell them about geography one day, gathering everyone around an atlas and spinning his old globe to show where India was and where America was. Another day he would try to teach accounting or he would talk about the planets and gravity, switching from topic to topic with little continuity, leaving the children with a jumble of information with no relevance. His favorite thing to teach was Indian history. He would start from the Indus Valley civilization and go all the way to Nehru. He spent days talking about Chanakya and King Chandragupta Maurya, and would get very emotional when he spoke of the British Raj.

At the age of thirteen, listening intently to the exciting stories Ramanandam would tell, Kokila was mesmerized. He was the most brilliant man under the sun to her. Vidura was also immensely proud of his father and would show off about how many people came to the *ashram* to visit him, honor him, and seek guidance from him. He didn't speak that highly of Charvi and claimed that his father was the real *guru* of the *ashram,* the true saint.

And because Vidura believed that, so did Kokila.

"He sleeps around," Chetana told Kokila one night when they were getting ready to go to sleep.

"What? Who?"

"Ramanandam Sastri Garu. And with prostitutes, young girls," Chetana said casually.

"And who told you, your whore mother?" Kokila asked, furious at the accusation. It was a mean thing to say to Chetana, only meant to hurt her, because it was one thing to call someone's mother a whore, but it was quite another to say it when it was the truth. It was no secret that Chetana's mother, Ambika, was a prostitute who had had Chetana when Ramanandam Sastri's sister had advised against yet another abortion. Ambika had not wanted to take care of her daughter and had left Chetana at the mercy of the world. Taruna had brought her as a baby to Ramanandam Sastri and Charvi, and Chetana had been with them ever since.

"Everyone knows about Sastri Garu," Chetana said, blinking back tears. "Why do you think Charvi doesn't even talk to him?"

That wasn't quite true. Kokila had seen Ramanandam Sastri and his daughter talk to each other on many occasions, but it was obvious to everyone in the *ashram* that there were dynamics at play between them that no one knew of.

Even though Kokila didn't believe Chetana, her fertile young mind started to concoct scenarios, fueled by gossip, each time Ramanandam stepped out of the *ashram*.

According to Vidura, his father went to the library, met with friends, and wrote at the beach. They all seemed valid reasons for Ramanandam to leave Tella Meda, but Kokila continued to think about the prostitutes he allegedly visited.

The only prostitute Kokila had ever seen was Chetana's mother, Ambika. She had come just once to Tella Meda since Kokila started living there. Ambika looked like a normal woman, except she had silk underwear. Kokila had sneaked into Ambika's room with Chetana to go through her suitcase. The underwear was silky, with lace on it, and the brassiere, oh, that was just indecent. Kokila hadn't even known clothes like this existed and seeing them had lifted another curtain that separated her from the real world.

The *saris* in the suitcase were garish, pink and yellow, cheap, with golden flowers on them. There were two lipsticks in the suitcase, one dark red and another dark pink. Chetana stole the dark red one despite Kokila's protests. Everyone knew that women who wore lipstick were not from good families.

"Do you know that Taruna Auntie, Sastri Garu's sister, tied her tubes?" Chetana whispered.

"What does that mean?" Kokila asked.

"I don't know, they go inside the body and tie the tubes that create babies," Chetana said. "After me, no one wants that bitch to get pregnant again."

For years Kokila thought of Chetana's mother as a bitch, a dog in heat, her tongue lolling as she copulated with male dogs outside Tella Meda. Dogs weren't allowed inside the *ashram;* they were foul creatures who ate their own feces and mated with their offspring and their siblings. Charvi hated dogs.

"I hate her," Vidura announced one night. He and Kokila often sneaked out in the night to go for a walk on the beach.

Vidura's feelings for Charvi were ambivalent. Kokila was constantly confused because sometimes he would speak highly of her and other times he would talk like his older sister Lavanya and call Charvi the worst kind of fraud. His feelings transferred to Kokila and she never quite worked out how she felt about Charvi. Sometimes she thought her to be the godliest and most serene person she knew; other times she thought Charvi was just ordinary, pretending to be someone greater.

"What did she do?" Kokila asked, barely able to conceal her curiosity. Everyone in the *ashram* craved glimpses of Charvi's life beneath the façade of the *guru.*

"She actually believes she can heal people," Vidura said, kicking sand with his bare feet. "I don't. But this man, some doctor or something, came by a month ago from Bangalore, do you remember?"

Kokila nodded even though she didn't. So many people came to the *ashram* that it was hard to keep track of all of Charvi's devotees. Only those who stayed in Tella Meda made an impact, however small.

"This doctor said he gets headaches and Charvi . . . she touched his forehead or something and today that doctor sent a letter saying that his headaches are completely gone," Vidura said, sneering a little. "And Charvi believes it. She was trying to stroke Chetana's stomach because she has a stomachache. How can she believe any of this?"

Kokila didn't know what to say. She didn't mind it so much that Charvi believed in herself and now had elevated herself to a touch healer. How did it matter?

"And you should see Nanna. He is just so proud that his daughter has these powers. Even he believes her," Vidura said resentfully. It became clear to Kokila that Vidura was jealous of the attention Charvi got from their father.

"And when I said that she's a fake, he yelled at me. He slapped me. My father never hit me before, but now he did it because of *her.*" There were tears in Vidura's eyes. "How can he believe that she is a Devi? And why do all these people who come to Tella Meda think so? She keeps saying that Tella Meda is not an *ashram* but it is, isn't it?"

Kokila agreed with him. Regardless of how Charvi wanted to see Tella Meda, it was for all intents and purposes an *ashram*, a safe harbor for people (like Kokila) who had nowhere to go. And Tella Meda's religious leader was Charvi. Charvi knew that and wielded her power even though to everyone's face she claimed she wasn't a *guru*. This was what had made Kokila suspicious of her right from the beginning.

Kokila wrapped her hand around Vidura's and squeezed gently. "It's okay. It isn't like your father loves her more . . ."

"I don't care who he loves more. He's a sick old man," Vidura said, and pulled his hand away from Kokila's. "I don't care about him or anyone else."

"Not even me?" Kokila asked, tears burning her eyes. She couldn't bear it that he pushed her away.

Instantly contrite, Vidura put his arm around Kokila. "I love you,

Kokila. But you will be gone soon, won't you? Away to your husband's house and you'll be someone else's wife."

Kokila leaned into Vidura. "Maybe I won't have to go."

Vidura laughed. "Yes, you will. He is your husband and why won't you want to go?"

Because of you, she wanted to say, but didn't have the courage. Kokila told him the other truth. "Because this is the only home I have ever had."

"No, Tella Meda is not your home. It is no one's home," Vidura said caustically. "This is an *ashram,* not a home, Kokila. You should get out of here as soon as you can."

"Don't you like living here?" Kokila asked, stricken that he didn't like Tella Meda.

Vidura shrugged. "When we lived in Kavali we had a small house but it was ours. Now it feels like a hotel, not a real home. I rarely talk to my father, my sister is some unreliable *guru,* and I just don't like it here."

Kokila let the tears fall. Didn't he love her enough to like being in Tella Meda?

"Oh, Kokila," Vidura said with a smile. "I'm just angry. I do like living in Tella Meda. Ever since you came, it has been wonderful. But you'll leave me and go away."

"I will never leave," Kokila vowed.

That was the first and only time Vidura kissed her. It was a kiss on her lips, light, brief, brushing, like a gentle wind caressing the sails of the fishermen's boats in the early dawn.

It was her first kiss.

Blood streaked her white underskirt and was a damp maroon spot on her light blue cotton skirt. Kokila wasn't the one who noticed it, it was Ramanandam Sastri. He didn't say anything to her about it, just asked her to go talk to Subhadra.

"Oh, oh, oh," Subhadra chanted when Kokila came to her. "How embarrassing for Sastri Garu. Now come on, girl, we have to take you to the menses room."

She grasped Kokila's hand but Kokila wrenched herself free and pulled away from Subhadra. She didn't want to go to that wretched room; she didn't want to go to her husband's house.

Kokila ran as fast as she could and hid under the bougainvillea bush in the front garden. It was her and Chetana's secret place, a small cave underneath green leaves and paperlike pink flowers. Usually the cats congregated there but it was empty that day and Kokila sat huddled inside, hugging her knees close to her, not wanting to know what the wet feeling between her thighs was.

It would go away. If she prayed hard enough, wished it enough, it would go away.

She stayed there for two hours before Chetana gave the hideout away. She didn't tell easily; it took two slaps from Subhadra and a lot of coaxing from Ramanandam Sastri before Chetana revealed where Kokila might be.

"Come out now," Subhadra said as she tried to yank Kokila out of the bougainvillea cave. Her large frame wouldn't allow her to get inside the cave, so Subhadra caught hold of one of Kokila's legs and started to drag her out.

Kokila grabbed a thorny branch and held on tight even as blood started to spurt from the palms of her hands. She wouldn't go to the menses room, she swore. Tears started to fall like warm summer rain down her face, noiselessly.

"Amma Kokila," Ramanandam Sastri said softly as he bent down to look at her. Then he gasped. "Stop it, Subhadra, the girl's hands are bleeding."

Subhadra immediately pulled away but Kokila wouldn't let go of the branch. Her eyes were wide, wet, her lips trembled as she stood her ground.

"Why won't you come out?" Ramanandam Sastri asked, settling down on the grass outside the bougainvillea cave.

"No," she whispered softly. "You will send me away to my husband's house. I don't want to leave."

Ramanandam Sastri smiled and then nodded. "In this house you can do as you please. If you don't want to go to your husband's house, you don't have to."

Could it be that easy? *"Ottu?"* she asked.

Ramanandam Sastri nodded. "Promise."

The celebrations began the next day and Kokila was relegated to the menses room. Chetana wanted to visit but Subhadra put a stop to it. Only during the *puja* the next day could anyone speak with Kokila.

Subhadra explained to Kokila that from now on she would have bleeding every month. Girls had bleeding when they became women and were old enough to become pregnant and give birth. Married women went to their husband's house at this time and made a family with him. Subhadra didn't go into any details about the sexual aspects of marriage and said only that Kokila was a woman now and would have to start acting like one.

The night before the *puja* that would symbolize to one and all that Kokila had reached puberty, she couldn't sleep. She lay on the coconut straw bed and tossed and turned. The cotton cloth pad between her legs was getting heavier and she knew she had to go to the bathroom and make a new one with the strips of white cotton cloth Subhadra left for her. But the idea of washing out the old one and looking at the blood nauseated her, so she lay quietly, in fear, alone.

Chetana sneaked into the menses room late at night, bringing with her *chakli* and *boondi ladoo*.

"Tomorrow will be fun for you," she said. "Lots of gifts from everyone and your husband's parents will bring gifts too."

"They'll be here?" Kokila asked, fear surging despite Ramanandam Sastri's promise.

"They will," Chetana said. "Sastri Garu telephoned them from Dr. Vishnu Mohan's house to let them know."

The betrayal struck Kokila hard and the *boondi ladoo* turned from sweet to bitter inside her mouth.

"You'll start your own family now. You'll have to have intercourse now," Chetana said with a glint in her eye. "Vidura and I will come and see you sometime, okay?"

Kokila's resentment and fear grew. Already that bitch's daughter was laying claim to Vidura. Kokila knew that as soon as she was gone, Vidura would forget her—Chetana would make sure of it.

"Sastri Garu promised that if I didn't want to go, I didn't have to," Kokila said with false courage.

"You have to go, Kokila," Chetana warned, suddenly serious. "Here you will have no life. There you can have a husband, children. You will have your own home."

"But I don't want to go."

Chetana only shook her head. "If I had the chance you have, I would never stay here."

Oh, if only, Kokila would think many years later, when her hair had turned gray and her smooth skin had become wrinkled. If only she had listened to Chetana. If only she had left. But she was fourteen—what did she know? How could she have known that leaving would have meant a real life?

As Chetana promised, the celebration proclaiming her womanhood was a lot of fun. Subhadra put Kokila in Chetana's silk skirt and *terricot* blouse. The skirt was dark brown with a gold border, while the blouse was yellow and had a thin gold border sewed around the edges of the puffed sleeves. Chetana had worn the same outfit for her *puja* and didn't begrudge Kokila wearing it now. After all, when Chetana wore it, it had been brand-new.

Subhadra washed Kokila's hair with squeezed *rita* pulp and made her feet yellow with turmeric paste. Chetana put henna on Kokila's hands and feet; she made a design of grapes hanging on their vines on her hands and an intricate seashell design on her feet. It was like Kokila's wedding day all over again.

Narayan Garu, an old friend of Ramanandam Sastri who also lived in the *ashram,* gave Kokila a pair of silver anklets that had small bells on them. They had belonged to his wife, who had died several years ago. He had saved her jewelry for his son's wives but after they swindled him out of his own house, relegating him to Tella Meda, he had kept the anklets and a few other pieces of jewelry. Everyone in the *ashram* knew about the expensive trinkets that Narayan Garu kept safely locked in his room and it was a special honor, Kokila knew, to receive one of them as a gift.

"You be good to your husband, little bird," Narayan Garu told her.

In those early days he used to call her "little bird" instead of Kokila, which meant "cuckoo bird" in Telugu.

The silver anklets that were shining on her ankles were a going-away present. And it was the first of many such gifts. Charvi gave her a thin gold chain with an *om*-shaped locket on it. Chetana presented her with small black metal earrings that she had bought herself from money her mother had sent her. The money came rarely and in small amounts, so it was especially touching that she had used it for a gift.

Vidura gave her a white handkerchief surrounded with lace. "I found it at the cinema," he told her. "So I asked Subhadra to wash it and iron it for you."

It was a lovely handkerchief, delicate, and it smelled of roses. It was the most beautiful thing that Kokila had ever owned.

"Chetana and I will come and see you. Oh, but you might be too busy with your husband and household," he teased.

Kokila winced when he said Chetana's name like that, pairing it with his. Everyone was assuming she was leaving. Even Ramanandam Sastri gave her a going-away present, a leather-bound volume of Ramayana. It was an old book and the papers were thick and yellow and smelled. By giving her a present, Ramanandam Sastri squashed Kokila's hope in the promise he had made to her that she wouldn't have to go if she didn't want to.

After a festive lunch, she was asked to go to Charvi's room, where Kokila's in-laws were waiting.

"Amma Kokila." Her mother-in-law, a sweet-looking, slender woman, hugged her to her bosom. "We wanted you to come home after your father died, but it wasn't proper then. We are so happy you'll be with us now."

Kokila looked down at her feet and nodded. She was disappointed that her husband had not come. She had been curious to see if she would even recognize him.

"Vamsi's health is very delicate," her mother-in-law said to explain her son's absence. "We didn't want him to sit in a bus for several hours. He is a very gentle boy, not used to the outside weather much. But once you're with us, you can take care of him."

Kokila felt panic rise within her. They wanted her to take care of someone? She didn't know how to take care of people. She knew how to play in the afternoons and lie down at night and gaze at the stars.

"And you can cook, right?" her mother-in-law asked, and she didn't seem all that sweet anymore. "Your father said you were a very good cook."

My father lied, Kokila wanted to scream. She didn't know how to cook. Subhadra did all the cooking in the *ashram*.

"You cook your good food for Vamsi and he'll leave his delicate nature behind," her mother-in-law said with an all-knowing smile.

Kokila nodded vaguely and turned her head to look at Charvi, who was sitting quietly, looking older than her twenty-two years. There were already streaks of gray in her hair and a small droop to her eyes. Subhadra said that since Charvi's soul was that of an ancient, wise goddess, it sometimes showed on her face.

Kokila's father-in-law cleared his throat to halt his wife from speaking further.

"We would like to leave today evening, after tiffin," he said. "Pack your bags and be ready."

"Subhadra is making your favorite, *masala vada,* for tiffin," Charvi said, and rose to put a hand on Kokila's hair. "We will all miss you."

"Yes, we will," Ramanandam Sastri said as he came into the room.

Kokila started trembling when she saw him. *He promised,* she told herself, and then turned to look at her in-laws, her eyes bright with tears.

"You will come back and see them again," her mother-in-law assured her. "Don't worry. I know it's hard to leave but you will have a nice house and a husband."

Kokila saw Vidura and Chetana hovering by the door into Charvi's living quarters. They were holding hands.

Kokila turned and looked at Ramanandam Sastri. "I don't want to go," she said tearfully.

"Of course you don't," her mother-in-law snapped, her patience appearing to depart. "But you must. You are a married woman. You can't stay at some pitiful *ashram* for the rest of your life."

"I don't want to go to your house," Kokila said, spurred by anger that someone who knew nothing about Tella Meda was calling it pitiful. "I don't know how to cook. My father lied."

"You can learn how to cook," Charvi said softly, her eyes warning Kokila not to say anything more.

"Why don't you want to go, Amma Kokila?" Ramanandam Sastri asked. He put his hands on her shoulders and looked into her eyes.

"I want to stay," Kokila said, afraid now that if she left she would have to take care of her "delicate" husband.

"Are you sure?" Ramanandam Sastri asked.

"Yes," Kokila said firmly.

Ramanandam Sastri let go of Kokila and turned to face her in-laws. "I can't force the girl," he said.

"Nanna," Charvi began, and then fell silent, shaking her head.

"But she's our daughter-in-law," Kokila's father-in-law said angrily.

"I can't force her," Ramanandam Sastri repeated.

"What is wrong with you, you stupid girl?" her mother-in-law demanded. "Are you an idiot? You are married. You can't stay in this low-life *ashram* all your years. What do you think will happen here? Nothing! Do you know the kind of people who live here?"

Kokila nodded but looked at her turmeric-stained feet.

"Some prostitute's daughter, this teacher whose sister is an abortion doctor . . ." Kokila's mother-in-law waved her hands as she spoke. "All losers and discards. You want to live with them?"

"Yes," Kokila said.

"Then you can't come back later and say 'Where is my husband,' okay?" the mother-in-law yelled. "We have another girl in mind, and we will get our son married to her immediately. So don't show up and demand your rights."

"I won't," Kokila said, happiness blossoming inside her. She lifted her head a little and saw Chetana, who looked sad now and was shaking her head. *She's just upset that now she can't have Vidura to herself,* Kokila thought gleefully.

"This is your bad influence, Sastri Garu." The mother-in-law now turned on Ramanandam Sastri. "We knew it was going to be trouble when you brought her here. We know all about your sister and family, *chee-chee*. And this *ashram* . . . we should have known something like this would happen."

They left on that note. No one told Kokila she had made a mistake, though she caught several pitying looks from the others when they thought she wasn't looking. She later found out that Ramanandam Sastri had given strict orders to leave Kokila alone and let her be happy with her decision.

At first she was happy. But then her chores continued, the looks grew more pitying, and even worse, Vidura began to turn away from her. And then, just like that, he stopped talking to everyone.

When Chetana and Kokila told Ramanandam Sastri they were concerned about Vidura's silence and how much time he was now spending alone, he assured them it was just a passing phase.

But it wasn't a passing phase.

Kokila tried to talk to Vidura several times and each time he shunned her. And each time it tore at Kokila. It was not just that he didn't want to talk to her; it was as if he was angry with her for not having left with her husband. In addition, he seemed angry with Charvi and Ramanandam Sastri. He wouldn't say anything but every time Charvi or his father was nearby he would leave, bitter anger in his eyes.

"He's just a boy," Subhadra said. "And he's turning into a man; it's the change that makes him behave like this."

Kokila wasn't sure what was going on with Vidura, and every time he walked away from her without a smile or any form of acknowledgment it was an arrow through Kokila's young heart.

"Stop crying for him," Chetana told her when she caught Kokila weeping by the *tulasi* plant in the courtyard. "If he doesn't want to talk to you, why bother?"

Kokila didn't know how to explain to Chetana that she had stayed in Tella Meda for Vidura. She had stayed because she loved him.

"You won't understand," Kokila said.

"Yes, I will," Chetana said confidently. "So he and you went for a few walks on the beach at night and he kissed you? He and I also went on walks and he kissed me too. One day he even touched my breasts. That's not—"

Anger and betrayal flashed within Kokila. "You are no better than your mother."

Chetana sighed and instead of fighting with Kokila spoke patiently. "I saw you and him on the beach one night. I never went with him after that, even when he asked. I love him too, Kokila. But he was with you and me at the same time without us knowing about it. What kind of a person does that make him?"

Through the red haze of anger Kokila could somehow clearly see what Chetana was telling her.

"But you let him touch your breasts," Kokila accused.

"And you let him kiss you," Chetana countered.

"I love him," Kokila said, the anger seeping out of her.

"I love him too," Chetana said with a sad smile.

"He lied to me," Kokila said, her heart breaking. What had she done? She had given up her husband to be with a boy who had no loyalty.

"What did he lie about?" Chetana asked.

Kokila tried to remember what it was Vidura had lied about, but there was nothing to remember. "I just assumed," she said weakly. "I thought if I stayed for him . . . but he told me that I should have gone with my husband, that I was a bad Hindu wife. Am I a bad Hindu wife?"

Chetana snorted. "You are not a wife anymore."

Even though he had broken Kokila's heart, she was prepared to forgive Vidura, if only he would speak with her and not be so remote. But Vidura isolated himself more and more from the people around him. And three months after Kokila had her first menses, Vidura ran away from Tella Meda without saying anything to anyone.

Kokila never saw him again.

27 May 1964. Pandit Jawaharlal Nehru, the architect and first prime minister of modern India, passed away at the age of seventy-four.

28 May 1964. A slow-moving funeral cortege containing the body of Jawaharlal Nehru inched through the streets of New Delhi. A million and a half Indians lined the route to pay final respects to their beloved leader.

A Modern Woman

Vidura ran away on the twenty-seventh of May, 1964, the day Jawaharlal Nehru, the first prime minister of India, died.

Ramanandam Sastri was destroyed.

He was like a walking corpse, going up the stairs every day to stand on the terrace under the splintering sun, watching and waiting for his son to come home.

Telegrams had been sent out, letters had been written to relatives, friends, anyone Ramanandam could think of. Most of them replied apologetically that they didn't know Vidura's whereabouts. The inspector of Bheemunipatnam also investigated but no one had seen Vidura with his battered suitcase filled with his belongings. Vidura's room, one of the small rooms across from the kitchen, was bare except for his bed and an empty Godrej steel cupboard. He had managed to take everything away but no one knew when, no one knew how, and most important, no one knew why.

There was speculation that he had been kidnapped and taken away to the docks where young boys were used as slave labor. Some thought he had seen something untoward and had run away because of fear. And some thought that he was just a crazy boy who had left his nice home for God only knew what. Everyone believed he would come back and they tried to console Ramanandam Sastri with that hope. But he was inconsolable, both because of Vidura and because of Nehru.

Kokila cried for days after Vidura ran away. It didn't seem fair that she was allowed to stay in Tella Meda but had to lose Vidura. Chetana was morose as well but less affected, Kokila thought, than herself. A gloom settled on the *ashram*. The ringing voices of play and laughter vanished, as if Vidura had taken not only his belongings but also the happiness out of Tella Meda.

Kokila found it hard to wake up in the morning and start a new day. She found it hard to find sleep in the night. She would lie down on the terrace and stare at the stars above and wonder if maybe Vidura was looking at the exact same stars at the exact same time. Maybe through the stars and moon she could reach out to him and ask him to come back home.

She wondered if he'd left because of her. Had he been so repulsed by her refusal to go to her husband's house that he had left Tella Meda? She could confide in no one about how she felt, how remorse and guilt at being the cause of Vidura's departure ate at her. If Chetana was upset, she didn't show it, and Kokila was coming to believe that Chetana wasn't upset or even disturbed anymore. Chetana seemed to have gotten over Vidura's leaving very quickly. When once Kokila mentioned that Chetana didn't seem to miss Vidura, Chetana serenely said, "Those who are gone are gone. I have to live my life now. My mother left—you don't see me cry about that, do you? And she was probably a whole lot more important to me than Vidura."

Kokila had experienced similar losses when her parents died, but this was different. They had died, their bodies had been burned, there had been closure. Vidura had left a raw open wound that didn't heal and Kokila feared it never would. Kokila stopped going to the beach in the evenings with Charvi. She couldn't bear to be there without

Vidura. As it started to become obvious that Vidura would never come back, something within Kokila shriveled; laughter, which used to come easily, wouldn't come at all. She felt older and seemed to have little interest in the idle times and nonsense of her old life.

To pass the time, Kokila started doing more chores at Tella Meda. Everyone except Charvi did their own washing; Subhadra did Charvi's and the other common linens. Kokila took over that responsibility. She would wash and dry and iron everything accordingly, nagging Chetana to help.

She even started helping Subhadra in the kitchen and coaxed Chetana to do the same. Cooking three meals a day for the people who lived in the *ashram* plus the inevitable guests and devotees who came unannounced was a full-time job and Subhadra welcomed their help in chopping vegetables and serving the food.

Chetana woke up late each morning but Kokila made it a point to be up early and do the morning *puja* with Charvi. Her faith in Lord Venkateshwara Swami had increased since Vidura ran away. She started to believe that everything had a divine reason and everything happened for one's own good. It was the only way she could cope with Vidura's desertion.

Breakfast was never an elaborate affair, as Subhadra just steamed *idlis* and served them with leftover *sambhar* and coconut chutney. Sometimes she would make lemon rice, curd rice, or tamarind rice with rice left over from the previous night's dinner.

Kokila and Chetana would help clean the dishes after breakfast and then start cleaning the verandah. Clothes had to be washed every other day, and Chetana helped, but reluctantly.

"Once I get married, I'm going to get a maid to do all this work for me," Chetana would say.

Then they would help Subhadra prepare lunch, do the dishes, and then repeat the process again for dinner. In the middle they would help clean the rooms and the terrace and also work in the garden with Narayan Garu, who loved the plants as if they were his own children. The small vegetable garden that Narayan Garu tended produced tomatoes, peas, carrots, coriander, mint, and various gourds. It was a lifesaver for Tella Meda, especially on the many days when there was no money to buy vegetables and Subhadra would have had to serve just rice and pickle if it hadn't been for Narayan Garu's vegetables.

Despite all their work, Chetana and Kokila still managed to find free time. Gradually they returned to their habits of spending many an afternoon gossiping, playing cards, reading Telugu film magazines, and going for matinees at the cinema when they could get money from Subhadra. Since neither Kokila nor Chetana had any income, it was always a matter of begging and nagging hard enough to melt Subhadra's heart so that she would part with a few *paisas* from her meager monthly pension.

Vidura used to accompany them in all their activities but as time passed, both Kokila and Chetana couldn't imagine how it had been with a third person intruding on their friendship.

Three months after Vidura ran away and Nehru died, *she* came to the *ashram*. She was an odd woman, everyone thought, a little too modern, too masculine. Her name was Vineetha Raghavan and she was an old friend of Ramanandam Sastri. Hearing of his loss and needing some peace herself, she arrived at the *ashram* unannounced. This was her first visit to Tella Meda.

She wasn't just Vineetha Raghavan, she was Dr. Vineetha Raghavan. And she wasn't a sick people's doctor but an engineer, a scientist.

Amongst all her father's friends, Charvi disliked Vineetha the most. It was Vineetha's bizarre friendship with her father that irked Charvi no end. Theirs was a special relationship, one she had never been able to pierce through or look into. Charvi was not sure and didn't care if they were having sex. That wasn't important. It was their emotional bond that grated on her nerves and kept her awake at night. For Charvi there was only one man in her life and to have another woman claim a place in his heart was torture.

Vineetha didn't care what anyone thought of her. It was enough that she had achieved what she set out to achieve. One of the first women scientists to be offered a post at the Bhabha Atomic Center, the first nuclear power plant in India, Vineetha felt she had done justice to the *lakhs* of *rupees* her wealthy father had spent in sending her to university in America. She had met Ramanandam Sastri at a party in Hyderabad several years ago when his wife was alive and the children were still young. The party was thrown by a literary friend and several writers and wealthy readers had been invited. She had immediately taken to the feminist writer, who was more than ten years her senior. Those who thought that they were having a sexual relationship couldn't have been more wrong. But it wasn't platonic either; there was a spark, something neither Vineetha nor Ramanandam could define. It was a cherished friendship and one both counted on.

In the past few years, however, they both had been too busy with their lives and their friendship had thinned with time. Vineetha had not had time for anyone, including herself, once she started working at the nuclear power plant. For years, Vineetha along with other scientists had worked to make India stronger, but now, after Nehru's death, the political dark clouds were settling on the Bhabha Atomic Center. Dr. Homi Bhabha, the founder of the nuclear program in India and a good friend of Vineetha's, had gone to New Delhi to speak with the new prime minister, Lal Bahadur Sastri, who, unlike the late Jawaharlal Nehru, didn't condone India becoming a nuclear power.

"He takes *ahimsa* too far," Vineetha complained to Ramanandam. "Doesn't believe in weapons and war, he says. Nehru didn't either and now we have China holding on to Indian territory."

"I believe in Gandhi and *ahimsa*," Ramanandam reminded her.

"But you can't believe in it blindly," Vineetha said. "India has to protect her borders. Anyway, I'm not here to think about the politics and the problems at work. I'm here to relax and spend some time with you."

"What do you think of my Charvi's *ashram*?" Ramanandam asked, looking around the courtyard where they were sitting and the rooms that spilled around it. "Isn't it serene?"

Vineetha followed his line of vision and couldn't see the serenity. The house had obviously been built for opulence, but opulence had to be maintained; this house looked like an old woman who in her youth used to be beautiful.

The whitewashed walls were dirty and the tiles in the courtyard seemed dull and old; obviously no one was polishing them as they were supposed to. The clothes that hung on the clotheslines were faded and inexpensive. The rooms seemed cluttered with things and the entire house was unkempt. The instruments in the music room were battered and old and the *veena* that Charvi played every evening during *bhajan* really needed to be restrung. It was worse in the evening because all the bulbs in the house were of low wattage to save money, and in that stale yellow light the house looked even more destitute than it did in the harsh light of day.

The food served at Tella Meda was simple, almost boring, Vineetha thought, and she wondered if no one got tired of eating *sambhar*, rice, and mango pickle all the time. And then there were the bathrooms. Vineetha shuddered as she wondered how she was going to get through the next two weeks with bathrooms that looked like they belonged next to a hut, with their rickety doors, damp walls, and cold and rough cement floors. The toilet was just a hole, which probably had never been cleaned, and the flush on top with a lever on it did not always work, which meant that you had to go out, fill a bucket with water from the taps in the bathroom or outside, and use that water to flush.

She was not really a snob and could adjust to any life, Vineetha believed, but here the stench of poverty and neediness was overwhelming, especially when she had to stand so close to it.

Always before, they had met in Hyderabad or Bangalore, where Vineetha had homes. When Ramanandam's wife was alive, Vineetha hadn't come to his house because she didn't want his wife's feelings to be bruised. After her death, she had continued to stay away rather than endure Charvi's almost blatant disdain. It was obvious to everyone that Charvi was very possessive of Ramanandam. And why shouldn't she be? She had no other man in her life and never would. Ramanandam had named her a goddess and had therefore thrown her into the land of spinsters and loneliness. The only man in Charvi's life was Ramanandam and she needed him, almost desperately.

So this was the first time Vineetha had come to Ramanandam, to

Tella Meda. Here everything seemed different. Ramanandam seemed different.

"How do you keep it going? This is a huge house and you have . . . many people here." The term she wanted to use was *free-loaders* but since Ramanandam himself could be considered one of those living off his daughter's asceticism, she couldn't be direct.

"There is my pension, there is no rent on the place, and everyone chips in," Ramanandam said, not feeling any shame in openly discussing his lifestyle. "And many devotees come by and leave an offering for Charvi. Everything helps and we don't need much. We're simple people trying to get closer to God and live our lives the way we want to."

Religion and money, Vineetha thought, walked hand in hand often enough, which made her wary of the former and appreciate an abundance of the latter.

"It seems like a sad place," Vineetha said. But that was not entirely true. It was not just a sad place; it was a desperate place, as the people who lived within the walls of Tella Meda filled it with their hopelessness.

"It is sad, my son is gone," Ramanandam said, his eyes filling with tears.

"I know," Vineetha said, responding to the devastation in his voice. "I can only imagine your anguish."

Ramanandam sighed deeply. "I never thought my heart could break this much. I never knew pain could be this sharp, this intense, and this all-encompassing. I feel like my insides have been scraped."

He seemed to have aged so much since she'd last seen him. But Vineetha suspected that most of the gray hair on his head had sprouted in the three months since Vidura disappeared.

"Why do you think he ran away?" Vineetha asked. They had talked about Vidura briefly when she first arrived but it had been a superficial conversation, meant only to soothe Ramanandam.

He raised his hands in defeat. "I don't know. I don't know and it is making me mad."

"You must know something," Vineetha said.

"I don't know," Ramanandam repeated in exasperation.

"Children don't just run away, Raman, there is always a reason," Vineetha prodded.

"I wish I knew, I wish I could tell you," Ramanandam said.

"What does Charvi say?" Vineetha asked.

"She hasn't spoken to me since he ran away. She blames me, I think, though she hasn't said anything," Ramanandam told her. "I can see her heart breaking but I can't do anything. I have searched for the boy . . . Does this pain ever go away? Is there ever any ease?"

Vineetha raised her hands and turned her palms toward the skies. "Maybe God knows the answer to that. But time will heal and you never know—he may come back."

"How? How will he come back?" Ramanandam asked in frustration. "It's been too long. Anything could have happened to him, anything at all."

"You have to keep faith," Vineetha said, though she knew it was just platitudes she was offering him. It had been three months and no one had heard anything from or about Vidura. She knew as well as Ramanandam that the chances of them finding Vidura were not very good.

"I keep trying to remember what I did, what I said, was it me? Why would he run away?"

"You are a good father," Vineetha said firmly.

"I'm so relieved to hear you say so," Ramanandam said. "Because I have doubted myself and . . . I'm so glad you're here. Just having you with me eases me."

"I had to come," Vineetha said with a smile. "Through all my difficult times I knew I could count on you for support. I had to come here and see if I could be of any help to you during yours."

When Vineetha was growing up it was unheard of for a woman to leave her home country, get an education, stay unmarried, find a job, and continue to stay unmarried. Now that she was perceived as being well beyond marriageable age, her family had given up on finding her a husband and tried to hide her scandalous behavior behind superficial talk about "one of the great women scientists of India." Vineetha knew that her mother would have died happier if her only daughter had been married with children.

In America and even back at home it had been difficult and almost impossible to explain that her interest in men was limited to the superficial. Even though some believed her to be homosexual, she was not. Ramanandam told her that not everyone is destined to be with a soul mate. He never found his, he said, even though he married and had four children.

At her age Vineetha felt that she didn't have to make any more excuses to society. Her life was what she made it and if it wasn't the life society would want her to have, that was not really her problem. "My dear feminist," Ramanandam called her.

Though she loved Ramanandam and respected him, his declaration that Charvi was a goddess had never sat well with her. She openly criticized Ramanandam for forcing the poor girl into a life that no one should have to live, unable to make her own choices, unable to marry or live on her own terms. But Ramanandam didn't see it that way. He truly believed that Charvi had been born with the spark of divine knowledge within her. Siddhartha had become Buddha after gaining knowledge one night while meditating under a banyan tree, but Charvi had been born with that knowledge.

Naturally, among Ramanandam's three daughters, it was Lavanya that Vineetha was drawn to. It was Lavanya that she kept in touch with through the years. Manikyam, Ramanandam's eldest daughter, deemed Vineetha a corruptor of Lavanya because of the closeness they shared.

"Lavanya is becoming just like *her,* Nanna," Manikyam would warn her father. "Look at Lavanya—no husband, no marriage, and she goes with men, even married men, just like your Vineetha."

"In this house we don't cast stones," Ramanandam would say quietly but firmly to her, even though Lavanya's promiscuous life had disappointed him. It was one thing to believe in women's rights and liberation and it was quite another to have sex outside of marriage, especially for his daughter. "Lavanya is living the life she wants to live and you are living yours, Charvi hers, and Vineetha hers as well. You have no right to judge or question what they do with their lives."

A week after Vineetha came to the *ashram*, Lavanya came as well. These days Lavanya was living in Madras. One rumor said she was a mistress to some married movie producer, another was that she had married a man of lower caste in secret, and yet another was that she was living in some hotel with the wrong kind of clientele. With Lavanya there were always rumors and usually they were well-founded ones. She rarely visited Tella Meda, so the residents of the *ashram* usually only heard the rumors despite the fact that she was family.

Upon hearing of Lavanya's visit, Manikyam arrived with her two sons, Ravi and Prasad. They were good-looking boys but completely spoiled.

"Did you say something to Vidura?" Lavanya demanded of Charvi. "You must have. Why would a boy just run away?"

"Why this suspicion?" Charvi asked, surprised at the accusation. "I'm just as worried as you."

"Oh, you mean you can't look into your crystal ball and tell us where Vidura is? What, the goddess doesn't have that power?" Lavanya demanded.

"I never said I'm a goddess," Charvi said humbly.

"See, Vineetha, how she turns it around," Lavanya said, her words hot and angry.

"There is nothing to turn around. He is gone and there is a deep pain inside all of us. Why he left? I don't know. When he left? I don't know. If I knew, I would openly tell everyone. I have nothing to hide," Charvi said softly.

They were sitting at the empty dining table outside the kitchen. Charvi was sipping Darjeeling tea while Vineetha was drinking a glass of water.

"I should've taken him away with me," Lavanya said as tears filled her eyes.

"You couldn't have," Charvi consoled her. "Your job takes you all around the world. You couldn't have given him a home."

"And this is home?" Lavanya asked. "This . . . place with the people, this is home? This is not a home, Charvi, this is a free inn for losers."

"You should ask our father why Vidura left. Maybe he can help you," Charvi said quietly.

"Oh, now you want to blame him? Well, I don't. I blame you for this hocus-pocus you are throwing at people." So saying, Lavanya left the table.

"She doesn't understand that saving Vidura is not in my power," Charvi said sadly. "He chose his destiny and his age doesn't have anything to do with it. He decided what he wanted to do and why. How can she blame me?"

Vineetha didn't want to get embroiled in a fight between sisters but for the first time she was not on Lavanya's side. It seemed unreasonable and unfair to blame Charvi for the actions of a confused teenager.

"She is just very upset and doesn't know whom to blame so she blames you," Vineetha said. "Why do you think your father would know why Vidura left?"

"He knows," Charvi said in her serene, goddesslike voice.

"Do *you* know why he left?"

Charvi shook her head. "I can't read people's minds. But my father knows."

"I asked him. He would have told me if he knew," Vineetha said, though she wasn't sure if Ramanandam would indeed tell her the truth about Vidura. As close as they used to be, the past years had put a strain on their relationship. She had been busy with work and he with setting up Tella Meda as an *ashram* for his daughter.

"Sometimes there are some truths that are more bitter than the *neem* fruit. He may believe that he doesn't know because he doesn't want to," Charvi pointed out.

"But you know, because you are the *guru* of Tella Meda."

Charvi laughed softly then. "You have always said that I was a fraud."

"Don't you think you are a fraud?"

Charvi shook her head. "By whose definition? I only have to worry about the woman I see in the mirror every morning and that woman is clear of blame, deceit, or any fraud. Do you look at yourself and see the woman others make you out to be or do you see yourself as you truly are?"

Vineetha smiled, pleasantly surprised by the woman Charvi had become. "If I cared about what people think I wouldn't be working alongside Homi Bhabha at the atomic power center; I would be married and a mother."

"And if I worried about what people thought I would have to wear orange clothes all the time and chant as if I were possessed," Charvi said with some amusement. "The other day a couple came to me because they are childless. I told them I will pray for them but there was nothing else I could do. They asked me if I could chant a few words and sway my head and give them some holy ash. Holy ash from a goddess, the husband had been told, would cure his wife of her barrenness."

Vineetha drank some water and wondered if she had misjudged Charvi all these years.

"What did you tell them?"

Charvi shrugged. "I gave them some holy ash and told them that I was not a goddess and that they would be better off seeing a doctor."

"But they still come flocking to you, despite your being so candid," Vineetha pointed out.

"I can't control the movements of others. I can't define their motives," Charvi said as she rose from the table. "You will have to excuse me now; it is time for my meditation."

Vineetha continued to sit at the table and watched Chetana braid Kokila's hair. They were so young, so bright and radiant, their eyes full of excitement and yearning to learn about the world.

When she was that young she also had had the light of hunger burning brightly inside her. She had wanted so much and now she had it all, yet there was a stunning loneliness because of the knowledge that after her nothing about her would remain. She believed in the soul not as a spirit but as a memory that resided in others. Children and grandchildren carried their parents, grandparents, and great-grandparents forward in their minds, and so a part of those who had died stayed behind in the world.

She didn't believe in the reincarnation nonsense, as she knew that humans were carbon-based life-forms and once they died they disintegrated like all other carbon-based life—there was no difference. A tree died and nothing living was left behind; similarly when a human died, life went away. It was as simple as that.

"Do you wear pants all the time?" Chetana asked. She was the daring one, Vineetha thought, the beautiful one. The one whose mother was a prostitute. The other girl, the one who didn't want to go to her husband's home, she was shy, quiet. Ramanandam had told her about all the residents of Tella Meda, given her the reasons for their living in the *ashram*.

"Most of the time I wear pants," Vineetha replied.

"Do you pee like a man, then?" Chetana asked, and was shushed by Kokila.

"No," Vineetha said, amused.

"Then why do you wear pants? Isn't it easier to lift a skirt and squat rather than have the pants hanging around your ankles?" Chetana wanted to know. Kokila was getting very agitated and tried to drag Chetana away before she asked any more embarrassing questions.

"Just because it's easy for you doesn't mean it's easy for me," Vineetha said patiently. "And I like pants. I can sit how I like and not worry about anyone seeing my underwear."

"But you don't look pretty in them," Chetana said. "Don't you want to look pretty?"

Vineetha pondered the question for a long moment. "I don't know," she said honestly, because she really didn't know if she would give up comfort for pretty clothes.

"Come on, Chetana, Subhadra wants us in the kitchen," Kokila insisted, and dragged her friend away.

"Why did you ask her those questions? They were rude," Kokila admonished Chetana after they were in the kitchen.

"Do you think Ramanandam Sastri and she are doing it?" Chetana asked, and Kokila groaned.

"Is your mind always in the gutter?"

"He has to do it with someone. My mother told me once that men just have to do it all the time, at least once a day, or their *lingam* shrivels." Chetana spoke with an air of confidence.

"Your mother is a lying whore. I wouldn't believe everything she says," Kokila said wearily.

"But she knows a lot about a man's *lingam*." Chetana giggled. "Have you seen one?" she asked, and Kokila shrugged.

"You have, you dirty girl. Tell me!" Chetana demanded with glee in her eyes.

Kokila made a sound and looked around to make sure Subhadra was occupied in the other end of the kitchen, then brought her voice down to a whisper. "I saw Narayan Garu's once."

"Really? How?"

"He was wearing that thin *lungi* of his, the blue one with red peacocks on it, and it fell open when he was sitting down. It was . . . I can't talk about this," Kokila said, her ears burning with embarrassment.

"How was it?" Chetana asked, undeterred by her friend's embarrassment.

"What?" Kokila asked, confused.

"His *lingam*."

"It was small and . . . dark," Kokila said, and called out to Subhadra before Chetana could ask any more questions.

That evening Charvi insisted that Kokila come for the evening walk with her. Kokila didn't have the heart to refuse. Charvi had been depressed since Vidura ran away but with the arrival of Dr. Vineetha Raghavan, Charvi seemed to be even more withdrawn. Lavanya's visit had not helped either.

Kokila didn't like the eldest sister, Manikyam, much and she definitely didn't like her two sons, Ravi and Prasad, who always spent the summer at Tella Meda. When they were younger they used to constantly whine and fight, but as they grew, the whines grew into angry outbursts, tantrums, and hysterics. Chetana spent more time with Ravi than Kokila liked but no one could ever stop Chetana from doing what she wanted. Prasad was almost always out of Tella Meda, whiling away the day and whistling at young girls as he sat with some rowdy friends of his by the cinema. If anyone bothered to tell Manikyam about her sons' behavior she would accuse the person who told her of being jealous of her sons.

Ravi always came up with ways of looking underneath girls' skirts and into women's blouses. Manikyam fondly called it child's play and naughtiness. Kokila couldn't understand how Manikyam could condone their foul behavior. It was always a relief when summer ended and they left to go back to Visakhapatnam.

Kokila didn't mind Lavanya much. She rarely came to Tella Meda, so Kokila didn't have to spend much time with her. Lavanya seemed to be angry all the time, which was so different from Charvi, who was never angry. Even when she was insulted by someone, Charvi would answer with dignity in a very calm tone. Kokila respected Charvi for her ability to control her emotions and hoped she could be as sedate and controlled someday.

"Vidura spent a lot of time with you," Charvi said to Kokila as soon as they reached the beach. "Did he say anything to you?"

Kokila bit her lip, not sure if she should hurt Charvi's feelings by telling her what Vidura had said the night he kissed her.

"Say anything to me? About what?" Kokila said evasively.

"About wanting to run away," Charvi replied patiently. She could see that Kokila was nervous talking about Vidura. "You can tell me anything. I won't take offense."

Kokila sighed. "He once told me that he hated . . . I don't think it's important. He just ran away, maybe he'll come back—"

"It's important to me," Charvi interrupted softly. "Tell me what he said. If someone should know, it's you."

"Maybe Chetana . . ."

"Chetana isn't silent enough to listen to what others say. So even if Vidura tried to tell her, I'm sure she didn't hear anything. You would. You are sensitive, you were close to him, and if anyone should know . . ."

Appeased by the compliment and by the disparaging words for Chetana, Kokila decided to tell Charvi the truth. She quickly realized, though, that she shouldn't have. Charvi might be a *guru*, a calm goddess, but she was still very human.

"Vidura said he hated Tella Meda because it was not a real home. And . . . and that he hated you for believing you were a *guru* and he was upset that Sastri Garu also believed you. He felt that because of you he was not close to his father anymore. He was angry that you thought you had the power to heal because he didn't think you did," Kokila said hurriedly. As the words came out and she heard them, she sensed how empty they were. They had achieved nothing. They were vague emotions, the ramblings of an angry boy, and Kokila had presented them as fact, as Vidura's true feelings, as the reason for his running away.

"Do you believe in me?" Charvi asked Kokila, surprising her.

When Kokila gave her a blank look, unable to understand her question, Charvi sighed.

"Do you believe that I am a goddess? That I have the power to heal?" she asked, and when Kokila merely looked at her feet, not answering, Charvi's much-touted control snapped. "Maybe you should run away too. You obviously hate my house and me as much as Vidura did."

Charvi spun around and left Kokila standing alone on the beach. By the time Kokila caught up with Charvi and tried to apologize it was too late. Charvi was wearing her serene *guru* face and wasn't listening to Kokila or her apologies.

Vineetha was upset after reading the newspapers. Prime Minister Lal Bahadur Sastri was publicly talking about scrapping the Indian nuclear program by saying that it was adversarial and would raise fear of war among India's neighbors.

She had sacrificed home and family for the atomic center. She had worked so hard to make India stronger and now Lal Bahadur Sastri was talking nonsense.

Vineetha was worried not just about losing her job but also about wasting a lifetime's work.

Unsettled and just a little tired of being in Tella Meda, she decided to take a walk on the beach and then go visit Lavanya, who was staying at a friend's place a few roads away. As a policy, Lavanya never stayed overnight at Tella Meda. A big part of it was pride. She didn't acknowledge it to be a home and refused to be part of the wayward and hopeless bunch that gathered there.

When Vineetha reached Lavanya's friend's house she was told that Lavanya had already left town. There had been an emergency at work and she had been called away. Vineetha was not convinced. What kind of an emergency could an air hostess be called away for? *We don't have enough smiling woman sashaying down the aisle, could you come and help us a little?*

When Vineetha came back to Tella Meda, Subhadra offered her tea, which she sat in the kitchen to drink while Subhadra started to grind water-soaked *urad dal* and rice for *idli* batter in the large stone mortar and pestle.

"Her brother is gone missing and she's gallivanting around. She doesn't even come home for three months because she's abroad. Doing what?" Vineetha muttered, suddenly resentful of the woman who had been her friend. "She and her ridiculous job."

"Lavanya feels her job is important," Subhadra said. "Just like you think your work is important."

"My work *is* important," Vineetha said sharply. "My work is of great importance to India, unlike Lavanya's. Her work isn't going to make a difference, a real difference, in anyone's life."

"And how is your work going to change the life of the beggar on the street or my life or anyone else's life?" Subhadra asked.

"My work is going to change India's standing in the world," Vineetha said.

"And I will still have to wait in the ration line to buy sugar," Subhadra said. "Look, what is important to you is not important to us. We live in the real world and in the real world no one cares if India has a big bomb or not."

"I'm not helping India make bombs, I'm helping her make energy so that every village in India will have electricity," Vineetha snapped at Subhadra, and set her half-filled glass of tea on the floor with force. It tipped and the tea spilled onto the floor. Vineetha didn't bother to pick it up.

"My life has meaning," Vineetha said.

"I am glad that you feel it does," Subhadra said gently. "We all should feel our life has meaning, otherwise there would be no need to live another day. I didn't mean to insult you, anyway. I am just upset . . . you know . . ."

Vineetha all but stomped out of the kitchen, not sure why she was so defensive about her work.

What did these people know? Vineetha thought angrily. They were so embroiled in their tawdry little lives, what did they care about India and her problems? These were lowly people, interested only in their own lives, not caring about the society, the country, the larger issues. As long as they got three square meals a day they didn't care who lived or who died.

The people and the place were suffocating her. Not having felt quite so out of her element ever before, Vineetha decided to leave Tella Meda.

Ramanandam heard about her decision and came to ask why she was leaving in such a rush.

"I don't know why, but I feel unsettled," Vineetha confided. "I can't read the newspapers without losing my temper and this house of yours is morose, Raman."

That surprised Ramanandam. "Why do you say that?"

"Everyone is stuck with their small problems," Vineetha said. "Your lives are . . . your lives are entangled in the ordinary and everyone seems so sad and lost."

"Small problems?" Ramanandam asked carefully, his voice quivering a little.

"Well, yes," Vineetha said. "I'm not saying your son running away is a small problem, but—"

"My son, my only son, my child is gone. I can't find him, I don't know why he ran away, and you think that is maybe a small problem?" Ramanandam asked, looking even more aged than he had just a few days ago when Vineetha first came to Tella Meda.

"I just said that it is *not* a small problem . . . Regardless of the size of your problems, I'm feeling stifled in this house of yours," Vineetha told him honestly. "Everyone seems so upset about the boy running away and yet no one seems to know how it happened. Don't you think that's strange?"

"Yes, I think it's very strange that he ran away and none of us can fathom why," Ramanandam said. He was almost yelling at Vineetha.

Vineetha closed the suitcase she had been filling up with all her belongings. "Why did he run away, Raman?"

"I don't know."

"You must know something," Vineetha said. "Charvi believes that maybe you do."

Ramanandam shook his head violently. "If I knew, don't you think I would've done something by now?"

"Maybe the truth is bitter . . . embarrassing," Vineetha suggested.

"What the hell do you mean by that?" Ramanandam demanded. "Bitter? Embarrassing? What did you think happened? He saw me do something terrible and ran away to hide from my sins?"

"Maybe," Vineetha said wearily.

"Maybe? How can you say that?" Ramanandam asked.

"Look, I don't know," Vineetha said. "But when children run away it isn't from happy homes. They run away because there is trouble at home, with their parents."

"Why did you come here? To sling mud at me? To insult me in my own home?" Ramanandam asked, agitated.

"I thought I came to support you," she said bitterly. "But I really can't. Your son is gone and . . . Raman, this *ashram* of yours is depressing. Everyone here is a failure and you know what? Being with them, standing next to them, you seem like a failure as well."

"This *ashram* is a safe haven for lost souls," Ramanandam said defensively.

"Including yours," Vineetha said in full agreement.

"Charvi is a *guru,* but you're probably too blinded by bitterness and rage to see the light of divinity within her," Ramanandam said angrily. "But one can't blame you. Women like you, women who have no God, no husband, no children, and no family, tend to be bitter and dried-up old maids."

Vineetha gasped. He had revealed what some had suspected were always his true feelings. The last threads of friendship holding them together unraveled.

"I came here with the good intention to help you, God knows why, but I can't stand to be with you and be party to your pitiful life. And yes, Raman, it is a pitiful life. Living off scraps left by visitors and anointing your own daughter a *guru* so that she can be the breadwinner, pretending to be open and kind but truly condemning those around you to a life of restriction and poverty—all of it is depraved," Vineetha said, and wondered why on earth she had come here in the first place.

"You are nothing but a whimsical rich bitch," Ramanandam said, furious with her.

"There is no reason for name-calling," Vineetha said calmly. "Here is some money for this stay. Isn't that what visitors leave behind?" She hadn't meant to give it to him—she had intended to give it to Subhadra, who took care of such matters—but pride propelled her and she threw the heavy envelope on the bed.

It was the last and only time Vineetha came to Tella Meda.

12 March 1967. Indira Gandhi became the prime minister of India for the second time.

13 May 1967. Dr. Zakhir Hussain was elected the third president of India, the first Muslim to hold the post.

The Goddess

*E*ventually time healed the wound Vidura had inflicted on Tella Meda and even though the wound itched at times, it didn't bleed anymore.

Charvi missed Vidura but as the years passed, his memory started to fade just a little. She felt some guilt for not remembering him as she used to but that passed as well.

Charvi's relationship with her father improved after Vineetha Raghavan's departure. Ramanandam never asked Charvi why she thought he knew the reason for Vidura running away and she never told him about her suspicions either. Till the day he died, Ramanandam claimed he knew nothing and Charvi never questioned him.

It was during the monsoon season, when rain was slamming the coast and the threat of a hurricane loomed large, that the white man with his signature American backpack and Levi's jeans arrived. Mark

Talbot was a photojournalist for *Life* magazine and was taking a vacation in southern India. A friend of his mentioned Bheemunipatnam and Tella Meda, and Mark wrote a letter to Charvi and asked for an invitation to visit.

He had been to other *ashrams* of famous Indian *gurus* and had seen their opulence, the numerous devotees, and the religious following. He was surprised by Tella Meda. It seemed barren, normal, like a home, just as Charvi had told him in the letter.

"This is my home," she had written, "and you are welcome to come and visit. I am not an Amma or a goddess, I am just Charvi. My home is open to anyone who is in need and by need I don't mean in need of salvation, for I do not know how to provide that. My home is a refuge for those who need a home, for those who are looking for some peace in their lives. It is by the Bay of Bengal and at night when you look at the waters, the waves look like white frothy birds frolicking on the night-darkened sand.

"My home is a place of religion but I don't believe in imposing my beliefs on those who come here. My God is not everyone's God and I believe that religion and prayer are private matters. You are welcome to pray with me and I will be happy to include you in my sermons about my God, but if you are not interested you will not be shown the door at my home.

"I don't know about the photographs you wish to take as I am a very private person and would be uncomfortable. But you are welcome to take photos of Tella Meda. The house is a beautiful piece of architecture and emanates a serenity I have not felt or seen elsewhere. It is a beautiful home with a clean soul. I hope you will see it as I do. We look forward to your visit in September, but I must warn you that the monsoon season will have taken hold of us by then and hurricanes may strike, submerging us in water.

"But I can promise you peace and excellent but simple south Indian food. Regards, Charvi."

Mark had been touched that she called herself just Charvi and no title of "Amma," "Guru," or "Bhagwan" anointed her name. His friend had told him that she was just twenty-five years old but mature for her age. She even looked older, his friend had said, with some gray-ing hair and wrinkles beneath her eyes, but she was a beautiful woman, with the goddess shining on her face.

He had not believed his friend, who had recently taken a Hindu name, but with one look at Charvi Mark became a believer. This woman was Devi, Amma, Circe, Goddess, Venus all blended into one. She was light-skinned and unlike most Indian women could pass for a foreigner easily. Her eyes were not dark but light brown, filled with mystery. But it was her voice that undid him.

When she talked about Indian mythology, the Upanishads, the *Bhagavad-Gita*, he was enchanted and he realized that at the age of forty he was experiencing a schoolboy crush on a woman who was be-lieved by all around her to be a goddess.

Kokila and Chetana couldn't keep their eyes off the white man. They both thought he was the most handsome man they had ever seen and Chetana boldly dressed up in her best half-*sari* to attract his attention. Not as bold as Chetana, Kokila would watch from behind doors and windows.

Mark Talbot was quite popular with the ladies of the *ashram*. Sub-hadra thought he was a wonderful man and spoke to him in her prim, accented English. Since Kokila and Chetana spoke very little English, Chetana struggled to learn as fast as she could.

But it was Charvi who fell in love with him. It was not the white skin, the tight pants, or anything else superficial that drew her to him, it was his photographs. He took pictures of Tella Meda and at the local photo studio used the darkroom to process the film himself. The house was magnificent. It looked better in his photos than it did stand-ing in reality. The Bay of Bengal looked like a lethal water mass in one photo and a serene tropical paradise in another. This man was full of contradictions and he spoke intelligently of Indian culture and tradi-tions. He seemed to understand religion even though he claimed he wasn't religious.

He never judged Charvi's role in Tella Meda, never questioned her godliness, and never implied that he thought her to be fraudulent or that he believed she was an Amma. He treated her with respect and Charvi could see the attraction he felt for her. His cologne, his voice, the smell of his soap, everything filled her with longing. Sometimes she would pass on meditation in the afternoon and instead think about him. She would lie in bed at night and wonder how it would feel to have him touch her, there, here, everywhere.

Another resident arrived two days after Mark Talbot did. Renuka was an acquaintance of Subhadra's, and also a relative in a convoluted way. Her husband had just passed away and, not wanting to spend her golden years with her sons and their "bitchy and ungrateful" wives, she had decided to come to the *ashram*. Subhadra warned her that she would have to pay some kind of rent and help with the day-to-day operation of the *ashram*. The rent as such was meager and Renuka's husband's pension helped pay for it but when it came to doing work around the *ashram* she couldn't seem to find anything that she wanted to do.

Finally, they settled on the cleaning and maintenance of the *puja* room, where all the musical instruments were also assembled. Renuka could play the harmonium and for the evening *bhajan* she would play in tune with Charvi's singing and playing of the *veena*.

Not having known Charvi since she was a girl, Renuka didn't have the same blind devotion for her as Subhadra did. She saw the things others didn't want to or couldn't see. She believed in tradition and was old-fashioned. After her husband's death she shaved her hair off and now wore only a thin white *sari* to cover her body. Chetana and Kokila spent a lot of time in the beginning peeking at her limp breasts hanging under the *sari,* as she wore no blouse. She stayed in a small room in a corner, wanting the smallest and least desirable room, and ate simple (and special) food without spices.

It was customary for widows to eat plain food and live simply. Even though Ramanandam told Renuka that in Charvi's *ashram* she could let her hair grow and wear colored *saris,* Renuka wasn't going to change the course of her life. It didn't take her long to start disliking the easygoing way of Tella Meda. It seemed wrong and sinful that those 17–18-year-old girls, Chetana and Kokila, would just prance around and talk to men of all ages. And one of them was a prostitute's daughter? Oh, Shiva, Shiva, what had the world come to!

But her biggest problem was what she saw happening between

the white man and the *guru* of the *ashram.* She watched them like a hawk. For morning *puja* she made sure she was there along with Sub-hadra to ensure that nothing foul went on between the two. Charvi was a good Brahmin girl and a *guru.* Associating with these immoral white men was wrong in so many ways. Renuka decided that once she had been there awhile she would take some control of Tella Meda and not allow men like this to come and stay. No matter how much money they left behind, it was not right to have a white-skinned man stay in the *ashram* where so many young girls lived.

Charvi barely noticed the arrival of Renuka. She was so con-sumed by her discussions and walks with Mark Talbot that everything else whittled into nothing. After the first few days, even the guilt she felt at her attraction for him passed and now there was a glow on her face. There was a change in the pace of her heart and a freedom she felt for the first time. *This must be love,* she thought. *This must be the love that they talk about in the books: incandescent, self-illuminating, fulfilling, and almost painful.*

"During the great battle, *The Mahabharata,* cousins were at war. The hundred Kaurava brothers were fighting against the five Pandava brothers. Armies had been amassed and the war was to begin. Arjuna, a Pandava, was torn. His charioteer was Lord Krishna, who saw the pain his friend and disciple was going through. They had been prepar-ing for battle for days, weeks, years now, yet at the time of reckoning, Arjuna couldn't imagine lifting his bow and shooting arrows at his own cousins, at his teacher, at people he grew up with, at his friends and family.

"It was then that Lord Krishna took his godly form and rose . . . See that picture there, Mark?" Charvi pointed to a painting in the music room.

It was a beautiful re-creation of the battle described in the great epic, *The Mahabharata.* Armies were scattered on either side of an empty strip of land where Arjuna kneeled in front of a large Krishna who took his original form and showed the world and Arjuna that he was indeed a reincarnation of Lord Vishnu.

"That is Arjuna, he who is kneeling, and Lord Krishna . . . well, he doesn't need to be described. He is God, eternal, all-encompassing," Charvi said with a small smile. "This is where Lord Krishna imparts the *Bhagavad-Gita* to Arjuna. *Bhagavad-Gita* literally means 'the divine song' and it is here he tells Arjuna that you have to put your personal feelings aside and fight the good fight."

"So . . . it was sort of a civil war," Mark said. "America had one as well."

"*The Mahabharata* was about a war between good and evil. What were you fighting over?" Charvi asked.

Mark grinned. "Money."

"I thought the great American Civil War was to free black slaves in the South," Charvi said with a twinkle in her eye, challenging him with what she knew of his world. She lived in India but she was well read and wanted to show off.

Mark nodded. "That was part of it as well . . . or rather it became part of the issue. The South wanted to protect its cotton industry and wanted a decentralized government and free trade. The North was more industrial and didn't believe in a decentralized government because that would mean loss of tax income from the wealthy South."

"And I thought it was about freeing the slaves," Charvi said, feeling foolish for wanting to impress Mark.

"It was. As the issues remained unsolved, slowly but steadily one of the biggest issues to stand out was slavery," Mark explained. "In the North, slavery was abolished in 1804, almost fifty years before it was eliminated in the South."

"So in this case we can assume that the North was trying to free the black people and make your country more just," Charvi said, and when Mark nodded she smiled. "It was the same in *The Mahabharata*. The Kauravas were hell-bent on destroying goodness, on submerging the Pandavas. It is a matter of principle—you fight for what you believe in and you have to fight for the good of the people, of the society, of the world."

Charvi spoke passionately, excited and exhilarated by their conversations. Mark was an intelligent man and he was a mine of information. She loved to translate his Western experiences into her knowledge of India and Hinduism.

Mark was cognizant of the fact that these morning *puja* sessions were the most entertaining and invigorating conversations he had had in a long time. Charvi was passionate about the *Bhagavad-Gita* and the Upanishads. She was well read and he couldn't make her stumble on her words, no matter how hard he tried. This was not a mere twenty-five-year-old girl, this was a learned woman. Maybe there was a goddess inside her that gave her the confidence and the knowledge that made her so sure of her convictions.

"Are you married?" Charvi asked him when they were walking on the beach one evening.

Renuka trailed along suspiciously. They spoke in English and she couldn't make out what was being said. It annoyed her. What if they were saying improper things? Oh, she wished she had brought Subhadra along to translate. But Subhadra was mortified that Renuka could think that Charvi, who was chaste and unmarked, would be having an unsavory liaison with a devotee.

"No," Mark said. "And you, are you never supposed to marry?"

Charvi turned to look at the rolling waves of the Bay of Bengal. "I don't think there is a written law but what could I give a man? I'm submerged in my prayers and meditation. I'm here to serve the people. I don't think I have anything to offer one man."

"You are a young, beautiful, intelligent woman. You have a lot to offer," Mark said.

Charvi blushed. "I am just a normal woman," she said shyly.

"You are one of the most fascinating women I have ever met," Mark said honestly.

"And you are the most fascinating man I have ever met," Charvi said honestly and just a little boldly.

His words fueled her attraction and her words fueled his.

Renuka kept watch but could not understand what they were talking about in English. But she could see what was going on, though. She wasn't blind or stupid; she could see that the girl was laughing and tittering, while the man was . . . why did he keep shoving his hands inside the pockets of his jeans? What did he have to hide? And couldn't he wear loose pants like all those boys wore these days? She could see the shape of his buttocks clearly and . . . *chee-chee*, Charvi never should have allowed this white man to stay in the *ashram*.

In the end even Charvi felt that it would have been wiser not to have allowed Mark Talbot into Tella Meda and her life because when he left, he broke her heart. And it would have been smarter to have kept Renuka out of Tella Meda because she brought along with her the stubborn, old-fashioned ideas Charvi detested. But the mistake had been made and Charvi could hardly turn the clock back and send a destitute widow such as Renuka out of her home and onto the street.

Ultimately, it wasn't Renuka's reaction to Mark that offended Charvi, it was her reaction to Chetana. Charvi had known Chetana since she was born. There was a deep affection that had pooled inside her because of proximity and the knowledge of the circumstances of Chetana's birth and life.

So when Charvi heard Renuka screaming so loud that Tella Meda shook with its intensity, and came into the courtyard just as Ranuka slapped Chetana, she took a step back, not having seen physical abuse before and unsure of what must be done. Usually, her father would come and clear up the mess, but since Vidura had left, he spent more and more time inside his room, rarely coming out, even eating his meals in his room.

When Renuka slapped Chetana again, Charvi moved into action.

"Stop it," she said with as much dignity as she could, and pulled Chetana away from Renuka.

"How dare you?" Chetana yelled at Renuka as tears streamed down her face. "I can do what I want to do. You're not my mother." Chetana's body shook with the shock of being slapped by a veritable stranger.

"What's the matter?" Charvi asked, though she could guess. This was about the lipstick Chetana had painted on her lips, probably in hopes of enticing Mark. Chetana had never told where she got the lipstick, but still . . . *How could a little red paint cause so much commotion?* Charvi thought.

"She wears lipstick like that whore mother of hers," Renuka said.

Her face was constricted with anger and her thin body was shaking under her white *sari*. Her back was slightly bent and Charvi noticed the bitterness in her stance.

"She can wear whatever she wants to wear," Charvi informed Renuka, and decided to ask Subhadra to explain the rules of Tella Meda to the old widow. "If you ever, and I mean ever, strike anyone again under my roof, you will have to leave Tella Meda."

"You don't teach right from wrong and she'll end up like her mother, selling her body for five *rupees* on the street corner," Renuka cried out. "I care about what happens to them when they grow up. You . . . you are too busy shaking your ass around that white man."

Charvi had to wait five seconds before she could pull a calm façade over the anger that was quickly claiming her. "Chetana, ask Subhadra to come here," Charvi instructed in a controlled voice.

Once Chetana left to get Subhadra, Charvi told Renuka regally, "You are not the voice of morality in my house. You are not to assume that role. If I feel something is amiss, I will deal with it. If you feel something is wrong, you can tell me about it and I will decide if it is worthy of attention. What I do is not your business and it is not for you to judge. What Chetana does or Kokila does is their own business. In Tella Meda we mind our own business. You will not strike anyone, child or adult, in this house. This is a Gandhian house; we don't permit any violence."

Subhadra came running out of the kitchen, leaving Chetana with Kokila for consoling. "What? What happened?"

"Nothing," Renuka said before Charvi could speak. "This woman does not care if that little girl walks around with red paint on her lips like a slut. Well then, why should I care? Let their lives go down the drain. I won't be responsible, you will."

Charvi smiled at the woman's foolishness. "We all make our own destiny and no one is responsible for another's decisions and their lives. Subhadra, please explain to Renuka the rules of living in Tella Meda. If she doesn't follow them, she must leave by the end of the week."

Chetana's affection for Charvi turned into devotion after the scene with Renuka.

"I don't like that Renuka," Kokila said. "She actually told me that I was worse than a widow because my husband left me."

"You left your husband," Chetana said with a smirk. "And you must have enjoyed telling her that."

Kokila's mouth curved into a smile. "Yes, very much, and then you should have heard her. She went on and on and on about bad morals and how God will strike me down for my sins. If she doesn't like Tella Meda she should go and stay with her children."

Chetana lowered her voice to a whisper because they were sitting in the courtyard. Subhadra was hanging wet clothes on the clotheslines and Narayan Garu was reading aloud from a book to Ramanandam Sastri.

"I heard that her children don't want her. She has nowhere to go," Chetana told Kokila. "And Subhadra told me that the woman only has some pension coming, that's all."

Kokila nodded. She wasn't surprised. Why would someone with money and kind relatives live in Tella Meda? Everyone in the house lived there because they had nowhere else to go, no one else to take them. Except her, of course; she had rejected her husband and his house to stay at Tella Meda. She didn't dare regret that decision even though sometimes she wondered why she had stayed, especially since Vidura was gone.

"Oh and that old hag said something about Charvi getting very friendly with that white photographer," Chetana whispered.

"Maybe something is going on between them," Kokila suggested, and Chetana immediately shook her head.

"No, that simply can't be true. Charvi is . . . she's a goddess, Kokila, and she doesn't have passions like we do. She is a higher person and she's godly," Chetana said. Kokila made a face. Usually, Chetana was happy to talk about Charvi but since Charvi had stood up for her against Renuka, Chetana was feeling especially loyal toward her.

"She's still human and humans have emotions. She certainly spends enough time with that white man. And so what if she finds him attractive?" Kokila said.

Chetana shook her head vigorously. "We find him attractive because we are lower beings; she doesn't. Her interest in him is purely religious."

"Right," Kokila muttered sarcastically. "Religion is why she goes on long walks with him and sits next to him during meals. Religion is why she smiles as soon as he says something in English."

"You're just like Renuka, you know, always criticizing Charvi," Chetana admonished.

That evening Renuka didn't follow Mark and Charvi on their walk on the beach. Charvi was tempted to tell Mark about Renuka and what happened in the house that afternoon but it felt too domestic. And then she realized that she had no one to talk to about the small things in life, about seeing a bird fly or a young man sneak a kiss from a girl behind the big boulder on the beach. She had no one to gossip with. She was supposed to be above the usual chitchat anyway. She had to talk about lofty subjects, important matters.

"Do you ever wish for the world to stop?" Mark asked Charvi.

"What a strange thing to wish for," Charvi replied thoughtfully.

"I mean, do you ever wish that you could stop your life and then change course?"

"You mean like changing buses during a long journey?"

"Yes, exactly," Mark said, pleased that she understood.

Charvi shook her head. "It's not a matter of wishing. I couldn't even if I wanted it."

Mark shook his head. "What if you could? Would you want to?"

Charvi thought about his question and then shrugged. "It's pointless to speculate over something that can never happen. I believe it's a waste of time. Would you want to change your life?"

Mark nodded. "Sometimes I wish I had a wife and children, a house in the suburbs like some of my friends. Other times I wish I had done more with my life professionally than I have. I wish I were more successful."

"But that is living with regrets," Charvi said. "Regrets are a good way of drying up the energy within."

"Yes, yes, you are right," Mark said.

"I don't know much about your profession but the photos you have taken of Tella Meda leave me . . . speechless. You make my house look more beautiful than it ever has looked through my naked eyes," Charvi said. "The photos I have seen are a testament to your art and your craft."

Mark laughed softly. "But those photos were easy to take. Your house is full of energy. There are vibes all around it and it feels alive. I have never been this compelled to take so many pictures of an inanimate object, a house, before," Mark said. "You were right when you said in your letter that it has a soul. Your house has a soul. I wonder if the walls move at night and whisper to each other."

"It has a soul but it is not haunted," Charvi said, laughing at the image of the walls whispering to each other.

But when she went back into her room, she thought she could hear the walls talk. They were warning her, cautioning her against falling in love.

Did she really swing her ass around Mark? Charvi wondered about Renuka's accusation. She had walked close to him today, his arm had brushed against hers and his roughness had caressed her softness. There had been a sensation akin to death and birth. Charvi had almost turned to face him and let him read all the pent-up affection and love inside her. She had so much to give, so much to offer, yet she felt her hands were tied. She had duties, Tella Meda, the people who came every Sunday for advice, help, and prayer. She couldn't turn her back on everyone. Could she?

As it always was, Sunday was a busy day. Devotees and those seeking help, salvation, more money, children, better children, male children—everyone with a need who believed in Charvi came to Tella

Meda. They were all seated in the large temple room. Charvi played the *veena* as she sang *bhajans* and Renuka (still angry with Charvi and everyone else at Tella Meda) reluctantly played the harmonium. Narayan Garu was not very good at the *tabla* but still accompanied Charvi on it. The devotees chanted after Charvi as she sang in praise of Lord Venkateshwara Swami and Tella Meda was alight with the glow of devotion.

Before lunch, the devotees stood in line and touched Charvi's feet as they asked for her blessing. She hugged each one and touched their foreheads with her hand. Devotees would discuss among themselves how the hug purified them and how her hand on their forehead brought immense peace.

Subhadra rallied Chetana and Kokila, along with some of the regular attendees such as Dr. Vishnu Mohan's wife, Saraswati, to prepare and serve lunch to all the devotees. During lean times, Subhadra just cut up the fruit the devotees brought along as offerings for Charvi. She served it with tea. But this week the white photojournalist had already paid for his stay and the money would go a long way in keeping mouths fed at Tella Meda for a few months.

The Sunday meal was simple: *bhindi* curry, *sambhar* with sweet potatoes, spinach *pappu,* mango and tomato pickle, and curds. Kokila and Chetana laid out banana leaves all around the knee-high dining table in the verandah. Once the thirty people were seated, they first put salt on each green banana leaf. Chetana came with a bucket of *bhindi* curry and put some on each banana leaf with a large steel spatula. Kokila followed with the rice and Subhadra with the *sambhar.* The spinach *pappu* came next, along with the mango and tomato pickle.

Another steel bucket of rice was emptied onto the banana leaves while people ate, talked, and shared their problems. The only member of the *ashram* not there was Ramanandam Sastri, who had stopped coming out of his room for meals after Vidura ran away. The regular visitors asked after his health and sent a prayer to God for Vidura's safe return.

"I'm hungry," Chetana declared when Subhadra handed her a bucket of curds, the last course of the meal.

"We eat after they have finished."

"But I'm hungry *now*," Chetana said peevishly.

Subhadra ignored her and gave Kokila a plate stacked with sliced mangoes. It was monsoon time; mangoes were not in season and the ones on the plate were a weak shade of yellow. "Here, you take this."

"Chetana, go," Subhadra ordered, and Chetana walked out of the kitchen onto the verandah.

"Why do we have to do this?" Chetana demanded as she forcefully dumped lumps of fresh yogurt on piles of rice settled on banana leaves next to remnants of pickle, *sambhar*, and *bhindi* curry.

"Just let's finish serving so that we can eat," Kokila said as she put one slice of mango on each banana leaf.

"Next she'll say that we have to make coffee for everyone and *then* we can eat," Chetana complained. "I'm telling you, I'm going to get married soon and get out of here. Then I can eat when I'm hungry, not wait for everyone to finish."

"And who's going to marry you?" Kokila asked as she placed a slice of mango on the last banana leaf.

"I'll find someone," Chetana said, and her silver anklets hummed as she went back into the kitchen.

Mark sat next to Charvi at the table and was pleasantly surprised by how many people showed up every Sunday. They all brought money, fruit, pieces of cloth, or vegetables from their garden, anything that they thought they could offer the goddess. Charvi took everything without drama and Mark wondered how she felt about accepting what he thought was charity in the name of God.

He had been in India long enough and had seen enough of it to understand the intricacies of life in India, where poverty—real poverty, where people went hungry—was only a step away. You just had to walk out of your nice or not-so-nice home and you would step into large puddles of penury and destitution. Beggars on the streets, young children who were filthy and skinny—it was a world apart from what poverty meant to him in America.

And yet, despite the struggle to make ends meet, he had seen that woman in the kitchen at Tella Meda put out a feast every Sunday so that every devotee would be fed. And it was probably because of their generosity that many homeless, hungry people came to their doorstep and were accepted as equals, seated next to the goddess at the table if there was enough room, or at rows of banana leaves placed in the courtyard in front of thin coconut straw mats.

He didn't know what to make of Charvi. On one hand he felt that she was cheating these good people out of money and gifts, and on the other he saw her as a benevolent soul who gave food and shelter to the hungry and the homeless.

Charvi accepted everyone, whether they were able to pay their way or not. No matter how he analyzed the situation, he couldn't figure the woman out. He couldn't understand how she, who was quite intelligent, could allow people to believe she was a goddess.

After lunch Mark helped Subhadra and Kokila with the dishes. Feigning a headache, Chetana had gone into the room she shared with Kokila to rest and avoid doing any more work for the wretched devotees of Charvi. *Poor Chetana,* Kokila thought, amused. She would be so upset that she didn't get a chance to wash dishes with the white man.

"No, no," Kokila said when the man didn't properly scrub the big pot used for making rice. "This like. This, you do," she tried to explain in her broken English.

She showed him how to get to the corners of the pot with the piece of coconut straw used for cleaning the dishes.

"Thanks," Mark said, and continued to clean.

"Everyone will be very scandalized that a man is cleaning the utensils," Subhadra told him. "But I think that since men eat, they should also clean."

"I agree," Mark said. "My father always did the dishes at home, my mom always cooked."

Kokila looked expectantly at Subhadra to translate what had just been said, and the older woman complied. Kokila was impressed. She didn't know any men who knew what to do in a kitchen besides eat.

Later, Chetana was livid that she had missed talking to Mark.

"Did he say anything about me? What did he say?" she grilled Kokila.

"He just washed the pots and that's it," Kokila said wearily. "Anyway, he's leaving in two more days."

"If I could speak in English, I'd have snared him," Chetana said saucily. "I'd make him marry me and take me away."

"Why do you want to leave Tella Meda so badly?"

"Why do you want to stay?"

Kokila shrugged. She had wanted to stay because of Vidura, but also because this was the only real home she'd ever had. Now when Chetana talked about marriage and a husband and leaving, she was still reluctant to leave. Where would she go? Why would she go?

"I want a rich husband, someone who will buy me everything I want, and take me to fancy places on holiday. Like Lavanya. She goes all over the world in big airplanes," Chetana said with dreams in her eyes. "And even this white man, he has been everywhere. Subhadra said she saw pictures he took in Africa. Do you know where Africa is?"

"Hmm," Kokila said, though she wasn't really sure.

"They have big wild animals there and only black people. You know why they are black?"

"Why?"

"Because it's very hot there. It isn't too hot here, that's why we are brown. In Africa it's very, very hot and they are all burned black," Chetana informed Kokila. "And it's very cold in America, that's why they are all white."

"So, is Subhadra looking for a boy for you?" Kokila asked, changing the topic.

Chetana shook her head. "No one is looking; I'm looking for my own husband. And I think . . . no, I'm not telling you anything yet. When the time is right, I'll tell you."

Kokila couldn't bear not knowing what Chetana had been about to tell her and nagged her to reveal her secret. She didn't succeed, though, and finally gave up.

He had promised that he wouldn't take any photos of her, but as she stood under the moon on the terrace Mark felt helpless and grabbed his camera. He was on the beach looking up at the house and she was standing up on the terrace, looking ethereal, like a fairy princess, dressed in white, her hair loose and flowing around her shoulders and the full moon lighting her.

He usually didn't take pictures of people who explicitly told him not to, but here he decided to make an exception.

The next evening, his last, when they went for a walk on the beach, Charvi was quiet and somber.

"I will miss you," she admitted to him, and waited, hoped, wished for him to say something. She wanted him to take her away from Tella Meda, this life. She suddenly wanted to see Africa with him, the big elephants and the tall giraffes. She wanted to see New York City and she wanted to see his home in a place called Kansas. She wanted the impossible because even though he was attracted to her, she knew he would never stake a claim and she couldn't let him. But what if he did? What if that magic happened?

"I will miss you as well," Mark said. "I saw your house under the light of the full moon last night and it *was* studded with diamonds."

"I'm glad that you had this opportunity," Charvi said. "Will you come back?"

Mark shrugged. "I'll try. I'll try my best."

The way he said it made it obvious to Charvi that he wouldn't be back. This was an interesting vacation but not one he'd care to repeat. The world was full of places he hadn't yet seen that he would visit instead.

"I hope you will come back," Charvi said softly, her voice not the voice of a goddess but that of a young woman trying to tell her first love that her heart was available.

If Mark noticed her breathlessness, her heart on a platter, he didn't say anything.

"I have to ask you something and I hope I won't offend you," he said, and Charvi nodded eagerly.

"You cannot offend me, ask away," she said with a big smile, trying to contain the small quakes in her heart.

"How do you feel about accepting what your devotees leave behind when you don't believe you are a goddess?" Mark asked, carefully placing his words in the sentence, not wanting to hurt her feelings because of the language barrier or his insensitivity.

Charvi looked stunned and Mark immediately started to apologize. She held up her hand and shook her head.

"You don't owe me any explanations," Mark said before she could speak, eager to make amends. She had been wonderful company and he didn't want her to think that he was some jerk right before he left.

"I can't control the desires of others, only mine," Charvi said in a low voice. She had hoped he would ask a different question and her heart splintered into a hundred pieces. "I can't make their decisions for them, I can only make mine. I take what they offer because not to do so would hurt their feelings. They bring me gifts with such purity that it would be small of me to turn them away. Do you understand me?"

Mark nodded even though he felt what she said was a load of bull served with a dollop of rationalization, but he didn't want to press the matter.

The next day he left and as tradition required, he even touched Charvi's feet. He did it because he had seen everyone else do it, and also because he did respect her. She was a smart woman making her way in a man's world in the best way she could and in the process she was helping others. He admired her even though he believed she was not being entirely truthful.

"I'm so glad I came," he said, and then, just as he swung his camera bag over his shoulder, he leaned over and brushed his lips against her cheek. "Be well, Charvi."

A month after he left he sent her a framed photograph. It was her picture as she stood on the terrace under the light of the full moon.

Kokila was beside Charvi in the temple room when she opened the package and gasped at the image in front of her. This was not Charvi at all; this was a sensuous woman, out of a black-and-white movie, a woman waiting for her lover. There was slumbering passion in her eyes and face.

"You look . . . different," was all Kokila could manage before

Charvi hurriedly took the picture and the letter that came with it inside her room.

The accompanying letter from Mark Talbot was brief.

"Dearest Charvi, I'm sorry to have taken this picture, but I couldn't resist it. I have kept one copy with me but I will not publish it anywhere or let anyone else see it. It will be for my eyes only and I am sending you one so that you can remember me and yourself when the moon was whole. Best wishes, Mark."

Charvi never fell in love again and until the day she died she convinced herself that she could feel the brush of his lips against her cheek—the soft brush, the caress, the power of it. She never saw or heard from Mark Talbot again.

21 January 1969. The first Indian-built electronic digital computer was commissioned.

12 March 1969. The Reactor Research Center was established at Kalpakkam in Tamil Nadu.

The Lost Father

*D*r. Vishnu Mohan, who lived three houses down the street, came running to Tella Meda at five in the morning. There was an urgent phone call for Ramanandam Sastri from a relative. It was about Vidura.

It had been five years since Vidura ran away. He was nineteen years old now and the relative said he had seen Vidura. He had talked to him on a train, but then in one of the worst railway accidents in the history of Andhra Pradesh, the train had crashed. He didn't know if Vidura had survived or not but he thought it would be prudent for Ramanandam Sastri to come to the outskirts of Ongole, where the toppled train lay, to see if maybe Vidura was one of the two hundred dead people who were being piled up and taken away. Another four hundred were being treated at the hospital for injuries.

It took Ramanandam Sastri fifteen hours to reach the wreck site. Kokila came along with him, insisting that he not go alone. The man had become frail in the years since Vidura left. He spent more and more time indoors and spoke very little. When Subhadra told Kokila and Chetana that Ramanandam was going to find Vidura, Kokila knew that there was a good chance that he would find only Vidura's dead body. Her love for Vidura and affection for Ramanandam propelled her into demanding that he take her along.

She shouldn't have come, Ramanandam thought when the taxi dropped them off where the red and brown train lay in a heap. Bodies were scattered everywhere even as rescue workers in khaki clothes moved as many as they could.

Kokila went pale when she saw the severed arm of a little baby in front of her by the railroad tracks. The baby's hand was still holding a small rattle. Kokila's body started to shake and nausea filled her. She had never seen such carnage before and she wished she'd never had to. There were so many dead people, so very many. One of them could be Vidura.

She had been determined to come with Ramanandam and take care of him but as she stood shaking, she knew she shouldn't have come.

"You sit here, Amma Kokila," Ramanandam said gently as he led her away from the carcasses and the stench of death. Ramanandam found a rock for Kokila to sit on and turned her away from the scene of the crash. "Stay here," he instructed, and she nodded, too horrified to do anything else. There were tears rolling down her cheeks and there was shock written on her face.

Ramanandam wanted to stay and console her but there was an urgency to find his own son, if he was indeed in the train. His relative, an old man who was married to a second cousin from his father's side, had sounded confident that he had seen and spoken with Vidura but when Ramanandam had asked him for a physical description, the old man had been vague.

"Those who are alive have been transported to a hospital in Ongole," one of the doctors told him. "The dead, they are here, except for those that have already been burned. But you can go through belongings . . ." The doctor pointed to another pile of suitcases and boxes, half-burned, half-broken.

Ramanandam wanted to go to the hospital first and see if Vidura was there, alive.

"You also have to remember there were eight hundred people on the train and many people left without a scratch on them. Your son could be one of them," the doctor said. "I'd start with the dead, as we need to start burning bodies as fast as possible. Then you can go to the hospital and see. It's a matter of time."

Ramanandam rubbed his hands on his smudged white *kurta*. He hadn't even taken the time to change. He had rushed out after the phone call, dressed in his slept-in *dhoti* and *kurta*. He hadn't brushed his teeth and there was a bitter taste on his tongue. He had long ago stopped shaving regularly but the beard still bothered him and he kept scratching his chin and cheeks, wishing for a razor.

As he reached the first body of the many lined up under white muslin sheets throughout the field Ramanandam pulled his spectacles out of his pocket and placed them on his nose. He couldn't summon his hands to lift the first white sheet smudged with dirt and blood. So he stood there, in front of the first body for a long time, hoping the wind would blow the sheet away and he would see that the face wasn't Vidura's. He hoped some other family member looking for his or her father, mother, brother, or sister would move the cloth so that the face would be revealed. But no one was coming his way and he stood rooted, unable to perform the simple task of looking at a face.

Finally, a policeman in khaki clothes came up to him. "*Sar*, we are very shorthanded. If you want to see the dead, do so fast. We're going to start burning from that other side in half an hour."

Ramanandam nodded and then waved his hand ineffectually. The policeman sighed and kneeled down and pulled the sheet from the face of the first body. It was an old woman, her face bashed in, dried-up blood crusted on her face and in her eyes. Ramanandam shook his head.

"Who are you looking for, *sar*?"

"My son," Ramanandam said.

"How old?"

"Fourteen . . . no, nineteen," Ramanandam said, and desperately tried to form Vidura's face in his mind. He could see a baby, a boy, but he couldn't see a nineteen-year-old or even a fourteen-year-old anymore. His memories of Vidura were warped and Vidura's face in his mind was like a fuzzy picture, burned around the edges, smudged in the center.

"Well then," the policeman said, and started to look at the bodies as fast as he could. "*Sar,* here is a young boy, is it him?"

Ramanandam raced down the bodies and came to the one the policeman was standing over. It was a boy, maybe seventeen years old, and he was not Vidura. The policeman helped Ramanandam look at every young male dead body on the field and though Ramanandam shook his head each time, the faces were blending into one another. One bloody face, one squished, one broken, one torn apart, one half-burned, one half-missing . . . the faces were going past him like a film reel and he couldn't remember if he had seen Vidura or if he hadn't. He couldn't remember his own son's face and wished he had brought a photograph along to help remind him.

"Thank you," Ramanandam said, taking the policeman's hand in his and leaving a ten-*rupee* note behind after all the bodies had been seen.

The policeman saluted him casually and walked away to help other relatives, who were swarming around the field.

"He isn't there," Ramanandam said confidently to Kokila, and knew he was lying. Even if his son was there, he wouldn't know for sure. He would never know if one of those bodies had been Vidura or not. He couldn't remember anymore. He was an old man, his eyes weren't that good, his memory was failing, and his heart was broken.

"Oh, I'm so relieved, Sastri Garu," Kokila said, and rose on unsteady legs. "I came to help you and here I am . . . Sastri Garu, are you okay?" Kokila immediately put her arm around Ramanandam as he started to collapse.

From the small roadside food stall that had appeared by the crash site to feed the relatives and policemen, Kokila bought Ramanandam a cup of tea, a glass of water, and a *masala dosa.*

Ramanandam just sat on the rocks Kokila had been sitting on, staring into space. He looked so frail, so old that Kokila wanted to hug him to her and tell him that she would do what she could to make this time easy for him.

"Here," she said, and held a piece of *dosa* dipped in coconut chutney to his mouth.

She fed him patiently and made him drink tea and water from time to time. He ate half the *dosa* and Kokila ate the other half. She hadn't had anything to eat in almost a day and was ravenous.

"Now let's go to the hospital," she told him, and he nodded.

She had to hold his arm and lead him. He seemed not to have the will to do anything. If she'd left him, he would have sat on that rock forever, Kokila thought. A bus was taking the relatives of the people on the train to the hospital, which was an hour away. Many victims of the crash had died midway to the hospital and the policeman on the bus warned the relatives that they would have to see more dead bodies in the hospital morgue.

Ramanandam didn't speak at all and Kokila didn't ask him any questions either. She held his hand as they rode in silence all the way to the hospital, knowing that they might find Vidura there, dead or alive. And then there was also the chance that they would not find Vidura at all: What then?

When they reached the hospital there seemed to be miles of people in long lines around it, crying, sobbing, screaming, demanding answers, urinating against the walls, kicking stones. Kokila held on to Ramanandam as they were jostled around in long queues.

The wounded were everywhere, spread on the floor, lying on filth, resting on small beds that were stained with blood and dirt, sitting on chairs. Their bodies were in different stages of disintegration. Some just had a few scratches, some had blood pouring out of their wounds still, and on some the blood had dried to a brown crust. Some were conscious and crying in pain, some were blissfully unconscious, and some were dying.

This was somehow worse than the train wreck where only the dead lay. Here it was harder to accept that Vidura might be one of the bleeding lives lying in all that filth and muck.

They didn't find Vidura among the living.

Kokila threw up the half-*dosa* she had eaten when they came out from the morgue. Ramanandam put his arm around her and she leaned into him. Vidura wasn't among the dead in the hospital either.

They waited outside the hospital with other relatives who hadn't found their loved ones, and even those who had, for a bus that would take them to the Ongole railway station. Kokila and Ramanandam would have to wait for ten hours, until two in the morning, when the train for Visakhapatnam would arrive. From Visakhapatnam they would have to take a three-hour bus ride to Bheemunipatnam.

Kokila wasn't sure if she was happy or sad that Vidura was not among the dead or the living. To have found his body or seen him wounded would have at least meant that she would have seen him. Now nothing had changed: he was still gone and she still didn't know whether he was dead or alive.

"Maybe he was never on the train," Kokila told Ramanandam when they were at the railway station, sitting on a small wooden bench waiting for their train. She had bought *idlis* from the station canteen and had fed him bite after bite. He still wore a wooden expression on his face and his eyes were the eyes of the dead.

"Maybe," Ramanandam said, and managed a weak smile. "You shouldn't have come, Amma Kokila. There are dark circles under your eyes."

"I couldn't let you go alone. I love him too," Kokila said simply, and held the cup of coffee she'd bought for him against his lips.

On their way back in the bus from Visakhapatnam to Bheemunipatnam, they held hands again. This time it was Ramanandam who reached out for her. When they walked back to Tella Meda from the bus station in Bheemunipatnam, Kokila was almost sad that the intimacy she had shared with Ramanandam in the past days was now over.

"Thank you," Ramanandam said before he opened the metal gate leading into Tella Meda's garden. The gate was rusty and made a lot of noise when it was opened; it would alert those inside, waiting to hear about Vidura.

"You don't have to thank me," Kokila said shyly, suddenly conscious of her boldness in feeding Ramanandam and holding his hand.

"Yes, I do," Ramanandam said, and brushed his hand over her head. "God bless you."

Subhadra came running out as soon as the metal gate opened. She stopped when she saw Ramanandam's face.

"No," she cried out. "He can't be dead."

Ramanandam waved his hand and looked at Kokila, silently asking her to take care of the questions. He disappeared into his room while Kokila spent two hours telling everyone what happened.

"Bad business, boys running away from home," Renuka said sternly to Kokila after everyone had left and they were sitting alone at the dining table in the verandah. "Bad business. It means there's a devil in the house."

"Means no such thing," Kokila told her. "He ran away and that is terrible, but there is nothing wrong with this house."

"But why did he run away?" Renuka demanded.

"If you hate it so much here, why don't you just leave?" Kokila asked angrily. "All you have done is speak ill of Tella Meda and all of us who live here. You don't seem to like it around here that much. I think you should leave."

"How you talk," Renuka said as tears filled her eyes. "Insulting a poor widow like this. Shame on you."

"Oh, the tears might work on Subhadra, but they won't work on me," Kokila said, still angry that this woman had slapped Chetana, twice, and now was talking about the devil living in Tella Meda. "You talk nonsense like that again, I will tell Charvi that you hit me."

"You will lie? You rotten girl! No one will believe you!"

"Everyone in Tella Meda will believe me and trust me. They will all be happy to see your bony back," Kokila said, and left the old widow alone.

Kokila checked on Ramanandam for the next few days regularly. She was the one who took him his food, fed it to him, and even brought warm water into his room so that he could wash up. She cut fresh flowers from the garden to bring some of the outside world into his room.

It frustrated her that no one seemed interested in helping Ramanandam get through his grief. It had been five years since Vidura had run away, and Ramanandam was still mired in the loss. Perhaps if others had helped Ramanandam more, he would be better. Kokila resolved on that day that she would be the one to help Ramanandam.

"Chetana, you look fine," Kokila snapped when for the fifth time that afternoon Chetana put on a different *sari*, even trying on some of Kokila's. "You're just going to the cinema; no one cares how you look."

Chetana arranged the pleats of the white *sari* with a blue border on her shoulder. It was fake silk but looked almost like the real thing. Chetana had recently had two blouses made, one white with a blue and gold border around the sleeves and the neckline and the second black with red flowers and mirrors embroidered on it. She had begged and borrowed money from Subhadra, and Kokila couldn't understand the fuss. It wasn't like anyone saw what she wore because she was at Tella Meda all day long.

"It's not just the cinema," Chetana told Kokila with barely suppressed excitement.

"Then what?"

"You can't tell anyone," Chetana said as she went and sat next to Kokila on her bed. They were in their room and Chetana had been admiring herself in the old steel cupboard mirror. Her blouses, petticoats, *saris,* and half-*saris* were scattered everywhere on the floor.

"Tell what?"

"I'm getting married," Chetana said, and then a laugh spilled out of her. "I'm going to get out of here."

Kokila stared at her, not able to think of anything to say for a very long moment. "To whom?" she finally asked.

"Uh-uh." Chetana shook her head. "I'm not going to tell you. Come with me to the temple tonight. We're getting married there."

Kokila sighed and put a hand against her forehead. "Why can't you tell anyone? You could get married here, in Tella Meda. Ramanandam would be happy to do that for you."

"Ramanandam? You are calling him Ramanandam now? What happened to Sastri Garu?"

Kokila shrugged. "Who is the boy, Chetana?"

Chetana gave her a sly smile. "You promise you won't tell any-one."

"Yes, *ottu,* I won't tell anyone," Kokila said.

"I'm getting married to Ravi," Chetana said.

"No!" Kokila cried. "Are you mad? He's one year younger than you. He's my age, Chetana, and he's spoiled. I hear that he already drinks and smokes. And Manikyam will kill you if you marry her son without her permission."

"And what about your precious Ramanandam? You think he'll care that his grandson is marrying the daughter of a prostitute?" Chetana demanded.

"Wise men like him see beyond the tragedy of birth. But I think if you marry like this, in stealth, you'll hurt his feelings, Subhadra's feelings, and Charvi's as well," Kokila said confidently.

Chetana made a face and picked up a red *sari* that was lying on the floor. "I'm twenty years old. I have to get married. Or do I have to spend the rest of my life here?"

"I'm not saying you shouldn't marry Ravi. All I'm saying is that—"

"You're jealous that I'm getting married and you have to live here and serve *sambhar* and whatnot to everyone at every meal before you can eat," Chetana cried out. "You don't have to come to the temple. I'll manage without you. But don't you mention a word of this to any-one or I'll kill you."

As Kokila had predicted, the news that his grandson had eloped and married a ward of his caused the already sad Ramanandam a consid-erable amount of pain.

"That boy grew up here," he said, patting his knee. "And now he marries without saying a word to me? I wouldn't have cared whom he married but he should've at least . . . Oh, Kokila, why are all my chil-dren hurting me so?"

Kokila sat down beside him on his bed and took his hand in hers.

"They seem to be really taken with each other. Maybe she'll straighten him out."

"Maybe," Ramanandam said, and smiled at Kokila, lacing his fingers with hers. "You are my savior, my Garuda. You carried me out of trouble."

"And you gave me a home," Kokila said, smiling back at him.

"Then we're even?"

"No. I will never be able to repay you," Kokila said. "But you should come to the courtyard and say something. Manikyam is yelling at Chetana, and Charvi just shut the door of her room. Subhadra is crying and Renuka . . . ah, well, she's telling Manikyam that she said so."

Ramanandam shook his head. "I can't, Amma Kokila. Why don't you go and tell them how I feel?"

"You have to come," Kokila said sternly. "Come this one time and if things get too bad, I'll bring you back. After all, I am your Garuda. And if you're really good out there, I'll coax Subhadra to make *kesari* for you."

Ramanandam reluctantly came into the courtyard. The scene was as Kokila had described. Chetana stood defiantly next to her new husband. Ravi was a good-looking boy with fair skin and silky hair that fell on his forehead. He stood there lazily until Ramanandam came out and then he stiffened a little.

"Nanna, see what has happened? My son is ruined. Married, they say. How can a nice Brahmin boy marry some Devdasi?" Manikyam sobbed, her hands going up in the air dramatically.

"Manikyam," Ramanandam said softly to stop her from screaming any more, "it's done."

"It can be undone," Manikyam said, looking at Chetana with hatred. "There are no witnesses to this alleged wedding—"

"It can't be undone," Ravi said evenly. "Amma, we're married and—"

"Your father will disinherit you. You still have to start college—how will you do that if we kick you out of the house?" Manikyam demanded.

"He'll get a job," Chetana said coolly. "And we'll rent a nice house in Visakhapatnam and live as a couple."

"What kind of a job will a metric pass get?" Manikyam yelled. "You whore—"

"Amma, watch what you say, she is my wife now," Ravi said. "And if you don't want to help us with money, I will get a job."

"You can stay here," Ramanandam suggested wearily. "Until you find your feet."

"No," Chetana said, and Kokila could see panic set into her. She had married Ravi clandestinely and in a hurry because she wanted to get away from Tella Meda, not stay here. "We will rent a house . . ."

"We have no money," Ravi hissed at her. "For now we can stay here and then find a place when the time is right."

Manikyam started sobbing even more loudly. "My husband is so angry, Nanna. He doesn't want to have anything to do with Ravi or this house. He blames you and so do I. I sent Ravi here in summer holidays in your care and you allowed this to happen? How could you, Nanna?"

Kokila leaped to Ramanandam's defense. "It isn't like he knew."

"Did *you* know?" Renuka demanded, looking at Kokila pointedly.

"She did not," Chetana answered for Kokila. "No one knew because we didn't tell anyone. We knew that this was how you'd all react."

Subhadra, who was sitting quietly by the *tulasi* plant, rose, shaking her head. "I thought you were my daughter," she said to Chetana accusingly. "I thought you were mine and then you do something like this without even telling me?"

Chetana looked at her surrogate mother for a moment and Kokila thought she would apologize but she also knew that Chetana was stubborn. She had plotted this, planned this to the last minute, and she had achieved her goal. She wasn't going to apologize for trying to make a life for herself. She would see it as her right and even her obligation to get married to a man who could give her a better life and get her out of Tella Meda.

"What am I going to do, Nanna? We are ruined. Our good name

is destroyed," Manikyam said, crying. "Oh, Ravi, the dreams I had for you. You could have gotten a good wife with a lot of dowry. Now you're saddled with this whore's daughter. You'll go nowhere in life."

Manikyam's husband, Dr. Nageshwar Rao, came to the *ashram* the next day, hoping to dismiss the marriage. In front of Ravi he frankly asked Chetana how much money it would take to end the "alleged" marriage.

Kokila didn't know where her loyalties lay anymore. Chetana was her closest friend. They had known each other from childhood, yet at this time she couldn't stand behind her; nor could she go against her. Kokila couldn't condone what Chetana did. She had cold-bloodedly hurt everyone who cared for her. But it was a terrible insult to have your father-in-law ask you what your price was, and Chetana, who had stood with a stiff neck despite everything that was said, was also shaken up.

The man had asked her her price, as if she were no better than her mother. But she was. Chetana wanted a home, a husband, dignity. She wasn't going to settle for less.

"I didn't marry him for money," she said, and Kokila knew she lied. She had married him because his family was wealthy and because she had known they would not turn their back on their oldest son. Chetana was confident that Ravi's parents would bring him home and she would go with him. She hoped to live like a queen in their big house in Visakhapatnam.

"Then why did you marry him?" Nageshwar Rao asked. He was a dark, fat man with a balding head. He wore big steel-rimmed spectacles and had a round face. It was a mystery how he and Manikyam could have produced boys as good-looking as Ravi and Prasad.

"Because I love him," Chetana said, and her father-in-law laughed.

"What do you know about love? You are a little girl . . ."

"I'm twenty years old," Chetana said defensively. "We just want a chance to live our lives happily."

"If you stay with her, you are not my son," Nageshwar Rao said to Ravi, who shrugged.

"I was never your son. Prasad has always been your son. Maybe my brother will give you what you want. I'm going to do what makes me happy," Ravi said nonchalantly. "If you don't want us to live with you, we'll live at Tella Meda."

Nageshwar Rao pursed his lips and looked straight at Ramanandam, who was slouched on the floor. They were sitting in the temple room by the musical instruments. Charvi was there as well, though she didn't say anything. She hadn't uttered a single word since Ravi and Chetana came to Tella Meda and announced they were married. She looked forlorn and sad, as if she had been personally betrayed.

"Charvi, will you let them live here?" Nageshwar Rao demanded.

Charvi looked at her father and then at Chetana. "They need a home. I never turn away the needy."

"Sastri Garu, I have done everything you have ever wanted me to do. This time, however, I cannot abide by your word and take Ravi home with me," Dr. Nageshwar Rao said politely. "I hope that after living in hardship for a while Ravi will leave this woman and come home."

He turned to his son and patted him on his shoulder. "You are my eldest son and I love you. You can always come home, as long as you leave her behind. I will not tolerate a girl from a lower caste in my house."

Chetana and Ravi were given one of the empty rooms reserved for guests in the front of the house. The room had two doors, one opening to the front verandah and another to the one that surrounded the courtyard.

Subhadra and Kokila made the bed with new white sheets that Subhadra had been saving for an important guest. She was crying as she put the pillows inside the cases and smoothed the creases on the sheets.

"How could she not tell me?" Subhadra kept saying as she wiped fresh tears with the *pallu* of her *sari*. "Kokila, you don't do such a thing, okay?"

Kokila nodded. "Who will marry me, Subhadra?"

"You should've gone with your husband. He married again. Already has a son, and is expecting another child," Subhadra told her.

Kokila tried to feel some regret at what she had thrown away but she couldn't dredge up any. Tella Meda was home and she couldn't imagine living elsewhere even with the pain of Vidura's departure.

They ripped petals off roses Narayan Garu had painstakingly grown in the front garden and spread the petals all over the bed. Subhadra lit sandalwood incense and left a plateful of *ladoos* and other sweets by the bedside.

"You spray rosewater around the room," Subhadra said, handing a silver perfumed water sprayer to Kokila. "And I'll get the almond milk ready. You make sure Ravi is here and we will send Chetana in. It is her wedding night—so what if Manikyam doesn't want to take her home? She can have a good life here until they get it all sorted out. You know, don't you, that Manikyam will take them back?"

Kokila didn't know any such thing but wisely didn't say that. From what she had seen of Manikyam's husband, it didn't seem likely that he would accept Ravi unless he left Chetana. Oh, what a web Chetana had woven and how trapped she was in it. Poor Chetana—she had wanted to leave Tella Meda but now she had to stay, for God only knew how long.

Chetana was dressed in one of Subhadra's white silk *saris* for her *shobhanam* night. Kokila had braided her long hair and put a garland of jasmine flowers on the braid.

"I'm so happy," Chetana told Kokila as she gazed at her reflection in the mirror she was sitting in front of. "I'm a married woman, Kokila."

"I wish you all the happiness in the world," Kokila said, hoping that despite all the warning signs, somehow this marriage would work out.

"He loves me and soon that bitch of a mother of his will ask us to come and live with them. He'll go to college and become a businessman and I . . . Oh, Kokila, I'll get out of here and live in a real house, in *my* house," Chetana said with stars in her eyes.

Chetana took the warm glass of almond milk Subhadra gave to her and started walking toward her new bedroom, where her husband waited. Her silver anklets made music as she walked with Kokila.

"Are you terribly jealous?" Chetana asked happily just before she entered the room.

"Yes," Kokila lied so as to not disappoint her best friend.

Ramanandam was furious. Gone was the dejected man. In his place was a man who was pacing his room, his hands locked behind his back.

As soon as Kokila came to his room with dinner, he snarled at her. "I have been waiting for an hour," he accused.

"We were getting Chetana ready for the first night," Kokila said, pleased that he wasn't sitting on the bed, as usual, with a wooden expression on his face.

"Ah . . . what could I expect from Chetana? Like mother, like daughter," he said wearily, and sat down on the bed. "Did Subhadra make *kesari* again?"

"Yes," Kokila said. "You are very angry."

"Yes," he said as he stuffed his mouth with rice and *sambhar*. "She married my grandson."

"She is very happy and so is he," Kokila reminded him. "And he's already a wayward boy. Marriage will straighten him out. She'll make sure he's straightened out."

Ramanandam shook his head. "Manikyam ruined his life with too much pampering. Both those boys are . . . Maybe Prasad will have the better sense to marry the girl his parents put in front of him."

"And I thought you believed in the individual's right to choose their own spouse," Kokila teased him.

"How do you know what I believe in?"

"I read your first book," Kokila told him, and saw the surprise on his face.

"What else have you been doing behind my back?" he asked as he continued to eat, his anger abated.

"Nothing," Kokila said shyly. "I think you're a wonderful writer."

"I haven't written in a long while," he said.

Kokila sat down by his feet and looked up at him. "I think you just need to be inspired. After Vidura . . . Ramanandam, you have so much to give the world with your writing. Why would you stop?"

"I am Ramanandam now?" he asked, amused.

Kokila put a hand against her mouth. "I—"

"It's okay, you can call me Ramanandam," he said, and set his plate down on the floor beside her. He washed his hands with his glass of water and pushed the plate aside.

He sat down on the floor next to her and took her face in his hands. "You think I can write again?"

"Yes," Kokila whispered, the blood pounding inside her at Ramanandam's closeness. When had this happened? she wondered. When had she lost her heart to this man?

"Will you be my muse?" Ramanandam asked.

Kokila nodded and closed her eyes.

She felt his breath close to her face and she could smell the *kesari* he had just eaten. He kissed her then; their lips locked and Kokila felt her universe implode.

The next morning Kokila hurried from Ramanandam's room like a thief and slid into hers, which was two rooms away. An empty room and that of Subhadra lay in between. No one saw her as it was still dark.

She had left him sleeping and naked. Her heart pounded as she remembered what they had done, what he had done to her. It was craziness, she decided, utter madness to have done what they did.

She lay down on her bed as the first rays of the sun kissed Bheemunipatnam. She hid her face in her hands and a laugh burst out from inside her. It was the laugh of a girl who had just discovered the brilliance of love.

It would be years before Kokila realized that what happened between Ramanandam and her was not love. It was the need of an old man to prove he was younger and the need of a young girl to protect her benefactor and make him feel younger.

3 December 1971. The third Indo-Pakistan war officially commenced and a national emergency was declared by Indian president Zakir Husain. The first night of hostilities commenced with Pakistan bombing several Indian airfields. The Indian ships *Rajput* and *Akshay* left Visakhapatnam harbor when they obtained a sonar contact. They fired several depth charges, and then a loud explosion was heard off the Visakhapatnam beach. The Pakistani submarine *Ghazi* (a *Tench*-class submarine obtained from the United States in 1964) came to grief.

17 December 1971. The war ended on this day when a cease-fire was called between India and Pakistan.

Casualties

*E*ven though the war was taking place in the northern part of India, there was a tense atmosphere everywhere. Rumors were brewing about big Pakistani rockets that could be launched all the way from Karachi and land on southern India.

Just a few days before, the sound of war had reached Visakhapatnam when a Pakistani submarine was destroyed by Indian ships off Visakhapatnam harbor. Windows had rattled and it had felt like a small earthquake had shaken the world. No one had ever believed that the Pakistani army could find a way to come so far south and the level of fear had increased all over the country.

"They have very powerful bombs," Ravi was telling poor frightened Subhadra, nervous Renuka, and unperturbed Puttamma, the maid who had been hired recently to clean the bathrooms and the outside verandahs. "We can all die. Tella Meda"—he snapped his fingers—"will be gone, just like that. Poof!"

Subhadra and Renuka listened intently, while Puttamma was not buying it. "India is most powerful," she said. "No one can touch us."

Ravi shook his head. "What do you know? Go, get to work and stay out of talk that you know nothing about."

" 'What do you know?' he says," Puttamma said angrily as she left to clean a bathroom. "I know plenty. What does he know? Idiot, son of a whore, talks to me like I am no one. Thinks he knows everything. Useless drunk! Son of a whore that—"

"Puttamma, what's wrong?" Kokila asked as she came out of the bathroom, a towel around her wet hair and her *sari*-wrapped body still a little damp after her bath.

Puttamma gargled in her throat and spat on the tiled floor. "It's that boy Ravi, telling stories to Subhadra Amma and Renuka Amma. That boy is up to no good. Chetana should've had better sense than to marry that loser."

"What stories is he telling?" Kokila asked casually as she removed the towel from around her head and shook her hair. Water sprayed around her as she started rubbing the moisture out with the towel.

"About the war and how those Pakis can come kill us here," Puttamma said. "You have lovely hair, Kokila Amma. Someday a man is going to come and make a grab for you."

Kokila ran a hand through her wet waist-length hair and laughed. The sun was shining on her face when she turned her head and her eyes fell on the man who had already grabbed her.

He was sitting on a cloth chair in the verandah in front of his room, comfortable, watching her. She turned away from him, afraid someone would see. But how could they not see what was going on? Were they all blind? Could no one see how happiness glittered in her eyes? How she smiled all the time?

"I say, why scare those poor women, eh?" Puttamma continued. "War is happening way up in the north and he says they'll throw bombs down here and kill everyone. I say, why make stories that make no sense? I say—"

"What are you bitching about now?" Chetana asked, her perfumed Lux soap in one hand and a white towel hanging over her shoulder. "Are you done cleaning? I need to take a bath."

"Your husband is a no-good fellow," Puttamma told Chetana, who sighed.

"He is *my* husband, I'll worry about him, you worry about yours," she said. "So, how is your husband?"

"Which one?" Puttamma asked on a harsh laugh. "My third husband left yesterday. Ran away, that son of a whore, took my copper pot and gold earrings with him."

"You don't have gold earrings," Chetana pointed out.

"Well, he thought I did, stupid bastard," Puttamma said slyly. "You go take a bath now. I will clean up after you are done. Kokila Amma, I'm going to go to the garden to smoke a *bidi*."

Kokila nodded. "I'll come along. I have to get some flowers for the temple room. And you can tell me all about your third husband."

Kokila knew Ramanandam was watching her as she walked toward the garden with Puttamma. He was always watching her. It was unnerving, flattering, exciting. Her heart felt like it was on a giant wheel, up and down, up and down, and every time the excitement mounted and mounted.

Since that first night they had been together, Ramanandam and Kokila had spent countless nights together, sometimes in his room, sometimes in hers. She used to share her room with Chetana but with her married and staying with Ravi, Kokila was alone in her room.

For two years now she and Ramanandam had been lovers. Two years of great joy, torture, and uncertainty. Sometimes Kokila would wonder where all of this was going. Other times she didn't want to know. No one seemed to notice the change in her behavior or her status in the *ashram*. Kokila had taken over so many responsibilities. She kept the books, paid the bills, did the accounting. The money from devotees and the residents didn't go to Subhadra anymore, who always used to make a mess of the finances, but came to Kokila. She used Ramanandam's room to store the books and keep track of money.

Maybe that was what everyone thought she was doing in Ramanandam's room. *Yes, that is what they must think,* Kokila decided. She wasn't sure how she would feel if her relationship with Ramanandam became public knowledge. She wasn't sure what others would say, especially Charvi, who was possessive about Ramanandam. Chetana would probably be appalled and hurt at not being made privy to such juicy information about Kokila's life.

Chetana had related in full, excruciating detail to Kokila the events of her *shobhanam* night. She had told Kokila everything, but Kokila had not told her about Ramanandam. But what could she say? She knew that her relationship with Ramanandam would not be accepted. Ramanandam was thirty-nine years her senior and they were not married. He said he didn't believe in marriage as an institution and after his wife died he had sworn that he wouldn't enter that fraudulent institution again. He didn't judge those who believed in marriage and even admired their faith in the partnership but said he felt he couldn't bind himself like that again.

"If two people love each other, why do they feel the need for their relationship to be validated by society?" he told Kokila.

In any case, Kokila couldn't imagine marrying Ramanandam. She didn't think of him as a husband, even now, even when they did those secret things that made her blush.

So who was Ramanandam to her? Lover? Father figure? Protector? Benefactor? All?

Puttamma enjoyed smoking her *bidi* very much. You could usually find her walking down the street, *bidi* in mouth, as she yapped away with a companion. She knew everyone in Bheemunipatnam and lived in one of the thatched huts that filled a part of the small town. The poor, the hungry, the wretched ended up there, scraping through life.

A gutter went through the area where the thatched huts were; it was considered the bad neighborhood, where the red-light district more or less survived and toddy shops lined the perimeter. Despite the poverty and the desperation that thrived in the slum, there was a certain sense of happiness that prevailed. Marriages, a girl's first step into womanhood, childbirth, death—everything was celebrated with great gusto. Songs would be played at full volume on loudspeakers late into the night and early into the morning and toddy would flow from the shops along with the drunks. Whenever Kokila found herself passing the slum she wondered if she would've ended up there if she hadn't found Tella Meda and then she would realize she would have ended up in her husband's home if she hadn't found Tella Meda. She wasn't sure if she was distressed about having stayed. Sometimes she craved the security, the normalcy, of a husband, a home and family.

At Tella Meda she had a roof over her head but not the respectability of a married and decent woman. People in Bheemunipatnam knew the life stories of most of those who lived in Tella Meda. Everyone knew that Kokila had refused to leave with her husband and that Chetana was a prostitute's discarded daughter. Every drunk in town had made a play at Kokila and Chetana while they were out in the bazaar or at the cinema, anywhere outside the protection of Tella Meda. Women looked at them with a combination of scorn, pity, and disdain. It was one thing to visit Tella Meda as a devotee of Charvi, quite another to live in Tella Meda. Those who lived in Tella Meda lived there because they were outcasts. As a child Kokila had seen the beautiful house by the beach as a place where there was always food, even if in meager amounts, and clean clothes, four walls, and a roof. As a child Kokila had thought that would be enough. As a woman she had begun to realize that by choosing Tella Meda she had rejected a respectable life as a wife. By choosing Tella Meda she had condemned herself to live on the sidelines of society.

"I see Ravi there all the time, at Mangalam's toddy shop," Puttamma gossiped as she smoked the thin brown cigarette filled with tobacco, hand-rolled in a *temburni* leaf and secured with a string at one end. She was standing in Tella Meda's front garden with Kokila.

"Chetana said he stopped going a week ago," Kokila told her. Usually she didn't indulge in gossip but sometimes it was hard to resist and after all she was a woman, wasn't she?

"Stopped? I saw him last night, piss-faced drunk. Manikyam

Amma will be so sad to hear that her son is traipsing down to the toddy shops and"—Puttamma's voice dropped to a whisper—"going to Sundari's room."

"No," Kokila gasped. "No, Puttamma, you must be mistaken. Chetana would never allow Ravi to go to a prostitute."

"Uh-uh." Puttamma only made a sound and continued to smoke her *bidi*.

"Are you sure?" Kokila asked.

Puttamma nodded.

"Poor Chetana. If she finds out . . ."

"She knows," Puttamma said, surprising Kokila.

"She knows?"

Puttamma nodded smugly. "Came by three days ago in the afternoon and yelled the place down. Called Sundari names. Told that *munda* to keep her hands off her husband and find someone else to . . . Well, Chetana never did have a clean mouth."

Kokila was shocked. Maybe there were things that Chetana didn't tell her anymore. She was obviously embarrassed by Ravi's behavior. And then Kokila wondered if she was embarrassed about Ramanandam and if that was why she kept their relationship a secret. Was it a dirty thing they did? Yes, it was a dirty thing. Unclean, impure, without the benefit of marriage, a sin, and yet she loved him and loved being with him. Yes, she was embarrassed, but not enough to walk away from him.

"This is terrible." Kokila sighed. "We need to do something. I will ask Sastri Garu to speak with Ravi. He will listen to his grandfather."

"Whatever you say," Puttamma said, obviously thinking that Ravi was a lost cause and no one could help him. "Maybe Charvi Amma could talk some sense into him. She is such a bright light in all our lives. I come here to clean so that I can catch glimpses of her. She is such a goddess, looks so beautiful and peaceful. Once, I touched her feet and she put her hand on my forehead . . . ah, what bliss."

"Ay, Puttamma, the verandah is dirty, dirty, dirty," Subhadra called out from the kitchen window that looked into the front garden. "Stop smoking that disgusting thing and get to work, woman."

"Coming, coming." Puttamma threw her *bidi* on the grass and stepped on it with her bare right foot. "That Subhadra Amma, she has no patience. I'm here all day, so I take a *bidi* break—what's wrong, eh, I ask, what's wrong with that?"

She muttered all the way back into the house while Kokila picked flowers and tried to figure out how to solve this crisis with Ravi and Chetana.

"You know I believe in personal freedom," Ramanandam said clearly as he stroked her naked arm and then cupped her small breast.

Kokila shrugged his hand off by moving her body. "This is not about personal freedom, Ramanandam, this is about wasting one's life."

"It's his life," Ramanandam said with a smile, and kissed her softly on the mouth. "If people knew about you and me, don't you think they would try to tear us apart?"

She couldn't win an argument with him. He was smarter, wiser, and not afraid to use his advantage.

"For Chetana's sake you must talk to Ravi. He can't wander around brothels and toddy shops. I thought he was going to start college but . . . Manikyam sends money and he spends it on toddy and women and nothing is left to go to college with," Kokila said angrily. "And you won't do anything about it. He's your grandson. If you won't try to steer him onto the right path, who will?"

She sounded like a nagging wife; it was there in her tone, her demeanor. Instead of getting irritated Ramanandam was amused.

"This is not funny," Kokila raged at him.

"You are beautiful," he said, and kissed her. "You are so beautiful, so young, so soft . . . I can't believe that I have you with me like this. When you are gone in the morning I can't believe you stayed all night. It feels like a dream, like a fantasy."

Kokila softened immediately. These were words she lived to hear. All day she would listen to his voice and remember his words and remember his hands and remember the slide of his body into hers.

When Chetana told Kokila about sex it sounded like a rushed thing, a physical thing, but with Ramanandam there was affection, there was love, and most of all, there was beauty.

Chetana had always thought sex to be an ugly thing. How could it not be? Her mother had been in the business of selling it and Ravi didn't even bother to take Chetana's clothes off when they did it. He just hiked Chetana's *sari* up and undid his pants. Kokila felt sorry that Chetana would never know the ecstasy of love and she couldn't explain it in words anyway. And what would she say? *Sastri Garu is a wonderful lover? Chee-chee,* just because they were doing it didn't mean she had to announce it to the world.

"I'll ask Charvi to talk to Ravi, then," Kokila said thoughtfully as Ramanandam started to doze off.

He chuckled. "You never give up, my little tigress," he said before falling asleep.

Charvi was no better than her father.

"This is a personal matter, Kokila. If Chetana came to me, I could help. If Dr. Nageshwar Rao or Manikyam Akka came to me, I would try to talk to them and then ask them to talk to Ravi. But we shouldn't interfere in someone else's marriage and life," Charvi said. "I don't think drinking is . . . And going to brothels? He is really going to a prostitute? Well, everyone has their *karma* to contend with."

Kokila didn't understand why Charvi couldn't just talk to Ravi and see if maybe she could lead him away from bad women and alcohol. What was this nonsense about personal matters? Everyone at Tella Meda always interfered in everything, yet now they were pretending that they didn't?

"Just talk to him," Kokila said in exasperation. "He's your nephew. Just talk and see if you can't convince him to start college, that's all."

Charvi smiled. "You're a good friend to Chetana. I'll see what I can do. But he's chosen his path. Only he can make the changes in his life to make the wrongs right."

Kokila didn't say anything to that. Even though she agreed that only Ravi could change his life, she didn't think that help was unwarranted. The strongest people needed help and Ravi was such a weakling.

"I'll try and talk to him tonight after *bhajan*—if he's there, that is," Charvi said in a placating tone.

"Thank you," Kokila murmured, and left Charvi to do whatever it is she did all day in her rooms.

Lately, Kokila was starting to get frustrated with Charvi and everyone else in the *ashram*. The more she looked at the finances, the more she was depressed. Narayan Garu had not paid his "rent" in four months. Renuka hadn't bothered to give Subhadra any money for eight months now. Ravi and Chetana had promised to put some money into the running of Tella Meda but they had not. Kokila now knew in intimate detail how much money Manikyam sent to her son without her husband's permission and where that money went. But Kokila felt she couldn't demand that anyone give money because she didn't add any income to the Tella Meda finances either.

She needed a job, she decided. She talked about it to Subhadra, who was instantly enthusiastic and had several suggestions.

"You can talk to this woman, she comes to the temple every Wednesday afternoon and distributes raw ingredients for *papads* and takes back the finished product," Subhadra explained. "You go there tomorrow. You can sit right here in Tella Meda and make *papads*. This girl, she's eight months pregnant, her husband is a soldier, he's in the war. She makes thirty packets every week and gets thirty *rupees*. It's good money."

When Kokila asked Chetana to join her she was reluctant but went along with her to the temple on top of the hill all the same. It was the same temple where Chetana had married Ravi and the priest nodded at her when he saw her.

"How is your husband doing?" he asked, and Chetana murmured appropriate words in response.

"One of these days I'm going to say my husband's a drunk who can't get his *lingam* up at night. Maybe then they'll all just shut up and stop asking me how Ravi is doing," Chetana said angrily.

Kokila wisely kept silent. These days it was better to not offer any marital advice to Chetana, as she would go into a rage. Charvi's conversation with Ravi had never taken place and Kokila didn't press the matter. She herself tried to talk to Ravi but he made a blatant pass at her, which made Kokila realize that Ravi was probably as unredeemable as everyone said he was. Maybe Chetana could save his soul but Kokila seriously doubted it.

Kanka Lakshmi was a large, matronly woman who wore a handwoven white cotton *sari* with an orange border. She sat on a chair while the women who made *papads* sat on the floor in a corner of the temple. Two large gold rings adorned her ears and a diamond nose ring flashed as she spoke. She wore gold bangles and a big thick gold chain, but it was not a *mangalsutra*. Kokila didn't think the woman was married.

A large dark man carried supplies into the temple and carted away the finished packets of *papads* to a three-wheeled yellow and black auto rickshaw at the bottom of the hill. Kanka Lakshmi spoke in a manly and stern voice. She chastised the women who hadn't made enough *papads* and those who had ruined their ingredients and produced bad *papads*. She even fired one woman, accusing her of stealing ingredients and using them in her kitchen instead of for the *papads*.

Radhika was eight months pregnant and the only woman who was praised for her good work. She rented a room in a house owned by an elderly couple near the temple. She was waiting for her husband to return from the war. The rumor, of course (which had already reached Chetana and Kokila, who had been at the temple for less than an hour), was that Radhika was carrying an illegitimate child and the husband at war was just a fabrication to cover up her sin.

Radhika was a demure woman with beautiful fair skin. If you didn't look at her belly, she didn't look pregnant at all. Her arms and face were still thin and she had a healthy glow about her. She talked very softly and often smiled shyly. How anyone could think this woman was sleeping around and conceiving illegitimate children, Kokila wasn't sure. She looked like a nice woman, a wife and a mother-to-be.

Kanka Lakshmi asked Radhika to stay back with the new women who wanted to make *papads*. There were four of them, including Chetana and Kokila.

"It's very simple," Kanka Lakshmi said. "Radhika, can you make some so that we can show these women how it is done?"

Radhika immediately went into action. "I'll make plain *papads* and then those with chili flakes in them, okay?" she said sweetly.

She measured flour, salt, oil, a tablespoon of turmeric and water and poured them into a big steel bowl. Then she kneaded the mixture until it was a soft dough. "Now you have to roll out the *papads*," she explained, and pulled out a wooden base and a thin rolling pin. Efficiently, she rolled out fifteen *papads* in no time, and then made more dough, this time adding red chili flakes from a packet.

"We give you everything you need. If we want you to make *papads* with chili flakes or black pepper, we will provide you with the ingredients," Kanka Lakshmi told all the women.

Radhika made three more *papads* and then set the dough aside.

"Sometimes if you don't put in enough water or too much, the dough gets lumpy or dry, then you have to be careful and add more flour or water accordingly," Radhika told the four women watching her carefully. "Now, you try," she said to Kokila.

Kokila hadn't cooked much in her life but she had participated in all kitchen duties at her father's house and at Tella Meda, so Kokila started out easily.

"Excellent," Kanka Lakshmi said when Kokila made *papads* and put them side by side to let them dry. "Once you are done, you leave them in the shade, never in the sun, and let them dry for a whole day. The sun will ruin the *papads* so don't leave them outside without paying attention. And then you stack them one on top of the other and put them into the packet that we give you."

Kanka Lakshmi showed them how to seal the plastic packet with a burning candle. That seemed to take some effort to get the hang of but all four women were hired to make five packets of *papads* each for the first week.

"If you do well, we'll ask you to make more," Kanka Lakshmi told them. "We give you enough ingredients for the *papads*, so don't use them in your kitchen. I will not tolerate thievery. You get paid one *rupee* for each packet and there are twenty-five *papads* in one packet. I pay more than the others do. They pay only seventy-five *paisas* per packet. So, do a good job and you will make good money."

Chetana was also excited now because it had been easy to make *papads* and money was in short supply, what with Ravi spending it on toddy and that whore Sundari.

"We live in Tella Meda," Kokila told Radhika as they all packed up to leave. "Do you want me to carry your supplies?" she asked politely, because despite being healthy, the woman was still eight months pregnant.

"Thank you so much," Radhika said. "I live right down there." She pointed to the houses on the street below. "It's the stairs, to get up and down from the temple, that are difficult for me."

The temple was up on a hill and it took thirty stairs to get up. But from the top of the temple you could look down and see all of Bheemunipatnam and on a clear day all the way to Visakhapatnam.

Radhika made tea for Chetana and Kokila when they got to her room. The kitchen area had been set up in one corner of the room with a pump kerosene stove and a few other essentials. A small coconut-straw bed leaned against a window, which was where Chetana and Kokila sat. There was an old three-legged chair leaning against the wall, and a straw basket that had been modified to be a baby's bed next to the kitchen area. An old black Philips radio sat on a rickety wooden table in the kitchen area. There wasn't much but the small room seemed overcrowded.

"The landlady is very nice," Radhika said. "They rent out two rooms, one I took and one two college boys have taken. They are just horrible."

Chetana sipped the tea quietly, looking around for evidence that the woman did have a husband. So far she could see absolutely nothing that indicated the woman was married, except for the *mangalsutra* she wore, which didn't mean anything anyway.

"It must be hard being on your own," Kokila said sympathetically.

Radhika nodded. "Very hard. In the beginning every drunk on the street would come and knock on the door. And those college boys . . . I am eight months pregnant and they still . . . The nonsense they talk!

But the war is going to be over soon, they say on the radio, so my husband should come back home. I don't think he'll be back before the baby is born, but I hope he will."

Chetana set her teacup down and saw a small framed picture on the windowsill. "Is this your husband?" she asked of the man in an army uniform.

"Yes," Radhika said, and smiled shyly. "This was taken right after he was commissioned. That was when we got married. We knew each other since we were children. We were almost neighbors growing up. Our parents are still very angry. My parents don't want to see me and . . . They are Brahmins, you know, and I'm a Reddy, so it wasn't a marriage either side approved of."

Chetana was immediately compassionate. She understood parental disapproval in the face of an intercaste marriage. If she had been a Brahmin, Ravi's parents would have been less against their marriage, but her being a Devdasi was unacceptable to them.

"You can come and stay at Tella Meda if you like," Chetana blurted out without thinking.

Kokila nodded as well. "There are a lot of people there and you won't have to be alone and there will be no college boys to bother you."

Radhika seemed to think about it and then shook her head. "I don't know, the landlady is very nice and she has promised to get the midwife and take me to the hospital when I'm ready to deliver. If something happens, I will definitely consider it. Thank you for making the offer."

They talked for a while longer and then Kokila and Chetana walked back to Tella Meda.

"Do you think she didn't want to stay at Tella Meda because she's heard stories about it?" Chetana asked.

Kokila made a noncommittal sound. "It isn't the best place for a woman to live in, Chetana."

Chetana sighed. "I don't blame her. If she comes and lives in Tella Meda, people will be absolutely sure that she's carrying an illegitimate baby."

"Poor thing," Kokila said. "It's so sad that she should be alone when she's eight months pregnant."

"What is wrong with parents? Why can't they just love their children?" Chetana demanded angrily. "If I have a child, I would never push that child away, no matter what he did."

A child? Kokila wondered if she would ever have a child, if it would be even possible for Ramanandam to give her a child. She had talked to Ramanandam about pregnancy; after all, it was a practical matter to discuss. Ramanandam told her that he was too old to make more children. Also, he'd had some disease when Vidura was a boy that killed his seed. Kokila didn't ask him if there had been others since his wife died and if that was how he knew that he couldn't father any more children. What he had done with other women was his business, and she couldn't stand to hear about them anyway.

Both Chetana and Kokila were hired to make more *papads* by Kanka Lakshmi after they returned with the finished *papads* the next week. Their quota was increased and since Chetana and Kokila worked in tandem, they easily made forty packets a week, but it took up all their free time. Every week they'd go to the temple with the finished *papads* and come back with more raw ingredients. On the way home they would drop by Radhika's room as she grew larger and larger, waiting to deliver anytime now.

One night Chetana and Kokila made *papads* by candlelight in the kitchen. A storm was raging and rain was crashing around and on the house with fury. Lightning and thunder had cut off the electricity.

"Isn't this fun?" Chetana giggled. After dinner they had played cards and talked and then when everyone went to sleep they decided to make *papads*.

Chetana kneaded the dough while Kokila rolled out the *papads*.

"It will take a long time to dry these if it's going to rain like this tomorrow as well," Kokila said.

"We can dry them in one of the guest rooms under the fan," Chetana suggested. "No one is here anyway. And probably no one will come until the monsoon is over."

"I hope someone comes before that," Kokila said wearily. "We're

SONG OF THE CUCKOO BIRD *99*

short of money. No one is paying their rent on time and people who come and stay are so stingy. Some of them pay well, like that professor from Guntur. He is very nice. And that doctor from Madras, she always leaves something good behind. But then there is that family who comes from Kurnool, that man with the limp and his ugly wife . . ."

"And those ugly children," Chetana said, and made a face. "I hope Ravi and I have nice-looking children . . . fair, yes, I want them to be fair. And since Ravi and I are both fair . . ."

Not really paying attention to what Chetana was saying, Kokila went on. "Well, the ugly family stays for two weeks and leaves *twenty* rupees behind, as if that should help in any way. Why bother to leave anything? And—"

"I think I'm pregnant, Kokila," Chetana interrupted her suddenly. "No, I know I'm pregnant."

"That's wonderful," Kokila immediately said with a smile. "That's just wonderful. When will the baby be born?"

"I've missed two monthlies now, so sometime in May or June next year," Chetana said, but there was no happiness in her voice. "I've known for a while now but I didn't want to say anything. I hoped . . . I thought that the baby would go down my legs and—"

"Chetana," Kokila cried out. "How can you say something like that?"

"I can because my husband is a wayward fool who is right now at some whore's house or lying on his face in some toddy shop. And because I'm still here, living in Tella Meda. Is this where my children will also end up? What of this child? Will he get to go out or will he also live off Tella Meda?" Chetana asked in a strangled tone.

Kokila was about to put an arm around her when they heard the pounding on the door. They waited to hear if maybe it was thunder but the pounding noise came again and they both ran through the verandah to the front door.

"Chetana, bring the lantern from the kitchen," Kokila said, not sure if she should open the door in the middle of the night. "Who is it?" she asked, and opened the door as soon as she heard Radhika's voice.

The poor woman was clutching her belly; she was soaked to the skin and in pain.

"Come in," Kokila said as she ushered her into the temple room. "Chetana, let's get her to my room."

They helped Radhika into Kokila's room. They were all wet from going through the courtyard.

"We have to get you out of these wet clothes," Kokila said, and started to remove Radhika's *sari*. "What happened? Why did you come all the way here in your condition?"

Chetana held up the lantern closer to Radhika and Kokila saw that mingled with the rainwater on the floor of her room was blood. Her legs went lax with fear. They had to get Radhika to a hospital . . . but on such a night, how could they?

"Get Subhadra, now," she ordered Chetana. "And get some towels from the closet in the temple room."

Chetana had seen the blood as well in the dim light of the lantern and didn't ask questions. She ran out into the courtyard, in the dark, to wake up Subhadra and get towels.

"My baby," Radhika moaned. "What about my baby? I have to go to a hospital . . . I need a midwife."

"The baby will be fine and you'll be fine," Kokila lied as she briskly got Radhika out of her wet clothes and put a blue nightie over her. She didn't know what to do next so she asked her to lie down.

Radhika screamed suddenly but the noise was drowned out by the raging thunder outside. "I think something is wrong. Something is wrong with my baby," Radhika cried out. As the pain subsided sobs racked her body. "And he's dead, Kokila, what am I going to do?"

Kokila knelt beside Radhika and took her hand in hers. "Who's dead? The baby? The father?"

Radhika nodded. "I got a telegram today. They said he died and . . ." Fresh tears flowed down her cheeks as pain wrapped itself around her abdomen again.

Subhadra and Chetana came back then with towels and a lantern. "Oh my God," Subhadra said, and sat down beside Radhika on the bed. "Amma Radhika, what are you doing here in your condition? Come, come, tell me how you feel."

Radhika shook her head and then clutched her stomach. More blood poured out of her along with some fluid, soiling Kokila's bed.

"I'm going to go get Doctor Garu," Kokila said. "Chetana, you get Charvi out here."

"Charvi? What can she do?" Chetana asked.

"Keep her calm," Kokila replied.

"Take the lantern with you. I'll get a new one for here," Chetana said, and held the lantern up to her. "Oh, you stupid girl, why did you come here in all this rain?" she admonished Radhika gently as she used her *sari* to wipe the sweat building on the young woman's forehead.

"Those college boys were getting rowdy and . . ." Radhika started crying again, in pain and in agony. "And that telegram. My Raja is dead, they said, in the war. What am I going to do, Subhadra Amma?"

"Have the baby," Subhadra said sternly. "And Lord Venkateshwara Swami will take care of the rest. You are a smart girl and if nowhere else, you can come and live here in Tella Meda."

Chetana felt panic rise within her. Would her childbirth also be this traumatic? And what if Ravi died or left her? Would her children's fate also be sealed within the beautiful walls of Tella Meda?

It took longer than Kokila expected to reach Dr. Vishnu Mohan's house. It was just three houses away but the lantern's dim wavering light was little help in navigating puddles and stones on the way.

Dr. Vishnu Mohan didn't delay when Kokila said that there was a nine-months-pregnant woman at Tella Meda who was bleeding. He quickly brought along his black doctor's bag and an umbrella, which was a futile gesture against the torrent of rain and wind. They walked as quickly as they could, as quickly as the howling wind would allow them, to Tella Meda.

"A big pot of hot water," Dr. Vishnu Mohan instructed. "We will need to wash her and the baby. Good, you already have towels. You might want to get some more pieces of cloth that you use when you have menses. She's going to bleed a lot more after the baby comes out."

Charvi was holding Radhika's hand, sitting next to her and talking to her in a soothing voice. Ramanandam was standing by the door asking how he could help. Even Renuka was helping by finding clothes for the baby. She had brought her son's baby clothes with her to Tella Meda as memories of the past and now was offering them for use.

Narayan Garu could sleep through an earthquake and was continuing to sleep through the storm. No one saw the point in waking him up as there was nothing he could do.

"You can't push right away," Dr. Vishnu Mohan was telling Radhika while Subhadra rubbed Radhika's feet to keep them warm.

Ramanandam came along with Kokila into the kitchen while she got water heated on the gas stove. "Damn this war," Kokila said furiously. "That poor woman has lost her husband. Now she has to take care of a baby all by herself. Her parents and his parents don't want anything to do with them because they're not of the same caste."

"She'll be all right," Ramanandam said softly. "She can stay at Tella Meda."

"And what kind of a life would that be? Living off someone else all the time, not having your own home?" Kokila demanded.

"Is that how you feel?" Ramanandam asked, and Kokila softened.

"No, but that's how Chetana feels and I understand that. I chose to stay here—I can't now start regretting my decision." She smiled the smile she saved for him and his thoughts. "And there is you."

"I would be lost without you," Ramanandam confessed. "Here, let me help you carry that."

They carried the big pot of hot water into Kokila's room in the rain. Radhika was starting to push now and each time she did, she cried out, so loud that you could hear it over the thunder and the rain.

Vishnu Mohan Raasi, named after the doctor who birthed him, was born at six o'clock in the morning after ten hours of labor. He was a big baby, weighing four kilograms (Subhadra guessed by holding a sack of rice in one hand and the baby in another), and had black hair covering his entire head.

"You have to nurse immediately," Subhadra told Radhika. "This helps get all the blood out of your womb."

As Radhika nursed sitting on a cushion on the floor, Kokila

changed the sheets on her bed and Chetana brought in some incense to burn to get the smell of birth and blood out of the room. Charvi watched mother and daughter intently, pleased that she had played a part in this miracle.

"You must go to the hospital tomorrow and have the baby checked properly," Dr. Vishnu Mohan told Radhika. "I'll come along with you. If your husband is in the military, you should have been close to a military hospital, Amma. It was foolish of you to walk all the way to Tella Meda in a storm."

"I know, but I wasn't thinking," Radhika said, looking at the wonderful boy in her arms. "Maybe this was how it was supposed to be."

Dr. Vishnu Mohan smiled. "Maybe you're right."

The storm cleared out the next day as suddenly as it had set in.

"Even Lord Krishna was born on a stormy night," Subhadra said to the baby as she massaged his entire body with mustard oil. She had hiked up her *sari* and put the baby on her thighs as she rubbed oil on him and told him the story of the birth of Lord Krishna.

Still frail after having lost so much blood during childbirth, Radhika slept most of the day with Dr. Vishnu Mohan checking in on her and giving her medication to help restore her strength. Once she was better, he insisted that she go to the military hospital in Visakhapatnam to make sure everything was all right with her and the baby.

"Let me, let me," Chetana insisted when Subhadra was done washing and oiling little Vishnu Mohan. "It's my turn."

"No, no, it's Charvi's turn now," Subhadra said. "She already said she wanted him after I was done."

"Why don't I take him to her?" Chetana offered slyly.

Everyone at Tella Meda was fighting to hold the baby, cuddle him, change him, and take care of him. Radhika felt blessed.

"Thank you so much for your help," she told Kokila when she brought food for her. "I had no family and now my son is being held by so many people with so much love and care."

"You can stay here," Kokila offered yet again. "It won't be the life you would've had with your husband, but it will be a good life. We will be your family and . . . But it won't be the same."

Tears sparkled in Radhika's eyes. "I know," she said as the tears rolled down her cheeks. "I have to let his parents know and my parents know."

"He's a son's son, his parents might come around," Kokila suggested, and Radhika shrugged.

"It doesn't matter. I am terrified of the future and sad that Raja is dead but mostly I'm angry that he left me to deal with all of this on my own," Radhika said. "And I am so happy that my son is here. Each time I hold Vishnu Mohan, I feel the world has opened to me. And I'm so sad that my Raja will never be able to hold his son, that I won't be able to see him hold our son."

Radhika stayed at Tella Meda for almost two months before another telegram arrived, this one with an apology for sending out a wrong message previously. Her husband was indeed alive, though he had been injured when a bomb went off. He was now recuperating in a military hospital in Jammu. He would be sent home within a month's time.

Though everyone was happy to hear that Radhika's husband was alive, they were also saddened that little Vishnu Mohan would be out of their lives. The baby had brought great happiness to Tella Meda. But after Radhika left everyone became busy and excited as they prepared for Chetana's baby, who would be born in a few months. The birth of little Vishnu Mohan became just one of the stories about Tella Meda told to devotees and guests who came to visit and pay their respects to Charvi.

28 July 1972. India and Pakistan signed the Simla Pact, settling border disputes in Kashmir.

17 December 1972. A new line of control in Kashmir between India and Pakistan was agreed to.

The Whore's Daughter

Chetana first noticed Ravi when she was fifteen. After that she made sure he noticed her as well and it wasn't a difficult task. Ravi was a good-looking boy, tall, well built like a wrestler, and not that intelligent. But it didn't matter to Chetana. She knew he was Manikyam's son and everyone knew that Manikyam's husband was a wealthy doctor in Visakhapatnam. He had his own clinic and famous people went to him with their ailments.

Whenever Manikyam came to Tella Meda she wore diamond earrings, fat gold chains with diamond pendants, thick gold bangles, and expensive *saris*. Chetana couldn't imagine how Manikyam, who had a fat pockmarked face due to a battle with smallpox as a child, could have found a man as wealthy as Dr. Nageshwar Rao to marry her. She knew that it had been something Ramanandam Sastri set up because Dr. Nageshwar Rao was a great admirer of Ramanandam's brand of literature. Still, they seemed an incongruous couple and she believed the rumors about Nageshwar Rao having a mistress safely ensconced in a lavish house in the other end of the city.

Manikyam, however, never showed any signs of being the sad wife pining away for her husband. She was like a fat cow all decked out in the finest jewels and clothes. And Chetana thought that if Manikyam, as ugly as she was, could find a wealthy husband, then her own good looks should find her one as well. She understood that her family background limited the number of well-bred bridegrooms she could choose from. It wasn't a secret that she was Ambika's daughter. It wasn't a secret that no one, including Ambika, knew who her father was. No boy from a wealthy family would ever come to ask her hand in marriage, so she did what she knew she had to do—she ensnared.

It wasn't difficult. Ravi and his brother, Prasad, came to Tella Meda every summer to spend the three hot months with their aunt, Charvi, and grandfather, Ramanandam Sastri. It was also a time for Manikyam to present herself at Tella Meda with all her successes. Not only had she married rich, she had produced two sons, two boys who would bring her husband's family name and blood into the next generation.

"She's almost twenty," Manikyam had said in distress to Charvi a few months before Chetana married Ravi. Chetana, who had been cleaning the verandah in front of Charvi's room, had overheard their conversation with amusement.

"With every passing year we grow older," Charvi had replied sternly. She didn't like to gossip and Manikyam liked to do nothing else.

"We need to find a good boy for her and get her settled," Manikyam said in exasperation. "Otherwise her mother's colors will show. What if she starts behaving like Ambika? Can we take that risk?"

Charvi had made a harsh sound then. "Chetana is not like her mother. How can you talk like this? You've known her since she was a little girl and you still . . . I don't want to discuss this anymore."

It wasn't just Manikyam who was wondering. Renuka often talked about it as well. "Two unmarried girls in the house . . . Shiva, Shiva, what are we going to do?"

Chetana enjoyed all the worry and speculation. No one knew of her relationship with Ravi. No one knew the secret things they did in the garden in the night, behind the big rock on the beach, behind the temple on Sunday mornings when he went there with Manikyam. No one knew, not even Kokila. Chetana had never kept any secrets from Kokila. But this was important. Ravi was talking about marriage. He was in love with her, Chetana knew, but he was also frustrated and desperate to have her on their first night or before, if she would allow it.

For Chetana it was a victory. She had Ravi exactly where she wanted. But whenever she asked Ravi to talk to Manikyam and his father about her, he would find an excuse not to do so. And Chetana knew, the minute she succumbed to Ravi, she would be no better than her mother and she was *never* going to be like her mother.

"Come on, we'll get married soon. How does it matter if we do it now or later?" Ravi demanded, his breath rough as he once again tried to push Chetana's *sari* up her thighs.

"No," Chetana said softly but sternly. "You know we can't. We have to be married."

Ravi sighed and rolled onto his back. It was almost two in the morning. The stars were twinkling above them and the bay was rushing in and out against the beach. They used the terrace for their late-night rendezvouses. Sometimes there would be guests in Tella Meda who would insist on sleeping on the terrace and on those days Ravi and Chetana would find privacy in the bougainvillea cave in the garden.

Finally, Chetana convinced Ravi to marry her and she thought that all her problems would be solved. She would leave Tella Meda, live in a big house, and be a legitimate wife. But then all her plans were thwarted by Ravi's father.

Now she was pregnant. And she prayed to God for a boy as she sat with Charvi every morning for *puja* and on Sundays in the temple room all day with other devotees. A boy, she knew, would ensure that she could leave Tella Meda, move into her in-laws' home, and hopefully straighten out Ravi. A girl would mean that nothing would change. She patted her growing belly all the time, telling her baby to be a boy. It had to be a boy; anything else was inconceivable.

"Rub your belly with almond oil," Renuka advised. "I did it regularly and had two sons."

Charvi frowned at that. She had disliked Renuka for years, ever since Renuka had accused Charvi of being too friendly with Mark Talbot. In Renuka she saw the whole society that stood against her and what she thought she could have had with Mark.

"The baby's sex is already decided," Charvi informed Renuka curtly. "That happens during conception itself. So no matter what you rub your belly with, Chetana, the baby will be what it has to be."

"Nonsense," Renuka said bluntly. "I had two children, I know about these things. You keep to your meditation and prayers, Charvi Amma, and leave baby matters to us mothers and married women."

The insult in Renuka's words was unmistakable and Kokila felt sorry for Charvi.

They were all in the kitchen helping Subhadra make massive amounts of *chakli* for the upcoming Sunday *puja,* when they were also planning to have Chetana's *seemantham.* Kokila and Subhadra had talked about it at length and decided that they would make it very festive and not let Chetana feel the lack of a mother or a mother-in-law. Traditionally in the seventh month of a woman's pregnancy, her mother or mother-in-law would arrange the *seemantham,* inviting married mothers to bless the pregnant woman and her unborn baby. But Chetana's mother was not traditional, nor had Chetana's marriage been a traditional one.

Kokila had insisted that Charvi write a letter to Manikyam to invite her to the *seemantham,* and despite not wanting to interfere in the matter, Charvi had written the letter. That had been three weeks ago and Manikyam still hadn't responded.

"I don't care if it is a boy or a girl as long as the baby is healthy," Subhadra said as she dropped the batter from the *chakli* press into a big wok filled with sizzling peanut oil. She made swirls from the yellow chickpea flour batter in the oil.

"I care," Chetana muttered as she broke a still-warm *chakli* and bit into it. "I want a boy and we even have a name picked out. We plan to name him after Ravi's father and call him Nageshwar."

"And what if it's a girl?" Charvi asked.

"It won't be a girl," Chetana said determinedly. "Maybe you can pray for me and make sure it's a boy."

Charvi smiled and then nodded. "If it's so important to you, I definitely will. But what has to be will be and whatever happens, it will be for your own good."

Kokila was placing the *chaklis* inside an aluminum tin carefully, so as to not break them. All this talk about babies and their sex put her on the edge. It made her angry and she could feel a heat rise within her. She wished Chetana would just have the baby and be done with it. Then no one would talk about it all the time. It was driving her mad. Everywhere she looked there were babies, pregnant women, and married women.

"Kokila, take some hot-hot ones for Sastri Garu," Subhadra said as she placed a newly fried batch into a colander to drain any excess oil. "He likes them hot. Also, make some tea for him. He didn't eat any breakfast or lunch. That man is starving himself."

"He is writing," Kokila said quietly as she went about making tea.

"Writing?" Charvi asked surprised. "Really?"

"Yes," Kokila murmured, and cursed her slippery tongue. She shouldn't have said anything. Now they would know, or at least they would wonder.

"I don't know why a man his age should do any work," Renuka piped up. "And I must say, I don't like his writing all that much. All that freedom for women, what good can come of it?"

As if she had been waiting for Renuka to step into it, Charvi turned on her with the delight of a five-year-old with a tin full of *boondi ladoos*.

"He writes about equality and how men and women should stand shoulder to shoulder," Charvi began. "If women are just supposed to passively go about their lives, the society as a whole will suffer. I'm not saying that everything my father says is correct, but I believe that freedom for women is the only way India can step into the coming decades with her head held high."

Kokila was glad that tea was ready and stepped out of the kitchen leaving the argument behind. Subhadra handed her spatula to Renuka and came out with Kokila.

"Kokila?" Subhadra called out as she stood up. "I . . . There's something I want to talk to you about."

Kokila nodded and then waited.

"Come here." Subhadra clasped Kokila's arm and all but dragged her away from the kitchen toward the other side of the courtyard to ensure that no one would overhear their conversation. They stood directly under the sun and Kokila had to squint to see Subhadra's face.

"I don't know how to say this," Subhadra said, and then looked around. Kokila saw her eyes dart toward Ramanandam's room and she froze. She clutched the hot glass of tea she was holding, not feeling the burn on the palm of her hand.

"I . . . ," Subhadra started again, and then smiled uneasily.

"If you don't know how to say it, then maybe it is best if you don't say it," Kokila said in a rushed voice. *No,* her mind screamed, *Subhadra can't know.* And then she thought more reasonably and knew that Subhadra could know, probably did know. She could have seen Kokila slip out of Ramanandam's room or seen Ramanandam leave hers. They were careful but not overtly so; after all, it had been going on for three years now and they were comfortable with each other and felt secure in the knowledge that no one knew.

Subhadra licked her lips and Kokila started to walk away.

"I know," Subhadra blurted out. "I just . . . I won't tell anyone but I wanted you to know that . . . I know . . . about you and Sastri Garu."

Kokila turned around looking at the tiled floor covering the courtyard. Slowly she lifted her gaze to look at Subhadra. They stood silent for a while and then Kokila shrugged. "Say what you have to say. Just say it."

Subhadra smiled. "I've never seen him so happy. You're good for him."

Kokila wasn't sure she had heard correctly. "What?" Kokila asked lamely, and then sighed. "I thought you'd call me all sorts of names if you ever found out."

"No," Subhadra cried out. "Never. I would never begrudge you or him this happiness. I just don't want you to worry that people will find out. I know, but I won't tell anyone." Then she smiled. "Go give him his tiffin."

Ramanandam said he was busy when Kokila knocked, so she left the plate of *chakli* and a glass of tea outside his room. She wanted to rush in, tell him what Subhadra just told her, and tell him about the relief she was feeling, but she knew she would anger him by interrupting his work, so she didn't.

Recently Ramanandam had started writing again. This time he was writing a novel, he said, but he wouldn't tell Kokila what it was about regardless of how much she pestered him. Kokila was flattered when Ramanandam confessed that it was because of her that he was writing once more. He told Kokila that she was his muse, his inspiration, and without her, his world would simply stop revolving.

After dinner, Chetana and Kokila went for a walk, as they had started to do every day since Chetana announced her pregnancy. It gave Chetana the opportunity to get away from Tella Meda and spend some time alone with Kokila.

"What happened last night?" Kokila asked, having heard a commotion and noise in Chetana and Ravi's room then. Chetana shook her head. She didn't know how to explain what was going on in her bedroom with Ravi. She didn't have the words to admit that marrying Ravi had been a mistake, getting pregnant a monumental act of stupidity, but she had done both.

The good looks that attracted her to Ravi had made him popular in the red-light district, especially with the prostitute Sundari. Chetana wondered if some married woman had cursed Ambika for luring her husband away and that curse had been transferred to her. All her life Chetana had worked toward not being her mother and it looked as if it had worked—she wasn't a whore, she was a wife. But she was a wife who stayed at home while her husband whored around.

The fights between Ravi and Chetana had also increased. The fights that once had led to rolling on the bed, sweaty with sex, now led to black eyes and ripped clothes. He never hit her, Chetana told herself, not really. He got angry and pushed her around, but he never used his hands to beat her. The black eye had been an accident when she fell and hit the bedpost. Yes, he had pushed her but she had made him so angry. And she could always make him so angry. Maybe she was abnormal, she told herself, maybe she needed too much attention, maybe something was wrong with her. No one had really ever wanted her. She didn't know who her father was, and her mother had only brought her into the world to avoid yet another abortion. Vidura, whom she had loved with a pure heart, had run away. Subhadra loved her because she had no children of her own, and Kokila . . . well, Kokila was probably her only true friend. The only one who cared for her, flaws and all.

"Did he hit you again?" Kokila prompted, and Chetana shook her head again.

"Dr. Vishnu Mohan said that the baby was growing well," Chetana said vaguely. "He didn't think that when Ravi pushed me he hurt the baby. He thinks maybe I should get a divorce."

Kokila stopped walking and turned to face Chetana. They walked on the pavement by the road, as Chetana still didn't like getting sand on her feet.

"He didn't say that, he never would," Kokila said confidently. "Why are you lying to me?"

"So he didn't," Chetana muttered angrily. "I did and that old coot said that I should just wait it out and once the baby was born Ravi would become different, good. My foot he'll become good. Why do people think that having a baby will change them?"

"Having children does change people," Kokila said, and Chetana made an irritable sound.

"It changes how you live and sleep and eat but you are still you. Ravi isn't going to become a kind and loving husband because we have a baby," Chetana argued. "But if he pushes me around again I will . . . that's it."

"I don't think Ravi is going to hurt you again," Kokila said. After the first incident, both Charvi and Ramanandam had spoken with Ravi. It was one thing to ask him to change his life, which they did not want to do, but quite another to ask him to stop hitting one of the daughters of the house.

"At least not where anyone can see," Chetana said sadly. "There are other ways of hurting people, Kokila. The mind is softer than the body."

They walked in silence and then all of a sudden Chetana made a choking sound. "What am I going to do? My husband is never there and now I'm going to have a baby. What am I going to do if Manikyam doesn't accept the child?"

"Stay at Tella Meda," Kokila said.

Chetana laughed harshly. "And do what? I have no one to take care of me, of my baby . . . what am I going to do?"

"We will take care of your baby and you," Kokila said soothingly. "Tella Meda is always there for you."

"Always there," Chetana agreed. "If there was anyone else, anywhere else, who would take care of me, I would've left. I would've left Tella Meda a long time ago."

Kokila didn't say anything, just nodded in agreement.

"Why can't I be at the *seemantham*?" Ravi demanded teasingly a few days later.

Kokila was stringing a garland of jasmine through Chetana's hair. Chetana was dressed in a beautiful red and green silk *sari* with heavy gold embroidery. The *sari* had been a gift from Charvi for the *seemantham*. The jewelry Chetana wore, a gold and ruby necklace, bangles, earrings, and armband, were all borrowed from Dr. Vishnu Mohan's wife, Saraswati, who was saving the jewelry for her granddaughter, who was now ten years old and lived in London with her parents.

"Only women are at *seemanthams*," Chetana replied with a smile. It was one of the good days, Kokila noticed. Some days the couple would be like a newly married one, loving and adoring. Other days, Ravi would be drunk.

"Maybe I can hide and watch the secret things you women do," Ravi suggested. He sat down in front of Chetana and took her hand in his. "My mother will be here soon. She sounded very happy in the letter."

"Children have a way of making everything better," Chetana agreed.

And it had indeed become easier in the last few days because Manikyam had finally responded to Charvi's invitation to the *seemantham* and said she would definitely come to bless her daughter-in-law and unborn grandchild. She had, however, made apologies for her husband, who was too busy to travel.

"Maybe we can go back to Visakhapatnam with her," Ravi said with a smile.

In the past years Tella Meda had lost its appeal for Ravi. He wanted to go back to his father's house, where money was in abundance. Of course, he was adamant about not going to college or getting a job, which frustrated Chetana. The little money she made by making *papads* for Kanka Lakshmi was hardly enough to live on but Ravi took part of that as well. He had also been caught stealing money and after the loss of a few hundred *rupees,* Kokila had started locking up the safe in Charvi's room where the meager Tella Meda money was kept, and hung the key at her waist.

"Do you think your parents will take you back?" Chetana asked, her eyes glittering with excitement.

"Why else do you think my mother is coming?" Ravi asked with a broad smile. "There will be gifts and presents for you and the baby and we can go back home."

"What do you think, Kokila? Is Manikyam coming to take us with her?" Chetana asked.

"I think you shouldn't get your hopes up," Kokila said honestly. "Why don't you just enjoy the *seemantham* and not worry about these other things?"

"You don't think Manikyam will want her grandchild with her?" Chetana demanded angrily.

Kokila sighed. "Look—"

"Why can't you just be happy for me?" Chetana interrupted. "Ever since I got pregnant you've been . . . you've been strange . . . and—"

"You're imagining things," Kokila said softly. "I'm very, very happy for you. And I do hope that Manikyam will accept you and your marriage. I just don't want you to get hurt if she doesn't. That's all."

"Oh, she will take us home. I know my mother, trust me," Ravi said.

Kokila tied the last knot to secure the jasmine flowers on Chetana's hair. "All done," she said. "Here, put the *kumkum* on and we can start the *seemantham* as soon as Charvi is done with *puja*."

"You look beautiful," Ravi whispered, and then winked at Kokila. "Isn't my wife beautiful, Kokila?"

"Yes," Kokila said tersely. Kokila didn't like Ravi, didn't like the way he looked at her, didn't like the way he treated her, didn't like the way he talked to her.

"I need to go to the bathroom first," Chetana said, happiness written all over her face.

As soon as Chetana was out of earshot, Ravi leaned over Kokila, who was picking up the remaining flowers and cotton thread. "But she isn't as beautiful as you," he whispered. He stood so close to her that Kokila could feel his breath against her neck.

"I have to get ready for the bangle ceremony," Kokila said without looking at Ravi, and walked away.

Manikyam came during the bangle ceremony. Dozens of glass bangles were collected in a straw basket in the temple room. Married mothers invited for the *seemantham* slid bangles onto Chetana's wrist.

Manikyam kissed Chetana on the forehead, her eyes glistening with tears, and she slipped four gold bangles onto Chetana's wrist. "I wanted to give my daughter-in-law these when Ravi got married, so here they are now."

Chetana, already overwrought and emotional because of the pregnancy, burst into happy tears. *Everything is going to be all right,* she told herself, and then looked at Kokila. She didn't seem happy at all for her. Why couldn't she be happy? Even when she and Ravi got married, Kokila had been full of warnings. *She must be jealous,* Chetana decided. *Jealous that my marriage is finally working out and now my mother-in-law has brought me beautiful gold bangles. Thick, beautiful gold bangles.*

Kokila would never get married, never leave Tella Meda, never have a *seemantham*. Even as Chetana felt sorry for her, she felt haughty. Kokila had decided not to go to her husband's house—this was her *karma*.

Charvi watched the proceedings with unconcealed joy. Even though she was not a married woman or a mother, her status of *guru* allowed her to slip bangles on Chetana's wrists and bless the mother-to-be. Traditionally, widows were not allowed to be at festivities but at Tella Meda no such distinction was made. Still Renuka stayed in her room, refusing to smear the happy ceremony with her widowhood.

After the bangle ceremony, Manikyam poured fragrant oil on Chetana's head and then drew a parting through Chetana's hair thrice with three stalks of *kusa* grass that were bound together. She chanted, *"Bheer, bhavar, svah"* while tears rolled down her cheeks. She seemed deliriously happy that she was to have a grandchild soon.

Kokila brought a basketful of fruit out from the kitchen and placed it next to Chetana's chair. Chetana spread the *pallu* of her *sari* and women dropped the fruit on it, blessing her with a fruitful womb.

"My little girl is so big now," Subhadra whispered to Kokila, sniffling a little, holding her tears back. "She's going to have a baby."

Kokila didn't know what to say because she was worried about the baby. What would happen to that child? Even if the baby was a boy, there was no guarantee that Ravi's father would accept the son as heir. And if the baby was a girl . . . only problems would come of that.

"Both my girls are happy," Subhadra said, smiling at Kokila. "You are like my own daughter as well."

Kokila nodded at the empty words and a heat started to spread through her. She was no one's daughter, no one's wife, no one's anything.

Finally, the *seemantham* was over. The guests left, Chetana changed into a cotton *sari,* and life at Tella Meda went back to the way it always was. Subhadra cooked dinner, Kokila and Renuka helped, everyone talked about how wonderful it was that Manikyam had come for the *seemantham*. Everyone was also sure that Manikyam was here to take her son and his wife back with her. Manikyam had not said anything and no one had asked her directly.

It was inevitable that someone would finally ask and an answer would have to be given. It was Narayan Garu who paved the way for the heated fight that night.

"So, Manikyam, taking Chetana and Ravi back with you, eh?" he asked without malice, and it wasn't really a question; he was absolutely certain. "We will miss them both very much."

Manikyam looked uncomfortable. She pushed her plate aside and stared at the untouched food.

"I'm thinking of starting college in Visakhapatnam once we're home," Ravi said, not for a moment doubting that Manikyam or his father would not be amenable. "And with the baby, Chetana is going to be busy, so it will be a good time for me to study. I'm thinking of doing my B.Com. and looking for a job as an accountant. Nanna keeps saying he needs someone to take care of the accounts at his clinic and I can start working there while I go to college."

"And I will help you with the household work," Chetana said demurely. "And you can watch your grandchild grow, right in front of your eyes."

"Yes, yes," Ramanandam said as he finished his meal. "It is a great joy to see children grow, and a grandchild, that is extra special. So, when is Nageshwar Rao planning to come and take you all back? Or are you three going to go back right away?"

Manikyam cleared her throat and smiled uneasily. She looked at Charvi and then without warning burst into tears. In between sobs she told everyone that her husband didn't know she was here. She had lied to him, saying she was visiting a relative, and had come for the *seemantham*. He was adamant about not taking Ravi back if he wouldn't leave Chetana and she was desperate to see her son and make sure her grandchild was well taken care of.

Chetana's heart started to pound loudly. The sound was so deafening, she was sure everyone could hear it. She automatically looked at Kokila, who was standing at the kitchen doorway, waiting for everyone to finish eating so that she could clear the table and then eat dinner herself. She didn't look disappointed, Chetana thought angrily. Everyone else was disappointed; everyone else was arguing with

Manikyam that she should convince her husband and giving suggestions as to how she could go about it. Everyone had something to say
but Kokila just stood silently as if she had been waiting for this to happen. She had wished this. Just a while ago she had said that Chetana
shouldn't get her hopes up. She had looked at her with evil eyes, jealous eyes, and that was why Manikyam was saying these things.

Rage clouded Chetana's vision and she walked on unsteady legs
toward Kokila. "You cursed me," she said, loudly enough for everyone
to hear.

Taken aback, Kokila stared at her, shock written all over her face.

"You couldn't stand my happiness and you wished me ill,"
Chetana cried out. "Just because you are stuck here, you want me to
be too. Well, your wish came true. Are you happy now?"

Kokila tried to form the words to explain to Chetana that she
didn't understand what she was saying but nothing came out. How
could she defend herself against such fantastic accusations?

"It's not Kokila's fault," Charvi said, as surprised as Kokila by
what Chetana was saying. "These things happen. It's fate."

"Oh, really?" Chetana said, a twisted smile on her face. "And what
are you planning for me? Praying to God that I have a dead baby?"

"Chetana," Subhadra cried out, and even Ravi looked surprised.

Tears burst out of her eyes as suddenly as her temper had flared.
"Oh, Charvi, I'm sorry," she said, and kneeled down beside Charvi.
She put her head on Charvi's lap and started to cry.

Everyone consoled her. Only Ramanandam looked at Kokila's
startled and hurt expression.

That night, he came to her. He didn't knock, just entered her
room. She was folding her sun-dried clothes as she always did at night
before she went to sleep. There was stiffness in her body that she
couldn't expel. She felt as if a deep wound was bleeding within her. He
hadn't come to her for a few days now, as he was busy writing. That
added to what happened with Chetana and her talk with Subhadra
had wound her into a tight coil of anger and resentment.

"How are you?" Ramanandam asked.

Kokila nodded but didn't say anything, her attention focused on the red and yellow cotton *sari* she was folding carefully so that the creases would not be too obvious and she wouldn't have to pay the man who pressed clothes on the street corner one *rupee* to iron it.

"Manikyam said she will try and talk to Nageshwar Rao. I'm planning to go to Visakhapatnam and talk to him myself," Ramanandam said.

"When do you leave?" Kokila asked without emotion.

"I'll leave with Manikyam tomorrow," he said. "I'll come back soon."

"Okay," Kokila said, and turned her back to him as she started stacking her clothes in Vidura's old Godrej steel cupboard, which she had been using ever since he ran away.

"Don't be like this," Ramanandam said, and put his hand on Kokila's shoulder. "What's wrong?"

"Nothing is wrong. Why do you ask?" Kokila demanded, and closed the *almirah*. "So, do you want me to take my *sari* off or are we just going to talk?"

Ramanandam sighed. "Maybe I should leave."

"Okay," Kokila said, still angry that when Chetana had accused her, he hadn't comforted her, hadn't come to her until now, hadn't defended her.

"Did you want me to say something to Chetana for yelling at you? Comfort you while everyone was watching?" Ramanandam demanded angrily.

Kokila cleared her throat. "So you *do* know what is wrong? Then why did you ask?"

Ramanandam shook his head. "She's a pregnant woman; they are usually volatile. She didn't mean what she said."

"Well, that makes me feel better."

"Do you want to take the risk and let everyone know about us?" Ramanandam demanded. "If that is the case, let's take this fight out into the courtyard so all can hear. I'm not the one who is afraid of letting others know, you are."

"Of course I am. I am the woman in this relationship," Kokila spat out. "And Subhadra knows."

"She knows?"

"Oh yes, she knows," Kokila muttered. Ramanandam sat down on Kokila's bed and looked at the floor as he ruminated over what Kokila had just revealed.

"How do you feel about that?" he asked after a long while.

Kokila shrugged. "Subhadra didn't seem to be upset. She thought that it was just wonderful because you were so happy." Bitterness laced her tone. The more she thought about what Subhadra said, the angrier it made her. Here was a woman, a sort of a mother to Chetana and her, and yet she thought there was nothing wrong in a twenty-two-year-old girl having an illicit sexual relationship with a sixty-one-year-old man. Would a real mother be so blasé? Kokila didn't think so. A real mother would be torn apart that her daughter's life was going to amount to nothing. Subhadra thought it was all right for Kokila's future to be sacrificed at the altar of Ramanandam's happiness.

"We are happy together," Ramanandam said carefully. He could sense her anger and silent rage. He didn't know the reason but he was attuned enough to her to know that somehow Subhadra had bruised Kokila's feelings. She was angry and this had more to do with what Subhadra had said rather than with Chetana's outburst.

"Are we? Really?"

"I am very happy," Ramanandam said, still in that careful voice.

At his soft tone, at his nonchalance, Kokila felt more anger. "Well, I'm not happy," she declared for the first time to him. "I'm never going to have a husband, a family, children, nothing. I'm going to be here in Tella Meda and we'll be *happy* until you're ill or dead, and then what am I going to do? Light a lamp in your memory for the rest of my life?"

Ramanandam pursed his lips and hurt swam in his eyes. "If I could be younger for you, I would," he said simply.

His words made Kokila's anger disappear. She had never thought that their age difference plagued him. If she worried about her life, he probably worried about it as well. He loved her, she had no doubt, and loving her would have made him think about the same things she thought about. She sat beside him in the bed and took his hand in both of hers.

"I love you just the way you are," she whispered, tears brimming in her eyes, a response to the pain she knew she had caused him. "I don't want you to be younger."

"But you wish you didn't love me so that you could love someone else," Ramanandam said with a sad smile.

For an instant, just for an instant, she thought to lie but then decided that being honest with Ramanandam was as important as being with him. "Yes," she said. "But this is my *karma* and I have to endure it. And loving you is no endurance."

"My skin is wrinkled, I'm old, I don't give you pleasure in bed or out. I don't shower you with flowers and jewelry. I don't take you out to the cinema and I don't marry you or give you children. And you tell me that it is no endurance to love me?" Ramanandam asked.

"Yes," Kokila replied.

"You humble me," Ramanandam said, and kissed both her hands. "I think you should come along with us when we go to Visakhapatnam. We're going to be uninvited guests in my son-in-law's house. I don't know what he will do when he sees Chetana and Ravi. She will need you for support, despite what she said to you today. And I want you to come."

"Why?" Kokila asked.

"Because I don't want to be away from you," Ramanandam said quietly.

"Then I'll come," she responded, and leaned over to touch her lips to his.

As Ramanandam predicted, Chetana profusely apologized to Kokila and insisted that she come along with them to Visakhapatnam.

"We'll all go in Manikyam's white Ambassador," she said excitedly. "And"—she looked around the rooms of Tella Meda from where they stood in the courtyard—"this is the last time I will live in Tella Meda."

The three-hour drive to Visakhapatnam was tense. Chetana was the only one with an air of smugness about her. Kokila, Manikyam, Ramanandam, and even Ravi were nervous.

"I hope he'll accept," Manikyam said tightly.

She was sitting next to Chetana in the backseat of the large car. Ravi was sitting next to the driver, while Ramanandam and Kokila were squeezed next to each other. The driver had been with the family for years and Manikyam didn't worry about being discreet in front of him. Wearing a white pair of pants, a white shirt, and a white cap, he looked like he was a driver for rich people in movies. Kokila had been amused to see him, while Chetana felt that all her dreams were about to come true.

She'd always known Ravi's parents were wealthy. She had seen the driver and the car before, but she had never thought that she would ride in the car, sitting next to Manikyam as an equal. And she was an equal. She was a married woman, a pregnant married woman. She was as legitimate as Manikyam and it didn't matter who her mother was. She felt very satisfied now for marrying Ravi and for having a baby in her belly. Just a few days ago she hadn't been sure about either; now she was beaming with uncontainable joy. It was spilling out of her and she had to restrain herself from crying out and thanking God aloud.

"When I told him that Chetana was pregnant he was not very happy," Manikyam continued. "He told me that I shouldn't go for the *seemantham*. But I couldn't stay away."

"Nanna will want us to live with him," Ravi consoled. "He wouldn't want his pregnant daughter-in-law or his grandson to live in Tella Meda."

Manikyam smiled at the thought. She had been craving grandchildren and now one was being made right next to her. She was overjoyed and she was scared of what her husband would do; the two emotions were tearing her into pieces.

"Nanna, you be careful with him," Manikyam warned Ramanandam. "He's still very angry about the marriage."

Ramanandam nodded but he wasn't overtly concerned. Even though Nageshwar Rao had not abided by Ramanandam's wishes and accepted his son's marriage, he still wrote to Ramanandam once in a while and was always polite. Nageshwar Rao was an intelligent man who would never allow his emotions to overrule his etiquette.

The house, as Chetana had seen in photographs Manikyam brought to Tella Meda and imagined in her mind, was opulent. It was all white, with columns in the front verandah, which had a jasmine creeper sprawling over it. Tall coconut trees surrounded the large compound on which the house stood. A temple sat in the middle of the garden with a large marble idol of Shiva in the center. Chetana couldn't wait to see the inside of the house. Were there fountains inside like there were in rich people's houses in the movies? Did they have large paintings and vases? Silk cushions and velvet sofas?

Chetana didn't get the opportunity to find out.

Nageshwar Rao met his uninvited guests at the verandah and seated them there. It was a large verandah with white wicker furniture and comfortable cushions, but it was still an insult. He wasn't letting Chetana enter his house. When Chetana had to use the bathroom, she was directed to the one outside the house, which was used by servants.

Ramanandam could barely contain his rage.

"It isn't you," Nageshwar Rao said, facing Ramanandam. "I can't accept Ravi's marriage to this woman and I can't permit her to soil my house. You know, Sastri Garu, her mother is a common prostitute. We don't even know who her father is. You are welcome inside, but she'll have to remain out."

"None of us will step into your house if she isn't allowed in," Ramanandam said. "She's going to have your grandchild, Nageshwar. How long are you planning to keep this feud going?"

"If I don't accept the marriage, the legitimacy of this child is already in question," Nageshwar Rao said, undeterred by Ramanandam's tone. "Manikyam should've known better."

"You read my books and you appreciate what I write about equality for all. You say you believe in what I say about individuals being allowed to do as they please, women being allowed to do as they please, and yet you can't accept Chetana as your daughter-in-law?" Ramanandam demanded.

Nageshwar Rao nodded and then spoke gravely. "Your ideas and your ideology are commendable and I respect both you and your work. But that doesn't mean I welcome them inside my home."

"You are nothing but a hypocrite," Ramanandam said. "Let's go," he said to Kokila and the others.

"Ravi," Nageshwar Rao said, "you can stay, but without her."

Chetana stared at her husband and Kokila stood away from both Chetana and Ramanandam. She felt like screaming at Ramanandam for bringing them all here and making them suffer through this humiliation. She glared at Manikyam, who stood with her head hung low. What did she care? Her husband would forgive her, but Chetana . . . Kokila felt a shaft of pain within her when she saw Chetana go pale as she looked at Ravi with unblinking eyes.

"I'll stay," Ravi said, and walked into his father's house without looking back at his wife, seven months pregnant with his child.

18 May 1974. The first underground atomic device explosion by India
was carried out successfully near Pokhran in Rajasthan (Thar Desert) at
8:05 AM. India was the sixth nation to explode an atomic bomb.

The Good
Wife

Ananta Devi had heard from a friend that
Charvi could make a barren woman fertile, and Ananta Devi was
craving a male child because her husband was craving one. Afraid that
he'd leave her and find a new wife, Ananta Devi along with her six-
year-old daughter, Manasa, decided to travel all the way from Hyderabad to Bheemunipatnam to experience Charvi's magic.

Ananta Devi had been to fertility doctors, saints, *sadhus,* Babas,
anyone she could think of to make her pregnant again. She prayed at
the temple once every day and kept a fast once a week and sometimes
twice a week to convince the gods to bless her with another child, a
male child.

The first time, she had gotten pregnant easily. She had been married less than three months when her monthlies stopped and the nausea began. Now if only Manasa had been a boy, she wouldn't have

been this frantic. But Manasa was a girl and everyone knew girls were the property of others. She and her husband needed a male child, an heir. Her womb refused to make another baby. It was wrecking her marriage. Her young daughter was also starting to notice that her father wasn't interested in her and her mother was always depressed, always praying at the temple or performing elaborate *pujas* at home. Ananta Devi's faith in God was unshakable and she was sure that if she prayed enough, Lord Shiva or Lord Vishnu or Goddess Parvati would grant her the boon of a male child.

Growing up suffocated by her father's disinterest and her mother's obsession for a male child, Manasa had already become an introvert. She kept to herself. She didn't play much, just followed her mother like a little dog and did as she was told.

Kokila's heart went out to Manasa when mother and daughter arrived at Tella Meda. She was a beautiful little girl who realized that she was unwanted by both her parents. But all was not lost, Kokila discovered; there was still a spark inside the girl.

Despite saying that all people are equal, Charvi usually gave special attention to celebrities and the wealthy when they came to Tella Meda to pay her their respects. She probably didn't even realize that she discriminated but those around her did. Kokila didn't complain. Happy rich people meant fatter envelopes at the end of their stay and more money and gifts in future months if their wishes came true.

Charvi sat in the temple room with Ananta Devi and Manasa while Kokila stood at the doorway watching. Charvi put her hand on Ananta Devi's belly and chanted prayers. In the past years the demure Charvi who had shied away from anyone calling her a *guru* had changed. She still told everyone, politely, that she wasn't a *guru* but she had also started playacting. She would put her hand on barren bellies, aching heads, and hearts. She believed she had the power to heal. Not everyone who left Tella Meda wrote back letters thanking Charvi—in fact, most did not—but those who did were remembered and created an illusion of Charvi's godliness and successful healing powers.

"Ananta, your womb is rich, I see no reason why you shouldn't have another child," Charvi said, and Kokila had to hold back a snort. How would Charvi know whose womb was rich or not?

"But it has been six years now," Ananta Devi said, biting her lip as tears fell down her cheeks. "My husband is losing patience and I'm afraid he'll discard me and find a second wife to bear him a son."

Oh, to say such things in front of a child, Kokila thought as she looked at Manasa, who didn't respond to what her mother said. But even if she heard it a hundred times it probably didn't make it easy for her to live with the knowledge that if her mother didn't produce a brother, Manasa would be cast away along with her.

"We'll do the Maha Devi *puja.* You must keep your eyes closed and focus on Goddess Parvati. She is a benevolent goddess and will listen to your prayers," Charvi said, and then continued to chant Sanskrit *slokas.*

"Manasa, did you hear?" Ananta Devi demanded in a loud whisper, and her daughter nodded. "Pray to Maha Devi and ask for a brother. Okay?"

Manasa also folded her hands like her mother, but opened her eyes in the middle of the *puja* and looked around with pure glee. Her eyes fell on Kokila and she shut them tightly, afraid that she'd been caught. *Ah, there is the spark,* Kokila thought with a smile. She was being naughty, and Kokila was pleased that Manasa's selfish parents had not destroyed the child in her completely.

Looking at Manasa, Kokila wondered about Chetana's six-month-old daughter. Chetana had named her Bhanumati at Charvi's insistence.

"Manikyam will be pleased if you name your daughter after our mother," Charvi had coaxed. Charvi didn't speak much of her pious mother, though she kept an old black-and-white photograph of her in her room. It was obvious that she deeply respected and loved the mother she hadn't known very well.

Chetana had been too depressed to argue. Manikyam wrote a letter to Charvi explaining the situation. A lawyer had been hired to nullify Ravi and Chetana's marriage and a new match was being arranged for Ravi. Nageshwar Rao's sister had a daughter of marriageable age and she was still willing to marry her off to Ravi, despite his recent escapade with a prostitute's daughter.

> Dear Charvi,
>
> I am deeply wounded by what happened. But with Ravi also claiming that maybe the child is not his, I'm recovering from the incident. As my husband said, the marriage is not really valid, therefore how can the child be? And we have to consider Chetana's background. If her own husband is casting doubt on her fidelity, who are we to think otherwise? I hope Chetana will find refuge along with her daughter at Tella Meda as so many others have. Please tell Chetana that she can keep the gold bangles. When I gave them to her I thought she was my daughter-in-law and even though now I don't, I would like her to have them.
>
> Ravi has started college and is getting ready for his wedding. We hope that you and Nanna will come and bless the couple. Anuradha is a very nice girl and we are very happy that she will be our daughter-in-law. Please give my regards to Nanna, Subhadra, and everyone else. I hope to visit Tella Meda soon.
>
> Your ever-loving sister,
> Manikyam

Charvi wrote back a scathing response.

> Dear Manikyam Akka,
>
> It pains me to read your letter. Its contents are jarring. Ravi and Chetana were married and set up household in Tella Meda, under my roof. Ravi's claim that Bhanu is not his daughter is false and I can't believe you are perpetuating this lie. I expected Ravi to say and do many things, even leave his wife and child, but to accuse Chetana of infidelity makes him, in my eyes, subhuman.
>
> You and your husband have your karma to contend with. As you know, Venkateshwara Swami watches everyone and we all pay for our sins and receive rewards for our good deeds. Happiness will not be at your doorstep, I can assure you, no matter whom you marry

*Ravi off to. What you're doing to Chetana is morally wrong and I
will not associate with you or your husband anymore. Please do not
come to Tella Meda again, as you are not welcome.*

*Nanna does not send you his regards and we're all insulted and
humiliated at your and your husband's behavior. Goodness must
indeed be dead in this world if you will cast away a grandchild
because of her mother's caste and family background. You and I
grew up in the same house, yet I find that I don't know you at all
and don't care to know you anymore either.*

Charvi

Manikyam wrote many more letters pleading for Charvi to forgive her but staunchly maintained that Bhanu was not her granddaughter. Charvi never spoke to her again.

Chetana just lay in her bed all day, staring at the ceiling. She had
moved back in with Kokila and Bhanu slept with Chetana on some occasions. Usually, it was Renuka who took care of Bhanu.

It all started when Chetana didn't respond to a crying Bhanu, who
was then just three months old, for almost an hour. Unable to stand
the cries of the baby any longer, Renuka went inside Chetana's room,
where she lay next to the baby, not picking her up or comforting her.

Renuka picked up Bhanu, who wailed some more. "The poor girl
is hungry," Renuka said acidly. "Come on, Chetana, feed her."

"I don't want to," Chetana said calmly. "You can feed her if you
want or leave her here. She will shut up when she falls asleep."

Horrified that a mother could be so cold, Renuka took Bhanu to
the kitchen and angrily told Subhadra what Chetana was doing.

"Thin milk for now," Subhadra suggested nervously, and quickly
mixed some milk with water.

"How do we feed her?" Renuka asked, speaking loudly to be heard
over Bhanu's hungry cries.

"A spoon . . . a small spoon," Subhadra said, and picked up the
brass one used to give everyone holy water.

Both women sat down on the floor and tried to feed Bhanu with
the spoon. The first few attempts were futile, as the milk flowed down

Bhanu's chin, but slowly Bhanu started to slurp the milk with her small rosebud mouth and stopped crying.

After Bhanu was fed, Kokila was immediately sent to the market to buy formula and a bottle with a nipple. The formula was expensive but for once no one at Tella Meda seemed to care about the cost. The baby's health was of paramount importance. Two bottles with nipples were bought and Subhadra sterilized them every night by putting them in boiling water. Everyone who wanted to pick up Bhanu had to wash their hands. Bhanu's clothes were washed separately from other clothes with a soft detergent.

Not willing to leave Bhanu with the disinterested Chetana, Renuka started to put Bhanu to sleep in the kitchen in one of the wicker baskets used to carry fruit during the day. She made a bed with white towels and muslin for the baby. Soon all the baby supplies that were in Chetana's room were moved to Renuka's as Bhanu started sleeping there at night.

Having a child to take care of altered Renuka's personality. The bitter widow who had come to Tella Meda became a loving though strict guardian to Bhanu.

Kokila was disappointed. She had expected Chetana to be a wonderful, caring mother, everything Ambika was not, but Chetana was just as callous. Kokila had tried to reason with Chetana but a severe depression claimed her and she was beyond reason. Chetana rarely ate or took a bath. She just lay in the bed staring at the wall or out of the window with blind eyes.

Kokila wanted to talk about the problem with Ramanandam, but he wasn't interested in hearing about the Tella Meda "gossip," as he put it.

Their age difference struck Kokila the most when he wouldn't listen to her problems and would instead talk about the larger issues regarding how the nation was dealing with one matter or other. He talked about politics and government and the enemies at the borders of India. Kokila didn't care about any of that. She had lived in the closed world of Tella Meda for so long that the larger issues of the world weren't relevant to her. She needed to talk to someone about waiting in the ration line for over two hours only to find that there was no sugar left. She needed to talk to someone about paying double to Puttamma's new husband (the fourth or fifth, she wasn't sure) for sugar, which he sold on the black market along with other essentials such as rice and oil.

She needed Ramanandam to listen to her talk about Chetana and how Bhanu was growing up without any attention from her mother. She needed him to listen to her and not just talk all the time. At times when he would drone on about the Congress Party or, worse, about his days in jail during the British Raj, Kokila had to resist the impulse to ask him to shut up.

Running Tella Meda, keeping track of guests both expected and unexpected, and helping with the cooking and cleaning was a full-time job for Kokila. Between that and making *papads* for Kanka Lakshmi, Kokila could not spend an appropriate amount of time worrying about Ramanandam's detachment from the real world or Chetana's detachment from her own flesh and blood.

Bhanu was growing up well, learning how to sit and trying to crawl. She was a lovely little girl, one who would never grow up to be as pretty as her mother, but she would be pleasant-looking. Kokila couldn't understand how anyone could think that Bhanu was not Ravi's daughter. She had Ravi's mouth and Manikyam's eyes and she smiled just like Ramanandam. She was a vocal child and made loud noises as she played by herself in the kitchen and the temple room while Renuka and Subhadra worked.

Charvi also spent a lot of time with Bhanu, talking to her, singing to her, letting her bang on the *tabla* and harmonium in the music room. Charvi had an abundance of patience with Bhanu. But Charvi's main concern was how Chetana was disappearing into herself with every passing day. She tried to help Chetana but besides getting a polite smile and nod, Charvi didn't get very far.

Kokila worried about Bhanu more than she did about Chetana. Would Bhanu grow up wondering why her mother couldn't love her? How could Chetana not be interested? If Bhanu were hers, Kokila knew, she would never let anyone take her girl away from her. As such, she contented herself with fighting to hold Bhanu and give her a bath. Renuka was a possessive surrogate mother. Bhanu wasn't getting her mother's love but she had enough mothers in Tella Meda to be happy and content, at least for now, until she grew old enough to see what was happening with her real mother.

Manasa didn't have Bhanu's luck. Her mother barely noticed her. She was too busy trying to have a son and there were no surrogates to take the role of mother with Manasa.

"Maybe if she stayed with her husband and kept household with him, she would get pregnant," Subhadra commented angrily when Manasa was shushed for speaking while Charvi imparted words of wisdom to Ananta Devi. The girl barely spoke and even when she did she was silenced. "Going to saints and *sadhus* is not going to get her pregnant."

"Manasa, come here," Kokila called out to the girl, who was sitting at the dining table in the verandah, listening to Charvi talk with her mother. "Do you want some *ladoo*?"

Manasa pursed her lips and looked at her mother expectantly. She waited for almost five minutes for her mother to say something, to at least look away from Charvi. Then she just rose and ran to Kokila.

"Is it coconut *ladoo*? I don't like *boondi ladoo*," Manasa said belligerently.

She knew her mother was too engrossed in whatever it was Charvi was saying. Her mother was always engrossed in what everyone was saying. Why wouldn't God just give her a baby boy?

Manasa didn't really want a brother but tried to want one because her parents wanted one so much. Her father would yell at her mother and call her a no-good wife and they would fight all the time. Ananta Devi might bow her head in front of *sadhus* and *gurus,* but at home she fought with her husband with great passion. He would then storm out of the house while Ananta Devi would cry and yell at Manasa for being a girl. So whenever her parents would have a fight, Manasa would hide someplace where her mother wouldn't be able to find her.

Whenever Manasa complained about anything her mother scolded her very harshly and even slapped her out of frustration. After all, didn't Manasa get the best clothes, the best earrings, the best bangles, the best everything? Why couldn't she be happy with all of that?

"Coconut *ladoo* with raisins in it, that's what I like," Manasa continued. "Do you have that?"

"Yes, we most certainly do," Subhadra said, and pulled out two *ladoos* from an aluminum tin.

Manasa sat on the floor next to Kokila, who was cutting *brinjals*. "Are we having *brinjal* curry tonight?"

"Hmm," Kokila murmured.

"I don't like *brinjal*," Manasa said. "Can't you make anything else?"

"Well, there will be sweet *pulusu*, plain *pappu*, and curds you can eat with ripe bananas," Kokila said.

Manasa wrinkled her nose.

"This is a coconut *brinjal* curry, it's very tasty," Kokila continued.

"I don't like *brinjal*," Manasa repeated. "My father doesn't like *brinjal*."

"Oh," Subhadra said, and sat down on the floor as well. "Have you eaten *brinjal* before?"

Manasa nodded and then shrugged. "I don't remember. But if my father doesn't like it, I don't like it too."

"You have to make your own choices," Kokila said. "Everybody likes different things."

"My parents don't like me," Manasa said in the same tone she had used to tell them that she didn't like *brinjals*. "Amma says that Nanna would love me if I were a boy. But I can't be a boy. I have long hair and I wear frocks."

"Your parents love you just the way you are," Subhadra said as she looked through the doorway at Ananta Devi with disgust.

"No." Manasa shook her head as she bit into a *ladoo*. "But that's okay. Once Amma has a boy, Nanna will stay at home more and he'll be happy. They won't fight so much. I don't really want a brother but I think I might just have to get one to get some peace in the house."

She spoke with a precociousness that brought a smile to Kokila. "If your mother allows, would you like to come to the beach with me?" Kokila asked. "We can collect seashells and you can make something with those shells for your father."

"Like what?"

"Like . . . a greeting card," Kokila suggested. "You can stick the shells on a piece of paper and make a card. What do you think?"

Manasa shook her head. "Amma doesn't like it if I go anywhere. Nanna doesn't like it. He thinks girls should be at home and go to school and nothing else."

"I'll ask your mother," Kokila said, and looked at Subhadra sadly.

When Manasa ran back to sit next to her mother, Subhadra sighed. "Poor little girl."

"I feel so bad for her," Kokila said as she cut the last of the *brinjals.* "You think Bhanu will be like her?"

Kokila shook her head. "Bhanu has all of us and . . . Chetana will get better too. She's just depressed and she'll—"

"She's just like her mother. Ambika left that little girl without ever hugging her or kissing her and Chetana is doing the same. I should've known this would happen," Subhadra said bitterly.

Away from her mother, Manasa was a lively girl with a vivid imagination. She filled the plastic bag Kokila gave her with seashells, some shaped like conchs and others flat, all in vibrant colors. When the bag was full they sat down on the sand and Manasa started to arrange some of the seashells on the sand.

"This is a peacock," she said as she put shells together to form a bird. "I like peacocks. Amma has many peacock feathers. They are so beautiful, blue and violet and shiny. Do you like peacocks?"

"Very much," Kokila said. "But I like swans best."

"I have never seen a swan," Manasa declared.

Neither had she, Kokila realized. "I've seen pictures in books," she said with a smile. "Which flower do you like the best?"

"Roses," Manasa answered immediately. "I like big red roses that smell so wonderful. Amma makes rosewater with the roses in the garden and we spray it on everyone when we have a *puja* at home."

"I like roses too," Kokila said. "I like yellow roses best."

"They're nice too," Manasa said as she put the finishing touches on her peacock. "Isn't my peacock pretty?"

"Very. But we can't take it back with us like this," Kokila said regretfully. "Back at Tella Meda, we can find you some paper and you can make a new peacock on it."

Manasa shrugged. "It's okay. Will the waves come this far and take the peacock into the water?"

Kokila nodded. "During high tide the waves will come all the way here and beyond. See that mark there?" Kokila pointed to a scar on the rocks behind them. "The water sometime comes up to there."

"Will we drown then?" Manasa asked, stricken.

"No, no," Kokila assured her quickly. "High tide happens at certain times only. And it won't happen now."

"How can you be so sure?"

Kokila picked up a seashell and drew a big circle on the sand. Then she drew another little circle over the big one. "This is the earth," she said, pointing to the big circle. "And this is the moon." She pointed to the small circle. "The water rises because the moon pulls it up. So when the moon is directly on top of the earth, it pulls the water away from the earth. But the moon is not on top now. So there is no high tide now."

"Then the water rises at night only," Manasa said thoughtfully, "because the moon is out in the night only."

Kokila sighed. "Not exactly. The water rises every twelve hours. Even if we can't see the moon during the day, it's still there, just hidden by the light of the sun. The sun is very, very bright and even though the moon is in the sky, the sunlight blocks our view of the moon and the stars. It makes the sky blue and gives us light."

"And in the night the sun hides and the moon can be seen," Manasa said, then squinted to look at the evening sky. The sun was still up, the sky was still blue. "So, the moon is hiding," Manasa said, smiling suddenly. "Maybe my father's love is hiding too and once the sun is gone, I will be able to see it. Once the sun is gone he'll be nice to me."

Kokila pulled Manasa close and hugged her tight. *No,* she wanted to tell the girl truthfully. *Your father is a bad, bad man who will never be nice to you, no matter how many sons your mother has. He will be nice to his sons but he will always ignore his daughter.*

When Kokila and Manasa came back a woman was sitting in the temple room, talking with Charvi. She looked so much like Subhadra that for a moment Kokila thought she was Subhadra. But this woman was younger, slimmer, and just a little different.

"Kokila, this is Chandra, Subhadra's sister," Charvi introduced. "Can you go talk to Subhadra and bring her here?"

Chandra smiled uneasily at Kokila. "She refuses to come out, you see, and . . . I would really like to meet with her."

"I have tried," Charvi said, raising her hands defensively. "She won't listen. Maybe she'll listen to you."

Manasa went to look for her mother, while a curious Kokila went into the kitchen. Why would Subhadra not want to see her own sister?

Subhadra was cooking dinner, as she usually did at this time. Her movements were brusque and efficient and lacked the smoothness she usually had in the kitchen. She closed the lids of the aluminum pans sharply, banged harder with her spatula, and in general was making quite a racket as she cooked.

For an instant Kokila thought of not saying anything. Why should she involve herself in Subhadra's problems with her sister? Kokila hadn't even known that Subhadra had a sister and in the ten years or so she'd lived at Tella Meda, this was the first time the sister had come to visit.

"What?" Subhadra demanded of Kokila, who was standing at the kitchen doorway. "What do you want?"

"Do you need some help?" Kokila asked as she came inside.

"No, get out of here," Subhadra said curtly. "I don't need any help."

"Okay," Kokila said. "Where's Bhanu?"

"Renuka took her up to the terrace to put her to sleep," Subhadra said. "And Chetana, that stupid girl, is still lying in your room, doing nothing. She was a bad wife and now she's a bad mother."

"Okay," Kokila said, not sure what Subhadra was talking about.

"That Ananta Devi, she might be hurting her daughter by wanting a boy, but she's a good wife. She abides by her husband's wishes and is trying to fulfill his heart's desire," Subhadra said, anger brimming in her voice. "Chetana's not a good wife at all. You too are a bad wife."

"I'm no one's wife," Kokila said.

"You should have gone to your husband's house," Subhadra responded, now really sounding angry. "You stayed. Why?"

"Because I was young and foolish. Now he's married and is living a happy life. What has this got to do with you seeing your sister?"

"I was a good wife," Subhadra said, all the anger suddenly draining out of her. "A very good wife."

"I didn't know you'd been married," Kokila said, realizing that she knew very little about Subhadra. Even Chetana knew nothing. And they had never bothered to ask or find out. Subhadra was Subhadra, not all that interesting to know about.

"I was married for three years. He wanted children but I couldn't have any," Subhadra said, and then shook her head. "That's not true. Actually . . . I couldn't sleep with him."

Kokila cleared her throat, feeling the embarrassment a child feels in knowing that his or her parents have sex.

"What? I'm human, I have needs," Subhadra cried out. "What?"

"Nothing," Kokila said, feeling very self-conscious. "What happened?"

"I . . . he couldn't do anything with me. The doctors said that I was too small and that I needed surgery but that didn't help at all," Subhadra said. "He was frustrated . . . I was frustrated. It was not a good marriage, but I was a good wife."

Kokila tried to stem her curiosity. She'd seen Chetana and Radhika push out babies from their small vaginas that seem to have expanded to allow the passage. It seemed improbable that any woman couldn't have sex.

"So, you're just small?" Kokila asked, not liking the image of Subhadra's tight vagina inside her mind.

Subhadra shrugged in exasperation. "Yes, just small, too small. I don't want to talk about that. I didn't want to talk to him or a doctor but I did both because I was a good wife. And then he married my sister. I was still a good wife. I didn't divorce him, just gave him permission to marry again. That's supposed to be enough. I was a good wife."

Kokila nodded. "Is that why you don't want to talk to your sister? Because she married your husband?"

Subhadra didn't reply and kept her face wooden.

"It was disloyal of her to marry your husband, I understand," Kokila said. "I can tell her that you don't want to speak with her. Is that what you want me to do?"

"Yes," Subhadra said, but as soon as Kokila turned to leave she put a hand on her shoulder to stop her. "She didn't want to marry him. I made her. I knew he'd marry someone else but I wanted him to marry my sister, not some other woman. I thought I'd feel better if he married my sister . . . if I arranged the marriage. But after the wedding, I left my job as a schoolteacher and came to live with Charvi."

"So you insisted that your sister marry your husband?" Kokila was confused. If Subhadra had arranged the marriage herself, how could she be against it?

Subhadra nodded. "She didn't want to but I made her. I was a good wife, Kokila. I wanted my sister to give my husband what I couldn't. They have two children now. One boy and one girl. The perfect family."

"So why don't you want to see Chandra?"

"Because she married my husband," Subhadra said, biting her trembling lower lip.

Kokila blew out air in exasperation.

"So what if I wanted her to marry him? I still hate her for taking my place," Subhadra said tearfully. "She writes regularly, I never write back. Now it's her daughter's marriage and she wants me to be there. How will that look? The old wife and the new wife at the same marriage *mandap*, blessing the bride? I don't want to intrude in their life."

"I don't understand," Kokila said finally. "She's nice to you, she invites you to her daughter's wedding, and she didn't want to marry your husband until you forced her to. What is the problem?"

"As long as I don't talk with her then she will always be a little sad about marrying my husband," Subhadra revealed. "If I have to live like this, she can bear a little pain for me."

Kokila raised her eyebrows and then shook her head. Subhadra, who had always seemed so selfless, was after all a normal woman with the same emotions that governed all humans.

"This has gone on long enough," Kokila said softly. "Come on, talk with your sister. Don't you think she has borne enough pain? Why make her pay penance for something that was not her fault to start with?"

"No," Subhadra said adamantly. "Tell her to leave and tell her that I won't come for her daughter's wedding."

"Have you thought how hard it must've been for her to marry your husband? She had to live in the same house you lived in, sleep with the husband you slept with, and live your life," Kokila said. "I think it must've been very hard to marry a man who was already married to her sister. She must've hated you for being there before her and for dragging her into your husband's life. I certainly would have. But she still invites you to her daughter's wedding. How can you be so petty?"

Subhadra shrugged. "I have to cook and you're wasting my time. Get out of my kitchen."

Narayan Garu was sitting at the dining table when Kokila came out of the kitchen. He nodded toward her. "We have a new guest today," he said.

Kokila smiled. "Subhadra's sister."

"I didn't know Subhadra had a sister," he said. "Will she be staying for dinner?"

"Yes, Subhadra's sister will be staying for dinner," Kokila said loudly, making sure Subhadra heard, which she did because she peeped out of the kitchen, looking horrified.

Kokila spoke with Chandra then and assured her that she wouldn't go back empty-handed. Subhadra, Kokila was sure, would soften at her sister's presence and would give in. Despite her feelings of jealousy and anger, Subhadra's heart was soft, like hardened *ghee,* and a little emotional heat was all that was required to melt it.

Chandra was a softer version of Subhadra but she also had that spine of steel Subhadra wore with grace. She spoke very softly and gently and had only good things to say about her older sister.

"My husband, my children, and I will be so happy if she comes for the wedding," Chandra said to Kokila. "And if you can make it happen, I will pray for you every day at the Venkateshwara Swami temple so that you have a happy and fruitful life."

Kokila didn't disabuse the poor woman of her notion that those who lived at Tella Meda did so because their lives were barren. No one at Tella Meda had prospects for a happy and fruitful life.

Kokila had been trying to get to talk with Charvi for a week now but with devotees and guests pouring in constantly, there just hadn't been time. Finally, after the evening *bhajan,* Charvi granted her an audience in her rooms.

"What's this about?" Charvi asked with a broad smile.

"Ah . . ." Kokila didn't know how to say what she had to say without sounding mercenary. "It's a delicate matter but an important one. I would like to talk to you without worrying about the niceties. I hope you won't take offense."

"Of course not, Kokila," Charvi said calmly.

"Last weekend, you didn't give all the envelopes with money to me," Kokila said, not looking away from Charvi's face. "We're going through a financially difficult time and we need all the money that is given."

"They leave the money for me," Charvi said, not a hair ruffled, not a tense speck in her eyes. "It's my money. The gifts are mine as well. I decide what to give and what to keep."

Kokila nodded. "I understand," she said, though she didn't understand at all. What did Charvi need the money for? "But we need the money to buy food for the devotees and the guests. All of us who live here pay for our stay, but with Chetana and Bhanu . . . expenses are a little high. Bhanu's formula costs so much money. And—"

"How dare you come in here and make me feel bad for keeping something that is mine?" Charvi demanded, still in a soft voice.

"I thought that everything belonged to Tella Meda," Kokila retorted, trying to not get angry. "And frankly, I don't know what you need the money for. All your desires are fulfilled. If you want to eat something, we buy it for you or make it. We buy all your clothes, slippers, jewelry for the temple room, everything. We buy whatever you need and everything you want. But if you're going to keep more than half of what people leave behind, it becomes very hard to please anyone at Tella Meda."

Charvi's eyes narrowed. "Just because you are sleeping with my father doesn't make you the queen of Tella Meda."

Kokila's ears started to burn at the words. Her heart was beating fast and she felt her legs turn to jelly.

"Oh, you thought no one knew?" Charvi demanded, the veneer of the peaceful *guru* slipping away. "You whore yourself to my father, that's your business, but don't come here begging for money."

"Begging for money?" Kokila finally found her voice. "In that case, you need to start paying for all your clothes to be starched and ironed. And the special food we have to buy for you? Raisins, almonds, pistachios, soy milk, and all of that. You will also have to pay—"

"Shut up," Charvi said, rising from the chair she was seated on "I'll give the money to Subhadra like I used to, but not to you, never to you."

"I maintain the finances of Tella Meda. That's why we have a maid now, that's why we have food every day. Subhadra, as wonderful as she is, is not capable of managing money. But if you feel more comfortable giving her the money to give to me, that will be all right as well," Kokila said in an alarmingly calm voice. Her insides were on fire; she didn't know how she would get past this. Charvi knew. Who else knew? Did everyone know? And did everyone think she was whoring herself with Ramanandam?

"I'll give the money to Subhadra," Charvi said serenely. "Make sure Chandra is comfortable. Thank you for talking to Subhadra and convincing her to speak with her sister. I wasn't successful in doing so and I'm pleased that you were. They are talking again and it's wonderful to see family united like this. Isn't it?"

The change in Charvi's tone of voice and words was jarring. Kokila left Charvi's room confused and feeling just a little battered.

The next day Chandra left Tella Meda after extracting a promise from Subhadra that she would attend Chandra's daughter's wedding in two months in Warrangal. Subhadra waved her sister away with tears in her eyes. She hugged her several times before she let her get into the cycle rickshaw waiting to take her to the bus station.

"All my life I turned her away from me but she forgave me and kept coming back," Subhadra said to Kokila. "Without you I wouldn't have spoken with her."

"Yes, you would have," Kokila assured her. "It might've taken you longer but you don't have a mean heart, Subhadra."

Subhadra sniffled and wiped her wet eyes with her *sari*. "I have a confession."

Kokila nodded, knowing what the confession would be. Subhadra had promised she wouldn't tell anyone about Ramanandam and her relationship, but Kokila knew that Subhadra didn't think of Charvi as just anyone. A goddess was meant to be confessed to and told the truth to.

"I know," Kokila said. "I understand."

Subhadra smiled. "You have a pure and clean heart, Kokila."

Kokila wasn't sure if her heart was all that pure or clean. In a way she did forgive Subhadra but she also knew that she would never completely trust Subhadra again. For all her goodness, Subhadra couldn't help how she felt about Charvi. Her loyalty to Charvi was beyond corruption.

"She already guessed and I just confirmed it. She already knew," Subhadra said in explanation. "She had an argument with Sastri Garu yesterday afternoon when you went to the beach with Manasa. He was very upset."

Kokila smiled vaguely. She hadn't seen Ramanandam almost all day, which was not unusual, especially since Chetana had started staying in Kokila's room again. And Kokila had been too tired to seek Ramanandam out in his room the night before.

But as soon as she could, she hurried to Ramanandam's room to make sure he was all right. The opinion of his godlike daughter mattered immensely to Ramanandam. He was as much devotee as father.

And now as Charvi grew older he was becoming more of a devotee than a father.

Ramanandam was sleeping, his arm covering his eyes, his body stretched tightly on the bed. He never rested, Kokila thought with a smile. He was always tense, always aware of the world around him. He woke up as soon as she came closer to his bed and let his arm slide away.

He didn't smile.

"How are you feeling?" Kokila asked.

Ramanandam shrugged and sat up on the bed. "Did she talk with you as well?"

Kokila nodded.

"She said some harsh words to me," Ramanandam said tightly. "Those words made me realize how cruel I'm being to you."

Kokila's heart started beating fast. Was it going to end today? Was it going to end because of Charvi?

"She told me that I shouldn't think of myself as the queen of Tella Meda because of us," Kokila said, and Ramanandam snorted.

"Queens don't work as hard as you do," he said, and the compliment soothed Kokila. But he still hadn't said anything to make her believe that their relationship was over or would have to be even more clandestine or maybe . . . maybe he would marry her? Would he? That possibility made her heart leap with joy.

"What are we going to do?" Kokila asked as she moistened her lips.

"Nothing has to change. Of course, if you have any issues . . ."

Kokila stared at him, her disappointment evident even as she tried to hide it behind a bright smile. "No, I have no issues."

"I can't give you more," Ramanandam said in frustration. "Why do you keep asking me to?"

"I have never asked anything of you," Kokila said quietly.

"Your silence, your face . . . I know what you want but I can't give it, do you understand?" Ramanandam demanded.

"Yes," Kokila whispered, and left the bitter old man alone in his tired room to ponder his life and its failures some more.

The next week, Kokila felt immensely guilty for the argument she'd had with Ramanandam. He came down with a high fever and vomited several times. Dr. Vishnu Mohan said that it was a viral fever and "it will go away in either seven days or a week." He used to always joke about viral fevers like that. No matter what you did, he would say, the virus is going to stay as long as it has to.

Their argument was quickly forgotten in the light of Ramanandam's illness. He once again started calling her his little tigress and confessed his love for her and she let him. However, Kokila felt that her role as his lover had already changed. His health had been deteriorating from the day she came to the *ashram*. She was his nurse now and she played that role with as much devotion as she had her previous one of lover.

Charvi didn't mention Kokila's relationship with Ramanandam again; no one mentioned it but everyone at Tella Meda knew. Renuka hadn't said anything but from her actions it was obvious she didn't approve.

"My Bhanu won't stay here any longer than she has to," Renuka said, glaring at Kokila one afternoon. "I'll get her married to some nice boy as soon as she is old enough and get her out of here. Look at your life. *Chee-chee,* young girls like you ruin your own lives. You have no one to blame."

Kokila didn't take affront. Renuka was entitled. The woman wore white, shaved her head in deference to her widowhood—how would she understand what it meant to be reckless enough to fall in love with an older man and consummate that love without marriage?

Chetana was amused. "You left your husband and you're stuck with an old man. My husband left me and I'm stuck with a young baby. It's destiny, Kokila, we were never meant to leave Tella Meda."

Ananta Devi left behind a thick envelope filled with money after her and Manasa's two-week stay at Tella Meda.

Kokila was sad to see the mother and daughter go. Despite her treatment of Manasa, Ananta Devi was actually a good woman, a good wife, trying to make her husband happy at any cost. She was prepared to do anything to get pregnant again and give birth to a male child.

It was a funny thing, Kokila thought, that pundits and people talked about love, devotion, respect, and obedience as being the cornerstones of a good marriage. No one said that the ability to have sex and give birth to male children were the most important things. Yet Subhadra had left her husband because she was unable to copulate with him, Chetana's husband had not come back to her because she didn't provide a male child that would have appeased his parents, and Ananta Devi was going from one *guru* to the other hoping to conceive. From where Kokila stood, it didn't appear as if love and devotion even mattered.

"Will you write letters to me?" Manasa asked Kokila before she left. "I'll write long letters to you."

"If you write to me, I will definitely respond," Kokila said. "But even if you don't write, I will write to you."

"*Ottu?*" Manasa demanded.

Kokila nodded. "Promise."

Manasa's letter came three months after she and her mother left Tella Meda.

> *Dear Kokila,*
>
> *We are all doing well here and I hope this letter finds you in the best of health and spirits. Amma is visiting Kanyakumari until the end of the month. I couldn't go as my teacher said that I shouldn't miss school anymore. I didn't want to go anyway.*
>
> *My father is very happy these days. He even plays with me and talks to me. He takes me to the store and buys me soft drinks and Cadbury chocolate bars. One day he even bought me a whole box of Cadbury Gems. He seems so happy now that Amma is gone and I secretly wish that Amma never comes back so that Nanna will always be this happy and always, always love me.*
>
> *I hear the servants talk about him getting married again. He keeps bringing this woman to the house. She eats with us but sleeps*

in the guest house. But I see my father go there at night after he thinks I am sleeping. The woman's name is Mallika and she is very pretty. She talks to me nicely and even combs my hair. Yesterday she took me to the bazaar and bought me three dresses. I like Mallika very much but I don't think Amma is going to be happy about her being here. But whenever I talk to her about my mother, Mallika asks me not to worry as Amma will be gone for a while now.

Amma writes short letters and says that she will be back soon but doesn't say when. I'm very concerned, but I'm also happy to spend this time with Mallika.

I miss you and Puttamma very much. Please give my regards to Charvi Auntie, Subhadra Auntie, Renuka Auntie, Narayan Garu Uncle, and Ramanandam Uncle. I miss playing with Bhanu, but Mallika says that there might be a new baby in our house as well and I can play with him.

Please write to me and come and see me in Hyderabad.

Love,
Manasa

The letters came in a timely fashion in the beginning and Kokila responded promptly to each. But as Manasa grew up and her memories of Tella Meda faded, the letters stopped coming. It was something Kokila had learned to accept. You could make friends with guests but it never lasted, even with regulars. Tella Meda stayed fresh right after a visit and faded away into oblivion soon after.

25 June 1975. President Fakhruddin Ali Ahmed signed the declaration of Emergency rule in India. Prime Minister Indira Gandhi announced that emergency rule would be implemented as early as the next day.

28 June 1975. As a response to antigovernment demonstrations, the Indian government imposed the toughest press censorship since independence.

The
Lepers

*R*avi came back to Chetana and Tella Meda when Bhanu was a year and a half old. His planned marriage to his cousin, Anuradha, had fallen through when she eloped with a boyfriend from a lower caste. Apparently, it was her affair with the lower-caste boyfriend that had prompted Ravi's aunt—Anuradha's mother—to accept Ravi as a son-in-law even though he was already married.

Ravi had stopped going to college, not that he ever really began, as he became involved with a Baba who provided him and his friends with inferior quality LSD and *ganja*. There were several Babas around the university who in the name of Rama and Krishna sold drugs to students. It was a common enough pastime and all of Ravi's friends from college indulged as he did. Manikyam and her husband were devastated, though. They had been sure that Ravi would put himself on the straight-and-narrow path as soon as he left the detrimental influence of Chetana behind. They cut off his allowance and threatened his independence. But Ravi started stealing money, first from home and then from his father's clinic. When Manikyam and Dr. Nageshwar Rao discovered the theft, they declared that Ravi had crossed too many lines.

Manikyam thought that if Ravi left Visakhapatnam and went back to Tella Meda, away from that fraudulent and dangerous Baba, he would start living a clean life. But even more than that, it was Ravi's influence on his younger brother, Prasad, that prompted Manikyam and her husband to shove Ravi out of their home.

Prasad started smoking *ganja* because of Ravi and then started drinking heavily as well. Dr. Nageshwar Rao knew that it was time to remove the bad apple from the basket before it completely ruined the good one.

Ravi had nowhere else to go, so he went back to Tella Meda, where he had a wife and a child.

The years had been difficult for Chetana. She hated Renuka with a passion because Bhanu preferred to be with that old widow rather than with her own mother. In an effort to reinvent herself, Chetana started learning how to be a tailor. In the town two women, sisters, Jaya and Sheela, ran a small tailor shop. The women were not considered to be "right," as they ran a side business from their bedroom, the room next to where the tailor shop was. But Chetana needed money and sewing was one thing she could do, so she worked with the sisters.

Ravi went back to his old life very quickly at Tella Meda. Manikyam continued to send money to Ravi without her husband's knowledge. Ravi continued to waste it. This time Chetana didn't seem to care what he did as long as he gave her half of the money Manikyam sent. They both spent most of their time outside Tella Meda.

"I work," Chetana snapped at Kokila when she asked where Chetana was all day. "I make money as a tailor. And here." She threw a few *rupee* notes and *paisas* on the floor. "Our rent for this month."

"Just give it to Subhadra," Kokila told her, eyeing the money with distaste.

Was it true? Were the rumors floating around Bheemunipatnam

about her friend real? Was Chetana also turning into a prostitute like her mother? Jaya and Sheela, the owners of the tailor shop, were known to be women who engaged in licentious activities with wealthy men. Their clientele was considered to be varied, including the inspector of Bheemunipatnam, a few politicians, and some other men who came from all over the region. They had loud parties in their house with foreign alcohol and Kokila wondered if Chetana was drinking as well.

"We all know you're the one in charge, so why should I give money to Subhadra? Maybe I should've hardened Ramanandam's *lingam*, and then I'd have been the woman of the house," Chetana said with a sly smile. "You're not lucky, Kokila, but you're very smart, I'll give you that."

Every time Kokila tried to speak with Chetana, the conversation ended with Chetana being angry and resentful. Confused by her friend's behavior, Kokila finally gave up. The relationship that had bound them together for years, through good times and bad, was breaking. Kokila tried to look back and see when it all had begun. Was it before Chetana's marriage? After? Was it when Bhanu was born? Or had their friendship been sloughing off even before?

Subhadra tried to explain to Kokila that Chetana was behaving like this because she was sad and depressed. Her life had not turned out the way she had envisioned and what it was now was painful and embarrassing to her. If she was lashing out at everyone, it was a sign that she needed help. But Subhadra had always supported Chetana, through all her shortcomings, all her mistakes, and Kokila paid little heed to what she had to say.

The beautiful walls of Tella Meda seemed to want to strangle Kokila; her sense of suffocation at being inside was so intense. With Chetana gone from her life, it was as if a limb had been cut off and the loneliness threatened to drive her mad. Ramanandam was always sick now and she was tired of taking care of him. A part of Kokila wondered if the reason he was so interested in having a relationship with her was because he knew he needed a nurse.

Ramanandam was having some heart and lung problems. He was getting more and more frustrated because he couldn't move around as freely as he used to. On some days he would get tired easily, would be breathless just after a short walk. But some days he would be normal, as if the sixty-four years of his life had not taken their toll. He looked frail and continued to lose weight, regardless of how much food Kokila was able to coax into him. He didn't sleep and his only lifeline, his writing, he confessed, was also becoming more and more incoherent.

His demands on Kokila's time sapped her energy. He wanted so much from her. He wanted her to stay with him all night and stay up with him when he couldn't sleep. He wanted her to listen to him talk about his glory days and he wanted her to not express an opinion or tell him about her life, which was moving at a completely different pace than his. The situation had become so bad that Kokila made excuses to not be with him. She loved him but his sickness and neediness were throttling her.

It was when Kokila was all but ready to jump into the well in the backyard that she met Dr. Shankar Gurunathan. He was well known in Bheemunipatnam: the son of a wealthy Brahmin, he had given it all up to take care of leprosy patients camped in a small area just outside Bheemunipatnam.

A small clinic stood by the huts where the lepers lived and it was in this hospital that Dr. Shankar Gurunathan worked for the greater good of the people. The hospital was essentially two rooms and a verandah. The patients waited in the verandah and Shankar examined them in one room. If the case was very serious, Shankar would put them in one of the five beds available in the second room.

He was not just the doctor who doled out medication for the lepers, he was also their grief counselor, their messiah, their confidant, their father, their son, and anything else they needed him to be. He was always short on help and during every visit to Tella Meda he would ask Charvi if there was anyone she could think of who would like to join his cause. Charvi would politely assure him that she would definitely ask around but she never did. Despite Charvi's godliness and belief that all people were made equal, she found lepers repulsive. When Subhadra once wondered if she should help Shankar, Charvi ordered her to not even think about it.

"Leprosy is very contagious. If you want to help, send them some food but don't go there yourself. What if you get it? What will you do then?" Charvi said.

Maybe it was because Charvi was so against it, maybe it was because Kokila was feeling more and more stifled inside Tella Meda and its routine, but whatever the cause, Kokila volunteered her services to Shankar during one of his Sunday visits to Tella Meda.

"Are you sure? It is a very contagious disease," Shankar warned her, as he did all his helpers. Most never lasted more than a few months. "You will always have to wear gloves and a mask when you work with the patients. The risk is very high."

Kokila knew that leprosy was contagious. She had seen lepers with their fingers and toes falling off, their dirty clothes, their deformed bodies. She was afraid she would become one of them as well but something compelled her to curb that fear and accept the challenge.

"I'm sure," Kokila told him. "I'll be very careful. This is my chance to help people."

Shankar smiled. He had just lost one of his helpers to marriage and was shorthanded, as always. Kokila's offer had come at an opportune time.

"We open the clinic at eight in the morning. I see patients who come by at that time. At ten I make rounds around the huts. You will have to accompany me on those rounds. We have lunch at noon and then we stay in the clinic until four in the evening. You will get paid one hundred *rupees* a month. I know it isn't much but that's the best I can do," Shankar said.

"When do I start?" Kokila asked.

The reaction from Charvi and the others at Tella Meda was predictable.

"Well then, she can't come into the house if she goes there," Renuka was the first to say. "What if she gives it to Bhanu?"

"All of us will be at risk," Ravi claimed. "This is pure suicide. Why should she drag us all down with her?"

Subhadra was the only one who didn't see anything wrong with what Kokila was planning to do. "She's trying to help people. We all should have such big hearts."

"It's not a matter of a big heart." Charvi joined the criticizers. "This is a matter of her health, everyone's health. Leprosy is contracted by touch, breath, everything. We will all be at a very high risk. Kokila, I don't think you should do this. I'm sure Shankar will understand if you explain to him . . ."

"Explain what? That Charvi doesn't think I should go? Or that everyone is so scared that I will become a leper and give the disease to them? Someone has to help these people and if Shankar has managed to work there for three years without an infection, why should I be scared?" Kokila demanded.

"Shankar is rich—" Chetana began, but Kokila interrupted her with a glare.

"And being rich is some antidote to disease?" she asked, looking pointedly at Ravi, the son of a rich man.

"There is no cure, Kokila," Charvi tried again, and Kokila shook her head.

"There is. Shankar told me that they have done some research in Malta and—"

"That doesn't even sound like a real place. Malta? What kind of name is that?" Renuka piped up. "And I wouldn't believe anything that boy says. Too slick for my liking. Watch it, Kokila, you'll get infected too and then what? I say, stay at Tella Meda and be healthy."

Kokila wanted to scream that if she stayed at Tella Meda any longer, she'd go mad. She looked at Ramanandam, who hadn't said a word and continued to eat his dinner quietly. She never addressed him in public, never spoke with him freely. Their relationship, though not clandestine anymore, was still very private and discreet.

"Ramanandam, what do you think?" she asked softly but loudly enough for everyone to hear.

The fact that she'd called him Ramanandam and not Sastri Garu didn't go unnoticed. Even Narayan Garu, who was trying to stay out of the discussion, looked up in shock.

Oh, let them look, Kokila thought bitterly. *I'm good enough to sleep with him and I'm good enough to take care of him now that he's sick but not good enough to call him by his first name? If I can do in it private, why not in the open?*

"It's your decision. I don't believe in interfering in anyone's life," Ramanandam said, unperturbed by her use of his first name in public. "But I also think that you're taking a considerable risk, and of course, there is a risk to all of us if you bring it into Tella Meda."

Kokila felt a tightness fill her insides. She was numb. He was not her husband, not her lover, just an old man who used her, she thought. Because a husband, a lover, would have stood by her and supported her, no matter what the consequence.

"I didn't tell you all this so I could get your opinion on whether I should work at the clinic or not," Kokila finally said. "I told you as a courtesy. I will not be at Tella Meda from seven in the morning until after five in the evening. The daily things that I used to take care of will have to be taken care of by someone else. I will still manage the finances and all the other work on Sundays. I will also help with the cooking and the cleaning every evening."

"As if we'll let you anywhere near our food or clothes," Renuka muttered. "If you go there, don't come near me or Bhanu. Stay in your room. We'll leave food for you there."

Subhadra gasped at Renuka's rudeness. "Renuka, she's just trying to do some good," she admonished.

"Good or wood, I don't care. If she's going to get that disease, she can live in a corner," Renuka said, and from the expressions others wore it was obvious they agreed with her.

That night Ramanandam came to Kokila's room. Chetana was back with Ravi in one of the front rooms and once again, Ramanandam was visiting Kokila in the nights when he was not ill.

"I need to wake up early in the morning to go to the clinic," Kokila told him as soon as he came inside.

"It's not always sex I want when I come here," Ramanandam said, and closed the door behind him.

"Well, whatever it is that you have come for tonight, I can't give, as I need to go to sleep," Kokila said, feeling like a nagging wife. "Or did you come in thinking that you can have one more night? After all, from tomorrow I become a high risk for disease."

Ramanandam shook his head. "It's an ugly disease. I don't under-stand why you want to be part of this. Is it that boy Shankar?"

"Shankar?"

Ramanandam sighed and then smiled in self-amusement. "He's young, good-looking, and a good man. I wouldn't blame you if you were attracted to him."

Rage built up again inside Kokila. "You have a filthy and rotten mind. Why can't I just want to do something with my life, something good? Why is that so hard to believe? If I want to work in the clinic, there has to be some ulterior motive?"

"He's a young man," Ramanandam said quietly.

"There are a lot of young men everywhere," Kokila spat out. "I'm not attracted to any of them and actually, right now, I'm not even at-tracted to you. You and your free mind and Charvi's godliness have their limitations, don't they?"

"Charvi has nothing to do with this," Ramanandam warned.

Kokila opened the door he had just closed. "You can leave, and take your ideologies with you. I expected you to say that no matter what I did and where I did it, you'd support me."

"I do support you," Ramanandam said weakly, looking at the opened door with fear in his eyes. "Don't turn me away," he pleaded.

"I'm not doing the turning away, you are," Kokila said, biting back tears of frustration, sadness, and love. She loved him. He might be old, ill, and narrow-minded, but she loved him.

Ramanandam nodded and walked out of her room.

Kokila expected the first day at the clinic to be easy. It would just be about explaining the work; how hard could that be? When she looked back, she realized that the first day was the hardest. She'd heard stories about the leper slums, the lepers, the dirt and filth, the ugliness, the sadness, the disease, the decrepit bodies, and the crippled children, but seeing all of it firsthand was haunting in its intensity.

She hadn't expected to be fastidious about the gloves or the mask, but the first man who came into the clinic was rotting away and she put them on in a hurry.

"We have to put new dressing on your wounds, Ramanaih," Shankar said kindly to the man. "Why haven't you come for six months? If you don't take medicine, it will only get worse."

Kokila couldn't place Ramanaih's age. He wore a filthy shirt over a filthy *dhoti*. His bare feet were dirty and his toes were covered with bandages that were as filthy as his toes. Flies were swarming around his feet and he emanated a foul smell.

"Kokila, can you unwrap his hands and clean them in the potassium solution?" Shankar said. He'd walked her through the routine, shown her how to mix potassium in water in a white basin to make a pale violet mixture.

Kokila's hands shook as she removed the dirty bandage wrapped around Ramanaih's hands. Vomit threatened to spill out of her. His fingers were stubby, the thumb on his right hand was missing, and there was pus everywhere. She threw the soiled bandage in the dustbin with a lid and dipped Ramanaih's hands in the cleaning solution. Bits and pieces of skin and dirt floated away from his hands and Kokila had to look away. Her heart was hammering and all she wanted to do was run away, run as far as she could, so that she would never smell the stench of rotting flesh again.

She wanted to catch the red and yellow bus that had brought her here to go back to Tella Meda. But pride and pity kept her from turning her back on the dirty old man. If he could live with his disease, she could at least show compassion.

Ramanaih's hands didn't look much better when they were clean. A red rash was streaked all over what remained of his fingers. There were sores on his knuckles and Shankar made a sound of distress when he saw Ramanaih's cleaned hands.

"I told you to be careful. What happened to the thumb?" Shankar demanded.

Ramanaih mumbled something incomprehensible.

As Shankar put an ointment over Ramanaih's hands and wrapped them again he lectured Ramanaih on the merits of coming to the clinic regularly.

He had to come to the clinic to take his medicine. He lived in the huts, so why couldn't he just come by? And where was he when

Shankar went on his rounds? Ramanaih didn't participate much in the conversation, just mumbled an apology once in a while.

"You have to be careful," Shankar told him again. "The disease takes away sensation from your fingers and that's why you don't feel anything when one gets cut off. You better come regularly, okay? Now, Kokila Amma is going to give you medicine. Drink it now with water and she'll give you a packet for the next month. Take three tablets every day, in the morning, afternoon, and night. Okay?"

Ramanaih swallowed the pill Kokila handed him and put the packet of pills she gave him in his shirt pocket.

"Thanks, Amma, thanks, Shankar Garu."

"How is your daughter doing?" Shankar asked as Ramanaih was about to leave.

This time Ramanaih spoke clearly. "She is doing very well. Her mother has fixed her marriage with a boy from Guntur."

Shankar shook his head. "Your daughter is thirteen years old, Ramanaih."

Ramanaih nodded with a smile. "Good time for marriage, very good time."

"Good time, he says," Shankar said to Kokila when Ramanaih left. "Poor man, his wife and daughter refuse to see him. He goes by their house once in a while and they give him some food. He's not even contagious anymore but no one seems to care about that."

"Then why is he still . . . sick?" Kokila asked.

"Because he doesn't take his medication properly. But he's not going to give anyone leprosy now. The first two weeks of medication kills the disease-causing bacteria."

"What is bacteria?" Kokila asked.

"Bacteria are very small living things . . . like an insect, but so small that we can't see them with the naked eye," Shankar explained.

Kokila nodded. "And bacteria are bad?"

"Not all bacteria are bad," Shankar said. "There are bacteria inside our body that are very helpful. And curds, they are full of bacteria. After lunch I'll show you what curds look like under the microscope."

The first two hours at the clinic seemed endless to Kokila. Half-eaten men, women, and children came in and left after being treated and advised. How could a small insectlike thing that one couldn't even see with the naked eye cause this much havoc? Kokila wondered.

Shankar and Kokila ate together. Shankar brought tiffin from his house, where he had a cook, and had told Kokila that she could share with him and not worry about bringing her own lunch. The tiffin carrier had four compartments filled with rice, *bhindi* curry, *sambhar,* and curds. Shankar's cook had also sent a separate steel tiffin box with *payasam* in it.

During lunch Shankar talked about his plans for the clinic and how he was hoping to get funding from the Andhra Pradesh government to keep it going.

"Most politicians don't care about the patients because they don't vote. But this is a serious problem. Over a million people have leprosy in India," Shankar said, and then smiled. "Are you overwhelmed?"

Kokila nodded. "Terrified, also. And . . . a little disgusted. I just want to go home and never come back. I guess I'm not as good a person at heart as I thought."

Shankar patted her hand comfortingly. "I would have been surprised if you were not disgusted. It's a disgusting disease. It's an ugly disease. If you don't come back tomorrow, I won't be angry or disappointed. I understand that this is tough."

"Then why do you do it? Everyone knows you come from a rich family. You have a lot of money. Why do you choose to do this?" Kokila asked.

"While I was growing up, there was this boy I knew in school. His grandfather had leprosy and the grandfather was kept in a separate area and no one spoke with him or went near him. He was completely isolated. I didn't think anything of it then, but as I grew up and went to medical college, I knew what I wanted to do," Shankar said. "My parents have money—that's why I can choose to do this and not worry about putting a roof over my head. And these people who live here in these shabby huts are better off than my friend's grandfather.

At least here people have each other for company. That man died alone."

Kokila realized there was a vast difference between the man Ramanandam was and the man Shankar was. Ramanandam could talk about a lot of things but hardly put any of it into action. On the other hand, Shankar was doing what he set out to do. No matter how ugly the job, how tainted his reputation, and how isolated his life because of his chosen profession, he was still doing it, every day.

"How do your parents feel about this?" Kokila asked.

"They wish I'd get married but they're not against my work. My father is a doctor as well and he worked in Burma for many years while I was with my mother in India," Shankar said. "He also had the luxury to do as he pleased because his father was a wealthy landlord."

"So, are you going to get married?" Kokila asked.

Shankar smiled broadly and a dimple appeared on his left cheek. He was a personable young man, just a few years older than Kokila. She realized that Ramanandam was right in wondering if she was attracted to him because she knew she could be. If she worked with him every day and every day they had lunch like this, wouldn't she feel something stir in her heart? Wasn't there already a stirring? His goodness was not a façade and that to Kokila was his most attractive quality.

"Sometime in the future I would like to get married, but I have no plans right now," Shankar said. "So, do you want to see what curds looks like under the microscope?"

It looked like several thousand living worms were wriggling against each other.

"Oh," Kokila said weakly. "I'm never going to eat curds again."

Her first day at work had been agonizing, fun, informative, and blissfully tiring. When she came back to Tella Meda, Renuka stood guard outside.

"You will have to stay in your room," Renuka announced as soon as Kokila opened the gate that led into the front garden of Tella Meda. "Subhadra will bring you food but you will have to eat it by yourself and wash your plate separately and keep it in your room. You—"

"Who do you think you are, talking to me like this?" Kokila demanded as she closed the gate shut. "Who do you think you are?"

"Stay away from me, you leper," Renuka squealed as Kokila came closer to her. "And stay away from Bhanu."

"Then get the hell out of my way, you old bitch," Kokila cried.

Without washing her feet, as everyone always did after coming from outside, Kokila stormed into Charvi's room. Charvi was sitting at her study table, reading. She looked up and raised her eyebrows in query.

"Did you ask Renuka to tell me to stay in my room and live like a leper?"

Charvi shook her head.

"Then talk to her and tell her that I'm *working* with lepers—that doesn't make me one. And even if I did by some chance get leprosy, with treatment I won't even be contagious after two weeks," Kokila said. "Can you do that or are you so against me that this is what you've been waiting for?"

Charvi looked at Kokila for a long moment. "I'm not against you."

"You hate me. You think I can't see that? You think I don't know that you disapprove of what . . . of your father and me?" Kokila asked, a thin hysteria tainting her voice. She was tired and the meeting with Renuka had increased her emotional stress.

"I don't hate you," Charvi said softly. "You are not in isolation. If Renuka doesn't like that, she can live elsewhere. But at the first sign that there might be a problem, I want you to tell us and get treatment. I think you're very brave and very foolish. I am concerned, but I will never be against you."

Kokila stared at Charvi, all the wind knocked out of her at Charvi's simple words. She turned and left the room more quietly than she had entered it.

Puttamma didn't seem to care where Kokila worked and was ready to fight against anyone and everyone to protect Kokila.

"You are doing good, Kokila Amma. Don't let anyone stop you," she said. "Those people need help. Dr. Shankar is a god and you're his helper. It is a good deed. Your soul is clean."

"But what will we do if her body isn't?" Renuka demanded, and Puttamma waved her away with a flick of her hand.

"Some people's hearts are not clean. That's where the problem is," Puttamma retorted, her meaning unmistakable.

"Old bitch," Puttamma muttered to Renuka's back as she left the courtyard. "You need anything, you tell me, Kokila Amma. I'm very proud of you."

"Thanks, Puttamma," Kokila said with a smile. "It is hard work but I feel like I'm alive. I'm doing something worthwhile."

"Those who have small minds and small hearts can't understand," Puttamma said firmly. "I'm surprised Charvi Amma had any objection. But she is a higher being, she is such a great lady."

Kokila wrote to Manasa about the clinic and Shankar. She described the clinic as best she could, though she worried that this might not be the kind of thing one said to an eight-year-old. But Manasa wrote back saying that she was very happy that Kokila was helping out the "poor leper people." Then she added some news.

My brother is very beautiful. Nanna named him Manav, so that his name is like mine. Mallika left a few months after Manav was born and now Amma says that she is Manav's mother. I don't understand. I thought Mallika was Manav's mother. She grew big and fat with him in her belly. I heard the servants say that Mallika is from a poor family so she came to have Manav and Nanna gave her money and then she left. I miss Mallika. She was nice to me. But I'm supposed to say that Amma had Manav while she was in Kanyakumari. It's a lie but my father said that it was a good lie. I don't think they'll mind if I tell you the truth. And in any case, all the servants know.

Amma and Nanna don't fight at all anymore. Nanna is even nicer to me though we all have to take care of Manav all the time. We went to Kashmir for vacation this summer and it was very nice there. We stayed in a houseboat and Amma was so scared that Manav might fall into the water. I didn't want him to fall into the water but I thought it could be fun to see what would happen.

I bought you a sweater there. Amma said that it is a very nice sweater made with sheep's wool. A special sheep. And the sweater is called a cashmere sweater. I hope you will like it. I wanted to buy the red one but Amma said the blue one would be better.

Please give our regards to Charvi Auntie and everyone else. Amma bought Charvi Auntie a shawl as well that she will send separately.

I miss you very much. Maybe when you get married you will find a husband in Hyderabad and we can see each other all the time.

> *Lots of love,*
> *Manasa*

The sweater came at a good time. Winter was coming up on Bheemunipatnam and Kokila's old sweater had become too thin and worn. She decided to wear her new blue sweater for especially cold evenings, so that it wouldn't get old too soon.

Kokila stopped making *papads* for Kanka Lakshmi, who had fired Kokila after learning that she was working at the leprosy clinic. But it didn't bother Kokila. There was a pleasant rhythm to her days. She left Tella Meda every morning and came back in the evening. It was a relief to leave and a relief to come back.

She still didn't like going with Shankar to the huts but she steeled herself every day and went with him. She had become adept at not smelling the foulness of the disease and not cringing when parts of a finger broke off while she was cleaning a diseased hand.

The lepers who lived in the huts always came and chatted with Kokila. They asked questions about Charvi and Tella Meda. They talked about their children, their grandchildren, their wives, and their husbands. The loneliness and desolation they felt was assuaged a little by the presence of Shankar and Kokila. They loved Shankar. They called him their god and savior. Kokila couldn't understand how it didn't go to Shankar's head. People said the same things to Charvi and she behaved like she was a real goddess. Shankar seemed unaffected.

"But don't you feel proud?" Kokila couldn't believe how he could be so humble, how anyone could be.

"I see people die of this disease, lose their eyesight, their family . . . what should I take pride in? That I can stand being next to them?" Shankar asked.

His goodness attracted Kokila to him. This was a man with a clean heart, as Puttamma would put it. He had no malice, only the desire to help people. He helped everyone he could. He saw such despair in his line of work, yet every morning Kokila would see him come to the clinic with a smile on his face. He was ready to take on the day and its challenges.

At Tella Meda, things were easing. Ramanandam was still not coming to Kokila's room and she wasn't going to his. Kokila thought it was a lovers' spat and they would make up again. But with every passing day she felt that a distance was opening between them that she couldn't breach. And since she met Shankar, it was a distance she didn't want to breach. Shankar was interesting and enjoyable to be around. He was not torn in two inside or worrying about larger moral dilemmas. He did what he could and admitted that some things were beyond him. He worked hard at the clinic but also made time to visit his parents, go out with friends, and even go to the cinema. He invited Kokila to join him and she did.

They were becoming good friends and Kokila was starting to value that relationship. The hurt she felt at Ramanandam's departure was assuaged by Shankar's arrival.

But the gossipmongers had also started to talk. Of course, no one believed that Shankar, a doctor from a good family, would marry a girl from Tella Meda, but no one would really blame him for taking advantage of one. After all, the women living at Tella Meda were not the most respectable. Women like Kokila couldn't expect marriage and family; no decent man would marry a woman who lived in the *ashram,* an orphan, a discard of society who had spurned one marriage already. If a woman didn't have a good family to stand by her, all she could expect were shameful liaisons with men out to take advantage of her. Kokila heard the loud whispers, but she ignored them, which was easy to do after a lifetime in Tella Meda.

The rash came three months after she started working in the clinic. She wasn't the first to notice it. Her arms had been itching all day but she didn't think much about it. It was getting colder and her skin always itched when it was dry. As she scratched she didn't notice the red welts on her skin until Renuka pointed them out.

"There, you've got it," Renuka cried out, hugging Bhanu close to her. "Charvi, Subhadra, she's got it. Look at her arms."

Fear ran through Kokila. She couldn't have it, could she? Shankar said that it took three years before any symptoms would appear even if she did get leprosy, which was highly unlikely since she protected herself constantly.

Charvi looked at Kokila's arms and sighed. "I'll send word for Dr. Shankar. Until then, Kokila, please stay in your room. Subhadra, take her food there, in a separate plate."

Kokila was speechless. "But it could be anything. Shankar said that leprosy only comes three years or more after exposure. This is not leprosy."

Charvi held up her hand. "I warned you that at the first sign of trouble we'd have to do something."

"If you had to do charity, couldn't you find something safer?" Chetana said as she looked at the red rash on Kokila's arms in disgust. "So, are you going to start losing your fingers and toes now?"

Kokila sighed. "No. Nothing is going to happen. Look, this can't be leprosy, okay? Leprosy—"

"Until a doctor says otherwise, why should we believe you?" Ravi demanded. "You are so stupid, Kokila. Going there to help those people, what did you think you'd get, a medal?"

Ramanandam was also asked to come and look at the rash. He shook his head somberly. "I'm so sorry," he said to Kokila, and she felt frustration bubble over.

"It's just a rash. It's winter, I get rashes during winter," Kokila said. "This is not leprosy."

"But until we know for sure . . . There are other people here, a baby is here. We have to let Shankar come and take a look," Ramanandam suggested softly. "In any case, you said that there was medicine. You'll be fine."

"If you're so sure, why are you asking me to sit inside my room and not step out?" Kokila asked, her eyes filled with accusation.

"Because we don't want what you have," Renuka said. "Now go before we get it from you."

Disgusted, confused, and rejected, Kokila went into her room and closed the door. She wanted to leave then, she wanted to go away, as far away as she could, but she had no place to go. *I should've left with my in-laws when they came all those years ago,* she thought as self-pity rose within her. It seemed that no matter how long she stayed in Tella Meda she couldn't escape that decision she made years ago. Look how the people of Tella Meda treated her. Even Ramanandam, after all they had been to each other. She had given up her youth for him, had cleaned his vomit, his clothes, and . . . Oh, God, what was she going to do?

Puttamma came that afternoon, after she cleaned the bathrooms, with Telugu movie magazines and some fruit. She sat down at the foot of the bed where Kokila was sitting, still in shock that she had been discarded.

"That new actress, what's her name . . . ah, anyway, she's having NTR's illegitimate baby," Puttamma said with glee. "It's all here in the magazine. I bought it for you after they told me. You read and enjoy. And eat some bananas, they are supposed to be good for you."

"Thanks, Puttamma," Kokila said, and slid off the bed to sit on the floor but not too close to Puttamma. "What are they saying?"

Puttamma snorted and moved closer to Kokila. "I say it's not leprosy. I know all about leprosy. It takes a while to get to you. But it can happen earlier too. I don't believe you have it. It must be something else. Good people like you don't get such a disease. God isn't that unfair."

Kokila nodded. "They aren't saying anything nice, are they?"

"It's just that old bitch, Renuka, and that new bitch, Chetana," Puttamma said bitterly. "Both of them banding together. And that no-good husband of Chetana's . . . that man should drown in the bay and die. No-good son of a whore. You don't worry about anything. If they ask you to leave, you come and stay in my hut until you get settled. My husband just left with that bitch Girija, so you come and stay with me, Kokila Amma. I'll take care of you."

That evening Subhadra brought dinner for Kokila in the same plate used by women who had to sit out when they had their period.

"Shankar said he'll be here tomorrow morning," Subhadra said sheepishly. "He doesn't think it can be leprosy."

Kokila nodded. "You should go. Who knows what you'll get from me."

Subhadra wiped tears off her cheeks. "You did a good thing and a bad thing happened to you. Sometimes there is no justice."

After Subhadra left, Kokila stared at the food that she didn't think she could eat. She had done a good thing and a bad thing did happen to her. But the bad thing was not leprosy. The people at Tella Meda, the family she had started thinking of as her own, had made the bad thing happen. Forget compassion—they had rushed her out of their sight at the first sign of trouble.

That night Kokila didn't sleep and contemplated how she could leave Tella Meda and what she could do to live a better life. Though even as she thought, she knew that if she had leprosy, one of the huts in the leprosy slum might be her fate.

Shankar saw the rash and shook his head. "It's not leprosy," he said quietly.

Kokila took a deep breath and let the air out. She searched for Ramanandam among those standing outside her doorway. He wasn't there.

"Then what is it?" Renuka demanded, Bhanu held tightly in her arms.

"Maybe she got something else," Ravi said, and Chetana made an assenting sound.

"It's just a rash," Shankar said, and then sighed. He looked around Kokila's room and his eyes fell on the blue cashmere sweater Manasa had sent. "Is this new?" he asked.

Kokila nodded.

Shankar held up the sweater and looked at its label. "You don't have leprosy. You're allergic to the kind of wool used in the sweater."

"What if she has leprosy and you're just lying to us?" Renuka asked.

"Why would he lie?" Subhadra demanded, and came inside Kokila's room. "Chetana, go get Charvi." Then she hugged Kokila tightly. "Just a rash! By the grace of Lord Venkateshwara Swami, you're saved."

Kokila felt stifled within the embrace. It had been just one night since they started treating her like an untouchable, but that embrace already felt foreign. She stepped away from Subhadra, her face expressionless.

"Everyone please go back to your rooms and business," Charvi said in the queen-of-the-house tone she had perfected in the past few years. "Hello, Shankar. Chetana said something but between her overexcited utterances and nonsense I don't think I understood anything. What should we do with Kokila?"

The question struck Kokila like a tidal wave. *What should we do with Kokila?* Is that what Charvi had asked? And what did that really mean?

"Nothing," Shankar said calmly. "I think she should put some Lactocalamine lotion on her rash, but nothing else."

"Are you saying it's not leprosy?" Charvi asked carefully.

"It's not," Shankar replied. "It's just a rash that I suspect she got from this new cashmere sweater of hers."

"That was sent by a devotee of mine," Charvi said, and nodded. "They sent me a shawl too, which I, as you can see, am wearing regularly. I don't have any rash."

Shankar made an exasperated sound. "Everyone has different skin. Your skin is probably not as sensitive as Kokila's to cashmere."

"So you're saying she's more delicate?" Charvi asked.

"No, all I'm saying is that her skin reacts to the wool and yours doesn't," Shankar said. "And she wouldn't get leprosy so quickly. It takes at least one year, but usually four to five years, before someone starts showing symptoms. And she hasn't been at the clinic long enough yet. I can't believe you treated someone in your house like this."

Charvi raised her eyebrows in shock. Shankar was always polite and humble, and no one spoke to Charvi like this. If Kokila hadn't been feeling so numb inside, she would've taken pleasure in the words Shankar dispatched to Charvi.

"You're supposed to be a *guru*, a goddess with a big heart, and yet you shun a woman for doing good? She was only trying to help the needy. Kokila, if you want to leave Tella Meda, you can come and stay with me," Shankar said.

A hush fell. Kokila ran his words through her mind over and over again to ascertain that they had meant what she thought they had the first time she heard them.

"And how would that look?" Charvi demanded, her tone still polite, but there was anger and bitterness. "A young woman staying alone with a single man? And already Kokila has quite a reputation, what with—"

"That's enough, Charvi Amma." Ramanandam's voice pierced through Kokila's numbness. She hadn't even seen him standing outside her door listening to what was going on within. "Shankar, thank you so much for coming here. We will always be indebted to you. Charvi did what she thought was best for the people who live in Tella Meda and . . . we're very happy to hear that Kokila doesn't have leprosy."

Shankar ignored him and turned to Kokila. "I don't care what people say. My offer will always be open. You can come anytime and live with me."

"I don't think that will be necessary," Ramanandam said, his eyes darting toward Kokila.

They were all looking at her, Kokila realized. She had to say something to let them know what her decision was. She had to let them know if she was staying or leaving.

"I need some time to think about this," Kokila said, a quiver in her voice. "Shankar, thank you."

"Let me know when you have decided," Shankar said, and left

without saying good-bye to Charvi or Ramanandam. He never came back to Tella Meda again.

"I did what I thought I had to do," Charvi said to Kokila. "And I'm sorry that your feelings were hurt. I would very much like it if you would stay at Tella Meda."

After Charvi left, Ramanandam came inside her room and closed the door behind him. Kokila sank onto the bed and looked out of the window into the backyard, her heart hammering against her ribs. This had seemed like a prison just a day ago. This room had been suffocating. Now she was free again. She wouldn't have to live in some slum while her body disintegrated.

"How are you feeling?" Ramanandam asked.

Kokila barely noticed his presence. What she had been through had been tragic, almost akin to death, albeit emotional, and now she had a fresh perspective on life. Ramanandam was not going to be part of this new life she planned to lead.

"Healthy," Kokila said.

"I'm relieved that you are well," Ramanandam said, and approached her, his feet moving silently against the tiled floor. "I have missed you."

Kokila understood why he was here, knew what he wanted from her.

"You can't go live with Shankar. There will be too much talk and—"

"Just like there is talk about you and me?" Kokila asked. "You didn't seem to care much about the talk when it was you and me, yet now you worry about that same talk if it was about Shankar and me. Why?"

Ramanandam shook his head. He took her hands in his. "I love you."

"No," Kokila said with absolute certainty. "If you loved me, you would have been here with me regardless of my health. That is true love, where you can be with someone no matter how bad the situation is. You have never loved anyone except yourself. You disguise your selfishness with talk of independence but you don't fool me anymore.

I stayed in this *ashram* because this was the only real home I ever had and because . . . because of Vidura. I'm not going to stay because of you now."

"You can't just go live with some—"

Kokila raised her hand to silence Ramanandam. "I'm not going to live with Shankar. But I'm staying here not for you but for myself." It was true, she couldn't go with Shankar. The scandal of it would be unbearable without the protection of Tella Meda. And Shankar had not asked her to marry him; how could she go then?

"What are you saying?" Ramanandam asked.

"You and I cannot be the way we used to be," Kokila said calmly. "It was perverse then, but because I loved you, I could bear it. Now I don't love you and I know that you don't love me. Whatever we share now would just be lust and that would be even more perverse . . . it would be monstrous."

Ramanandam searched for words. This was his Kokila, he thought in shock, who was calling his relationship with her a perverse thing, something she recoiled from now.

"What will you do?" he asked.

"I don't know," Kokila said, but for once she was not afraid of the future. She would find a way, she told herself, to make a real life. And it would be a good life, she vowed.

Ramanandam left her room silently. So ended the relationship Kokila had always in some corner of her mind known was wrong.

1978. Dr. G. P. Talwar, founder and director of the National Institute of
Immunology in India, started research on the mycobacterium W
vaccine, which he believed would play an important role in the eventual
eradication of leprosy.

The Pilgrims

Chetana was pregnant again. Bhanu, who was
now four years old, was very excited about having a baby brother. She
would talk to Chetana's rounded belly and constantly asked when the
baby would come out.

Having lost Bhanu to Renuka, Chetana was certain that this new
baby would be hers. She would take care of this baby and never let
him cry and never ignore him the way she had Bhanu. Bhanu might
call Chetana Amma but it was Renuka who was the real mother.
Bhanu slept with Renuka, ate with her, and was bathed by her.
Chetana was not involved in Bhanu's life in any real way. It had bothered Chetana a lot more before she got pregnant again. Now she focused on this new baby growing in her belly, confident that she would
do right by him.

Ravi started writing letters to his mother again, telling her about
the new baby, the impending *seemantham,* and how wonderful it

would be if Chetana could have the new baby in Visakhapatnam in his childhood home.

This time Manikyam responded to the letters politely but without enthusiasm. She did start sending extra money to Ravi and Chetana. This time she didn't make the mistake of saying she would come to the *seemantham* or even suggest her husband would consider bringing the prostitute's spawn inside his home.

The news was not as disappointing this time to Chetana as it had been the last. Chetana had come to terms with Dr. Nageshwar Rao never accepting her marriage to Ravi and she had also come to terms with living in Tella Meda for the rest of her life.

The coconut trees swaying in the wind, the smell of the bay, the chatter of Puttamma, Ravi's philandering—everything was wrapped within a dull polyethylene bag. If Chetana didn't bother herself with the facts of her life, then how would it matter what the facts were?

Chetana watched Kokila carefully these days but didn't approach her. It had been three years since everyone had tried to drive her out of Tella Meda, afraid she might have leprosy, and even now, the bitterness of that clung to Kokila.

Chetana wanted—she could feel the want ram against her heart—she wanted so much to be friends with Kokila again, get back to a time when it was not all so complicated, when life was not a constant struggle, but each time she made an effort, Kokila, the changed Kokila, rebuffed her.

And Kokila had changed. Everyone talked about it.

"She isn't sleeping with him anymore," Renuka whispered to Chetana when once Ramanandam tried to talk to Kokila but she walked past him as if he didn't exist.

"Good for her," Chetana had retorted, not wanting to gossip about her old friend, though just a year or so ago, she wouldn't have been able to resist the opportunity.

"It seems she blames him for her leprosy," Renuka continued, unperturbed by Chetana's lack of interest.

"She didn't have leprosy, it was a rash," Chetana muttered.

"I think she doesn't want to sleep with him because he has cancer," Renuka said confidently. "A man has sickness like that and women like Kokila leave them. My husband had cancer and I nursed the man till he died."

"Amma, you are a great wife and a great woman, okay? Are you sure your husband died of cancer and not because you nagged him to death?" Chetana said sarcastically. "And Sastri Garu was diagnosed with cancer last year; Kokila cut off ties with him long before that."

"Three years ago, they stopped being together. I have been counting," Renuka said. "I tell you, Kokila is a weak woman to do what she is doing. No matter what you say. Leaving that poor man when he has cancer and needs . . ."

"He isn't her husband, okay?" Chetana interrupted a little angrily. "And, old woman, don't you have anything better to do than sit next to my ear and blabber?"

But it was not just Renuka with her malicious talk who discussed Kokila; Subhadra did too, albeit out of concern. Kokila had stopped going to the leprosy clinic, to everyone's relief, but had started a new career that kept her out of Tella Meda for a good part of the day. After the rash incident Kokila couldn't get herself to go back. Part of it was fear and part of it was also that she had gotten weary of seeing the lepers every day.

"Poor girl, she just goes to that typing school all day. She never sits with us and eats anymore. You should talk to her, Chetana," Subhadra would coax even though she knew that Kokila was completely unreachable. Subhadra had tried to get through to Kokila with apologies, food, everything, but hadn't succeeded.

Charvi had also tried to talk to Kokila but nothing came out of it. Ravi was the only one who was unconcerned.

"If she seems to hate us all so much, why doesn't she leave?" he would demand even as everyone would shush him. Guilt was heavy among those in Tella Meda who had tried to throw Kokila out when they were convinced she had leprosy. Even Renuka, who usually seemed to be untouched by regret, was tormented by her actions. They had been justified, she would tell herself and others, she had been protecting Bhanu, but it was no balm for the guilt.

Ramanandam watched Kokila with haunted eyes. At night he ached for her, during the day he wished for their old conversations. As his health failed, he found that Kokila had been not just his lover and muse but also his nurse. No one in the *ashram* paid much attention to him or his ill health now. Except for Subhadra, who would check on him once in a while, no one came to him to talk, to help.

The old days were indeed gone. Now those who came to Tella Meda came for Charvi. Ramanandam's writing was long forgotten. His old friends were dead or dying, like him. Vineetha Raghavan had written to him when she found out he had cancer and they had resumed some communications, but it was formal, unsatisfying, useless. Vineetha didn't care for him any more than he did for her. The only woman who had truly cared was now as if made of wood.

Kokila wasn't unaware of the speculation, the concern, the malice, or the ache of a lost relationship, but she didn't let any of it bother her. If she felt the impulse to go check on Ramanandam when she heard him cough, she curbed it. If she felt curiosity burst within her when Subhadra discussed Ramanandam's cancer and his condition in a hushed voice, she stifled it. Ramanandam had nothing to do with her.

He is a dying man, she would argue with herself, *a dying man who is alone.* But a strong force within Kokila believed Ramanandam's illness and loneliness to be divine punishment. She had given herself to an older man, completely and faithfully, yet he had not stood by her during her time of need. This was Lord Vishnu's justice and Kokila felt she shouldn't interfere with divinity.

Once she stopped going to the leprosy clinic, Kokila learned how to type and then became a teacher in the Telugu typing school. The hours were from ten in the morning until two in the afternoon. It was a good job that paid enough to cover her expenses at Tella Meda. It also gave her the opportunity to step out of the oppressive *ashram*. At Tella Meda she still managed the finances, more easily than she had before because no one argued with her anymore. If she told someone their rent was due, the rent would be made available or a clear excuse was given. The lengthy lectures on how Kokila should be less of a mercenary had stopped. Even Charvi gave the devotee money she wanted to part with to Kokila and not to Subhadra.

But it wasn't easy to hold on to the anger she felt for everyone, especially Subhadra, who constantly tried to make peace. It was petty, Kokila knew, but becoming the old Kokila again, who could talk to everyone and be part of the Tella Meda family, seemed like a defeat. She didn't know what she was winning by staying aloof but she couldn't fathom changing. Not yet. Anger that had bubbled within her initially had settled down to a steady stream of slowly fading hurt but there was resistance to becoming too close to anyone at Tella Meda again. It was self-preservation.

"He is very sick," Subhadra said to her while they hung washed colorful cotton saris on the clothesline. "Spat out blood yesterday. I saw it on his clothes. No one talks to him . . . and he only wants you anyway. Why don't you just—"

"Are these it? Are there any more clothes?" Kokila asked in a high-pitched voice, pretending Subhadra had not spoken. She could hardly stay calm in the face of blood, could she? Spat out blood? How much blood? What did that mean? How sick was he? Was he dying? When?

"Come on, Kokila, don't be like this," Subhadra admonished softly. "He loves you . . ."

"*Subhadra,*" Kokila warned.

"What? I'm not afraid of you. You can bully everyone in Tella Meda, but not me," Subhadra said. "He's sick. Very sick. He's dying, Kokila. There's nothing left to fight over."

Kokila walked away from the courtyard into the temple room, her head throbbing because of the heat, the wetness of the clothes she had hung on the clothesline, and Subhadra's words.

What was she supposed to do?

Kokila stared at the shining black and gold idol of Lord Venkateshwara Swami in the mahogany temple and folded her hands in prayer. *Sometimes it is just easy to believe that there is a god watching over and guiding you,* she thought. *Sometimes it is easier to just let go.*

It was common for people to make requests of Lord Venkateshwara Swami and promise to visit his home in Tirupati, or offer money for the temple *hundi,* or offer the hair on their head, if their request came true. Kokila had never asked for anything but as she stood in the temple room that day, for the first time she asked for something. Guidance, a divine sign, a symbol, anything that would tell her what to do. And if the wish came true? She was thinking what she could promise if her wish came true when the letter arrived.

The postman, Ramana Rao, had been delivering post to Tella Meda for over a decade now. He would come and sit down in the verandah and whoever was around would give him a glass of cold water from the earthen pot in the kitchen, along with tea or coffee and some snack. If there was no tea or snack available, there was always someone to talk with Ramana Rao and brighten his weary post-delivering day.

"Many letters today, Post Garu?" Kokila asked as she brought cold water in a steel tumbler.

Ramana Rao gulped down the water without touching the rim of the glass with his lips. He drank neatly, with not even a drop of water escaping down his throat.

"How are you doing, Kokila Amma?" he asked as he set the steel tumbler down. "No typing school today?"

Kokila shook her head. "They are closed on Saturdays."

"Very nice," Ramana Rao said, nodding. "They say that in America people only work five days a week. Saturday is a holiday for everyone. That's a good life, don't you think? Two Sundays, one after the other."

"Post Garu, how are you?" Subhadra came out to the verandah with a cup of tea and some *chakli* she had made the day before. "If you can wait five minutes, Renuka is making fresh coconut *ladoo*. You can take some with you."

"So nice of you, Subhadra Amma. Since my Parvati died, this is the only place I get any homemade food," Ramana Rao said as he bit into a *chakli*. This was the finest part of his day. Since so many people lived in Tella Meda, there was always post for someone or other and he always managed to get his *chai-pani* break with the nice women of the *ashram*. Once in a while he could see Charvi, making it even sweeter to come to Tella Meda.

"What, Madhavan is not making good food anymore in that canteen of his?" Kokila asked.

Ramana Rao sighed. "Too much water in the curds, the *sambhar* has no vegetables in it; the vegetables have too little vegetables in them and the *pappu* . . . always only tomato *pappu*. I told him, '*Array*, Madhavan, nice unripe mangoes out there, make some mango *pappu*.' He says, 'You buy the mangoes, old man, and I'll make the *pappu*.' What time has come? *Kalyug*, it is, Kokila Amma, it is a modern, evil time."

"You should come and eat with us on Sunday," Subhadra offered yet again, as she always did.

Ramana Rao shook his head as he got up to leave. "You are generous enough. I just come here for company and some *chai*."

Subhadra went inside to get some coconut *ladoos* for Ramana Rao, while he picked out the mail for Tella Meda.

"Only one letter, it's for Sastri Garu. How is he doing?" he asked.

Kokila stared at the blue envelope and nodded. "Good . . . he's good," she said vaguely.

"I heard he has cancer," Ramana Rao said as he clucked his tongue. "The nurse at the hospital is a friend of the postmaster's wife. She told him that Sastri Garu is very sick. No cure for such terrible diseases."

Kokila nodded, still looking at the envelope.

"The letter will cheer him up," Ramana Rao said. "Letters always cheer people up."

"You wait here for Subhadra, I'll take this to him," Kokila said without even looking at the postman.

It was a sign, she decided as she walked through the temple room and then the courtyard to reach Ramanandam's room. She flipped the letter around to see who the sender was and shook her head. She had never heard of the man before, but then she didn't know most of the people who wrote to Ramanandam.

Kokila knocked on the door, as she had been in the habit of doing when she and Ramanandam were seeing each other. Usually she didn't wait for an answer but this time, conscious of the change in her relationship with Ramanandam, she waited for his invitation.

When there was no response after the first knock, Kokila gingerly opened the door and peered in. He was lying on his bed and a smile curled her lips. She had seen him lying like this so many times, and she had loved him with all her heart. How could love that had been all-consuming wither away? True love, they said in songs and books, always, always stayed. Like the love Devdas felt for his Paro. Yet now when Kokila looked at Ramanandam, she felt the pinch of a forgotten relationship but not the engulfing feeling of love and ownership.

"Ramanandam," she called out softly, and walked toward him. He was lying serenely on his back, one hand thrown over his forehead, his eyes closed.

"There's a letter for you," Kokila said, and contemplated whether to touch him and wake him or to just leave.

She almost left, leaving the letter on the floor by his bed, but a slight dribble of saliva coursing down his chin made her look at him again.

"Ramanandam," she called out, this time louder than last time. "Ramanandam," she called out again, more loudly.

She pushed gently at the arm that lay on his forehead and it fell onto the bed.

He wasn't breathing, Kokila noticed for the first time.

He wasn't breathing.

His chest wasn't going up and down as it was supposed to. She held her hand against his nose and felt no rush of warm air. She put her hand on his chest and searched in panic for his heartbeat. There was nothing but silence. His body was quiet, no movement inside or out. She shook him but he didn't wake.

She backed a few steps away from Ramanandam, and when her heels touched the raised threshold, painted yellow and red to symbolize turmeric and *kumkum,* Kokila ran out of Ramanandam's room into the courtyard.

Chetana was watching her, her hand on her full belly. "What? Patched things up again?" she asked sarcastically. She was about to say more but caught herself when she saw Kokila's stricken face. "Is everything okay? Did he do something? What did he do?" Instantly protective of her old friend, Chetana put her arms around Kokila, who slumped down onto the courtyard tiles, which were heated through by the relentless sun.

Chetana went on her knees and held Kokila, confused, unsure of what had happened. As the first sob rose from Kokila, the words poured out as well. "He's dead," she managed to say, and Chetana held her more tightly.

They stayed there for a while, until Subhadra found them.

Ramanandam had died of a heart attack in his sleep. Only those who had not sinned, had lived a pure life, died such easy deaths, Subhadra said.

Tella Meda fell into mourning. Manikyam and her husband arrived and even though Charvi didn't speak with either of them, she asked Kokila and Subhadra to be cordial on her behalf. Lavanya came, as always angry and suspicious of Charvi. But even she didn't say what was in her heart because it was obvious to anyone who looked that Charvi was the most devastated.

She sat in the temple room all day long lighting lamps as they died down and making cotton wicks from small cotton balls. She refused to eat or drink or see visitors. She sat quietly, all day, praying at times, weeping silently during others.

"Vidura isn't here," she said to Kokila once. "He should be the one lighting his pyre."

It was the son's duty to light his father's funeral pyre. The father's soul went to heaven, regardless of his sins on earth, if his son performed all the *pujas,* cut six locks of his hair, and set fire to his pyre. In the case where a son was lacking, a son-in-law would suffice, and if there was no son-in-law, the pyre would be lit by a nephew. But there was no guarantee then that the soul would go to heaven.

"Poor Nanna, he died with a hole in his heart," Charvi continued even though Kokila didn't say anything. "Vidura never came back and my poor father . . ." She fell silent and then went back to staring at the black and gold idol of Lord Venkateshwara Swami in front of her.

Kokila went about her life in Tella Meda as if nothing happened and she convinced herself that nothing had really happened. Renuka,

Subhadra, and Chetana watched her carefully, concerned that she would have a nervous breakdown soon since she was holding herself so stoically, too stoically.

"She was upset when she found him dead," Chetana told Subhadra and Renuka. "But now? She is behaving as if nothing happened."

"She hurts," Subhadra said softly. "She hurts so much that she's afraid to let it show, she's afraid to feel it."

More than hurt, guilt besieged Kokila. She had let him die alone and she hoped that he had indeed died as peacefully as he had looked. She had shunned him when he needed her the most. Her heart ached when she remembered the Ramanandam of the past, the smiling, kind, loving Ramanandam. He had been a shriveled old man, lying dead on his bed, peaceful, still, gone. She wished she had let go of her anger before he died. She wished she could have talked to him, they could've at least been friends, and she could have said good-bye to him before he passed away.

But she couldn't go back and change her life. And because she couldn't, she refused to succumb to the tears that threatened to flow and the sorrow that wanted to overwhelm.

If Chetana had been the subservient and extra-caring daughter-in-law the last time Manikyam was at Tella Meda, this time she was the opposite. She didn't even talk to Manikyam until Manikyam asked her with bright eyes about the new pregnancy. Chetana was resigned to living in Tella Meda and in the past few years had even come to enjoy it. Ravi had been the wrong choice for a husband, she knew that now, and she accepted that this was her fate and she had to live her life with the load of her decisions.

"I don't know how all of you tolerated that. It's so disgusting to even think about. He was such an old man and she . . . she must've seduced my poor father," Manikyam said. Now that Ramanandam's body had been cremated, it was obviously not right to talk ill of him. The blame had to fall on someone else.

"Seduced?" Chetana asked angrily. "How could Kokila seduce a grown man? Your father went around with prostitutes, and then there was that woman . . . what's her name, Subhadra? That doctor from the big power factory?"

"Hush," Subhadra said, and then sighed when Chetana glared at her. "Her name is Dr. Vineetha Raghavan."

"Oh yes, and what about her? She and your father were *very* close friends. Poor Kokila, she took care of Sastri Garu. She fed him, washed his clothes, and cleaned up his vomit when he was sick. What seduction? He was years older than her, more experienced. I say she got the short end of the stick, caring for an old man and getting nothing in return but ill talk from the likes of you," Chetana said in a loud voice.

Manikyam snorted. "This is what I expect a prostitute's daughter to say. You have no moral values and you don't understand—"

"Moral values?" Chetana felt more anger surge through her. This woman whose son went around drinking toddy all day and cavorting with whores was talking about *her* moral values? This woman whose husband was known to have a "small house" at the other end of town was talking about *her* moral values?

"You were born in sin and you—"

"Why don't you just shut up?" Chetana said, her eyes now red with rage. Subhadra sighed deeply while Renuka waited gleefully for the action to begin, holding Bhanu close to her as they both watched the scene in fascinated terror.

"How dare you speak with me like this? Do you know who I am?" Manikyam was not about to let some whore's daughter get away with such a tone of voice. But the whore's daughter had nothing left to lose.

"I know who you are. You are a woman who cannot accept her own grandchildren because their mother is of a lower caste, and that to me is a lack of moral values. You are a woman whose son sleeps around with every whore in town. You are a woman whose husband has a whore on the side . . . Please, close your mouth, mosquitoes will get inside," Chetana said, enjoying herself now while Manikyam looked at her openmouthed in shock. "Next time you want to talk about moral values, go someplace where people don't know you and your family. I married your son and keep house with him, I know all about his moral values. What, you taught him to drink toddy all day long and sleep with prostitutes? Or did he learn that from his father?"

And with that Chetana crossed some imaginary line Manikyam had drawn. The slap was a surprise and Chetana sat in stunned silence alongside Renuka and Subhadra, while Manikyam seemed astonished that her hand had connected with Chetana's cheek. If it was some other woman, it would have ended there.

As soon as Chetana had her wits about her, she slapped Manikyam right back, hard, her fingers leaving prints on Manikyam's soft, fat, fair, pockmarked cheek, rocking Manikyam's jaw.

"Don't you dare think you can get away with nonsense like this with me," Chetana said as she left the kitchen, waddling with her seven-months-pregnant belly in front of her.

It was the first laugh Kokila had in months.

"It's not funny," Subhadra exclaimed even as laughter threatened to spill out of her. "Poor Manikyam, she didn't move for almost five minutes. And it didn't help that Bhanu started clapping and singing that Amma slapped Nannamma. Renuka had to take Bhanu away because she was laughing so hard. I had to sit and console that poor woman. Two of her teeth got loosened."

Kokila wiped tears from the corners of her eyes. "Manikyam should've known that Chetana has enough rage to give Goddess Kali competition."

Charvi, who had also heard the entire story from a sobbing Manikyam, whom she still refused to speak with, came into the kitchen to talk to Subhadra about the incident.

"It's not funny," Subhadra said again, her lips twitching.

"The handprint is still there, shining red against her pale skin. I had to listen to her for an hour, complaining about Chetana and how her teeth are still shaking." Charvi sighed and sat down on a wooden *peetha* that was painted yellow and used for sitting on while eating. "It is the most I have felt like laughing since Nanna died."

As soon as Charvi mentioned her father, Kokila rose to leave the kitchen.

"Kokila, your pain must be very deep," Charvi said then, and Kokila shook her head.

"I feel no pain," she said softly.

"Yes, you do," Charvi said. "No matter what, he was the first man you loved. His departure has left a wound inside your heart."

"What do you care? You called me—" The words burst out of Kokila as if they had been waiting for the opportunity all along, right there, in the back of her tongue.

"And I'm sorry for that," Charvi interrupted Kokila and surprised her. "It took his death for me to understand that what you shared with him is something only you could share with him. I could not be that woman to him, though I wanted to be everything to him."

"He thought a great deal of you," Kokila said, feeling compelled to give something back. "He respected you. You were the only woman he truly respected."

"And you the only woman he ever loved," Charvi said, and then she smiled, a serene smile. "I'm planning to go to Tirupati. After all these *pujas* and mourning, I feel like visiting Lord Venkateshwara Swami's home. I would like it very much if you would come with me."

Kokila stared at Charvi and then at Subhadra, who was smiling even as she wiped tears off her cheeks. This was the reconciliation she had been hoping for, Kokila realized. This was the apology she had been craving for the years since her leprosy scare. A part of her wanted to reject Charvi's request and get back on her high horse and look at those who lived at Tella Meda with disdain but another part of her, the part that had missed being part of a family, was ready to reconcile.

"I would like that very much," Kokila said, a small quiver of excitement running through her voice. It was going to be all right; the past would fade and bitterness would go away and she would not be lonely anymore.

"Good. I would like to leave sometime next week, before Rahukalam starts," Charvi said as she got up. She put a hand on Kokila's cheek. "And if you could find out about bus and train timings and buy tickets as well, I would be very grateful."

"She doesn't need company, just someone to take care of everything while she travels," Kokila said in amusement once Charvi left the kitchen.

"She could ask anyone for that," Subhadra said, and she was right. This was Charvi's way of bringing Kokila back into the family and her way of saying that now that Ramanandam was dead, he didn't have to be between them.

Chetana insisted on coming along to Tirupati, even though both Charvi and Kokila didn't think it was wise for her to travel in her condition.

"Women work in construction sites while they're pregnant and you're saying I can't get into a bus and a train? And if I need anything, Kokila is there to take care of me, aren't you, Kokila?" Chetana said to Subhadra, who protested the loudest.

"I'm not taking care of anyone," Kokila said firmly. "Everyone will have to take care of themselves. Got it?" She hoped Charvi understood what she was saying but Kokila knew that being a *guru* for so many years had spoiled Charvi. She didn't understand that in the real world you took care of yourself. In the real world, people didn't bring you water and milk when you wanted. In the real world, such people were called servants and they had to be paid to run errands. But Charvi's world was a strange mixture of truths she had accepted and lies she had come to believe. She wouldn't be able to grasp what Kokila was saying about everyone taking care of themselves. She really didn't know what it meant anymore. As the years had passed she had become more and more of a *guru,* comfortable with her status and with Tella Meda being an *ashram,* though vocally she would still protest those titles. But everyone knew it was only a farce, a pretense Charvi put up to relive emotions she'd felt as a young woman.

They took a bus from Bheemunipatnam to Visakhapatnam, from where they would take an overnight train to Tirupati. Kokila had made sure that the train tickets she had bought at the bus station allowed for reservation in the ladies' coupe of the second-class compartment.

In all trains in the second-class compartments there was a coupe, an enclosed room within the open compartment that was reserved for women. You had to have reservations, or have paid enough of a bribe to the conductor, to sit in that compartment.

Usually in trains there would be catering service, even if the food was almost inedible at times, but Charvi would have none of that.

"We will carry food with us," Charvi instructed. "I don't like eating outside food."

So Kokila packed a tiffin carrier with rice, yogurt, pickles, and other items that wouldn't spoil easily during the journey. They were to stay with Subhadra's sister, Chandra, in Tirupati. Since Chandra's daughter's wedding four years ago, which Subhadra attended, Chandra had become a regular visitor at Tella Meda. She never came with her husband, for obvious reasons, but she would come for a week every year. During the years, some of Subhadra's blind devotion for Charvi had rubbed off on Chandra, who was certain that a goddess had taken residence within Charvi's corporeal body.

Subhadra never went to Chandra's house; she just couldn't bring herself to. Her sister lived in the same home Subhadra had lived in with her husband. The memories were too painful and she didn't feel she had the emotional courage to take that step and accept Chandra's several invitations. But now that Charvi, Kokila, and Chetana were going to stay with Chandra, Subhadra's heart lightened. She made Chandra's favorite flour *ladoos* to take along as a gift, along with *chakli* and other snacks. Subhadra packed all the food in a good-size aluminum tin that Kokila wanted to complain about but couldn't find the heart to. Subhadra was unbelievably excited about this trip, almost as if she were going to Tirupati herself. She felt immense pride that Charvi would be visiting her sister and staying in her home when she went to Tirupati.

She had written a letter to Chandra giving her the time of Charvi's train arrival, so that someone would receive them in the train station. Subhadra had also given strict instructions regarding food, *puja* in the morning and evening, and how to treat Charvi in general while she was in Tirupati. *She is a visiting* guru, Subhadra wrote to her sister. *Treat her like you would treat Goddess Parvati.*

"Why does she need this whole trunk?" Kokila asked as she stared at the black metal trunk Charvi wanted to bring along with her.

"God knows," Chetana said. "We'll have to hire coolies every-where. You and I can't carry that and *she* won't carry anything."

Ultimately, the journey was a pleasant and easy one. They reached Tirupati at seven in the morning and Chandra, her husband, Shiva, and her eldest son, Madhu, were at the station to receive the visiting *guru.* All of them touched Charvi's feet at the train station despite the fact that the holy feet were caked in dirt thanks to the journey. This pleased Charvi immensely.

Two rickshaws were waiting to take them to Chandra's house.

"Madhu's wife is expecting their first child in two months," Chandra told Chetana as they rode in the rickshaw. "When are you due?"

"In two months," Chetana said, her eyes skirting around the city they had come to. This was her first visit to Tirupati, to a big city besides Visakhapatnam. Tirupati was completely different from Bheemunipatnam, which was really a small coastal village. There was a hubbub in Tirupati, throngs of people clamoring to get to Tirumala, where Lord Venkateshwara Swami's famous temple was located. There was devotion in the air and the smell of turmeric and *kumkum* wafted around them along with rotten food, open sewers, and spicy roadside food. *Idlis* and *dosas* with *sambhar* and coconut chutney were being sold by vendors along the train station and Chetana's pregnant belly was rumbling despite an early breakfast of cold rice and pickle in the train.

Tirupati was surrounded by hills that appeared blue in the morn-ing light. As Chandra talked about the plans she and her husband had made to take their guests to Tirumala, Chetana watched vendors pushing green coconuts, while others were selling fresh coriander and mint leaves. She and Kokila were in awe of the energy they felt in Tirupati.

"There are so many people here," Kokila said as she washed her feet in Chandra's backyard. Chandra's husband had drawn water from the well and filled two buckets for their guests.

"This is such a nice house," Chetana said. "Subhadra told me that Shiva's grandfather built it."

It was a nice house, Kokila agreed. It had a nice front yard secured with a small wooden fence. The gate was made of black metal and had obviously been freshly painted for the holy guest. It had an *om* design on it. The verandah was large and comfortable, protected from the eyes of those on the street with long coconut-straw mats that hung from the roof.

"We throw water on the mats and the verandah is cool all year around," Chandra told them as soon as Charvi complained about how hot Tirupati was compared to the seaside.

Beyond the verandah was a nice, big hall with a large radio playing devotional music. A large black-and-white television set was next to the radio. Madhu was doing well at the bank where he worked and Chandra joked that he liked to buy all the new toys. Since it was Madhu who had arranged a loan for a television manufacturing company, the company had rewarded him with a TV at a great discount. But as soon as Charvi spoke of her distaste for the newfangled medium, Chandra swore that they rarely turned the gadget on and it was there *just* for show.

The kitchen opened into the backyard. Green vegetables grew lushly in a small patch, and a *tulasi* plant stood center stage in a colorful tall cement pot. There was plenty of room to dry clothes. The bathrooms were situated in the backyard as well, away from the house, as was the norm in old houses. There were four other rooms, used as bedrooms. It was a large house and as she looked around, Chetana wished she had married a man who could've given her a normal house and family life like this. She had wanted riches and was now left with nothing. Oh, why couldn't she have had the life that almost everyone seemed to have? It seemed so easily within grasp but had been elusive for her.

After a breakfast of Charvi's favorite tamarind rice with fresh yogurt, Charvi went to rest in the cool verandah with Chandra fanning her, while Kokila and Chetana busied themselves in the kitchen. They were not the holy guests and it was customary for the women who came to visit to help with the household chores.

In the kitchen, Madhu's wife, Harini, was making lunch. She smiled shyly when she saw Kokila and Chetana.

"Is Charvi Amma outside? Does she like the verandah?" she asked, her eyes excited.

Chetana sighed at the blatant devotion in Harini's face and Kokila smiled. Chandra had obviously made sure that her entire family showed and felt respect for Charvi.

"She's in the verandah and she probably likes it," Chetana said. "Do you want us to help with something?"

"Why don't both you pregnant women just sit down while I finish with the cooking?" Kokila suggested, and gently took the knife Harini was using to cut the big green bottlegourd and slid the bowl with the chopped bottlegourd pieces toward her.

"I'll take some cold coconut water for her. My father-in-law cut some coconuts just this morning," Harini said, pointing to the coconut trees standing tall in the backyard.

"She'll like that," Kokila said.

As soon as Harini stepped out of the kitchen, Chetana snickered. "Next she'll say Charvi's able to walk on water."

"Oh come on, there was a time when you were just as smitten with Charvi," Kokila reminded Chetana.

"I was a child then. Now I have my own children, so maybe I'm wiser," she said, smiling. "Poor Charvi, is this all she will have in her life? Mad devotees and Tella Meda? No children, no husband . . . nothing?"

"It's more than I seem to have," Kokila said.

Chetana looked stricken. "Just because he died doesn't mean you're some lifelong widow. Even if you were married to him, you could find yourself another husband, which is exactly what you should do."

Kokila shook her head. "The one man I was legally bound to I left. The man I was illicitly seeing died on me. What decent man would want me for his wife?"

"Someone better than Ravi, I'm sure," Chetana said. "You could have a real life, a happy life. Don't give up."

"Give up what?"

"Hoping and dreaming," Chetana said.

Kokila marveled at her friend's resilience. Despite everything that had happened and all that had been beaten out of her, she could still hope and dream.

Chetana and Kokila reverted to their familiar roles of working in the kitchen and serving everyone while they were in Chandra's house. Chandra was flattered and pleased, while Charvi enjoyed everyone's love, affection, and tireless efforts on her part, as she always did.

It was decided that they would walk up the hills to Tirumala, the main temple, instead of taking a bus. Kokila tried to persuade Chetana and Harini that an eleven-kilometer walk was not good for them in their pregnant condition but to no avail. It was God's desire, the pregnant women said, that they walk on the *sopanamargas* from Alipiri, at the foot of the hills, to the house of Lord Venkateshwara Swami.

"The Lord will take care of them," Charvi said to the concerned Kokila. "It's his wish that they come to him and that they walk. It will be okay, just trust the Lord of the Seven Hills."

So the small group of men, women, and pregnant women started the journey.

"You're crazy and stupid," Kokila informed Chetana, who shook her head with determination. "Charvi might want to trust God but I think God wants us to trust our good sense."

"I made a vow that I would climb the seven hills to get to Lord Venkateshwara Swami. I need a wish fulfilled," Chetana said as she huffed and puffed up the *sopanamarga*. "Have you made a wish?"

Kokila shrugged. She had been thinking about it but could not come up with anything. Almost everyone who went to Tirumala to see Lord Venkateshwara Swami made a wish and a promise to do something if the wish came true. It was destiny and legend that if you made a wish and promised God that you would climb the seven hills to get to him, or shave your hair off and offer the hair to God, your wish would come true, but you had to fulfill your promise as well.

"I'm going to shave my hair off too," Chetana told Kokila, who gaped at her. Chetana was very vain about her looks and it was proof of her devotion that she was going to have her head tonsured.

"Why?"

"I told you, I made a wish," Chetana said.

"He can't make your baby a boy or a girl," Kokila told Chetana.

"Shiva and Madhu are both going to do *angapradakshinam*," Chandra told Chetana and Kokila. "You know, for the health of our grandchild growing in Harini's belly and all others to come."

Several hundred devotees every day would lie prostrate and roll down the Vimana Pradakshinam, which ran around the temple. *Angapradakshinam* was difficult because of all the rolling involved and was therefore a strong proof of devotion to Lord Venkateshwara Swami.

"They have to wake up very early and bathe in the Swami Pushkarini before they go to the temple," Harini told them, showing off about her husband and father-in-law's level of devotion to her unborn baby. "I want to wake up early too, for the Suprabhatam."

"And what time is that?" Chetana asked.

"At three in the morning," Harini said with a smile, and Chetana shook her head. It was one thing to be devoted, quite another to wake up before the sun did.

Kokila laughed softly at Chetana's expression. "And you want to tonsure your head and whatnot? You're not even ready to wake up early for the Suprabhatam."

"I'll wake up if you do," Chetana said.

"Have you made a wish?" Chandra asked Kokila, who shook her head.

"Nothing?" Chandra was more than surprised.

Kokila shook her head again.

Chandra smiled. "You must have a content life if you have nothing to wish for."

Chandra wasn't being sarcastic; she genuinely believed that Kokila had a satisfactory life. It baffled Kokila. She didn't have a content life, but a hopeless one. Those who had hope wished for something. What could she wish for? A husband? No, she wasn't going to be with another man ever again. Children? Hmm . . . yes, she would like children, but it was hard to have children without a husband in this world. So no, that wouldn't work either. As she went through a list of common desires in her mind, not one appealed to her. Everything she could wish for was already tainted by decisions she had made and she couldn't go back and change her life.

They had to stop often to rest because of Harini and Chetana. Charvi seemed to glow with the light of a devotee and a goddess. The result was a sublimely happy Charvi. She wore a smile on her face as she looked up at the temple, their destination.

"Whenever I come here, I'm filled with joy," Charvi told Kokila. "There's something, isn't there?"

Kokila nodded, unsure of the "something" Charvi could feel.

This was her first time in Tirumala. She had wanted to come for a long time and now that she was here and the chants of devotees around them were loud, she wondered what the fuss was about. Was this very different from praying to Lord Venkateshwara Swami from the temple room in Tella Meda? Did the Lord really care where she prayed to him from?

It took them almost all day to reach the top of the hills and the temple, and the free *choultry* where they were to stay. Shiva had pulled strings and managed to get two rooms for their group. One room was for Charvi and the other room was for everyone else. Shiva and Madhav were planning to sleep outside or in the hallway. The nights were balmy and it wouldn't matter where they slept.

Two bathrooms were shared by everyone in the *choultry* and Chandra cleaned the bathroom before Charvi went to take her bath.

"That is devotion," Chetana said cynically.

"If I weren't pregnant, I'd do it," Harini said easily. "You live with her every day, don't you see the light within her?"

Kokila and Chetana looked at each other in disbelief and shook their heads.

"Then why do you live in Tella Meda?" Harini asked, a little angry that they, who were so fortunate to see Charvi every day, didn't seem to appreciate her.

"We live there because we have no other place that will take us," Chetana said.

Harini didn't speak to either of them for the rest of the evening.

They ate at a small Brahmin canteen where they were assured that only Brahmins had cooked the food. Charvi wasn't particular, she said (after all, Chetana wasn't a Brahmin and cooked in Tella Meda), but when she was eating "outside" food, it would be so much better if she knew a Brahmin with his clean hands had cooked the meal she put in her mouth.

Replete after a dinner of rice, curds, *sambhar,* potato and cauliflower curries, mango and ginger pickles, and *payasam,* Charvi went to sleep with Harini in her room for company, while Chandra sat up with Chetana and Kokila playing cards.

"This is so blasphemous," Chandra said, even though she was smiling. She was obviously not as uptight as her pious daughter-in-law.

"Why?" asked Chetana, and pointed to the cards. Lord Venkateshwara Swami's serene face was plastered on the playing cards. "If they can put his face on the cards, then it must be okay to play with them. Think of it as a kind of prayer."

They played until late and then were woken by Shiva at two in the morning. After a quick bath they all went to the temple. After standing in line for an hour they were allowed inside the temple.

It was disappointing. There were so many people there that it was impossible to see the idol of the god.

The priest began to sing the Suprabhatam to wake up Lord Venkateshwara Swami and the devotees joined him, their hands held together in prayer. A tape recording of the prayer accompanied all of them.

There was jubilation within the temple when the first stanza was sung, a stanza memorized by almost all devotees of Lord Venkateshwara Swami.

Kausalyasuprajarama!
Purva sandhya pravartate,
Uttistha! narasardula!
Kartavyam daivam ahnikam.

O! Rama! Kausalya's auspicious child!
Twilight is approaching in the east.
O! best of men!
Wake up, the divine daily rituals have to be performed.

There was a palpable feeling of love for the god. It was three in the morning but instead of sleepy devotees, everyone present stood, mesmerized and submerged in prayer, the power of the Lord shining within them. *There must be some kind of magic,* Kokila thought, *when even Chetana who never wakes up before nine o'clock, can be bright at this hour of the morning, singing the song that will wake up Lord of the Seven Hills.*

After the prayers, Shiva and Madhav went to roll around the temple with the other devotees who were also performing the *angapradakshinam,* while the women stayed to touch the feet of Lord Venkateshwara Swami.

He was a large idol, handsome, beautiful in black, adorned with heavy gold and diamond jewelry. Something shifted inside Kokila at the sight of him and she closed her eyes. Sometimes you had to reach your destination to know the purpose of the journey.

May his soul rest in peace, she said inside her heart, and hoped that Lord Venkateshwara Swami heard her and granted Ramanandam, in death, the peace he never seemed to have had in his life.

Since Chetana wanted to shave her hair off, Kokila and she went to Kalyana Katha, where several hundred barbers were sitting in long queues shaving hair off the heads of hundreds of devotees. The hair was collected and then sorted and sold to the thriving wig businesses in Tirupati.

Chetana and Kokila stood in a long queue awaiting their turn. There were at least thirty heads that needed to be shaved ahead of them.

"Do you also want to have your head tonsured?" Chetana asked Kokila, who raised her eyebrows in response. "Are you sure?" she asked. "If you have any wishes, this will certainly ensure they come true."

"I don't believe in this promise-and-vow business. I don't think God is that petty," Kokila said.

"A lot you know," Chetana said, a twinge of nervousness bathing her words. "Do you think it itches after?"

"I think so," Kokila said, seeing a young girl with her head tonsured being led away by her mother. The girl was trying to scratch her head while her mother was holding a bottle of coconut oil promising to lather her bald head with it soon if she didn't scratch now.

"And how long do you think it takes for the hair to grow back?" Chetana asked.

"A year . . . maybe more," Kokila said. "Why? If you've made a promise then just do it, stop wondering about the consequences. It's just hair, it'll grow back."

When they finally got to a barber, Chetana all but ran away from him and his sharp razor without a word of apology.

Harini was even more disappointed with Chetana now that she had backed out of getting her head tonsured.

"My Madhu and father in law both did the *angapradakshinam*," Harini said. "If you make a wish, you have to fulfill the promise, otherwise . . . you can't cheat God, you know, ever."

"Oh, Harini, the good God above is not keeping track of such things," Charvi said before Chetana could give their hostess a piece of her mind. "Chetana did what she could do and that's more than enough. No good God will ever blame her for not shaving her hair off."

Harini was appeased because the words came out of Charvi, but Chetana still wondered what kind of punishment Lord Venkateshwara Swami would mete out now that she had backed out of her promise. Obviously her wish would not be fulfilled now, would it?

It was anticlimactic to sit in the train as it headed toward Visakhapatnam after their visit to Tirumala. After the noise of the city and the sounds of prayer, the rhythmic grunt and crunch of the train almost felt like silence. Chetana, Kokila, and Charvi were comfortably ensconced in the ladies' coupe in the second-class compartment with two other women. They were sisters on their way to see their eldest, dying sister in Visakhapatnam.

Both Gayatri Devi and Pushpa Lata were taken with Charvi and agreed that the light of the goddess did shine within her.

When she was younger Charvi had been reluctant to tell anyone about Tella Meda and who she was, but that had changed with the passing of years. She was a good-looking woman in her early thirties, unmarried, yet more independent than most women. She was confident now, sure of who she was and of her purpose in the world. She easily told Gayatri Devi and Pushpa Lata that her home was Tella Meda and she was the daughter of the late, great writer Ramanandam Sastri. She introduced Chetana and Kokila as women who lived with her, indicating that they were devotees and not just residents in her house.

Pushpa Lata had apparently heard about Tella Meda from a relative and immediately put two and two together. They started calling her Charvi Amma and she didn't seem to mind. They asked her advice on how to deal with their dying sister and she quoted *slokas* from the *Bhagavad-Gita*.

"She still doesn't call herself *guru*," Chetana pointed out to Kokila. "Still doesn't call Tella Meda an *ashram*."

"But she believes it now," Kokila said. "*You* certainly have changed your opinion about Charvi."

Chetana shrugged. "After living my life it is almost impossible to believe in anything spiritual."

"You have to believe in yourself," Kokila said. "That's all you need to do."

"Everything I have done hasn't worked out. Bhanu is with Renuka, Ravi is with every whore in town, and I tried to be a tailor, but those women were just whores. I thought they were my friends but, you know, Ravi actually went with one of them," Chetana said with a laugh.

"Really?" Kokila asked, shocked and curious as to how Chetana felt about Ravi going with a woman Chetana had started to consider a friend.

"I stopped going there once I found out," Chetana said.

"Why did you start spending time with them?" Kokila asked.

Their friendship had been strained in those days and she hadn't been able to question Chetana's ill sense in working with those tailor girls in Bheemunipatnam, well known for their side business of prostitution.

Chetana shrugged. "I needed to get away from Tella Meda. I needed to breathe outside. You know?"

Kokila nodded. She did know.

She got onto the train at the Ongole railway station.

It was a big station and Kokila filled the earthen pot they carried with water and bought some fresh mangoes and bananas. Since Chetana and she had no qualms about eating outside food, she also bought some *vadas* and *bajjis* for a snack.

Charvi ate only the fresh fruit, while Kokila and Chetana fell upon the spicy *bajjis* and *vadas*.

She sat in a corner of the ladies' coupe. Gayatri Devi and Pushpa Lata wanted to send her out on accord of her dirty clothes and smelly person but Charvi asked them not to. Her face was hidden by her *sari* and she was crouching in the corner. A small bundle of clothes was hidden under her arm.

Chetana and Kokila ignored her and continued to gossip and talk, while Charvi did the same with the two sisters.

It was almost ten o' clock at night and time for Charvi to retire when the ticket collector came by. The woman in the corner all but leaped out of her skin when he asked her for a ticket.

"No ticket, no train," the ticket collector said loudly. "Now come on. Next station is Bapatla, you can get off there. All sorts of people getting on the train . . ."

"I need to go to Visakhapatnam," the woman said, a quiver in her voice. "Please . . ."

"This is not a charity service, Amma. Do you have any money? Any money?" the ticket collector asked.

The edge of her *sari* covering her face fell off then and everyone in the coupe gasped. Half her face was covered with dried blood and was bruised.

"*Ayyo, papam,*" Kokila said, and went toward the woman, who cowered some more.

"Look . . . ," the ticket collector began, obviously melting at the condition of the woman.

"I have twenty *rupees*," Kokila said before the ticket collector could go on. "Will that do?"

The ticket collector looked at Kokila suspiciously and then nodded. The ticket cost more than that but he didn't say anything.

"Thanks," the woman said, and started to cover her face with the *sari* again.

"Amma, have you eaten anything?" Charvi asked, and when the woman didn't respond, she held out a mango and a banana.

"We have some *vadas* left," Chetana said as she looked for the food in her bag.

"No, no, it's okay," the woman said but as Chetana held the *vadas* under her nose, her protests died away.

Her name was Shanthi. She came from a small village in the Prakasam district. After she ate the food put in front of her she related her tragic story, one the other women had heard often.

"Some men have no shame," Gayatri Devi announced. "Beat you up like that . . . *chee-chee*. But Shanthi, how can you survive now? Things were bad but at least you had a husband. Now what will you do?"

"My sister is in Visakhapatnam. I'll live with her. I used to be the village tailor and maybe I'll do that in Visakhapatnam. They need tailors everywhere," Shanthi said.

"Is your sister married?" Pushpa Lata asked, and when Shanthi nodded, she sighed. "You don't want to be a burden on your married sister. Go back to your husband. His ways will change if God is watching you."

"Why will his ways change?" Chetana demanded. "My husband's ways didn't change no matter what I did. Don't go back, Shanthi, next time he'll beat you to death."

"How you talk," Pushpa Lata said, obviously scandalized. "A woman's place is with her husband, no matter how bad he is."

"What nonsense," Chetana said as she patted Shanthi's hand.

"Are you a good tailor?" Charvi asked, speaking for the first time since Shanthi told about her abusive husband and how she ran away from her village.

Shanthi nodded shyly. "I can make all kinds of blouses. All weddings in the village, they come to me. I make the best blouses and I have also learned how to make *chudidars*. Not too much demand but I make good ones, like Rekha wears in the movies."

Kokila looked at Charvi and saw the intent on her face. She might have changed, become more conceited, and believed she was a goddess, but her heart was still in the right place.

"We could do with a tailor in Tella Meda," Kokila said, and Charvi smiled at her. "We all live there. It's Charvi's home and she shares it with us."

Chetana grinned then. "And you and I can set up a tailor shop there. I can stitch *sari* falls, I have a very clean hand."

Shanthi looked at the women and suspicion clouded her eyes. It was not uncommon for madams to recruit unsuspecting young women for their brothels like this.

"She really is a *guru*," Gayatri Devi confirmed. "She is Ramanandam Sastri's daughter. Do you know who he is? A great writer."

Shanthi shook her head uncomfortably. She obviously had no idea who Ramanandam Sastri was and what being a great writer meant.

"I promise that this will be a home for you, not another hell," Kokila said, taking Shanthi's hand in hers. "It's not much but it has walls and it is secure."

Shanthi nodded, still unsure but realizing that she didn't have many options and this, if true, was a gift from God.

"You'll have to pay some rent," Chetana said. "But you can man-

age that with the tailoring. What do you say? Do you want to be part-
ners with me?"

"Yes," Shanthi said, and smiled for the first time since her husband
had beaten her. Sometimes fate brought you home. Years later when
she and Kokila would reminisce about her train journey to Visakhapatnam, Shanthi would always say that it was Kokila, not Charvi, who
convinced her that Tella Meda could be her home too.

14 January 1980. Indira Gandhi was sworn in as the prime minister of India for the second time.

16 July 1981. India performs a nuclear test.

30 November 1982. The world premiere of Sir Richard Attenborough's *Gandhi* was held in New Delhi to record audiences.

The Professor

*T*here was a slight chill in the air as Kokila climbed the small wooden stool to pluck flowers from the *neem* tree growing in the front garden. Narayan Garu had painstakingly planted three *neem* trees seven years ago but only one had survived. One had died as a sapling and the second had been torn off the ground during a hurricane.

Every year, Kokila was thankful that this *neem* tree had survived, because every January, for the Telugu new year, Ugadi, Kokila plucked the *neem* flowers for the traditional Ugadi *pachadi*. Dr. Vishnu Mohan and his wife, Saraswati, along with several others in the area, also got *neem* flowers for their Ugadi *pachadi* from the Tella Meda *neem* tree.

The Ugadi *pachadi* contained the three prominent flavors, sweet, sour, and bitter. The sweet was from jaggery, the sour from unripe mangoes, and the bitter from the *neem* leaves. Subhadra bought fresh jaggery from the market for the *pachadi* and some unripe mangoes from Dr. Vishnu Mohan's garden where six mango trees thrived and produced different and flavorful mangoes.

"Good year this year will be. I can just feel it, can't you, Kokila Amma?" Puttamma said as she sat on the grass smoking a *bidi*.

It was on the tip of Kokila's tongue to say that it was going to be just another year, like the previous years had been.

"It's just not the same, is it, without Sastri Garu," Puttamma said, mistaking the sadness in Kokila's eyes as being for the man who had died three years ago.

Kokila nodded and then smiled. "People go and people come."

And that was true as well. There were many new faces at Tella Meda. Shanthi had settled in nicely, taking the big room in one corner for her tailoring shop and living space. Chetana and she had come up with a system of stitching clothes and dividing the income. They were becoming popular with the locals as well as with guests who would come to Tella Meda for a week or two. The regular guests would bring various pieces of cloth along so that Shanthi and Chetana could make clothes from measurements they took then and there. It was a decent business and like the bruises on Shanthi's face, her past had faded away. She couldn't remember her life before Tella Meda and Kokila was happy that this life was better than the previous one.

Chetana had a second daughter and she was convinced that she had yet another girl because she had refused to have her head tonsured at Tirupati when she was seven months pregnant.

"I didn't fulfill the vow and see, another girl," she told Kokila. But she was smiling this time. This time she didn't care about Ravi's disappointment or anyone else's. This time she fed her baby and clothed her with a possessiveness that surprised everyone and hurt Bhanu, who was now seven years old and understood that Renuka was her surrogate mother while her real mother was busy with her sibling.

Chetana named her daughter Meena Kumari after her favorite Hindi movie actress. The name got shortened to Meena. She was only three years old now but she had her mother's determination and stubbornness.

"That girl, she'll be trouble," Puttamma announced to Kokila as she crushed her *bidi* and watched Meena stealthily follow one of the new cats at Tella Meda. This one was really a kitten, gray in color with dark stripes running over its little body.

"She's a good girl," Kokila immediately defended Meena as the little girl pounced on the cat. It screeched in fright and ran away from its tormentor. Meena chased the cat into the house, making growling sounds.

"No, no, this one has malice in her soul . . . just like her mother. Mark my words, she will grow up to be just like her mother," Puttamma said clearly. Her affection for Chetana had not increased in the past years.

Puttamma thought that a woman who couldn't keep her husband in line was not a good woman or a strong woman. "A bad wife is the reason a man strays from home," Puttamma said. "I know because I've had enough husbands stray from home."

"Ravi was spoiled long before he married her," Kokila told Puttamma. "You stay for some Ugadi *pachadi,* okay?"

"If Subhadra Amma is making it, it'll taste like *amrutam,*" Puttamma declared. Indeed, Subhadra's *pachadi* did taste like food for the gods.

Every year for Ugadi, everyone at Tella Meda wore new clothes and celebrated with a lunch of tamarind rice, fresh yogurt, rice, mango *pappu,* sweet *pulusu, gongura pachadi,* and plenty of sweet rice *payasam.*

Large amounts of food disappeared as many guests came to wish Charvi a happy new year and take her blessings so that their new year would be prosperous and happy.

This year, for the first time in her life, Kokila bought herself dangling gold earrings. They were small with a little hat hanging from a gold knob. A piece of red coral adorned the gold knob. The earrings cost her all her savings, but it was Ugadi and she had promised herself she would renew herself and try to be happy this year.

"Look at those earrings," Chetana had teased her. "Are you trying to impress someone?" she asked as she looked at the guest who had arrived just the day before.

Professor Manjunath Kaakateeya had been coming for a week

every summer for the past three years. Every year he would arrive, full of anecdotes and gossip. He was a lively man who was respectful to everyone but still managed to be playful. Chetana always insisted that he looked at Kokila with a man's eyes, to which Kokila only rolled her own.

This year, Professor Manjunath came early and he was quiet and hesitant. Something had happened to bring him here early, everyone was certain, but no one dared to ask.

"He always brings blouse pieces for his wife and daughters," Shanthi said with concern. "Nothing this time."

"Maybe he has had some bad news," Subhadra said as she squeezed out tamarind pulp for the tamarind rice. "Even Charvi was talking about it. It isn't healthy to be this sad during Ugadi. It's the time of renewal. Ah, poor man, God knows what happened."

Ugadi at Tella Meda was always a festive occasion. Devotional music played on the radio, accompanied by the smell of *payasam* that had been simmering for hours. Kokila could almost taste the new year, it was so palpable. This year she would turn thirty. She was an old woman already, in her middle age, with nothing to show for her years. It was time she turned her life around, she told herself. And so she had started with the earrings.

"Kokila, *you* should talk with the professor," Subhadra suggested.

"Yes, Kokila," Chetana teased. "You must, you must."

"Unlike you gossipmongers, I like to mind my own business," Kokila said smoothly, and left the kitchen, her new earrings swishing just a little as she walked with a bounce.

And she would have minded her own business if he had at least shown up for lunch. Just before they started serving, Manjunath came up to Kokila and said he wasn't hungry and was going for a walk. There was such desolation in his expression that Kokila wanted to follow him out and ask what was wrong, how she could help. But she decided that it was none of her business and there were so many guests to take care of she didn't have time for Manjunath and his problems. The Ugadi lunch was boisterous and happy, and Kokila vowed to not let Manjunath's sorrow dampen her spirits.

It was a well-known fact that Dr. Manjunath Kaakateeya was a very bright man, teaching mathematics at Andhra University in Visakhapatnam. His oldest daughter had married recently while his youngest daughter had received top marks in the state medical entrance exam, EAMCET. She was studying to be a doctor in Osmania Medical College in Hyderabad.

When he had come to Tella Meda the previous summer, Manjunath had been gushing about his youngest daughter and how bright she was. Manjunath himself had studied in America on some kind of scholarship.

Charvi said that the Fulbright scholarship was given to exceptionally smart people and she was very flattered that an intelligent man such as Manjunath came to Tella Meda to find peace and solace.

"Vacation away from family," he would say. "But I tell them that it is a holy vacation and after all I'm coming to your holy home, Charvi Amma."

For his accomplishments, and the list was long, he was still very young. He had married young and had his first daughter when he was only twenty years old. He was considered a dynamic young professor who someday would become vice chancellor at Andhra University. The vice chancellor position was a political one but most people in the know had already decided that Dr. Manjunath Kaakateeya was the man for the job.

He respected Charvi. He sat with her during *bhajan* in the evening and he prayed with her in the morning. During the day, he spent time chatting with Narayan Garu and the women of the house. He went for long walks and came back with seashells and wildflowers for everyone. He helped with the cooking on Sundays and was always full of charming wit. An excellent human being, everyone said. When Manjunath visited, Dr. Vishnu Mohan, who lived two houses away, had his meals at Tella Meda. Even his wife, Saraswati, would spend more time than usual at the *ashram*. Such was Manjunath's appeal. Everyone liked him and everyone knew him as a cheerful man who brightened the day, so it was especially noticeable when he came to Tella Meda without his humor and welcoming smile.

He sat in the temple room for hours, watching Charvi meditate or staring at the idol of Lord Venkateshwara Swami. His walks were getting longer and he would return with a heavier face than the one he left with.

"He didn't eat lunch," Kokila told Subhadra.

"The rumor is that he got some girl pregnant," Renuka said, and both Kokila and Subhadra glared at her. "Saraswati said something about it. She talked to some friend of Doctor Garu's at Andhra University and he said so. I'm not making up stories."

Kokila sighed. "But you don't even know if this is true. Why say things like this and ruin a man's good name?"

Renuka sighed, big tears filling her eyes, as they always could on command. "Everyone blames me because I'm a widow. Maybe he did get a girl pregnant, why is that so hard to believe?"

"Because he's a good man," Subhadra snapped at Renuka. "Sometimes, Renuka, you just . . . You have a big mouth and one day it will hurt you. Now, why don't you go out of my kitchen and leave me to cook dinner in peace."

Renuka made a face and sighed a little before walking away. Having caused mischief, she had accomplished her mission, it appeared.

That evening, during *bhajan,* Saraswati confirmed the rumor.

"A young girl committed suicide," Saraswati whispered to Subhadra and Kokila.

Chetana craned her neck as she was sitting behind Saraswati. "Really? How young? A student?" She was full of questions. Gossip was always welcome at Tella Meda.

Saraswati nodded. "Eighteen-year-old girl, they say. That's how old his youngest daughter is. I thought he was a good man . . . *cheechee,* now I find this out. It's just not right that he's here in the presence of Charvi."

"I don't believe it," Kokila said, a little miffed that they all were turning against a man they had always been friendly with. "He seems to have too much integrity to do what you accuse him of. And who is this friend of yours in Visakhapatnam who told you this?"

Saraswati shook her head. "Not Visakhapatnam. Vishnu's friend is a professor at the Regional Engineering College in Warrangal. Well, he used to be a professor there, ten years ago, but he still has good contacts and he heard this from a friend whose sister is married to a professor who works at Andhra University."

Chetana laughed softly. "Looks like this story has been through so many mouths that there is probably more *masala* in the story than story."

"No, no, it really happened," Saraswati claimed, her voice rising above a whisper. Charvi didn't say anything but paused in her singing and looked straight at Saraswati, who became quiet immediately.

After the *bhajan*, Saraswati profusely apologized to Charvi for speaking during her singing and was immediately forgiven, though Charvi did hold her hand up to silence Saraswati when she tried to implicate Kokila and Chetana as well.

Manjunath didn't come for dinner that Ugadi night and neither did he show up for the special *bhajan* in the evening. He sat quietly in the backyard by the well, smoking cigarette after cigarette.

Subhadra saw him from her room's window and asked Kokila to go find out what was wrong.

"I'm scared he'll jump into the well," Subhadra said truthfully. "Whatever he did, he did. What do we know? Just go and check on him and make sure he comes inside. That well doesn't look deep but it is. You jump in, you die, not just end up with broken bones."

Kokila wanted to tell Subhadra to go talk to him herself if she was so worried but she knew that Subhadra would never interfere in a stranger's personal business quite so blatantly.

Kokila had always thought that Manjunath was a good-looking man. He was tall and broad-shouldered and looked more like a big construction worker than a Brahmin professor. The white and yellow cigarette looked small in his large hands. His spectacles had slid down his nose, his *kurta* was smudged with black streaks, and his dark pants had not been ironed before he wore them. There was a week's worth of stubble on his face and his hair looked greasy and dirty, as if it hadn't been washed in a while.

As soon as Manjunath saw Kokila, he politely dropped the cigarette on the grass and crushed it under his blue rubber slipper.

"I'm sorry I missed *bhajan,*" Manjunath said, his voice a little scratchy because of too much smoking and lack of sleep.

Kokila shook her head. "Don't worry about it." She knew she should say something else but didn't quite know what to say. She barely knew this man. He came once a year for a week or two and during his stay he chatted with everyone and it wasn't like when he talked with Kokila he spoke with any extra closeness.

"I'll go to sleep then," Manjunath said when he realized that Kokila wasn't going to say anything more and the uncomfortable silence was not being broken.

"Okay," Kokila managed, and watched him walk away.

She felt miserable. She should've said something, she knew, but what could she say? *You seem different this time, Manjunath Garu? Any problems in your life you want to share with everyone at Tella Meda?*

She hoped that he'd talk to Charvi. She was the *guru* of the *ashram* and the one who could give advice and offer salvation. This wasn't her problem, Kokila decided; she had many problems, but Professor Manjunath was not one of them.

That changed eventually.

It was during his third week in Tella Meda that Kokila saw him crying on the terrace in the night.

Subhadra and Kokila had left chilies to dry on the terrace and forgot to bring them down in the evening after the sun had set. Just before she went to sleep, Kokila remembered and rushed upstairs with a flashlight to bring the chilies to the kitchen. If left all night, they'd get wet again in the morning dew.

He was sitting in a corner, his head bent and hidden on his knees, his body shaking as small sobs escaped him.

Kokila wouldn't have even noticed him in the dark. But as soon as she heard a sob, she turned the flashlight toward the sound. His head came up in shock.

"Manjunath Garu?" Kokila said as she looked curiously, wanting to make sure it was indeed him. *Is he crying?* she wondered with a little fear. Would she have to console him? Did she know how?

He cleared his throat and covered his face with the back of his hand to avoid inspection and the glare of the light. "Yes. I was just resting here," he said in a clear voice.

"Oh," Kokila said, and turned the light away from him. She quietly folded the muslin cloth on which the red chilies lay and packed it neatly so that she could carry them downstairs without dropping any chilies on the way.

Curiosity burned within her. She wanted to ask him why he had been crying. She wanted to ask him if she could help, though she couldn't imagine how she could help. What would she say? And what if it was true that he had made some girl pregnant and she committed suicide? No, no, it was better not to get involved. She couldn't help this man.

Kokila put the flashlight on top of the muslin. Holding the cloth with both hands, she started to walk toward the stairs.

"Please wear a sweater, it gets cold at night these days," she said because she felt she had to say something.

"Thank you," Manjunath said, but made no move to get up and go downstairs to get a sweater.

This is not my problem, Kokila told herself repeatedly. *Whatever that man did, it is his business and it is not for me to judge.* Those who looked at her relationship with Ramanandam from the outside probably also believed that it was morally wrong. Maybe Manjunath had been in love with that student. And maybe they had had sex. Sex wasn't a bad thing. Sex was a basic human function, Ramanandam would always say. People could call it making love and all sorts of other things but sex was a base function. All animals had sex, just like people.

As Kokila put the chilies in the kitchen, her heart beat just a little faster.

Sex?

Oh my, she hadn't thought of that for years now . . . almost three, four years. Even before Ramanandam died, sex had started to become an occasional thing, not like it had been in the beginning. The urgency was gone in the later years. And the heat had deserted them as well. But she remembered the first few times vividly. The feel of his body sliding into hers . . . Kokila shook her head to disperse the thoughts. They were shameful. They must be shameful.

Suddenly, all she could think about was Manjunath having sex with some young college girl. Their love must've been just as illicit as hers and Ramanandam's had been. Her breasts tightened at the thought of Manjunath lying naked on top of some young girl. Maybe he had grunted and so had she. Maybe . . .

Kokila was mortified. Here she was, standing in the middle of the courtyard, in the middle of the night imagining some man naked and having sex with a girl. As she tried to clear her mind again, it struck her that Manjunath was not having sex with some young girl in her mind; he was having sex with her. She looked down at her feet, unable to move, deeply disturbed by her traitorous body. Where had this come from? She was a pious woman. Wasn't she? She did *puja* in the morning, in the evening. How could this be happening to her? With Ramanandam it had been love. She wasn't in love with Manjunath. Then why was she having these thoughts about him?

This was all Chetana's fault. She kept saying Manjunath looked at her this way and that. It was Chetana who had put this in her head. She used to barely notice Manjunath during his visits. Now all she did was notice him. And why did Subhadra have to ask her to help him? Why couldn't she have asked Charvi? Oh, what was she going to do?

Kokila sat on her bed and looked out of the window that opened into the courtyard and watched for Manjunath. He wasn't coming down and it was getting colder. He could fall sick, she told herself. It was just noble and human of her to take a blanket for him. Or a shawl? Didn't she have a nice shawl somewhere?

Kokila opened her Godrej cupboard and started to look for a flesh-colored shawl she had bought some years ago. It was not real wool, just some synthetic material, but it was warm enough. She smiled in triumph when she found it.

She looked at herself in the mirror on the Godrej cupboard before leaving her room to go up to the terrace again.

She didn't take the flashlight this time, convinced that the moonlight would show her the way. She tried not to think that maybe she would look more attractive under the moonlight, that the creases age had given her face would be hidden by the gentle light of the moon. Maybe Manjunath would fall in lust with her as he had with that college student. *Maybe this is all just a big mistake,* she told herself even as she realized she couldn't stop herself from going to him. This was attraction, she knew, even though she refused to acknowledge it. Maybe Chetana had fed the illusion of attraction but it had always been there, small and insignificant. Now it was springing to life because he was a broken man.

Manjunath was sitting right where she'd left him, his head on his knees. He wasn't sobbing anymore.

"Manjunath Garu," she called out, and held up the shawl as his head lifted. "It's getting cold."

Manjunath took the shawl. "Thanks."

She could barely see him, hidden in the dark corner, the moonlight not as bright as she'd imagined. He probably couldn't see her. He probably just saw a shadow of her and how attractive would that be?

"Are you okay?"

Manjunath nodded again and wrapped the shawl around him and waited for her to leave.

"Are you sure you're okay?" she asked.

"Yes," Manjunath managed.

Kokila shrugged and started to walk away from him. If he couldn't ask for help, she couldn't give it.

"No," Manjunath called out after her. "I'm not okay."

Kokila immediately went back to him. "Why don't we go downstairs? I'll make some tea for you."

"She's dead," he said. "She tried to tell me but I wouldn't listen. Big professor, it would be too shameful. So I said, 'Nothing doing.' And then she hanged herself from the ceiling fan."

"I'm so sorry," Kokila said. So there had been a girl who killed herself because of him. Oh, the guilt. So heavy it must be to carry. Compassion replaced lust and Kokila took his hand in hers. "Sometimes we can't control everything, not even our own reactions."

"And there are consequences, aren't there? To reactions?"

"Yes," Kokila said.

Manjunath sighed. "I thought I'd come here to forget but I only remember, all the time. My wife . . . she's falling apart but I can't go to her. How can I? She blames me too. And it is my fault. She had warned me and pleaded with me, but I wouldn't listen. I was so sure of myself. What a waste, Kokila Amma, what a waste!"

"A life, no matter how long it has been lived, is not a waste. She gave something to you and to others and left something behind. You will all remember her and that's no waste," Kokila said, hoping her words would assuage, just a little. She wasn't Charvi; she couldn't find the right soothing words like the *guru* of the *ashram* could.

"You should talk to Charvi," Kokila suggested. "She will help you clear your mind and focus on what's important, today and tomorrow. Yesterday is past, but you can learn from it."

"But today is too painful and tomorrow unfathomable," Manjunath said, his hand clenching tightly around Kokila's.

They sat in silence for a long while and then he started to cry again. Kokila wrapped the shawl around both of them and he put his head on her breast and wept softly.

It was almost sunrise when they went downstairs to Kokila's room. He lay in bed with her, holding her close as he slept, and Kokila felt delight dance through her, even as she felt sorrow within for the weeping and inconsolable man she held in her arms.

Chetana was sitting with Kokila in the courtyard shelling peas when he stepped out of Kokila's room in the afternoon.

"Hmm," Chetana said, a smile playing on her face.

"Nothing, hmm," Kokila said. "He was upset, that's all." She wiped her hands on her *sari* and went to Manjunath.

"I slept too late," he said, smiling, just a little. It was his first smile in three weeks. "People will talk and—"

"That's okay. I kept some *upma* from breakfast for you. Would you like to wash up? I'll get some tea," Kokila said, feeling just a little shy, the intimacies of last night now embarrassing in daylight.

Manjunath nodded. "Yes, I'm hungry."

"Stop smiling like that," Kokila hissed at Chetana as she went into the kitchen.

It was almost impossible to keep a secret in Tella Meda and soon everyone knew that Manjunath had spent the night in Kokila's room. Most of the residents didn't mention the matter, but both Renuka and Subhadra did. Renuka was scandalized, while Subhadra told Kokila to be careful. The man's reputation had been smeared and from the rumors it was evident that he indulged in extramarital affairs all the time.

"I didn't sleep with him," Kokila said as she paced Shanthi's room in anger. "Why does no one believe me?"

"I believe you," Shanthi said as her feet worked the foot pedal of the Singer sewing machine to move the needle over the cloth. She was sewing a blouse for Subhadra to go with a new *sari* she had bought for Ugadi.

"And even if I did sleep with him, would that be wrong?" Kokila demanded.

Shanthi shrugged and moved the blouse cloth a little as she ran a small curving stitch over the bright yellow material.

"Would that be so wrong?" Kokila asked again.

"Yes," Shanthi said as she pulled the yellow cloth away from the needle and bent down to cut the yellow thread with her teeth. "He's a married man."

"I'm not married," Kokila said peevishly.

"Look, you have to do what you have to do with your life," Shanthi said, and then smiled at Kokila. "And you know that it is wrong. It's wrong to sleep with a man who isn't your husband, and especially wrong when that man is some other woman's husband."

Kokila sighed, all the fire going out of her. In the past three years, she, Shanthi, and Chetana had become close friends. It had taken Shanthi several months to open up and become the woman she was, but with Chetana by her side in the tailoring business and Kokila's friendship, slowly but steadily Shanthi had found herself.

"I want to sleep with him," Kokila confessed. "I . . . suddenly, I feel this attraction to him. Maybe I get attracted to sad, old men."

"Manjunath Garu is not old," Shanthi said.

"But he's sad and weepy, just like Ramanandam was. I have a weakness for weeping men. Maybe I believe that they are actually strong, like that actor Dharmendra in the film *Sholay,* and then when they are sad, my heart melts," Kokila said.

"Ravi goes about crying a lot and I don't see your heart melting for him," Shanthi said as she examined the now finished bright yellow blouse.

"First the man has to be a man. Ravi is not a real man," Kokila muttered. "He's found a new whore. Now he doesn't even give any money to Chetana. Blames her for Meena also being a girl, says that if she had been a boy, his father would have taken them home. Bad *karma* that family has. Have you heard about Prasad? That boy is going down the drain too."

Shanthi rarely indulged in gossip and merely nodded. She didn't know Manikyam or Ravi or any of the others Kokila and Chetana talked about very well. She had met Manikyam only a few times and kept away from Ravi, who made her uncomfortable with his lecherous ways. He had lost more weight and was thin, like an old, diseased, dying man. His skin was not as light as it used to be and had darkened because of the time he spent lying outside toddy shops, under the sun. His cheeks and eyes were sunken and the smell of toddy always clung to him.

Charvi had ordered him to take a bath as soon as he came into Tella Meda and had warned him that if he ever came for dinner or *bhajan* smelling like a toddy shop, she would throw him out of Tella Meda. He didn't pay much heed to her and she didn't make good on her threat. He was her sister's son, and as wayward as he was, he was still her family. Charvi could threaten him into making his life better but she would not show him the door. He didn't have any other place to go.

Charvi still didn't speak with Manikyam, but Charvi would listen to Manikyam rant and rave about her fate and how even though she had two sons, she had no peace.

Now the story was that Prasad had started drinking as well. He had finished his degree in commerce but refused to take up a job. Having thrown his older son out of his home, Dr. Nageshwar Rao was holding on to the younger one very tightly. They even got him married to a nice Brahmin girl from Srikakulam, the daughter of a well-known doctor and friend. But that didn't straighten him out. As luck would have it, their new daughter-in-law, Sita, miscarried three pregnancies and was unable to conceive after that.

"If only Prasad had children," Manikyam would wail. She was convinced that a grandson from Prasad would bring her family back to the right path of goodness and fruitfulness. But now Sita stayed more often with her parents in Srikakulam than in Visakhapatnam. She would go home for this festival and that marriage and stay for two or three months before returning. And usually it would take several letters, phone calls, and a visit from Manikyam before Sita would come home.

Sita's father had even warned Dr. Nageshwar Rao that if he didn't get Prasad to stop drinking there was a good chance that a divorce might have to be considered. But that was an empty threat. No self-respecting parent would encourage his daughter to divorce her husband, no matter what his flaws. And Sita didn't appear to have Shanthi's backbone, so it was unlikely she would leave her husband and start her own life.

And it wasn't easy to leave a husband, as Shanthi had learned. Soon after she left him, Shanthi's husband tracked her down through her sister in Visakhapatnam and came to Tella Meda to take her back home.

It had taken the strength of two male guests and Puttamma's fourth husband to push the violent man away from Shanthi and lock the front door of Tella Meda. Shanthi's husband stayed, camped out in front of the gate of Tella Meda, insisting he would only leave with his wife. Finally, Puttamma's husband had brought some of his friends to "talk" with Shanthi's husband and he left with a broken jaw and a black eye. That was two years ago and he hadn't bothered Shanthi since. Shanthi had not talked about the incident to anyone, though she confided in Kokila that she immensely enjoyed hearing about her husband's beating by Puttamma's husband and friends. Now he would know what physical violence meant.

With Subhadra's yellow blouse finished, Shanthi threw it toward Kokila. "Iron this for me, will you," she said, pointing to the small iron Shanthi had purchased to press the stitched clothes. It made the clothes look better and the customers happier.

As Kokila ironed, Shanthi got busy on a second blouse, this one for Chetana. "All fancy things she wants. Frills on the sleeve, low back . . . shameless, that girl is," Shanthi said with a grin as she read her note on the blouse cloth. "Low round cut and tight cup, that's what she wants. Why bother with a blouse? Just wear a brassiere and a *sari*."

"Chetana likes to show her body and her fair skin," Kokila said.

"She's lucky she stays so thin. My older sister had one child and that was it for her. She is fatter than Manikyam," Shanthi said, and then looked up from Chetana's blouse cloth to Kokila. "You know, happiness is short-lived. You were happy with Ramanandam but it didn't last very long. How long will there be happiness with Manjunath Garu, you think?"

Kokila ironed the yellow blouse sleeve carefully and thought about Shanthi's question. "However short-lived, happiness is happiness and I want to grab it with both hands every chance I get."

Everyone was appalled at the easy affection that flowed between Manjunath and Kokila during the next week. For once even Charvi interfered with a personal matter, something she never did.

"You will ruin your reputation and Tella Meda's," Charvi warned her. "The former I can do nothing about, but Tella Meda's integrity must be maintained. If people find out about you and Manjunath, Tella Meda will earn a bad name."

"I'm doing nothing to hurt anyone," Kokila protested. "I'm just offering friendship to a man who is in need."

"This man carries some deep pain," Charvi said. "Be very careful what you get into."

"I don't think he got a girl pregnant," Kokila said.

Charvi shook her head. "I don't care about rumors. I'm telling you what I see. He has a deep pain. He can't give you any happiness because he doesn't know what it means anymore."

It sounded too much like Charvi's regular prattle and Kokila ignored the advice. Maybe she shouldn't have, maybe she should've paid attention and stayed away from Manjunath. But her mind had already been made up, and even if her mind could be altered, her heart was decided and that Kokila couldn't and wouldn't change.

It felt like spring, spring after a very cold winter. Kokila ignored the fact that Manjunath was married, that he would be gone soon, that he was a sad man with a broken heart. It was joyous to have a man pay attention to her. It was fulfilling and satisfying to have someone of her own to talk to. And it was special to be the cause of a sad man's smile.

But the relationship didn't move beyond the boundaries of propriety. After that first night, Manjunath was cautious and careful about where he was seen with Kokila.

"Reputations are like clay pots. Once broken they can be mended but there is always a crack," he told Kokila.

She laughed at that. "This clay pot has been in pieces for years and cannot even be mended anymore."

It would have been impossible for Manjunath not to have heard about Kokila's relationship with Ramanandam. It was common knowledge in Tella Meda and most of Bheemunipatnam. Kokila was not a highly respected woman, but then except for Charvi, no Tella Meda woman was all that respected. Discards of society didn't enjoy the benefits of respectability.

"Are you leaving soon?" Kokila asked him when four weeks had passed and Manjunath's wife had written over five letters asking him to come back home.

Manjunath shrugged. "I'm not ready to leave."

She found him crying again on the terrace. Whatever burden he was carrying was immense and Kokila's heart tore itself into pieces for him. How could she help him? she thought desperately. There must be some way to assuage his pain.

She held him again, as she had the previous time, and he wept on her bosom.

"Tell me," she whispered as she stroked his graying hair. "It'll help to let it all out." She wanted to give him release but she was also curious.

Manjunath shook his head, his body trembling with pent-up tears.

"I heard some girl committed suicide because she was pregnant," Kokila said. "But I really don't know. It could be all rumors. If you don't tell me, how can I help you?"

Manjunath looked at her, his eyes bright with tears, glistening in the light of the moon, just a couple of nights shy of being full.

"It wasn't some girl, Kokila, it was my daughter," Manjunath said, and Kokila's eyes widened. Had he made his daughter pregnant?

"She didn't want to go back to medical college . . ." He paused and then shook his head. "There's nothing to say. She didn't want to go, I made her go, and she killed herself. It was my fault."

They went downstairs as they had the previous time and just like that time, Manjunath held on to her as they slept, trying to ward off his demons.

Kokila wondered if she should tell others the truth but this was Manjunath's secret and until he said it was okay, she couldn't tell anyone else about it. But Manjunath's secret didn't remain one for long. Dr. Vishnu Mohan and his wife, Saraswati, arrived the next day, somber and apologetic. Dr. Vishnu Mohan asked to speak with Manjunath in his room while Saraswati told everyone else what they had learned. Even Shanthi was huddled in the kitchen to listen to Saraswati and usually she stayed away from Tella Meda gossip.

"Manjunath's wife phoned last night," Saraswati said, wiping tears that were streaming down her cheeks. "She knows a relative's friend . . . Anyway, his daughter, you know, the one he keeps talking about? The one who went to medical college? She was raped. She didn't tell anyone except some of her friends."

"Who raped her?" Subhadra asked.

"Some man, she wouldn't say who. But he threatened that he would do it again if she told anyone and then he would kill her," Saraswati explained. "All this has come out now, from those friends of hers."

"Why didn't they do anything to help her?" Chetana demanded. "If they knew, they—"

"Hush. So what happened to the girl?" Subhadra asked eagerly.

Kokila listened in silence, pretending to focus on chopping green beans for lunch.

"She came home for the Dussera holidays and told Manjunath that she didn't want to go back. He thought she couldn't handle the studies and was scared of failing exams, so he insisted that she go back. They had a big fight and Manjunath said that he didn't have any respect for her if she wouldn't go back and he was really harsh to her," Saraswati said.

"Anyone would be," Renuka said. "Medical college is difficult to get into. He did what any father would do."

Everyone nodded and then focused their attention back on Saraswati to hear the rest of the sordid tale.

"She went back and ten days later hung herself from the ceiling fan of her dormitory room," Saraswati finished.

"Oh, the poor man," Shanthi said. "He's blaming himself."

"Well, he is a little to blame," Renuka said thoughtfully.

Chetana snorted. "But you just said that he did what any father would do."

"Well, first, he should just have gotten the girl married and not worried about medical school—fool. Not that important, education," Renuka said firmly.

"Was she pregnant?" Chetana asked.

Kokila was numb. Charvi was right, she thought, Manjunath carried a deep pain. Could there be a pain that was deeper than losing a child? And wouldn't that pain be blinding in its intensity if the parent felt he was to blame? Just like Ramanandam who never got over Vidura leaving, never came to terms with losing him.

Saraswati nodded. "And now he won't go home. He resigned from

Andhra University and his wife wants to come here but he has written to her asking her to leave him alone. His older daughter has written to him but he doesn't even respond. So they called us to see if we could help. Vishnu is talking to him. Maybe we can convince him to go home."

All the women focused on Kokila and she sighed.

"He isn't staying here because of me," she said. "Nothing is happening between us, so don't look at me."

"He seems to be taken with you. Maybe you could talk to him," Saraswati suggested, and Kokila shook her head.

"What should I say? He's a grown man, I can't tell him how to live his life," she said. "And he is not taken with me. We just talk, we're just friends."

Manjunath came to her room that night after *bhajan*. He had spent the evening elsewhere and came to her saying he was hungry.

Kokila hurried to the kitchen, prepared a plate of cold food for him, and took it back to her room.

He sat quietly and ate everything: the rice, the leftover green bean curry from lunch, the *sambhar* with sweet potatoes, the slightly sour yogurt, and the mango pickle.

He drank half the glass of water, used the other half to wash his hands in the plate, and pushed the plate aside.

"They told you what happened," he said.

Kokila nodded. "Dr. Vishnu Mohan's wife can't keep anything inside her."

Manjunath laughed harshly. "My wife's like that. She gossips all the time but has a clean heart, no malice."

Kokila nodded again.

"I have a wife, Kokila," he said, looking at her.

Kokila bit her upper lip, unsure of what to say, unsure also of what he was telling her.

"I love my wife. I love my daughters . . . both my daughters," he said. "And I killed one of them."

Kokila took his hand in hers. "No. It was fate. We can't always choose to make the right decisions because we don't know what the future holds."

"I shouldn't have forced her to go back," Manjunath said, holding Kokila's hand in both of his. "The pain is too much. I can't bear it. Sometimes . . . sometimes I'm sure I'll die of it."

Kokila put her arm around him and pulled his head toward her. "Let me help," she said, and kissed him tenderly on his mouth. He wrapped his arms tightly around her and kissed her back with desperation.

He was gone in the morning. His dinner plate was still in the corner where he had left it and her clothes were scattered by the bed. Kokila looked out of the window and judged the time to be around five. It was still early but the birds were singing softly, gearing up to chirp with more gusto.

It hurt her that he had left while she slept. He had sneaked away while she was sleeping, happy, in peace. She wished he had stayed, wished she could have woken up with him.

"I have a wife, Kokila," he had said, and she knew that whatever they would share would be temporary. And as Charvi said, he was unable to recognize happiness right now. It would take years of healing before Manjunath would be a happy man again and even then, the wound of losing his daughter would never quite heal. It would bleed occasionally and would always be a part of him.

Maybe he had left before she woke up to protect her reputation, Kokila wondered, and that thought erased the hurt. Yes, he was chivalrous enough to think of that.

She hastily put on her *sari* and ran to the bathroom to take a quick bath.

Fresh, smelling of her jasmine soap, Kokila tied a towel around her wet hair, feeling shy and gauche as if she were a new bride. Already, Tella Meda was coming alive. Charvi must be taking a bath as well, Kokila thought, as she got ready for the morning *puja*. Subhadra would be up soon to bathe and then cook breakfast.

Puttamma would arrive shortly and start sweeping the courtyard and cleaning the bathrooms. It was just like every morning but there was something special about today.

Kokila's silver anklets tinkled merrily, in tune with the swish of the gold baskets in her ears, as she walked up to the guest room where

Manjunath was staying. She looked around to make sure no one was watching. She should wait for him to come out, she knew, but the temptation to see him and feel as she had the night before was too heavy. Like sweet molasses, it clung to her senses.

She knocked on the door and then tested the doorknob. It opened and she stepped in, a smile on her face, as she searched for Manjunath on the guest room bed.

His feet dangled on top of the bed, his tongue was sticking out, his eyes were wide and bulging. His neck fell forward in an odd angle as he hung on a rope from the ceiling fan. The rope was familiar; it was the clothesline from the courtyard that everyone used to hang their clothes.

But she had been so happy, she thought as her body froze, suddenly incapable of any movement. *It isn't fair,* she almost cried out in indignation. *It isn't fair.*

She couldn't avert her eyes from his hideously disfigured face. She wanted to look away, turn away so that she wouldn't carry the image of him hanging lifelessly from the white ceiling fan, but even as she closed her eyes and tried to recollect the Manjunath from the night before, kissing her, suckling her breasts, touching her lips, she couldn't. All she saw was him hanging, his dead face a parody of what it had been when filled with life.

1984

31 October 1984. Indira Gandhi, India's four-time prime minister, was gunned down by two members of her personal security guard as she walked from her home to her office in New Delhi. She died after four hours of emergency surgery.

31 October 1984. Rajiv Gandhi, son of Indira Gandhi, was sworn in as prime minister of India by President Giani Zail Singh in New Delhi.

5 December 1984. Methyl isocyanate gas leaked out of a Union Carbide factory in Bhopal during the night. Casualties were extremely high.

Widows and Orphans

*I*t didn't seem appropriate to have a television in Tella Meda. Charvi didn't like the idea at all. She didn't mind the radio, but television? But the pressure to get a television was very high. Even the quiet Narayan Garu said he thought it would be nice to watch the news every evening, a Telugu movie once in a while. What would the harm be?

Finally the decision to buy a television was made, and then the argument began whether it should be a color TV or a black-and-white one. Chetana declared that if they wanted to buy a black-and-white TV, they needn't buy one at all. If one couldn't see the news anchor's lipstick color, what was the point? So despite the expense, everyone at Tella Meda agreed it would be better to get a color TV.

Then another discussion emerged. Where would the television be housed? Definitely not the temple room, but where else could the TV be placed so that it would be in the open and for everyone's use?

One of the three guest rooms with doors facing both the front garden and the inside verandah was suggested as the future TV room.

"No, no, no," Kokila said the day before the television was supposed to arrive. The electrician had promised to have the antenna up and running the same day so that the television would start spouting images and sounds as quickly as possible.

"Why not?" Renuka demanded. "Why do we need three rooms for guests?"

"Because they make sure that we all have food to eat," Kokila said angrily. Did no one realize how much juggling it took to maintain a house as big as Tella Meda? Everyone paid a minimal rent that barely covered food purchases for an entire month and there were other bills to pay: water, electricity, extra food purchases for the Sunday lunches and festival days. Puttamma had to be paid for cleaning the bathrooms and the courtyards, a job that no one offered to do. Now that Narayan Garu had become too old to work in the garden, Puttamma's son from her first marriage, a thirteen-year-old boy, Balaji, came to remove the weeds, water the plants, and cut the grass. He wasn't paid much but it was still an expense.

Ever so often a musical instrument would need to be replaced or fixed, a bulb would have to be replaced, the water pipes fixed, a door hinge repaired . . . the list was endless. And then there was Charvi, an expense all in herself with her increasing demands for special food and clothing. Guests came and usually left some money behind. But no big donations were coming into Tella Meda. Charvi was well known locally but not well known enough to have very wealthy people give thousands of *rupees* as they did to other, more popular *ashrams*.

"Oh come on, Kokila," Chetana said. "It will be nice to have a TV. You'll see."

"Yes, Kokila Atha," Bhanu pleaded. "All my friends have TV, I want TV too. This Sunday they're showing that Krishna movie with—"

"It isn't about movies," Renuka interrupted, and glared at Bhanu. "This is about education also. They show a lot of educational programs on television. Saraswati says that she has learned a lot from TV."

Kokila shook her head. "Find another place for it. A guest room is—"

"If we have extra guests, they can have my room," Subhadra said superiorly. "Will that do?"

Kokila sighed. Everyone was in on this scheme and no matter what she said it would not matter. They were all blinded by the lights the television promised.

V. C. Ramarao had his own television company in Visakhapatnam. The company thrived on local sales, on people who couldn't afford the twice-as-expensive BPL Sanyo, Samsung, and other brand-name television sets.

V. C. Ramarao's wife, Rambha Devi, was a conservative woman who believed in saints and *gurus,* unlike her husband, who thought all religious people to be fraudulent. Rambha Devi, however, managed to get enough money out of her husband's tight fists to donate to *ashrams, sadhus,* and the like by convincing him that ill luck would befall him if he wasn't charitable.

Rambha Devi visited Tella Meda often and it was really her idea that a television be installed there. She thought she would be able to convince her husband to give a sixty-five-hundred-rupee color television set for free to the residents of Tella Meda. As superstitious as V. C. Ramarao was, he was no fool. He wasn't about to just give away a good television for free. He agreed to give it for less than half the price and said he would throw in the installation for free.

Kokila grumbled about the three thousand *rupees* he was charging for the TV but admitted that the evenings would be a little less boring with the television showing movies and movie-song programs. Already, everyone was talking about the half-hour show on Monday evenings, *Chitralahiri,* which broadcast songs from old and new Telugu movies. It was one of the most popular television programs, in addition to Telugu dramas and Hindi serials, shown in the evening.

Rambha Devi came to stay at Tella Meda for a week to ensure that her husband didn't skimp on the installation. She also wanted to make sure Charvi knew that it was Rambha Devi's influence that had brought a color television into Tella Meda. And it was her husband's television company that had provided the TV.

The way she talked about it, the television had walked all by itself from Visakhapatnam (thanks to her husband) and no one at Tella Meda had had to pay a *paisa* for it, Kokila thought bitterly.

"Still, it's less than half the price," Subhadra said when Kokila complained that Rambha Devi made it sound like they were getting the TV for free.

"It's still three thousand *rupees*," Kokila complained. "Do you know how long we had to save for that?"

Subhadra nodded. "Yes, yes, but still, the installation is free. And if the TV goes bad, they'll even change it."

"They have to. It has a two-year warranty," said Kokila, now well versed in what came with a color television. She had spoken with the local TV shop owner and he told her that V. C. Ramarao's TV was not that good and that's why he was able to sell it for that price. The other color televisions cost thirteen thousand *rupees* or more.

"And do you know why his TVs are cheaper than others?" Kokila demanded shrewdly.

"Because he's a good man trying not to cheat his customers?" Subhadra put in with a smile.

Kokila made a face. "All you can think about is that Krishna movie on Sunday. So it's a total waste of time talking to you."

No one was on Kokila's side. Everyone wanted that television, even Shanthi, who was usually sensible, and they were all so grateful to Rambha Devi. It grated on Kokila's nerves. She was the one who had juggled the Tella Meda finances to ensure they had enough money saved up and could therefore use that money to buy a TV but did anyone say thanks to her? Did anyone show her any gratitude? Everyone was flocking around Rambha Devi. Shanthi was stitching blouses for free, while Chetana was stitching *sari* falls, a cotton lining at the bottom edge of the *sari,* for free, and Subhadra was cooking all of Rambha Devi's favorite foods. It was as if Rambha Devi ran the *ashram.* Kokila was resentful. She wished they didn't have the money to afford the TV and wished that the subject had never come up.

———

But on the day that the television was to be installed, there was a problem.

"I'm not lying. The money is not there." *How could they believe I'm lying?* Kokila thought angrily. She was almost in tears, hysteria humming beneath her calm voice.

Rambha Devi pursed her lips. "My husband insisted that you pay something for the television. That is not unreasonable."

"Kokila, I know you, you hid the money so that we couldn't have the TV, didn't you? You never wanted us to have the TV," Renuka demanded, glaring at Kokila. Kokila felt a pang. It was true she didn't want the TV, but she wouldn't hide the money.

"Kokila never lies," Subhadra snapped at Renuka. "Okay, where did you leave the money?"

Kokila swallowed the lump in her throat. Three thousand *rupees*! How could it be gone? Who would take the money?

"Right here." She pointed to the desk in Charvi's room. They had all congregated there once the theft had been discovered. Charvi herself was out for her evening walk.

"I took it out of the safe and put it there so that I could give it to Rambha Devi as soon as she finished her bath . . . and then the milkman came for his money. I went to pay him. I came back . . . the money was gone," Kokila said. "Look, I know the TV is important but . . . This has never happened before. I am always very careful with money."

Rambha Devi obviously didn't believe Kokila.

"My husband will never agree," Rambha Devi said firmly. "You will have to give three thousand *rupees* somehow, otherwise no TV installation today."

Bhanu's eyes filled with tears. The television was sitting in the new TV room that had been set up with chairs and mats, ready for the Sunday night movie just two days away.

"I won't ask the electrician to take the TV but he won't fix the antenna until the money is here," Rambha Devi said, sure that once she laid down her threat Kokila would find the allegedly stolen money.

"How could you do this?" Bhanu shrieked at Kokila, and ran away with Renuka following her.

"I just left it here for a minute," Kokila said, looking at Subhadra with stricken eyes. "Who could have taken it?"

"Well, you better find it by tomorrow, otherwise the electrician will take the TV with him, and then don't come and blame me for it," Rambha Devi said.

"All day you've been strutting around as if the television is a free gift to us and now you're becoming so stingy," Subhadra muttered.

"My husband said—"

"Look, the money got stolen. If you don't believe it, that's your problem. Kokila here doesn't have a printing press that will print out three thousand *rupees*. So if it's gone, it's gone. You can take the TV today and be gone if you like," Subhadra said angrily.

Charvi came into her room, her eyes scanning all the faces.

"The money got stolen," Kokila blurted out. "I put it here and then went to pay off the milkman and the money was gone."

"What money?" Charvi asked.

"The TV money," Subhadra said.

Charvi nodded and then shrugged. "It's just money. I'm sure it'll turn up. No one steals at Tella Meda. Someone took it by mistake, I'm sure."

"I'm sure too," Rambha Devi said, looking accusingly at Kokila.

Charvi looked pointedly at Rambha Devi. "Kokila can take money anytime she wants to. No one knows how much money is in the safe and no one governs her. But she has never taken a *paisa* from Tella Meda. She keeps everything running and I know some months she puts her own typing school money inside the safe. So never look at Kokila with such accusing eyes. God punishes such unfairness. Some eyes that look unjustly may go blind."

Rambha Devi was stricken. "I didn't mean—"

"It's time for my meditation before dinner," Charvi interrupted her, and then focused on Kokila. "Please let everyone know that there will be no television if we don't find the money by tomorrow. I hope that the thief has some conscience."

But no one came forward with the money.

"I saw Ravi out and about," Puttamma said as everyone sat in the courtyard to discuss the lost money.

"You always have to blame him," Chetana muttered.

But Kokila and Subhadra could easily see Ravi stealing. After all, he had stolen several times before from everyone at Tella Meda.

"When did you see him?" Kokila asked.

"He probably stole the money, that useless fellow," Renuka said. "You don't keep your husband leashed properly, Chetana, and see what happens?"

Bhanu sat quietly, unsure of what to say. Chetana's husband was her father and even though he rarely spoke with her and never ever played with her, he was still her father and she knew what a father meant. She didn't like it when Renuka called her father names, even if Renuka never referred to him as Bhanu's father, always as Chetana's husband. But Bhanu knew stealing was wrong.

"Let's not jump to conclusions," Kokila said, and then sighed. "Puttamma, where did you see him?"

Puttamma looked at Chetana and then at Kokila. "In the afternoon. When I was coming here, he was going to the city."

"That means nothing," Chetana said, incensed, as she shifted Meena from one hip to the other. It was not that she wanted to defend Ravi; she wanted to defend herself. As a wife, it was her duty to keep her husband on the straight and narrow. She had failed on that account, but if he had stolen the TV money? Oh, no, it couldn't be him. But even as she wondered who else it could be, Chetana was quite sure that the only person capable of stealing at Tella Meda was Ravi.

"He owes Simhan two months' bill," Puttamma said. "And Simhan threatened him last night, saying he'd break his legs if he didn't bring the money today."

"And who is this Simhan?" Rambha Devi asked, looking at Chetana with disdain. Her expression seemed to say, *Well, what can one expect from a prostitute's daughter?*

"He owns a toddy shop in the *kallu* compound," Chetana said indignantly. "My husband is a drunk and a womanizer. Happy now?" She ran inside her room with Meena wailing on her hip.

Kokila wanted to follow her but before she could, Chetana came back out, a red silk string bag in her hand. She dropped the bag on the tiled floor in front of Rambha Devi. The bag fell with a clang.

"That should be worth three thousand *rupees,* easily," Chetana said, and patted Meena on the back, trying to calm her down. "Just shut up," she told her daughter. At six years old, Meena was completely spoiled and cried to manipulate Chetana. It was easy to manipulate Chetana because she still felt guilty about not having taken care of Bhanu as a baby. So everything Meena wanted, Meena got because Bhanu had not asked anything of Chetana and never received anything either.

Rambha Devi opened the bag that lay in front of her and pulled out four thick gold bangles.

"Manikyam gave them to you. You can't give them away," Subhadra said, putting a hand on Chetana's shoulder. "They are your insurance for later on in life; don't waste them on a television."

Chetana shook her head. "Not on the television but on Ravi. This is the last money I waste on him." Chetana looked at Bhanu. "He's not a good man. We won't let him come back into Tella Meda again."

"Never in Tella Meda again?" Meena asked curiously. Bhanu had ambivalent feelings about her father, but Meena definitely didn't like him. Since she'd been born she had spent no time with him and saw him with jealous eyes. He was the man who made her sleep with Bhanu in Renuka's room, away from Chetana.

"Never again," Chetana assured her.

"Now, now, don't be rash," Rambha Devi said, weighing the bangles, assessing their worth. "He's still your husband."

"Are these worth a color TV or not?" Chetana demanded, speaking over Rambha Devi's advice.

Renuka looked shrewdly at the bangles then and snatched two away from Rambha Devi, who tried to grab them back. "Two are enough. These are thick, thick, and two are enough. Don't you think, Rambha Devi?"

Rambha Devi looked at the bangles in Renuka's grasp longingly. She didn't want them to think she was greedy or short of money, which she wasn't. It was just that the bangles were beautifully made, the design on them was intricate and two on each wrist would look so much nicer than one on each wrist. Still, Renuka was right, they were quite expensive and two should be worth three thousand *rupees*. And she could convince her husband of their value by simply not buying jewelry for the next two or three months.

"Yes, two are enough," Rambha Devi admitted grudgingly.

Chetana took the last two bangles from Renuka and put them on. They sparkled on her skin and she shook her head. The bangles were the only valuable things that had come out of her marriage and she had dreamed of so much more. She had dreamed of a big house, servants, a happy life . . . a life like Manikyam had.

And it had come to this.

The electrician from V. C. Ramarao's company hooked the color TV up in the TV room and the antenna up on the terrace. Everyone stood in the front garden admiring the antenna as it was put up. Almost every home in Bheemunipatnam now had an antenna sticking out. It was a status symbol and even some huts had antennas. But they had black-and-white televisions, while Tella Meda was getting a color one. It was a night for celebration.

The money had just been sitting there.

Ravi had come to beg Charvi for some and usually she gave him a twenty here and there, but this was a stack of notes, some crisp, some dull, and he knew he had hit a gold mine. This was the color TV money that everyone was talking about. And he did think that the drab and dull Tella Meda needed a television.

Ravi didn't want to deprive anyone of a TV and surely when the money went missing that devotee woman would give it to them for free. He felt no guilt or remorse for putting the money in his pants pocket. He hurried away before Kokila could spot him. They would get the television anyway and he would finally be able to pay back the money he owed Simhan.

Ravi had seen what happened to others who didn't pay the toddy shop owner what they owed. They were beaten, severely. Simhan was the only *kallu* shop owner in the area who allowed patrons to drink on credit. But he charged fifty *paisas* extra per bottle and if payment didn't come at the end of the month, legs were broken and faces were bashed in.

Ravi was afraid of Simhan. He was a large, dark man with a thick mustache. He looked like an *asura,* a demon, from an Amar Chitra Katha comic. And he had arms as big as tree trunks and a voice that scared Ravi enough that he always paid his debt, no matter whom he had to steal from.

This time Simhan had given him almost two months' grace period. The bill had risen and risen. Now he could not only pay off Simhan but also enter the brothel of Chamba, who had kept him out since he hadn't paid her whore two months ago. They said she had some fresh bait. Maybe for the money he was left with, he could get the fresh bait.

Sometimes when he was drunk he would wonder what he was doing in Bheemunipatnam, drinking and whoring about. He would wonder why he couldn't just go home and then he would drink some more because he'd remember that his father had kicked him out and that since he'd married that bitch Chetana, his life had gone down the drain like bad toddy.

All he could do to keep himself sane was to drink and when he was drunk, a whore made him happy, especially since Chetana hadn't allowed him to touch her for over two years now. And now he had the means to get toddy and a whore. Sometimes good luck just fell into your lap.

Ravi didn't come home that night and Chetana didn't get the opportunity to kick him out. She made a bundle of his clothes ready to throw out after him. The television was set up on a Friday and he didn't come on Saturday and neither did he come back on Sunday.

Though the television was turned on every evening from 7 PM after *bhajan* to 11 PM when the television station went off the air, it was Sunday evening everyone was looking forward to. Even *bhajan* had been postponed to 9 PM, after the movie, instead of at 6:30 after dinner. The movie with the superstar Krishna and famous actress Sri Devi would start at 5 PM and end at 9. There would be a small break for Telugu news for half an hour at 7:30 PM. That was when dinner was planned.

Charvi agreed with the new timing. She didn't watch many movies and rarely went to the cinema but even she couldn't stand up against the enthusiasm of the women of Tella Meda.

"Now let's hope the electricity doesn't go off," Subhadra said during lunch. For the first time she was not interested in the devotees and guests at Tella Meda.

"Our own television! It's so nice not to ask that Saraswati if we can come and watch this movie or that," Renuka said. "The fuss she made when I wanted to see ANR in *Sudigundalu.*"

"And when they showed *Missamma,* she made all sorts of excuses," Subhadra said angrily and with some satisfaction. Savitri was her favorite actress and *Missamma* her favorite movie.

"She behaves as if we're not good enough," Chetana commented. "We're good enough to eat with and gossip with but if we need something she turns her nose up. It's just Charvi whom she has any respect for."

"I never liked her much. She's so snobbish," Rambha Devi said, earning snickers from everyone.

"People living in glass houses shouldn't throw stones," Shanthi whispered to Kokila, who pursed her lips to stop from laughing.

But the electricity went out at 4 PM. Bhanu stood by a light switch, turning it on and off, on and off, hoping that by some miracle the electricity would come back on if she played enough with the switch.

"It's not summer anymore, so why do they still keep taking the current off?" she moaned. In the summer months, the electricity was turned off for several hours a day to save it. But even during the rest of the year, the electricity was never stable and it occasionally went off due to some malfunction or the other.

"Just leave that switch on. If the current comes back we'll know," Renuka told her.

They were all waiting in the TV room, anxious.

Kokila, who had shown little interest so far in the whole television melee, also was disappointed. What if the power didn't come back on? And after they'd done so much to get that television.

Puttamma came running to Tella Meda at quarter to five. Her breath was coming in short gasps and her *sari* was almost undone in her haste to get there.

"The current is gone," Subhadra said as Puttamma came huffing into the TV room. "So you didn't miss anything."

Puttamma shook her head and then looked at Kokila. "Amma . . ."

Kokila, who was sitting in a corner with Shanthi, walked up to Puttamma. She had to lean over to listen to what Puttamma had to say. She looked at Puttamma in disbelief.

"What? No current all night? Is that it?" Renuka asked. "What did you find out, Puttamma?"

"Oh, why is it that they should take the current off today?" Bhanu demanded, and so as not to be left out, Meena pouted as well. "I like Krishna so much and now we won't be able to see the movie."

"Chetana," Kokila said, ignoring everyone else. "Come with me."

"What happened now? I don't want to miss the beginning of the movie," Chetana said on a long sigh. "Did some more money go missing? I can give the last two bangles but that's it. I don't have any—"

Kokila took Chetana's hand and led her into the temple room.

"Puttamma just saw . . . Ravi is dead, Chetana," Kokila said bluntly, not sure how one should say something like this.

"Dead? Dead?" Chetana said, staring at Puttamma. When Puttamma nodded, Chetana nodded as well. "Completely dead?" she asked, just in case her question was misunderstood.

"Simhan got some bad toddy yesterday night and ten people died at the *kallu* compound," Puttamma said.

"Oh," Chetana managed to say despite the big lump that had appeared in her throat all of a sudden. She didn't know how to react. There was so much shock along with relief and surprise.

Now there would be a funeral. She had to let Manikyam know. And the body, that would have to be brought to Tella Meda. Or would Manikyam want the funeral in Visakhapatnam? No, no, here would be better. It was closer to where his body was. His father or brother would have to do the last rites. After all, Ravi had no sons, at least none she knew about.

"Where is he?" Chetana asked.

Puttamma looked uncomfortable and shrugged. "We can get him here and . . ."

"Oh, Puttamma, just tell me where he is," Chetana said, suddenly feeling very weary.

"At Champa's. He had money and she has a new girl. He died in her room. She's still screaming because he went into convulsions, vomited all over her. They want to get rid of the body right now. The police are looking into it as well. They've arrested Simhan for selling bad toddy, but you know how it is. He'll be out by sundown, selling more toddy from his shop," Puttamma said, the words rolling out of her mouth at full speed.

"Hmm," Chetana said, and then looked at Kokila. "What now?"

"I'll tell Charvi and then go to Vishnu Garu's house and phone Manikyam, or do you want to do that? Ah . . . Subhadra can—" Kokila stopped speaking and held Chetana close as her face suddenly crumpled.

"I'm a widow now," Chetana mumbled, and started to cry. "I was hardly ever a wife and now I'm a widow. Oh, Kokila, it isn't fair."

Puttamma looked at the two women with misery in her eyes. All the time she had cursed that Ravi to hell and blamed Chetana for his shortcomings and now that he was in hell, it was just sad. He had given no one any happiness in his life and even in his death his wife wasn't able to find joy. If her first husband had died on her, Puttamma would have celebrated. Instead the son of a whore had stolen her money and jewelry to run away with the neighbor's wife.

"Better to be a widow, Chetana Amma, than the wife of a bad, bad man," Puttamma said. Most people didn't think so but Puttamma had lived long enough and had spent enough time with no-good men that she didn't believe in the societal custom of putting up with a husband no matter how bad he was. If she had been married to Ravi, she would've beaten him and thrown him out of her life long time ago.

Chetana looked up from Kokila's shoulder at Puttamma, amusement in her eyes at the remark. "And he was a terribly bad man, wasn't he?"

"Oh yes," Puttamma said sincerely. "He was the worst."

"It would be so easy, wouldn't it, if we could all be as practical as Puttamma," Chetana said sadly.

"You have to learn to be practical to survive," Puttamma said.

"I have to tell the girls," Chetana said, and stepped away from Kokila. "You'll take care of the—" Chetana looked up at the ceiling fan in the temple room as it whirred to a start. "The current is back."

On cue, music from the TV followed. Applause and cheers from everyone in the TV room filtered into the temple room.

Puttamma rushed into the TV room and demanded that the television be turned off. At the curses everyone hurled at her for speaking loudly as the initial music of the movie began she said Tella Meda was in mourning and that it wasn't proper to watch movies when a woman had lost her husband.

Dr. Nageshwar Rao performed the last rites. His younger son, Prasad, stood by his brother's dead body wearing a white *kurta* and *lungi,* with breath that smelled of whiskey. He didn't indulge in toddy. Rich men's sons who married according to parental wishes didn't have to drink toddy, he had discovered. He could sit in his own home with his friends and drink foreign whiskey, peg after peg, without worrying about how to pay for it. He didn't quite see his brother's death in the light his father hoped he would. Prasad didn't believe that alcohol killed Ravi. It was *bad* alcohol and that whore's daughter Ravi had married that killed Ravi. Prasad's wife, Sita, didn't live with him anymore because when she did, she brought the house down every time he got drunk. And every time she nagged him he felt like he had to slap her around and then she would start crying and the misery would go on all night.

One night he beat her so much that there were huge bruises all over her face. In the morning when the alcohol wore off he was apologetic but she didn't want any apologies. She packed her suitcases and left. *Good riddance,* Prasad thought. Now his father-in-law was crying about divorce and as far as Prasad was concerned that was all right too. But Sita always came back because his mother always went to Srikakulam to bring her back. She would lure her back with new diamond jewelry, expensive *saris,* and whatnot. Prasad didn't care all that much where she was, but he was happiest when his wife went to visit her parents.

Marital sex had turned out to be a dud as well. At least his brother was lucky in that department, Prasad thought as he stood by his brother's pyre, imagining his brother's wife without her clothes. Oh yes, Chetana had nice lush breasts and even after two children, her waist was slim and her hips just wide enough to make a man want to hold her in between his legs. Why on earth had his brother been visiting whores when he had such a delicious piece at home? He understood why his father kept a fancy piece on the side. He just had to look at his mother to figure that out.

Prasad had seen his father's mistress several times in the market, in his father's clinic, in his father's car, other places. It wasn't like his father was discreet about her or anything. Her name was Menaka. People said that was her "movie" name and no one knew her real name. Menaka was not from Andhra but from north India. No one was sure where. She had bright, fair skin and an even and smooth face, unlike Manikyam's pockmarked visage. Her hair was always tied in a neat little bun with flowers decorating it. She wore high heels under silk *saris* that Dr. Nageshwar Rao bought for her and she always wore makeup and perfume.

Dr. Nageshwar Rao might not have been loyal to his wife but he had been loyal to Menaka. Since he met her on the set of a Telugu movie fifteen years ago, he had not slept with his wife or any other woman. Menaka had worked in films as an extra for a while but the roles soon dried up and so did her interest. With Dr. Nageshwar Rao paying her keep she didn't have the need to work for a living.

Prasad had never spoken with Menaka and never spoken about her either. Everyone in his family pretended she didn't exist and his father pretended Manikyam didn't exist; it was a perfect setup. Prasad had hoped for a setup like that for himself: a wife at home to keep house and raise the children and a whore on the side who was dynamite in bed. But his wife kept running away to her parents and he found that he couldn't quite support a mistress in style without a solid income. Money trickled down very slowly from his father.

Back at Tella Meda, where the third-day *puja* for Ravi was in full swing, Prasad wondered if now with Ravi dead Chetana might be available for an easy lay. Who would it hurt? And it wasn't like she was washed in milk. She was a prostitute's daughter, and she had been married to Ravi. How high could her standards be?

Prasad's first mistake was to make a pass at Chetana. His second was to make a second pass when Chetana ignored the first one.

"You son of a whore, you bastard, you think you can come and talk to me like that?" Chetana demanded, standing in the center of the courtyard, wet clothes needing to be hung on the clothesline still in her hand.

They had made her a widow the day before by breaking her bangles, wiping the *kumkum* from her forehead, and cutting five locks of her hair. She had refused to shave her hair completely off, as Renuka would have liked. The experience had left her jittery and uneasy. The future seemed bleak and in the middle of all of this she had to deal with her dead husband's brother's misbehavior?

"Didn't you teach your sons anything?" Chetana yelled in the direction of Manikyam, who sat at the knee-high table in the back verandah with Subhadra, Renuka, and Lavanya.

"What? What are you talking about, you crazy woman?" Manikyam demanded, though Chetana knew what she was talking about. She had seen the look in Prasad's eyes. Just because she didn't say anything about her son's bad habits didn't mean she didn't know about them. He had set his eyes on his dead brother's wife. Only Lord Venkateshwara Swami could cleanse the boy's sins now.

"This son of yours—"

"What? Now you're blaming me for something?" Prasad demanded, aware that if he didn't defend himself before the accusation was made, he would be in trouble.

"Yes, I am, you dirty-minded son of a whore," Chetana said loudly. "You think you can come here and talk about my breasts and my hips? These breasts nurtured your brother's children and you should show them some respect."

Subhadra clamped a hand on her mouth, shocked at what Chetana was saying, what she was claiming Prasad had said to her. Chetana was a new widow and already the vultures were circling. Men would never leave her in peace anymore. A young, beautiful widow like that, everyone would try to snatch a piece of her away. And a young widow living in Tella Meda . . . Subhadra shook her head at that thought. Already people looked down upon them for living in an *ashram*. Poor Chetana—they would tear her apart for also being a widow.

"What is this noise about?" Charvi stepped out into the verandah from the temple room, her eyes red and irritated. "You're disturbing my meditation."

"Now look what you did!" Manikyam said urgently and rose to lead Charvi back to the temple room. "Chetana is just upset."

Charvi, who had sworn never to speak with Manikyam again, turned away from her older sister and instead looked at Subhadra.

"You'd be upset too if your dead husband's brother came and made a pass at you," Lavanya said casually before Subhadra could say anything. "Manikyam, you did a poor job of raising your sons. That one died of bad toddy and this one . . . this one will die of stupidity."

Manikyam's face contorted with anger. "What would you know? You are a worthless woman, no better than that whore's daughter."

Lavanya shook her head. "I don't know why I bother to come here. Next time someone dies or gets married, you needn't let me know. I don't think I'd want to come."

"Okay, we won't tell you," Charvi said to Lavanya, and then turned to Chetana. "What happened?"

Chetana looked at Prasad with hatred. "He made a pass at me. Asked me if I'd like to spread my legs for—"

"This woman is lying, Charvi Pinni," Prasad said. "Come on, Pinni, you know I'd never—"

Charvi's eyes blazed. "Get out," she said clearly and firmly.

"What?" Manikyam's mouth fell open.

"You're asking me to get out?" Prasad demanded cockily.

"Yes, this is my home and there is no room for philandering, indecent men like you. Your brother was bad enough. He stole money from us, came home with alcohol on his breath, and treated his wife shabbily. I won't have you here too. Now get out," Charvi said. "And if anyone has a problem with that, they can leave as well. Now I'm going back to meditate. Please try to keep your voices down."

Everyone thought that Manikyam and Dr. Nageshwar Rao would leave with Prasad but they stayed even though they packed him up and sent him home in their car. Lavanya left with him, cursing him, Manikyam, Charvi, Tella Meda, and anything else she could think of.

Manikyam and her husband stayed through the thirteenth-day ceremonies and left only after all the religious needs pertaining to their son's death had been fulfilled. Dr. Nageshwar Rao came to speak with Kokila the day he and his wife were to leave. He had never bothered with more than a nod of the head for her in all the years she had known him. Kokila wasn't even sure he knew her name. Nevertheless, when he knocked on her door, she opened it and let him in.

"I wanted to talk to Chetana but after how Prasad behaved I find myself too embarrassed to speak with her," Dr. Nageshwar Rao said without preamble. He was known to be a straight man who spoke as he felt, so Kokila waited for him to get to his point.

He pulled out two small books from his pocket and held them toward Kokila. They were State Bank of India passbooks. Kokila took one and flipped through the pages.

"There is fifteen thousand *rupees* each for the girls when they turn eighteen," Dr. Nageshwar Rao said. "The money will grow by then and become more, and I think it will be enough to support them when they're ready to marry."

The passbooks were made in the name of Bhanumati Rao and Meenakumari Rao.

"Your grandchildren need more than money," Kokila said as she put the passbooks back in Dr. Nageshwar Rao's hand. "Chetana will never accept this money."

He shook his head. "They're not my grandchildren, not legally . . . but I would like to do this for them. Will you give them to the girls?"

Kokila thought about it for a moment and then agreed. No matter how Chetana felt about Dr. Nageshwar Rao and his money, this was for the girls, and Kokila wasn't about to turn away their future.

No one was really mourning Ravi; everyone had been maintaining a posture just until all the *pujas* and other formalities ended.

The television room that had been set up in such haste had not been used at all. But after the thirteenth-day celebrations, the adults pretended to cave in to Bhanu and Meena's insistent pleading for television and turned it on. It was a Wednesday evening, the day *Chitrahar*, a show with songs from Hindi movies, was broadcast. Even Charvi decided to come after *bhajan* to watch some television. After the difficult past few days, everyone was in need of some excitement and enjoyment.

"What is this?" Bhanu demanded angrily. Two women were sitting on the floor with *tanpuras* playing slow, classical music. "This is not some movie song, is it?"

"No," Renuka said, perplexed.

They all watched the boring music for a while and then there was a break for the Telugu regional news.

There was a shocked silence as they listened. Just that morning Prime Minister Indira Gandhi had been shot by her Sikh bodyguards. Ravi's death had distracted everyone and they had not heard yet. The country was in mourning for ten days. When the country went into mourning, Doordarshan, the government-run television station and the only one available in India, played only devotional music with breaks for the day's news.

"So, will there be just this boring music for ten days?" Meena asked, her eyes filled with tears. "I just want to see some songs. First he dies and we can't watch TV and now someone else dies and there's nothing to watch. It isn't fair."

Charvi sighed and started to walk back to her room. She passed Kokila, who had been finishing up in the kitchen and was hurrying to get to the TV room.

"No rush," Charvi said when she met Kokila on the way to her room. "Some Sikhs shot and killed Indira Gandhi, so they're only going to show devotional music for the next ten days. Bhanu and Meena are quite disappointed."

"They really wanted to watch some movie songs. First Ravi and now this . . . they must be very frustrated," Kokila said, feeling sorry for the girls.

"It's sad, isn't it, that they should compare the death of their philandering father with the assassination of a great leader and treat both deaths with less regard than movie songs," Charvi said wearily. "What has the world come to?"

Kokila wasn't really listening to Charvi but planning how to make it up to Bhanu and Meena. "Well, I'll take them to the cinema on Sunday for a matinee. That should make them happy," she decided.

"It probably will," Charvi said wearily, and went back to her room.

4 June 1987. A Swedish government inquiry determined that the Swedish company Bofors paid a commission to middlemen for concluding an arms purchase agreement with India. The identity of these middlemen was to be the subject of an investigation, an Indian government spokesperson said.

14 June 1987. Prime Minister Rajiv Gandhi ruled out the termination of the 17 billion *rupees* Bofors gun deal.

Surrogate Mothers

Subhadra was getting too old to cook all the meals alone. Her arthritis made it difficult for her to stand up and sit down. Once she sat down on the floor to cut vegetables or clean the rice she couldn't rise easily again. So it was the perfect time for Sushila and her daughter, Padma Lakshmi, to arrive at Tella Meda. A relative of Subhadra's in a very convoluted and distant manner, Sushila had lost her husband in a bus accident in Cuddapah. With nowhere to go and a nine-year-old daughter, Sushila wrote to Subhadra and was invited to live in Tella Meda.

Padma and Meena immediately became friends. Meena was delighted. It was not easy to make friends in school, as everyone knew she was Chetana's daughter and that she lived in Tella Meda. Mothers of several of the girls in her class had told their daughters to stay away from Meena. She found out because those girls had cruelly shunned her when she'd tried to make friends with them and they'd called

Chetana all kinds of names. Meena had a few friends in school, other girls who were not very popular and didn't have many friends. But having Padma in Tella Meda meant having a permanent friend whose mother would not ask her to stop speaking with Meena.

"Amma said that this is an *ashram* and people can come live here if they have nowhere else to go," Padma told Meena. The girls were the same age and both of them had lost their mostly absentee fathers recently.

"We also live here because Nannamma and Thatha don't want us to live with them," Meena said. "I don't like Thatha. I didn't like my father. I don't care that he is dead."

Padma didn't like her father either. "He used to shout at us all the time. And I don't have any Thatha and Nannamma—my father's parents died when he was a boy and my mother's parents died a few years ago, so we had no place else to go. Do you like living here?"

Meena shrugged. "It's okay. I don't like Bhanu. She's always so mean."

"Always angry," Padma agreed. "Why? What's wrong with her?"

"Don't know," Meena said.

Meena's skinny knee bumped against Padma's as they sat in the verandah, a yellow rice basket on Meena's lap. The rice basket was yellow so that the black of the stones and the white of the rice would stand out, making it easy to separate the rice from the unwanted stones. Open on one side, the wide and shallow basket had been used by Subhadra for years to glean stones from the rice. She would expertly hold the closed end of the basket and shake the rice within. She was so good at it that none of the rice granules would fall out of the basket, only the husk that hadn't been removed. Like magic, with every move, the stones hidden inside would rise above the white rice, making them easy to pick out and throw away.

Since Meena and Padma were too young to shake the heavy basket of rice, they had to sift carefully. It was their after-school chore. Subhadra had been reluctant to give any work to Meena or Bhanu, as she was so attached to them, but Sushila, who had already started training her nine-year-old daughter, decided that it was high time all the young girls in Tella Meda learned how to cook and do chores.

Bhanu wasn't about to let some new woman in Tella Meda teach her how to live her life. At fourteen, blossoming into a woman, Bhanu wasn't listening to anyone. Having been thoroughly spoiled by Renuka, Bhanu was growing up to be exactly like Chetana had been at her age, headstrong and adamant.

Bhanu resented that they all lived in Charvi's house and that Charvi was given special preference. Charvi didn't do anything at Tella Meda but everyone catered to her needs as though they were her servants. Bhanu wasn't like the others and she made sure that Charvi and everyone else at Tella Meda knew that. Her disdain for Charvi seemed to have grown out of nowhere.

"Why should I do any of this?" Bhanu demanded of Sushila as soon as she was given vegetable-chopping duties.

"Because you live here," Sushila told her firmly.

"Charvi lives here and she doesn't do anything," Bhanu pointed out slyly.

"Charvi is the *guru*. What are you?" Sushila asked. "Sit down and start cutting vegetables, otherwise we might have to ask Puttamma to stop coming so that you can start cleaning the bathrooms and the courtyard."

Kokila liked Sushila's frank manner. Unlike Chetana, Sushila wore white in deference to her widowhood, but unlike Renuka, she didn't shave her head. She was a tough woman in her mid-thirties who had been married to a man rumored to be a political thug in Cuddapah. She had a brisk manner and her skin was completely black. When Padma and Sushila walked together, everyone joked that they looked like a black *sari* with a white border because Padma was luckily very fair, like her father. She was a pretty girl and everyone was sure she would grow into a beautiful woman.

Bhanu disliked Sushila for her strict ways and disliked Padma as well. In her fantasies, Padma's face got burned and no one thought she was pretty anymore. The fact was that everyone around Bhanu was prettier than her. Meena was supposed to be just like Chetana, pretty-pretty; Padma was supposed to be beautiful. No one said any of those things about Bhanu. She was just Bhanu. And what kind of a silly name was Bhanumati?

Since Ravi had died Manikyam came to Tella Meda almost every month, clothes and sweets in hand for her granddaughters. She now openly called them her granddaughters. But even she was partial to Meena, calling her the beautiful girl, while calling Bhanu just Bhanu.

Chetana didn't notice Bhanu's resentment and even if she did, she couldn't be bothered by it. Shanthi and the tailoring business kept her busy, as did a young man who recently had moved to Bheemunipatnam from Vijaywada. He was the new cinema manager. Chetana had met him during a matinee show of a Chiranjeevi movie and after much flirting and eyelash batting, Chetana was now privileged to receive free balcony tickets for the first show of every movie. And she went, to the disapproval of Renuka, Manikyam, and even Subhadra.

"Nothing is free," Subhadra would warn Chetana. "You know what he wants? Beautiful widow like you, he thinks you're easy."

Chetana confided in Kokila that she was attracted to Srinivas. He was the antithesis of Ravi.

"Don't think because he's the opposite of Ravi, he's the right man for you," Kokila told her. "Don't rush into anything."

Chetana assured Kokila she wasn't about to rush into anything but she was not exactly telling the truth. On a trip to Visakhapatnam she used all her savings from the tailoring shop to have her tubes tied. She told no one, not even Kokila. She stayed at a ladies' hostel while she was there and chose a good hospital. She would not take the risk of ending up with infections and the like by going to a cheap hospital. Within a day she was healed and ready to go back to Bheemunipatnam. Chetana didn't want any more children but since Srinivas had started showering her with gifts and interest, she wasn't sure she didn't want physical relations with a man.

And it had been easy to get her tubes tied. The entire country was trying out the slogan "We are two and we should have two." Couples were encouraged to have only two children to control the population of India, which was threatening to surpass the Chinese population in a few years. A decade ago, Prime Minister Indira Gandhi had ordered forced vasectomies but now things were not so extreme. Now it was more subtle. There were advertisements on television promoting birth control pills and the IUD. The address of the hospital in Visakha-patnam where women could have their tubes tied was flashed on local TV all the time. Chetana had just copied the phone number and ad-dress and then phoned, discreetly, from a telephone at the cinema to get more information.

Physically she felt ready to start having sex with Srinivas; emotion-ally she wasn't sure if she would ever be ready for another man in her life.

While Chetana was working on ensuring that she never had any more children, Kokila felt the pang of lost time. She was thirty-seven years old, middle-aged, with no prospects of ever having a child of her own. Her menses were becoming irregular and she worried she would stop bleeding soon. There was a raging inferno of motherhood inside her, warm as breast milk and just as painful when not released. She wanted to be pregnant, wanted to feel a baby inside her womb, wanted to have someone who would love her as unconditionally as Meena loved Chetana. Even Bhanu loved Chetana. Chetana had turned away from Bhanu when she was a baby, but Bhanu still looked up to her mother, wanted her approval, demanded her validation, and fought her every step of the way.

Kokila wanted all of that, the good, the bad, the beautiful, but with every passing year she knew she was further from getting her de-sire.

It was the year that Doordarshan, the only Indian television station at the time, started to show the classic epic *Ramayana* that a regular and wealthy devotee of Charvi's showed up at Tella Meda with a baby.

Charvi, who had for the most part avoided television, was mes-merized by the story of Lord Rama unfolding so beautifully in color. Everyone at Tella Meda agreed that buying a color television had been a wise decision. In any case, black-and-white televisions were becom-ing less popular as color televisions became more affordable.

Even though the TV serial *Ramayana* was in Hindi and most resi-dents of Tella Meda didn't speak much Hindi, only Telugu, no one could be moved away from the TV room between nine and ten in the morning. Puttamma came to watch as well, her hands folded as if she were sitting in a temple.

Other devotees who came on Sundays to pay their respects to Charvi also joined her in the TV room to watch *Ramayana*. Even Subhadra and Sushila watched *Ramayana* while they ignored the preparation for lunch. The usual rhythms of Sundays at Tella Meda changed forever after that. The devotees were asked to come after 10 AM instead of at eight and lunch was served at one in the afternoon to allow for enough time to cook after the television program.

"Even you watch it," Bhanu accused Kokila, who was rarely found in the TV room except for Sundays. Kokila didn't understand the fascination and between dealing with the day-to-day business of Tella Meda and the Telugu typing school, she didn't have the time or the energy to sit in front of the television and try to grasp the story line.

"I watch *Ramayana,* yes," Kokila admitted. These days it was becoming increasingly difficult to speak with Bhanu. She picked fights on purpose, always wanting to needle anyone she could find.

"But you never watch other TV, so why do you watch *Ramayana?*" Bhanu demanded.

Kokila was thinking about what to say to that when she saw a man come into the temple room with a squalling baby in his arms.

"Oh, another crying baby," Bhanu said angrily. "Why do they bring their babies here? I hate babies."

"You hate everything these days," Chetana said with a smile, undaunted by her daughter's tantrums. Everyone went through some of this at this age, she told Kokila.

The man had come in a big black Ambassador. He had been to Tella Meda a few times before, usually with his wife. Bangaru Reddy was some politician from Hyderabad. Very wealthy, everyone said, and Kokila definitely believed that because he left at least a thousand *rupees* each time he came to pay his respects to Charvi.

"Are you well, Reddy Garu?" Kokila asked politely as she peeked at the baby's face.

Bangaru Reddy just nodded tightly.

"Whose baby is that?" Kokila asked, still peering. "A boy or a girl?"

"A boy," Bangaru Reddy said. "Would you hold him? He won't stop crying and . . . I don't know what to do."

"How old is he?" Kokila asked as she took the baby into her arms.

"Ten days," Bangaru Reddy said, and his Adam's apple bobbed. "I need to speak with Charvi Amma."

"Well, it is Sunday and some people are here to see her—"

"It is very urgent, Kokila," Bangaru Reddy said, panic lacing his voice. "I have formula and a bottle in the car, but he refused to drink when the driver tried. I should've brought a maid along but . . ."

"I'll take care of him," Kokila said, wondering where the boy's mother was.

The boy was beautiful. He was only ten days old but his skin wasn't wrinkled, and his eyes were wide and dark. Puttamma, who was also besotted with the baby at first sight, went and got the baby's formula and bottle from the car while Subhadra started to heat water to make up the formula for the weeping baby. Kokila settled down with the boy in the kitchen as all the women watched over him carefully.

He was obviously hungry because the minute the bottle's nipple touched the baby's mouth he grasped it in a tight suckle and soon emptied the bottle. Kokila watched in fascination. She had held Bhanu and Meena like this and several other babies and each time it had been special.

"What's his name?" Chetana asked as she stroked the baby's cheek.

"I don't know," Kokila said. "Just that he's ten days old."

"I think his name should be Karthik," Sushila said as she bent and kissed the boy's forehead. "He looks so bright and full of light, just like Lord Murugan."

"Yes, yes," Subhadra agreed, as she did often with Sushila these days. "Karthik would be a good name."

"Maybe he already has a name," Bhanu said. "Some stupid name, like Pentaayyah or something; what will you do then?"

"No one could name this beautiful baby Pentaayyah," Renuka said.

"Is Pentaayyah even a real name?" Meena asked.

"Sometimes when a couple is not able to have a baby they promise to name their children certain names if they do have a baby," Renuka explained. "It's tradition."

"Can't they promise to name their baby something nice? Why name anyone after *penta*? *Penta* means 'shit,' " Meena said, making a face.

Shanthi came into the kitchen then. She had taken up sitting by Charvi when the devotees came to see her. It gave her something else to do at Tella Meda besides her tailoring and she liked to listen to Charvi talk to the devotees and try to solve their problems. Some Sundays there were many and some Sundays no one came to Tella Meda.

"Kokila, Charvi wants to see you in her room," Shanthi said, and then was drawn to the baby. "Oh, can I hold him?"

"No, no, it's my turn now," Chetana said, and took the baby from Kokila.

Bangaru Reddy was wiping tears off his cheeks when Kokila came to Charvi's room.

"How is he?" Bangaru Reddy asked.

"He ate and now is almost asleep," Kokila said, but her eyes were focused on Charvi, who looked worried.

"Bangaru has come in the hope that he could leave that baby here, at Tella Meda," Charvi said, and a small sound escaped Kokila.

"Apparently, Bangaru's son had a small indiscretion with a servant maid . . ." Charvi shook her head, unable to speak for a moment. "The girl died during childbirth. Bangaru's son's wedding is set for next week."

Kokila nodded.

"Amma, I know what he did was wrong, very wrong, but should he pay for his small mistake forever? And it wasn't like that servant girl was a good girl," Bangaru Reddy said. "Please, I can't . . . I will have to leave him at an orphanage."

"Orphanage?" Kokila almost yelped the word. "No, no, leave him here."

Charvi shook her head. "Kokila, it isn't this simple. This is someone else's baby. We can't just—"

"What if I adopt the baby?" Kokila asked, and as the unplanned words came out of her she realized that this was the answer to her yearnings. "Can I adopt the baby?" she asked again with more confidence. "Then he can be my son. Will it be okay then?" She wasn't about to let little Karthik out of her sight. An orphanage? The poor little boy. No one was going to leave him in an orphanage.

"Are you sure?" Charvi asked. "This will be forever."

"Yes, yes," Kokila said, looking at Bangaru Reddy, whose eyes were spilling over again.

"I want you to think about it first," Charvi said. "Bangaru, why don't you wait outside for a moment while I speak with Kokila?"

As Bangaru Reddy was walking out of the room, Kokila realized that Charvi was against the baby being here.

"Are you sure you can take care of this baby?" Charvi asked Kokila. "Think carefully before you answer, very carefully."

Kokila shrugged. "There's nothing to think about. I want to keep the baby."

"What will you do when you go to your typing school?" Charvi asked. "Who will care for the baby then?"

"Shanthi will," Kokila said, even though she hadn't asked Shanthi. "Or Subhadra will, or Sushila will, or Chetana will. Or I will stop going to typing school. I can't let Reddy Garu put Karthik away in an orphanage."

Charvi's eyebrows rose. "Who is this Karthik?"

Kokila's lips lifted and she smiled sheepishly. "We were wondering what his name was and we thought Karthik was a nice name for him."

Charvi sighed. It was evident that Kokila was already attached to the baby.

But how could she be attached to a baby she had just met? Charvi understood that women had needs and that as age came their womb shrank and shrank, reminding them that it would forever be empty.

She had dealt with her desire of wanting a traditional husband and children and family. But it had never been this intense. There had been babies in Tella Meda and she liked to hold them and play with them, but now, in her mid-forties, she couldn't imagine being burdened with a baby for the rest of her life.

"I don't approve of this," Charvi said even though she knew that Kokila didn't care much about what she did or did not approve of. "It's an illegitimate child. God only knows what blood . . . I know, I know, Chetana is illegitimate and she's still a daughter of Tella Meda. But—"

"Charvi, I want this baby," Kokila said. "I need this baby."

Charvi nodded. "Okay, ask Bangaru to come in. You better look in the storeroom in the back for all of Meena and Bhanu's old things."

Bangaru Reddy was most grateful when he heard Charvi's decision to let his illegitimate grandson stay at Tella Meda.

"Every month, Kokila Amma, I will send you money. A thousand *rupees* for the boy, every month. But no one can know, you understand, don't you? Baby born out of wedlock . . . our good name will be destroyed," Bangaru Reddy said, not looking at Charvi because he was ashamed of what he was doing.

Kokila assured him she had no intention of telling anyone anything about Karthik's real parentage. "But when he grows up and wants to know? What should I say then?"

Bangaru Reddy seemed uncomfortable as if he had not thought about the boy growing up. "Why don't we worry about that then?"

So it was settled. There were no legalities involved, no documents to sign, but in the Tella Meda social court, where no judge sat, it was known that Kokila now had a son, Karthik, and he was beautiful.

The months flew for Kokila. Having a child was, she discovered, an intensely selfish experience. You could spend days, entire weeks only worrying about the child and caring for the child. When Karthik fell ill for the first time when he was six months old, Kokila had gone into total panic. He was sad, weepy, and uncomfortable and Kokila worried that he would never laugh again the way he used to.

Chetana and Shanthi took turns staying up with her and Karthik at night, but Kokila couldn't rest if he didn't. And when he did sleep, she was scared that if she slept he would slip away in his sleep. A few months earlier she had had only herself to worry about; now she hardly worried about herself, her appearance, her life, because Karthik was the center of her life and she didn't have time for anything else.

Charvi warned Kokila to not let her life slide away in caring for Karthik. "The boy will grow up and leave. What will happen to you after that?"

But that seemed so far away that Kokila couldn't focus on it because the needs of the present were overwhelming her.

She quit working in the typing school and used the money Bangaru Reddy sent for expenses.

Karthik was the most beautiful boy Kokila had ever seen. From his chubby hands to his dark eyes to his fair skin, everything about him was special, a delight. When he first started to sit up on his own, Kokila felt such pride surge within her that she forgot for a moment that all babies learned to sit on their own at one time or another. For her everything Karthik did was an indication that her son was a genius in the making. He was an easy baby, always happy and rarely prone to tantrums and crankiness.

"Ah, here comes the happy baby," they would say when Kokila took him into the kitchen. He rarely cried and ate everything put in front of him. By the time he was a year old, Kokila was mixing rice and plain *pappu* together, and fed Karthik with her fingers. He loved to eat *sambhar* from a spoon and cried out when he ate something too spicy, after which he'd gulp down cold milk from a glass.

Bangaru Reddy, as promised, sent a thousand *rupees* by money order to Kokila every month. The money was always sent in Kokila's name and the amount was always a thousand *rupees*. There were no letters or any other form of communication between Kokila and Bangaru Reddy. As far as he was concerned this was just a regular payment he made. He didn't care if his illegitimate grandson was dead or alive.

Kokila was actually glad that Bangaru Reddy was not interested in his grandson. Karthik was hers, and she didn't want Bangaru Reddy or his son to come and stake a claim. Not that they would, she told her-self. They had given up Karthik when he was just ten days old.

Karthik started walking on his first birthday, which was cele-brated as the day he came to Tella Meda. He walked unsteadily on bare feet saying "Amma" while he clapped at the antics of a cat or while Meena and Padma Lakshmi played with him. He had plenty of company at Tella Meda. Even Charvi spent time with him. He was a pleasure to be around; he kissed and hugged easily. His kisses were sloppy but his emotions genuine. Kokila was convinced it was she who had influenced Karthik's good behavior. He was a testament to her excellent mothering skills. So what if he hadn't come from her womb? She had done a better job than Chetana at least. When one looked at Bhanu, it was obvious someone had made a mistake in rais-ing her.

Bhanu's resentment for everyone at Tella Meda seemed to have been pooling inside her through the years and now only increased with every passing day. She was sixteen years old now and had just failed her metric exams. She wasn't planning to take them again and neither was she planning to go to college, as was becoming quite com-mon among girls her age. She wasn't sure what she was supposed to do besides wait two years and then get married when she was eigh-teen. She wasn't pretty like Chetana but by a quirk of fate her breasts were large and pushed out of her rib cage like two ripe and plump mangoes. Her skin was not as light as Chetana's or Ravi's but dark like Manikyam's. A couple of years ago she started to have pimples on her right cheek, which she tried to hide with face powder.

"You look like a whore," Renuka would say, and tried to rub the powder away with her *sari*.

Renuka was getting old now. Her bones hurt, she always said, and her eyesight was also weak. Her skin had wrinkled completely and now hung over her thin bones like a worn *sari*. Renuka knew that her time was getting near and she wanted to see Bhanu married before she died but at the rate she was going, who would marry her? But then what had Renuka expected? She was a whore's granddaughter and that kind of taint didn't leave the blood.

And Chetana was no better, according to Renuka. Instead of

being a good and pious widow, that woman was gallivanting around town with that cinema manager, Srinivas. She spent the nights away sometimes, making excuses and stories about going somewhere with someone, but everyone knew she was with that no-good bastard, Srinivas. He wasn't offering marriage either, which made him just as bad as Chetana.

Bhanu constantly hurled insults at Chetana about her new boyfriend but Chetana was so shameless that she didn't even pay heed to what her own daughter had to say. Meena would never say anything about her mother, whom she worshipped. But . . . *chee-chee,* this Chetana had no morals, Renuka thought, and wondered if somehow Chetana had passed that along to Bhanu from her womb.

"You be a good girl and you will marry a nice boy who will take you away from here. You be like your mother and you'll end up with some bastard like Srinivas and be here for the rest of your life," Renuka warned Bhanu.

But Bhanu wasn't listening. She liked boys. She trusted them and her ability to get them to do what she wanted them to do. Her mother had been stupid enough to marry a man like Ravi and now hook up with a man like Srinivas, whom everyone knew was engaged to his cousin in his village and would never seriously consider marrying a widow.

Bhanu was smart. She wasn't about to marry a good-for-nothing man like her father. She would marry a man who was already established. She wouldn't marry some young chit of a boy who needed his parents' permission to do anything.

And she already had someone in mind.

The Bheemunipatnam photo studio owner, Rajendra Babu, was ripe for plucking and he was interested in Bhanu. He would coax her into his studio and take pictures of her while her half-*sari* shifted just enough to allow him a glimpse of her ripe breasts covered by the thin cloth of a tight blouse. Bhanu asked Shanthi to stitch tight blouses for her so that she didn't have to wear a brassiere all the time. She was going to use those blouses to get her man.

Rajendra Babu, who was called Babu, was just over thirty years old. He had been married for two years but his wife had died just a year ago of some disease and he had no children. He did have a thriving photo business on the main street of the burgeoning town of Bheemunipatnam. He had a brand-new Bajaj scooter in the coveted blue color and a nice house right above his photo shop. The house had four rooms: one main room, a kitchen that opened to a small and narrow balcony in the back, one bedroom, and a small room that Babu used for storage. The main room had been nicely decorated by his wife with little dolls and pictures of Lord Venkateshwara Swami. The sofa was not too old either. Babu's wife had brought the sofa and the color TV with a remote control as part of her dowry.

Babu did small spreads and photographs for local businesses. And sometimes he also shot some women in the nude for an underground pornographic magazine run by a friend. There was a lot of money in the nude pictures business and besides it was not a hardship to take photos of naked women.

Bhanu obviously knew nothing about the nude pictures, though when she found out later on she was surprised but not really upset. She got angry at Babu and used her tantrum to get new gold earrings from him. Then she conveniently forgot what Babu was involved with.

Babu, on the other hand, couldn't believe his luck. This young, fresh virgin seemed to be interested in him. She hung around the photo studio and batted her eyelashes at him and let the *sari* covering her bosom slip by what seemed like an accident.

Like Chetana, Bhanu knew how to ensnare; unlike Chetana, she wasn't about to aim too high and end up with nothing. She finally drove Babu so mad with pent-up desire that he showed up at Tella Meda with his widowed mother and a proposal of marriage.

"She's just sixteen," Chetana said, staring at Babu with open disgust. The man was a disgrace. He was so much older than Bhanu and he looked like a lecherous fool. "It isn't legal to marry a girl off that young."

"Legalities can be dealt with," Babu said quietly. "If we have your blessing, the rest can be easily managed."

"Children these days, you have to let them do what they want,"

Babu's widowed mother said, and Chetana wanted to remind the woman that while her daughter was a child, Babu was no child.

"I don't think this is a proper match," Renuka said openly to Babu and his mother. "You're much older and she's just a—"

"Why don't you talk to Bhanu first?" Babu suggested politely.

Bhanu had prepared Babu for when he and his mother would come. He knew what he had to do to get that blouse off Bhanu's breasts. These old bats could say and do what they wanted but he was not about to give in and lose his chance with a fresh girl like Bhanu. So what if she was flirtatious and headstrong? Once he married her he would tame her. Babu wasn't worried.

When Bhanu told Chetana and Renuka she was in love with Babu and wanted to marry him, Chetana slapped her across the face.

"In love, it seems. Nonsense. You won't marry that old lecherous pig."

"I'm pregnant," Bhanu lied easily. "And he's the father."

The wedding took place at Tella Meda with no pomp or show, just the bare rituals. Chetana didn't have the money for a fancy ceremony and there was also reason for haste. Bhanu insisted that the marriage take place immediately and implied that her pregnancy was reason enough for hurry. Chetana suspected Bhanu was lying but was afraid to call her on it. What if she wasn't lying and the marriage fell through? An abortion was possible but . . . Chetana sighed. She hoped Meena would have the sense to not pull such a stunt.

After the marriage ceremony, as Bhanu packed her belongings, getting ready to leave for her husband's house, Kokila gave her the bank passbook Ravi's father had left in her care for his granddaughters. She had contemplated giving the passbook to Chetana and letting her do with it what she wanted but she knew that Chetana was angry enough and proud enough that there was a chance she would throw the passbook away.

"This is a lot of money," Bhanu said, and then looked at Kokila. "Does Amma know about this?"

Kokila shook her head. "She would kill me if she knew."

Bhanu grinned. "Amma likes money . . . but I think she hates

Manikyam's husband more. Why didn't you give me this money before?"

"I thought it would be wise to give it to you when you were ready for it. Are you angry with me for not giving it before?" Kokila asked.

Bhanu shook her head. "I would've just wasted it. Now it will help Babu and me have a better life. He has a good business but this is . . . Do you think I should send a letter to them saying thank you?"

"I don't think it's necessary," Kokila said. "In my opinion, the man doesn't deserve thanks. He did this, I think, to assuage his guilt for turning Ravi and Chetana out of his house. If he was truly penitent, he would've accepted Chetana and you and Meena after Ravi died. But he has chosen to not accept you as his granddaughter. Just take the money, make good use of it, and be happy."

"I'll keep it just as is and not tell Babu about it," Bhanu said. "I'll save it for a rainy day. Do you think that would be wise?"

"I think so," Kokila said, impressed with the maturity Bhanu was showing all of a sudden. "Do you think you'll be happy with Babu?"

Bhanu nodded eagerly. "I like him. I know he's not young and handsome, but I don't want that. I want a man who loves me. No, I want a man who worships me and will take good care of me. Babu will do that. I'm not going to spend my life waiting for a prince to ride down on a white horse to sweep me away. I'm not going to end up like *her,* sitting in Tella Meda, going out with men like Srinivas and having no home of my own."

"Chetana did the best she could," Kokila said in defense of her friend.

"She made mistakes," Bhanu said firmly. "I won't make mistakes."

When it was time for Bhanu to leave for her husband's house, she had tears in her eyes. She hadn't thought she would cry but suddenly she was swamped with sadness. She knew she would miss Tella Meda; she would miss Renuka, Chetana, even Meena. Now that she was leaving she could be benevolent. She even touched Charvi's feet on her way out, something she'd never done in her entire life. She was just sixteen and she had achieved the one thing her mother had never been able to do: she was leaving Tella Meda, forever.

"She is getting away," Chetana said as she wiped her tears after

Bhanu left. "Oh, Kokila, did you ever think that I'd have children who would grow up so much that they would get married?"

"Someday Karthik will grow up and get married too," Kokila said as she watched her son bounce around the courtyard.

"You let him marry whomever he wants and accept his wife, okay?" Chetana said, and Kokila smiled.

"He's too small for me to worry about the kind of woman he marries," Kokila said.

Chetana shook her head. "One minute they're born and the next they're grown up. I think Bhanu was lying about being pregnant."

Kokila was shocked. "How do you know?"

"She had bleeding last week, I think. She's cunning, that girl," Chetana said. "And Babu, they say he takes pictures of naked women in that studio of his."

"Maybe you should heed your own advice and accept whomever your daughter has married," Kokila said.

Renuka was sobbing quietly in the courtyard, sitting by the *tulasi* plant.

"She's sadder than I am," Chetana whispered to Kokila.

"She raised Bhanu," Kokila said, and Chetana nodded.

Whether she liked it or not, and she didn't like it at all, Chetana knew she had abandoned Bhanu as a baby and Renuka had picked up the responsibility. Chetana had always looked at Renuka with disdain, as a woman who stole her child, but now that Bhanu was gone maybe it was time she forgave Renuka for something she herself had forced her to do.

"It's okay," Chetana said going over and putting her arm around Renuka. "She lives close by, almost next door, she'll come and visit often."

Renuka looked up at Chetana and fresh tears started to roll down her cheeks. "She is like a daughter to me," she said.

"And you are like a mother to her," Chetana said as emotions choked her as well. She hugged Renuka close and they mourned the loss of their daughter.

5 March 1990. The Indian Government announced interim relief of 3.6 billion *rupees* to half a million victims of the 1984 Bhopal gas tragedy.

20 October 1990. The Andhra Pradesh government declared a five-day work week for all offices and educational institutions starting November 1, 1990.

The
Actress

*I*t was unimaginable that Subhadra would leave Tella Meda. She had been like the house, solid, never needing any repairs, self-sufficient and irreplaceable. She had been with Charvi for forty years now, a lifetime really, but at the age of seventy, she was starting to feel tired and burdened by the chores at Tella Meda. That didn't mean she relinquished control of her domain freely to Sushila without a grudge. Subhadra liked Sushila very much and in the three years since she had come to Tella Meda Sushila had become just as much of a permanent fixture as Subhadra had been.

"She doesn't make the *pulusu* the way we do," Subhadra confided in Kokila as she packed her things in two big black metal trunks and one big suitcase. "She doesn't cut the ladyfingers properly. They get sticky if you don't cut them correctly. And she has no idea of how to make *chakli* properly. She puts too much chili powder in the batter. I don't feel right about leaving like this."

Kokila had heard that long-term prisoners when freed had trouble adjusting to the idea of the world outside. They preferred to stay in prison rather than go out and live with real people in the real world. Subhadra was trying to find reasons to stay in Tella Meda rather than leave.

The telegram had come a month ago, announcing the death of Subhadra's husband, and her decision to leave had been made instantly, but the planning and procrastination had been constant. Subhadra missed the funeral of her husband but she didn't feel right showing up there in white when it was her sister who was really the widow. Her sister was the one, after all, who had stayed with Shiva for a good forty years. She had borne him children and had taken care of him when his health went bad. Subhadra had done none of that.

Subhadra phoned Chandra from Dr. Vishnu Mohan's house as soon as she got the telegram. Her usually calm and in-control sister was weeping openly, sobbing uncontrollably; she was completely devastated. "Come home, Akka," she pleaded. "I can't live here all alone."

It wasn't as though Subhadra didn't want to leave; she was excited about living with her sister and sharing her life. There would be children and grandchildren who would visit and she would be part of a real family again. And since Shiva was dead, Subhadra didn't have to feel uncomfortable about his presence. It was the perfect setup. Subhadra was thrilled that her sister needed her, but she wasn't sure what to expect.

"What if they don't take care of me?" she asked about Chandra's son, Madhu, and his wife, Harini, who lived with Chandra.

"They will," Kokila assured Subhadra. "Harini is devoted to Chandra and does everything according to her mother-in-law's wishes. And Madhu is a good boy. They'll take very good care of you."

Subhadra nodded as she dropped another stack of *saris* into the trunk. "I have missed her and it will be nice to live with her again, like when we were growing up."

"It will be very good for you. We will miss you here . . . I will miss you very much," Kokila said. "You have been . . ." She paused and bit back the tears. "Like a mother."

Subhadra came to Kokila and hugged her, crying herself.

"Can you come with me to Tirupati?" Subhadra asked when she drew away. "I'm scared of going alone. Chandra said she would send Madhu but that boy is probably devastated because of his father's death. I don't want him to have to come all the way here to accompany an old lady."

Kokila hesitated. She had a son now; life wasn't as flexible as it used to be.

"You can leave Karthik for a few days with Shanthi," Subhadra coaxed because Kokila looked so stricken. "Nothing will happen to him if you go away for a few days."

"I know," Kokila said in a low voice. "I have never been away for a night from him. And—"

"Please, Kokila," Subhadra said, and Kokila sighed. This woman had been like a mother, always there, always understanding, and now she needed something.

"I'll come," Kokila said with a smile. "You don't have to say please. I'll get one more ticket. But I can't stay there long. Just two, three days and then I will come back to Tella Meda. Okay?"

The day before Subhadra left everyone gathered to wish her a safe journey and bid her good-bye. There were tears and hugs, gifts and pieces of memories. It was a sad time at Tella Meda. Even Charvi had tears in her eyes. Subhadra had always been by her side, her strongest devotee and supporter. There would be a hole in her heart, Charvi told Subhadra, when she left because when Subhadra left she would take a piece of Charvi's life with her.

For Subhadra it was an affirmation that she had been a useful member of the Tella Meda family. Shanthi stitched several blouses for her, for free, and made some pillow covers to take for Chandra as a gift. Sushila, though she had been at Tella Meda the shortest, had become quite close to Subhadra because of working with her in the kitchen every day. She was dismayed that Subhadra would leave.

"I can't find the ingredients sometimes and if you aren't there . . ." Sushila hugged Subhadra and wept. It was a surprise to see her so emotional because Sushila was a no-nonsense person who did a good job in the kitchen and raised her daughter with a strict eye. No one had ever seen her get sentimental over anything and Puttamma always said there was something wrong with Sushila because she didn't even cry when she chopped onions.

The train journey to Tirupati was a difficult one. It was terribly hot that summer of 1990 and patches of sweat appeared on women's blouses, in the back, the underarms, right under the breasts. Thighs stuck to each other underneath light cotton *saris* and petticoats. Rivulets of sweat formed patterns on men's shirts. The fans within the train compartments provided little surcease against the heat and Kokila had to buy a small battery-operated fan in Vijayawada to stick in front of her face and neck. Subhadra fanned herself with a coconut-straw fan she'd brought along from Tella Meda.

They bought water at every railway station to ward off thirst and whenever they could they bought and drank coconut water. The ladies' compartment was packed and Subhadra and Kokila had to sit in the general second-class compartment. The train was crowded but at least now the new regulations had created a third-class compartment with sitting room only, while in the second-class compartments only those who booked a berth could lie down. A young couple was in the berths across from Subhadra and Kokila. They seemed to be newly married.

Subhadra took to clearing her throat when the couple appeared to forget that there were no doors to lock in a second-class compartment and people were sitting on the other side where they could see the obscene display of young love.

"I have seen men like him but that girl, *chee-chee,* she just doesn't seem to be able to keep her hands to herself," Subhadra whispered to Kokila when the young girl snuggled up to her husband and thought she was discreetly touching his crotch.

"Maybe they are not even married," the woman who had the window berth on the other side of the aisle told Subhadra. She was traveling with her young son, who slept all through the journey in the berth above his mother's.

"You think so? Not even married?" Subhadra asked, and then raised her eyebrows. "Some people have no shame."

They reached Tirupati at eight the next morning. The train was only one hour late. Both Kokila and Subhadra were tired and haggard after the sleepless night.

Madhu and Chandra were waiting at the train station to receive them. Chandra hugged Subhadra close and burst into tears while Madhu nodded toward Kokila and asked about Charvi's health. His wife, Harini, was at home because their younger son was sick, he said, otherwise they all would have come to receive them.

This time there were no rickshaws waiting to take them to Chandra's home. Chandra proudly introduced Subhadra and Kokila to her son's brand-new red Maruti 800. (Well, it was not really brand-new; it was used and about three years old, but it had never been in an accident so it was almost as good as new.)

"Turn on the AC, Madhu," Chandra instructed as soon as they got into the car. "Usually we don't turn on the AC. It takes up too much petrol, but for you, I think we definitely should."

Subhadra was terribly impressed. "So Madhu is doing well, is he?" she asked Chandra in a whisper.

Kokila was sitting in the front with Madhu while Subhadra and Chandra were sitting in the backseat. The car was quite small, especially compared to Manikyam's Ambassador, the only car besides taxis Kokila had ever been in. So even though Subhadra was whispering in the back, both Kokila and Madhu could hear her clearly in the front.

"He just became bank manager here. He is so young too," Chandra said proudly. "Doing very well. This car, he bought with all his money. Saved one *lakh* of *rupees* and bought the car."

"It was only eighty thousand *rupees*," Madhu told Kokila in a low voice. "She likes to say one *lakh* because it sounds better. And it isn't a new car. Three years old, that's why it was only eighty."

Kokila smiled at him. "I think you should be proud. Not everyone has a car, you know. I know only one or two people who have their own cars."

If Chandra was proud of her son and the car, Madhu's wife was downright snobbish about it. Her eldest son was now twelve and the youngest one was eight.

"I heard Chetana had a daughter," Harini said while Kokila sat in the kitchen with her to help with cooking. "She didn't tonsure her head, I remember. I had a son because Madhu did what he promised to do at Tirumala. It's all fate anyway. So, do you have any children? Marriage?"

Kokila nodded, too proud of Karthik to hide him away from the world. "I adopted a boy, Karthik. He's at Tella Meda now and I miss him very much. He's just three years old. Do you want to see a photo?" Before Harini could say yes or no, Kokila pulled out a photo from her purse. "Isn't he beautiful?" she asked.

"Yes, he is," Harini said uncomfortably. "Adoption? But you don't know what kind of blood is in the boy. It could be dangerous."

Kokila put the photo away immediately, angry and ready to jump to Karthik's defense. "What could be dangerous?"

Harini shrugged and laughed nervously, realizing that she had hurt Kokila.

"He is very beautiful," Harini said instead and then changed the subject. "I thought I will make mango *pappu* today. It's so hot, isn't it?"

Kokila stayed for two days only. She had a return ticket but Subhadra surprised her by changing it.

"First class? No, no, Subhadra," Kokila said. "I can't take it. First class is so expensive."

"It's a gift from Chandra and me," Subhadra said. "You came all this way to give me company and I want you to go back comfortably. You will be in a two-berth coupe and if there is another passenger, it will be a woman. It will be nice. Don't say no. This is my way of saying thank you. And you are like my daughter. Daughters shouldn't say no to their mothers."

Kokila had not been in trains often and she definitely had never been in the first-class compartment. The seats were made of gray leather and the maroon floors were actually clean. Each compartment had a door that could be shut and locked from the inside for privacy. Even the bathrooms at the end of the compartment were clean and shiny.

Kokila had the bottom berth but even if she had the top berth the rule was that she could sit down and look out of the window until after dinner. In any case, it wasn't always that both berths were taken. She could travel all the way to Visakhapatnam alone in the compartment and that thought perked her up immensely.

Even though she had been very reluctant to go, sure that she would miss Karthik too much, it had been nice to change the rhythm of her life. She constantly thought about Karthik and wanted nothing more than to feel his chubby arms go around her and to hear him talk, tell her about his day and kiss her. Still, it was good to have done something away from Tella Meda. It was nice to sleep through the night without Karthik waking up because of a nightmare or asking for water.

She thought about Subhadra and hoped that she would be happy with Chandra and her son. They seemed eager to please Subhadra and treated her with great respect. It hadn't sunk in yet but Kokila was sure that once she was in Tella Meda she would start to feel Subhadra's absence. In the beginning it would be painful and then slowly the pain would fade away. She wondered if she would ever leave Tella Meda. Maybe once Karthik grew up, she could go and live with him and his family. She would cook good meals for Karthik and his wife and his children, take care of them. She would make sure she got along well with her daughter-in-law. She wouldn't be like Manikyam and Chetana, fighting all the time. She would be her daughter-in-law's friend. Oh and she would have grandchildren now, she thought with a smug smile.

Right before the train left the Tirupati railway station the door to Kokila's compartment opened and her hope that she would have the coupe all to herself was crushed.

A woman wearing stylish sunglasses and smelling of sweet perfume stepped in. A coolie was behind her and she instructed him to put her suitcase underneath the berth. She carried a beautiful sequined black purse from which she pulled out a few *rupees* to give to the coolie.

She looked familiar, Kokila thought, but she couldn't place her. The woman had a big leather bag with her, the same color as her flesh-colored high-heeled sandals. She sighed as she sat down on the berth next to Kokila and opened her bag to drop the black purse in and bring out a bottle of water. She drank the water thirstily and put the bottle back in the bag.

"It's so hot, isn't it?" she said to no one in general. "Are you going all the way to Visakhapatnam?" she asked Kokila as she took off her sunglasses.

Kokila nodded with a tight smile. Where had she seen this woman before?

"I think I have the top berth," the woman said, and sighed again. "It was on such short notice that they couldn't find me anything else."

Kokila nodded again. She had heard this woman's voice before as well, she was certain of it. She just couldn't remember from where and when.

The woman pulled out a glossy magazine from her bag and put it beside her. Kokila looked at the magazine cover and then at the woman. Everything fell into place. This was Sharada, the legendary Neeraja from movies such as *Manchimanusu, Chinnawadu,* and others. Kokila had seen several of her movies, but she looked different on film, less stylish, because she always played the role of a traditional woman. The real woman wore a starched cotton *sari* in vibrant gold and red. She had a slim gold watch on one wrist while a bunch of shiny gold bangles adorned the other.

There were three or four strands of gold chains around her neck and diamonds studded her earlobes. She must have been wearing makeup because her face was lighter than her neck and there was lipstick on her lips. She had dark *kajal* around her eyes and her eyelashes seemed to be artificially long and thick.

Kokila couldn't understand why Neeraja would wear makeup while traveling, especially in such heat, and why a rich woman such as Neeraja would travel in first class and not the comfortable and better air-conditioned compartment. Maybe she wasn't rich anymore. She was a yesteryear star. Now she did mother roles and bit parts in movies. She still was talked about in magazines, like the one Neeraja was reading herself, but the fire was gone from her stardom.

Kokila felt gauche with her white-and-green cotton *sari* and her slightly graying hair. Neeraja's hair was completely black and she was at least fifty years old. Kokila always braided her hair and now tried to discreetly look at Neeraja's stylish bun to see how it was done. When she had been young, Kokila had hardly bothered with her looks. Everyone could see that Chetana was the beautiful one, the attractive one. Kokila never wanted to compete, not that she could. Kokila's skin was not as fair as Chetana's. It was what was known as wheatish color in matrimonial descriptions and though her skin was smooth, wrinkles were starting to show. She wasn't young, she was forty years old now. Her hair was supposed to be graying and her skin was supposed to be folding. Yet Neeraja didn't seem to be having any of those problems. Her skin still looked smooth, probably because of all those creams and lotions actresses were rumored to use to keep their skin looking young, and her hair was glossy, not like the women Kokila saw in Bheemunipatnam who dyed their hair themselves and the strands became wiry and stringy.

In the magazines Puttamma made Chetana read out loud to her as she went about her chores at Tella Meda it said that Neeraja was having some serious marital problems. She was married to a fellow thespian, Suman Kiran, who was known for his emotional films from the sixties and seventies. Now he played older brother and father roles in movies but they were always meaty roles and he was well respected in the industry. The rumor was that either Suman Kiran was cheating on Neeraja with a young film actress or that he drank too much and beat up Neeraja. Kokila suddenly wished she had listened more carefully to Chetana and Puttamma's movie-star gossip.

She wondered with just a little glee what Chetana and Puttamma would make of her spending the night in the same compartment with Neeraja. They both would be red-hot jealous!

"So hot," Neeraja said again, and smiled at Kokila. "They didn't have any seats in the AC compartment. These producers, you know, they ask at the last minute if I'll come here or there. They're shooting in Visakhapatnam, an outdoor set, and Rama, Rama, sometimes I think I should retire and not run around like this."

Kokila wasn't sure if Neeraja was venting or showing off, so she decided to keep quiet and listen. It didn't seem as if Neeraja needed her to respond anyway.

Neeraja seemed nervous though as she flipped desultorily through the pages of the magazine, her light pink polished nails a blur as the pages moved.

"It's so hot, isn't it?" she said again and Kokila nodded again. "So, are you going all the way to Visakhapatnam?"

Kokila wanted to frown. Hadn't she just answered that question a while ago?

"Yes," Kokila said, and looked out of the window. The landscape had changed from city to suburb to farmland. Cattle were being herded home as the day was coming to an end and the sky was vermilion like the *bindi* on a bride's forehead. Women were carrying pots on their heads and people were soon silhouettes against the dying sun. How different it all was! From the city with its new cars and open sewers to the almost beatific farms and villages. Kokila loved to look out of the window when in a train. She wished she had traveled more, seen more. She had never even been to Hyderabad, the capital of Andhra Pradesh.

They said Hyderabad bustled with life and there were so many people there that the city never slept. Most people who lived in Hyderabad had their own cars, refrigerators, and VCRs.

It had taken a devotee's special donation to buy a fridge for Tella Meda two years ago. There had been so much debate about the fridge that ultimately Kokila and Sushila had had to make a unilateral decision. Subhadra couldn't imagine why Tella Meda needed a refrigerator and had fought it for years. The children complained there was never any ice cream and the water from the earthen pot was never cold enough but Subhadra wouldn't budge. She wasn't about to cave in on any newfangled technology. They had managed fine for many years without a fridge; there was no reason to get one now. Sushila's argument that vegetables stayed fresh in a refrigerator longer was thwarted by Subhadra's demand that vegetables be brought fresh every day. There was no need to let them lie in a fridge to become limp. And what with the current being taken off all the time, the food would spoil despite being in the fridge.

Finally, Kokila and Sushila, after getting Charvi's permission, ordered the fridge and had it installed, right in front of Subhadra's horrified eyes. Once the fridge was there, everyone became accustomed to it almost immediately and by the time Subhadra left Tella Meda even she couldn't remember how they had survived without it.

In Hyderabad and other big cities there was no such argument and debate over household appliances. People saw refrigerators as a necessity. They also had big color TVs with remote controls and women drove around on scooters, just like the men.

Maybe someday she could go to Hyderabad too, Kokila thought, maybe not to visit, but to live. She and Karthik could have their own home with a TV and a fridge and everything else everyone in the big city had. When Karthik grew up . . . oh, who knew what he would become. Maybe he would live in Hyderabad, maybe Bombay or Delhi or some other big city. Or maybe he would go to America like so many Indians were doing these days. And Kokila would go live with him, in a big city in America.

As Kokila daydreamed, the sun set completely, leaving behind dark patches of night outside the train compartment's window. A knock on the compartment door reminded her again of her famous companion. Neeraja was still leafing through her magazine.

The ticket collector saw Neeraja and started to stammer, telling her how much he loved her movies and how he had watched a certain film more than fifteen times. Neeraja was charming and smiled often at the compliments and seemed quite humble about the praise. The conductor even forgot to ask either of them for their ticket and left with a big smile on his face. It wasn't every day that you got to speak with your favorite movie star while you were at work.

"They are always so nice—fans, you know," Neeraja said, and smiled at Kokila. "I have brought dinner with me. I can't eat this train food. I fall sick and I can't afford to fall sick. Would you like to join me?"

Kokila wanted to say yes. Imagine the stories she could tell about

eating the same food as Neeraja, with Neeraja. But she was too reserved for this kind of intimacy with a stranger.

"I brought my own," she said. Harini had packed a tiffin carrier for
Kokila with curd rice, tamarind rice, a few *chapattis*, some *bhindi* curry,
sambhar, and mango pickle. In a separate tiffin box, she had even
packed some *kesari* so that Kokila would have something sweet to eat
during her journey.

"Oh," Neeraja said. "Maybe we can eat together."

It would be rude to say otherwise and Kokila was starstruck
enough to want to eat with Neeraja. They brought their food out and
in companionable silence ate what they had.

Kokila eyed what looked like chicken in Neeraja's tiffin carrier sur-
reptitiously. Tella Meda was strictly vegetarian and Kokila had never
touched any kind of meat. Sitting this close to a piece of chicken
made her uncomfortable.

But Neeraja wasn't a Brahmin and she was wealthy, so it was obvious that she would eat meat, Kokila told herself.

After dinner they went to the bathroom one after the other to
wash their hands. Neeraja had brought some nice-smelling soap and
she offered it to Kokila for use after she was done.

The soap smelled of sandalwood and Kokila was impressed with
Neeraja's generosity. Here was Kokila, a veritable stranger, yet Neeraja had offered her food and soap. She seemed like a nice woman.

"I can't sleep these days," Neeraja confided in Kokila. "Do you
mind sleeping up so that I can stay down? If you can't, that's no—"

"Okay," Kokila said immediately. "Do you want me to go now?"

"No, no, whenever you're ready to go to sleep," Neeraja said with
a smile. "Thank you very much."

Kokila nodded. So this was why she offered food and soap, so that
she could get the bottom berth, she thought cynically.

"My husband says I talk too much," Neeraja said all of a sudden.
"I think I do. I have been talking and talking and you haven't said anything."

Kokila cleared her throat. What did Neeraja want her to say?

"So, where are you from?" Neeraja asked.

"My people are from a village near Simhachalam and now I live in Bheemunipatnam," Kokila said.

"So, your husband is not with you today?" Neeraja asked.

Kokila wanted to squirm. At Tella Meda no one asked such questions and she had little interaction with people from the outside world. Yet it was a pertinent question.

"Not married," Kokila said.

"Oh," Neeraja said, her tone suddenly accusatory and full of pity at the same time. "You've never been married?"

Kokila shrugged. "Long time ago. But I was just thirteen then."

"So, what happened?"

Kokila shrugged again. "He is now married to someone else, has kids and everything. I have a son, he is adopted, but he is my son. My Karthik. Would you like to see a photo?"

Neeraja agreed enthusiastically and made all the appropriate sounds when she saw Karthik's picture. He was so beautiful. He was so fair. Such a wonderful-looking boy. That smile of his . . . it was just so warm and loving. Anyone could see he was intelligent.

"I can't have children," Neeraja said after she returned Karthik's picture to Kokila. "In the beginning, I was so young, I made some mistakes and . . . you won't tell anyone, will you?" Kokila shook her head in earnest and Neeraja continued. "This is a bad business, the film industry and I made some mistakes. I had two abortions before I was even twenty and the doctor did something wrong. Now I can't have children."

"Oh," Kokila said. "I'm so sorry."

Neeraja's eyes were filled with tears. "So you live on your own with your son?"

Kokila then told Neeraja about Tella Meda. She listened in fascination.

"Do you think I could come there?" she asked. "Could I stay there for a few days? My shoot is only for two or three days in Visakhapatnam and I don't have anything lined up for . . . oh, months now. And I would love to meet Charvi. My life is in such chaos these days that . . . Do you think Charvi would maybe be able to help me? Maybe I could stay for a few days. What do you think?"

Kokila could only hope that a celebrity such as Neeraja would grace Tella Meda. It would be a matter of such pride and everyone would know that Neeraja was in Tella Meda because of Kokila, not Charvi. Even though she would never voice her feelings, Kokila was in awe of Neeraja. This was a movie actress and a part of Kokila wanted to jump up and down and tell everyone that she was talking to Neeraja, eating with Neeraja, and sleeping in the same compartment as her. And Neeraja had told her a secret about her two abortions before she turned twenty.

They talked late into the night. Kokila did most of the listening, greedily soaking in every word Neeraja uttered so that she could tell Shanthi and Chetana about it later on. It wasn't like her, she knew, but this was different. This was a famous movie actress who was baring her heart to Kokila.

"Suman is nice, but he is still a *man*," Neeraja said with a small laugh. "Do you mind if I change into my nightie? I am always more comfortable in that at night."

Kokila nodded and buried her nose in the magazine Neeraja had brought with her. She could hear the *sari* come off and fall next to her. The blouse followed. There was a rustle here and a rustle there.

"All done," Neeraja said with a smile as she started to fold her *sari*. She now wore a lime green nightie with smocking on the top decorated with tiny pink flowers. She even had a robe to go with the nightie; it was also lime green and had smocking on the pockets and the waist where a button held the lapels of the robe together. It was made of light cotton and filled the compartment with the smell of newness and jasmine.

"So, what were we talking about?" Neeraja asked as she sat down, her legs crossed. She looked like a little girl, eager for more conversation as if it were sweets.

"Ah . . . you were saying something about your husband," Kokila prompted. She felt silly. She was forty years old and here she was blushing like a schoolgirl because a movie actress was speaking with her. And she wanted to know more about Neeraja's husband, Neeraja's life.

Chetana would rattle on and on about the lives of movies actors and actresses that she read about in gossip and movie magazines. They had big mansions and big cars. Women smoked and drank and cavorted shamelessly with men. All actresses had to sleep with producers and directors to get movie roles. They were all unsubstantiated rumors but generally were accepted as fact.

"Ah, Suman," Neeraja said, and then sighed. "You know how it is. He is a major character actor now, big-name star, and he has power. You know how it is."

Kokila nodded vaguely. How would she know how it was?

"He has so many contacts and he owns a big part of Arpita Studios, so they all listen to him," Neeraja said bitterly. "He sleeps with all the young actresses. They know they have to if they want the roles in movies he produces. And he is shameless about it. Everyone in the business is shameless about it. They say it's cleaner in Bombay with Hindi movies . . . I don't think so. I think it is all bad. Filthy. Filthy. Filthy."

Kokila licked her lips, not wanting to say what she was thinking, but she couldn't help herself. "If it's so filthy, why are you still in it?"

Neeraja sighed again. "I have nothing else to do and one has to earn a living."

"But you must have lots of money and your husband is rich. Why should you work for a living?" Kokila asked boldly.

"You are so naive," Neeraja said with a small smile. "I have to live like a movie star and that costs money. I have a lot of money but I need to make sure I have enough for later on. And Suman's money is his money. We don't have that kind of marriage. We . . . Actually, we're getting divorced. Suman wants to marry . . ." Her voice choked up and tears filled her eyes. "He wants to marry that new actress, Vaijayanthi. That whore slept with half of Hyderabad and now he wants to marry her. We were married for twenty years, and now he wants children, he says. She can give them to him, he says. So I have to work and make some money. Otherwise what will happen to me in my old age? I don't want to be like Savitri, old and poor with no one to take care of me. It's so sad, isn't it, Kokila?"

Husbands leaving wives and marrying younger women who slept

around . . . Kokila wasn't sure if she was listening to the story line of a bad Telugu movie or real life.

"And now I'm playing mother roles. It's just so hard," Neeraja said, and started to weep openly.

After that the conversation was mostly about how terrible Neeraja's life was. She had a big house and a big car (several big cars, really) and lots of money, yet she claimed her life was pathetic and she just had to work for a living. All the awe Kokila had felt in talking to a movie actress faded into irritation as the night started to grow old. Finally, Kokila excused herself and went to the top berth and fell asleep, grateful not to hear about Neeraja's glamorous life anymore.

In the morning, Neeraja was dressed up and ready, as if she hadn't spent the night weeping and wailing. Her demeanor was stiff and she appeared not to want to have anything to do with Kokila.

When the train arrived at Visakhapatnam at six in the morning, Neeraja said a hasty good-bye while instructing a studio driver, who had come to the train station, to take her suitcase into the car. She didn't even offer Kokila a ride to the bus station or ask her anything else about Tella Meda and how she could come and visit.

By the time Kokila got home she had quite forgotten about Neeraja in her urgency to see Karthik again and hold his warm and soft body in her arms.

He came running to her as she walked into the courtyard, his little feet carrying him to her as fast as they could. Shanthi had dressed him in a pair of blue shorts and a white shirt. He looked like a little young man instead of a three-year-old boy.

"Oh, I missed you," Kokila said as she hugged him close and smelled Shanthi's Ponds powder on him. *My son*, she thought joyously.

"Amma, Shanthi said that we could make *ladoos* today because you were coming back," Karthik said. "And she said I can eat two *ladoos*. Can I eat two *ladoos*?"

He can do anything he wants to do, Kokila thought, *anything at all*.

"So, how was Subhadra doing when you dropped her off?" Chetana asked while they all got together to make *ladoos* in the kitchen that afternoon.

"Good. Chandra's son bought a car," Kokila said.

"Is it a Maruti? What color?" Chetana asked immediately.

"Red," Kokila said as she rolled the coconut, sugar, and fried flour mixture between the oiled palms of her hands.

"Karthik do it, Karthik do it," Karthik cried out, his hands dipping into the *ladoo* mixture, intent on making some *ladoos* himself.

Kokila gave him a small *ladoo* and he happily rolled it between the palms of his hands before tiring of the game, eating the *ladoo*, and then asking for more.

"Those cars are nice," Chetana said. "Not like those big, bulky, ugly Ambassadors. Premier Padminis are okay but Maruti, that's the car to have if you have to have a car."

"Right and you should talk about cars, our expert," Renuka piped up. She was sitting in a corner with a string of Rudrakasha beads, slipping one after the other between her fingers as she invoked the name of God. In between she would stop and tell everyone what she thought of them. Since Bhanu had left Renuka had become more and more ornery. She was waiting for Bhanu to get pregnant—the sooner the better, she thought, but Bhanu said they were being careful.

"I'm using birth control pills, we want to wait a while before we have children," she had announced to the scandalized Renuka. Women from good families didn't utter nonsense like that. Good girls got pregnant after marriage and that was that.

Chetana thought it was a sensible decision. Bhanu was a child herself and it would be good for her to grow up a little before having a baby. Bhanu had admitted easily and without any guilt that she had lied about being pregnant so that Chetana and Renuka would let her marry Babu. "As if I'd let him touch me before the marriage," she told Chetana a few weeks after the wedding. "You think he'd marry me then? Now he thinks when I let him do it that I'm doing him a big favor. And I don't let him do it every night. I think we can start with two or three times a week so that he doesn't get too used to it. What do you think, Amma?"

Chetana could only shake her head and wonder where Bhanu had learned such slyness. Whatever her reasons and methods, Bhanu's marriage to Babu appeared to be a happy one. Babu might take pictures of naked women for pornographic magazines but in reality he had eyes only for Bhanu. He brought her jewelry and *saris* and took her on vacation to Ooty and Goa. Every summer he would ask her where she would like to go and he would make it happen. Chetana had no complaints. It looked like her daughter had managed what she had been unable to do: find a husband who could afford to keep her happy.

"Srinivas is buying a car," Chetana said to Renuka. "A *blue* Maruti."

"So what if he's buying a car? He isn't your husband," Renuka said and muttered something under her breath that sounded a lot like "slut."

"Old woman, just sit with your Rudrakasha and don't worry about who's going to marry me," Chetana snapped at her, then turned toward the others. "So the car is going to have AC. And the windows, you don't have to roll them down. You press a button and they go down, whoosh, like magic."

"He must be doing very well if he can buy a car," Sushila said.

Chetana nodded with a broad smile. "All those tickets he sells on the black market, all that money he pockets."

"What a rogue, selling tickets illegally on the black market. If the cinema owners find out he'll lose his job," Renuka said.

"Everyone sells tickets like that," Chetana said. "It's good business sense. And Srinivas has made a lot of money with his good business sense. He's even thinking about building a house here."

"But is he thinking about marrying you?" Renuka asked.

Chetana sighed. "Maybe I am the one who doesn't want to marry him. Have you thought about that?"

"Why wouldn't you want to marry him? These days widows get married all the time and it isn't like you even dress like a widow," Renuka said.

"What is it with this old hag?" Chetana said angrily. "Always interested in my life and my children. Mind your own business, old woman."

"Ah . . . I met someone while I was coming back." Kokila changed the topic and when everyone looked at her expectantly, she told them.

"Neeraja? The actress? Really? Oh, I love her in *Chintamani*," Sushila said. "What was she like?"

Kokila frowned because she really couldn't describe what Neeraja was like. She told them what Neeraja had told her and how she seemed completely altered the next morning.

"Maybe she was drunk in the night," Chetana offered.

"No, no, she didn't have any alcohol with her and I would've smelled it," Kokila said. "It was very strange. One night she was friendly and nice and in the morning she was just cold."

"Maybe you said something to upset her," Renuka commented.

"Maybe you should shut up," Chetana snapped at Renuka. "She's just getting worse and worse. Mumbles to herself and—"

"She's just getting old," Shanthi said in a low voice and tossed a *ladoo* toward Karthik. He played with the *ladoo* for a moment before popping it into his mouth.

"He's not going to be able to eat any dinner," Kokila said as she wiped coconut crumbs from her son's face.

"So he won't," Shanthi said with a smile. "Once in a while you should eat just *ladoo* all day."

"Is Neeraja coming to Tella Meda?" Sushila asked eagerly.

"Why will she come? Kokila must've said something to insult her. That's why she didn't want to talk with her in the morning," Renuka said. "Mark my words, women who have no respect for tradition will all suffer in hell."

Everyone sighed and continued making the *ladoos* in silence.

A week later Neeraja showed up at Tella Meda in a big white Maruti 1000. She drove herself, which caused everyone to raise their eyebrows. It wasn't common, at least in Bheemunipatnam, to see women drive cars. Maybe in the big cities women were driving scooters and mopeds but in Bheemunipatnam, women walked or took the rickshaw or taxi and didn't go gallivanting around driving automobiles of any kind.

Neeraja was dressed in a light blue *salwar kameez* and looked ten years younger than her real age. She hugged a surprised Kokila as soon as she saw her.

"Oh, it's so good to see you," she said, and Kokila could only gape.

Sushila rushed into the kitchen to prepare fresh snacks and tea for the celebrity guest. Charvi was informed that Neeraja was in Tella Meda and had come to stay for a few days and had driven her car all by herself from Visakhapatnam to Bheemunipatnam.

Neeraja was polite and charming and answered everyone's questions about her movies and the actors and actresses she worked with.

"Kokila said this was a beautiful house and it is," Neeraja said. "And she said that you were a dear *guru*, a wonderful goddess," she said to Charvi, who lit up like Tella Meda on Diwali night.

Kokila had never said any such thing about Charvi to Neeraja, just that she was the *guru* of Tella Meda.

"Kokila is one of our longest-term residents," Charvi said. "And my favorite disciple."

Disciple? Kokila wasn't sure whom Charvi was talking about. And Charvi never called herself *guru* or those who lived in Tella Meda disciples.

Tella Meda was done up like a bride for the benefit of Neeraja. She helped cook in the kitchen, leaving Sushila speechless and prostrate in wonder. Shanthi couldn't help but be swept away. Bhanu came with Babu to see Neeraja but wasn't as much in awe as the others. Now if Amala or Ramya Krishna had been at Tella Meda, that would be different—they were her generation. This woman, she was old, and only other old people were interested in her.

The women of Tella Meda, however, did care. Even Puttamma spent her days at Tella Meda; thrilled beyond belief that Neeraja bothered to speak with her and even touched her hand. Puttamma was so humbled that she took a picture of Neeraja and put it along with the idols and photos of gods and goddesses in the small temple in her hut.

Charvi was acknowledging that she *was* a *guru* to Neeraja in front of everyone. No one seemed surprised or shocked the way Kokila was.

"My father, Ramanandam Sastri, he said he could see the goddess in me," Charvi told Neeraja in her soothing, musical voice. "And that's all I have ever known. I feel a light inside me, blazing fire sometimes, sometimes warm, but always present. I think that is the power of enlightenment."

Neeraja was taken with Charvi and thanked Kokila for opening this spiritual door for her. "My husband will be so pleased to see you," Neeraja said. "Next time, I will bring him along. He hates it when I go somewhere without him. You know how it is—after twenty years of marriage; you just get so used to each other that being apart is very difficult."

"I see so much happiness in your future," Charvi said.

"We never had children." Neeraja sighed. "But that was in God's hands. It hasn't mattered one bit to my Suman. We have each other, he says, and that's enough."

"You are so lucky to have a nice husband like that," Charvi told Neeraja.

Kokila wasn't sure who was the actress here, Charvi or Neeraja.

"She told me she and her husband were getting a divorce," Kokila said to Chetana.

"I told you she was drunk that night and that's why she was telling the truth. Now she's . . . Look at Charvi," Chetana urged with a broad grin. "She's holding her hand up and closing her eyes like she really is a goddess."

"Hush, the two of you," Shanthi said. She didn't quite believe that Charvi was a goddess but still respected her for her knowledge and kindness.

The three days Neeraja was at Tella Meda, Charvi transformed from somber lady of the house to transcendental goddess. She talked about God and how he spoke with her; she talked about how she had healing powers; she talked about how she could see the future. No one seemed surprised by the change in her and accepted it as a special situation because Neeraja was there.

And Neeraja transformed from the weepy woman in the first-class compartment to a happy actress who had a wonderful family life.

The evening before she was to leave, Neeraja came to Kokila's room while everyone was congregated in the TV room.

"You must think I'm a total fake," Neeraja said sheepishly as soon as she stepped into Kokila's room. She looked around and nodded uncomfortably. "It's a nice room. My room is nicer, though."

"We save the front rooms for guests," Kokila said. "You can sit if you like." She pointed to a wooden rocking chair she had acquired after she got Karthik.

"Am I waking him up?" Neeraja asked, looking at Karthik, who was fast asleep in Kokila's bed. After Karthik had come to Tella Meda Kokila got rid of her old metal cot and bought a bigger wooden bed with a good mattress. It would have cost a fortune but the owner of the furniture shop gave her a discount because the bed had been returned by a customer and because he was a devotee of Charvi. The bed was big enough for Karthik and Kokila to sleep in, with plenty of room for Karthik to play in the bed when he woke up in the morning.

"No, he sleeps like a log. He plays hard all day and then collapses," Kokila said.

"Is he starting school soon?" Neeraja asked.

Kokila nodded. "Next year. Nothing great here, you know, as it's a small town, but it's a good school and Sushila's daughter Padma and Chetana's daughter Meena are doing well there. They both want to become doctors."

Neeraja wasn't listening to her, Kokila realized. She was staring at the courtyard through the window.

"I don't want anyone to know about my problems. I don't know why I told you, but I hope you won't tell anyone," Neeraja said.

"Well some people at Tella Meda already know. I told them. I didn't think you would be coming," Kokila said defensively. "But whom else would I tell? And who would believe me?" *Especially after your performance,* Kokila wanted to add.

Neeraja shifted uneasily. "I mean the magazines. I don't want you to tell them what I told you about my past and my marriage. Look, I know I made a mistake in telling you too much. I should have kept my mouth shut but I was just so depressed and . . . Look, if you want some money, I can help. I—"

"I won't tell any magazines anything," Kokila said in disgust. "Now, if you could leave? I have a long day tomorrow."

Neeraja nodded and bit her upper lip nervously. "I didn't mean to insult you just now. I . . . I was planning to leave money for Tella Meda, but maybe I could just give it to you."

"You don't have to bribe me. I don't have any interest in talking to magazines about your sordid little life," Kokila said in exasperation. "You know what your problem is? You've forgotten how to be normal, just a regular person and not an actress."

Neeraja smiled then. "Everyone is always acting, don't ever forget that. Your Charvi is putting on a good act about being a goddess. See, we all do what we have to do to survive. Haven't you ever acted and become someone else to get what you wanted?"

Kokila thought back and came up empty. "No," she said triumphantly. "Unlike you and Charvi, I don't need to act to survive. I have more honest means."

"Living off charity? Is that what you're calling honest?" Neeraja demanded softly. "You're just as much a party to Charvi's acting as she is because you live off her acting. Look, I don't want to hurt your feelings or insult you or any of that. I like you. That's why I told you those things in the train. I just want to leave some money. Can I do that?"

"It would be better if you gave it to Charvi," Kokila said.

Neeraja then leaned down to kiss Karthik's cheek. "He is beautiful. Maybe I should think about adopting too."

"Maybe you should," Kokila said, even though she was unable to imagine how a woman who appeared to be as selfish as Neeraja could ever give a big part of herself away to a child.

"I think I'll come back here. Even though she acts a little, there is something inside her, isn't there?" Neeraja said.

Kokila nodded. "Yes, there is. She has a good heart and above all that is most important."

"Well, I should go. They have rented a VCR and a movie of mine," Neeraja said with a gleam in her eye. "Even though I am growing old,

I can watch the old movies and remember my youth. It's like I can become young again. I love these videotapes and the VCR. I can watch my movies all the time, if I want."

And she was chirpy again as she went to the TV room, excited about her movie.

Kokila left Karthik to sleep and joined the others to watch Neeraja become young again in a movie made a long time ago.

21 May 1991. Rajiv Gandhi, former Indian prime minster (1984–89), was assassinated by a suicide bomber. The assassination was rumored to be plotted by the Liberation Tigers of Tamil Eelam (LTTE), a separatist group.

Of Bombs
and Bullets

*T*hey killed him, they killed him," Padma said as she came running from the TV room into the courtyard.

"Who died?" Chetana asked, bleary-eyed. She had just woken up and was nursing a cup of coffee.

"A bomb exploded and he's dead," Meena said as she came running as well.

"This is what comes of letting them watch too much TV," Renuka said to Sushila. It was seven in the morning and the girls had made it a habit to watch the morning news while they ate breakfast before heading to school.

Puttamma was sweeping the courtyard and pointed a finger at Meena. "I heard too. Some LTTE people killed Rajiv Gandhi."

"Killed him?" Kokila said in surprise. "How?"

"Rajiv Gandhi? Dead?" Chetana seemed to wake up a little.

"A bomb, they say," Meena said. "A bomb went off and he's dead. They are showing it on TV."

Everyone rushed into the TV room and listened and watched the news in silence.

"Does this mean Doordarshan is going into mourning again?" Puttamma asked.

"At least ten days," Padma said. "He was once PM."

"True," Meena said, and sighed. "Ah, well, maybe we can rent the VCR and watch some movies on Sunday. Amma?"

"We'll talk about Sunday later on," Chetana said as she turned the television off. "Why don't you both go out and wait for your rickshaw?"

Padma and Meena shared a rickshaw with another girl their age, Ramya, who lived down the street. Since Padma and Meena were doing well in school, a lot of parents overlooked the fact that they lived in Tella Meda and allowed their children to associate with them in the hopes that some of Padma's and Meena's intelligence would rub off on their kids as well.

The rickshaw picked them up at 7:30 AM and got them to school ten minutes before the morning assembly began at eight. And then the rickshaw brought them home by 4:20 PM. If they were even five minutes late coming home from school, Sushila would start pacing the road watching for them. Chetana tried to tell Sushila that she worried too much but Sushila shut her up by making an oblique remark about Chetana's bad parenting skills.

The television was left turned on almost all day as news about Rajiv Gandhi's death came pouring in.

"Poor wife of his. First they killed his brother, then his mother, and now him," Charvi said sadly as she sat with the others in the TV room. "Tonight we will have a special *bhajan* and pray that his wife and children have peace and his spirit meets with his mother's."

"You think his wife will go back to Italy now?" Shanthi wondered. "Why would she stay in India?"

"Because of her children," Sushila said. "Her children are Indian and so what if she is Italian? Sonia Gandhi looks Indian enough to me."

"No, she doesn't," Chetana said. "Look at how pale her skin is!"

"Your skin would also be pale if your husband just died," Puttamma said.

"My husband did die and my skin never went that pale," Chetana snapped at her.

"Hush, we're trying to listen to the news," Meena and Padma both cried out in unison.

Bhanu, who was now five months pregnant, came to Tella Meda every morning after Babu left for the photo studio and went back in the evening when it was time for him to come home. She started crying as she watched images of Rajiv Gandhi's wife, Sonia Gandhi, wearing dark glasses on TV.

"The poor woman," she wailed. "What would I do if someone killed Babu? Oh, Amma, those poor children have no father now."

"But they have lots of money," Chetana said, uncomfortable with Bhanu being quite so emotional. Ever since she got pregnant Bhanu had softened considerably and Chetana couldn't stand that she cried all the time.

"What good is money if your husband is dead?" Renuka said.

"I'd rather have money than a husband," Chetana said, and sighed. "Now I have neither."

Soon details about the bombing started to filter in. A woman named Dhanu, whose photograph was shown constantly on TV, had been the human bomb that detonated next to Rajiv Gandhi.

"She touched his feet and then as he was lifting her up she turned the bomb on," Padma explained during dinner. "Her severed head is what they used to identify her."

"And all the pictures we see," Meena said, "those are taken of her severed head."

"We're eating, Padma, Meena," Sushila admonished. "Talking of bombs and bullets and severed heads . . . what has this world come to?"

"It is bad times, Sushila Amma," and Narayan Garu, who rarely spoke. "But I must say I support the LTTE on this matter. If Rajiv

Gandhi had become PM again the Sri Lankan Tamils would suffer more."

It wasn't that Narayan Garu was talking that was the most shocking, it was that he held political opinions. He was the only male left in Tella Meda besides Karthik. He stayed in his room most of the day and puttered around the garden with Puttamma's son, Balaji, who was the official Tella Meda gardener. He was a conscientious boy and seemed to have a lot of patience with Narayan Garu, who at eighty was getting crankier about the garden.

"The LTTE is a terrorist organization," Meena said immediately. She had been reading the newspaper and watching the news regularly, and she and Padma had discussed the matter at length.

"What do you know about anything?" Chetana said. The girls were all of twelve years old and they talked as if they knew everything. *But what does that Narayan Garu know either, the old man? He should just shut up and eat his food,* she thought as she watched Meena and Padma glare at Narayan Garu mutinously.

"They are not terrorists," Narayan Garu said, his voice actually rising. "Wait here."

He washed his hands in his half-eaten plate and went toward his room.

"Meena, he's an old man, don't agitate him," Chetana said.

"I think the girls should be allowed to voice their opinion," Sushila countered. "It's good for them to have opinions. So tell me, Padma, what is this LTTE all about?"

Padma cleared her throat as if getting ready for an oral exam. "The Liberation Tigers of Tamil Eelam were founded in 1975 to win the freedom of the Sri Lankan Tamils from the Sri Lankan government. The organization was started because Tamils started to feel that they needed to use nonpeaceful measures to gain independence from Sri Lanka."

Meena cleared her throat next and got ready to impart the rest of what they knew about the LTTE.

When she had gone to school, they never came back knowing so much about the world around them, Kokila thought. And then she looked at Karthik, who was playing with a piece of ladyfinger on his plate, and wondered how much more he would know than she did.

"Their leader is a man called Velupillai Prabhakaran and they say he has died *several* times. He's a difficult man to kill and people have tried very hard but he keeps surviving," Meena said. "Our social studies teacher told us that because Rajiv Gandhi sent Indian peacekeeping forces to Jaffna when he was prime minister, the LTTE is angry with him. They were probably afraid that he would become PM again, and why wouldn't he considering how badly VP Singh has done? That's why LTTE killed him."

Narayan Garu came back with several pamphlets in his hands. "Here, see this," he said, and put them down in front of Meena and Padma, who were sitting next to each other. "This is what Rajiv Gandhi did to the Sri Lankan Tamils."

Meena and Padma both glanced at the pamphlets and nodded in tandem. "These look like propaganda pamphlets. The LTTE are known to use brainwashing techniques to recruit new members for their organization."

"These pamphlets tell the truth," Narayan Garu said, and spit flew from his mouth as he spoke. "Charvi, tell them, you know."

Charvi looked up from her food, surprised that someone was talking to her.

"What?" she asked, not having followed the conversation.

"The LTTE is helping Tamils," Narayan Garu said. "Tell these girls that."

"The LTTE is helping Tamils? Okay," Charvi said, and shrugged when Narayan Garu made a sound of protest. "Narayan Garu, I don't know anything about politics and it is beyond me. You should sit down and not get so agitated. It isn't good at your age."

"LTTE have assassinated many Sri Lankan leaders and so many Tamils have had to leave Sri Lanka to live in refugee camps since this civil war began," Meena said. "Violence is not how problems are solved."

"What would you know, you chit of a disrespectful girl?" Narayan Garu thundered. "How dare you go against what I say?"

Meena and Padma looked at Narayan Garu, unperturbed by his

anger. "We believe what we believe, and you believe what you believe," Padma said. "Our teacher said that people are divided about Rajiv Gandhi's assassination, but you have to admit that it wasn't right to kill the man."

Narayan Garu looked in disgust at everyone sitting at the table and walked into his room.

"Next time don't get into a debate with him," Charvi instructed with a smile on her face. "He's old and he's not going to change."

"Then he shouldn't try to change us," Meena pointed out.

Charvi nodded. "But he's set in his ways. You have to be the older one here and let him say what he wants."

Narayan Garu passed away that night in his room. Dr. Vishnu Mohan and the new local doctor, Dr. Lakshman Prasad, both determined that it looked like he had a heart attack. They weren't surprised as Narayan Garu was almost eighty and had been having heart problems for years now.

"It's just old age," Dr. Lakshman Prasad said.

"So it wasn't because he was angry?" Meena asked, her trembling upper lip caught between her teeth. "Padma and I . . . we argued with him yesterday and . . . we . . ." She burst into tears then.

"No, no, it wasn't because of an argument," Dr. Lakshman Prasad said, looking around at the women of Tella Meda for help in calming Meena down. "He was quite old, he was ready to go."

Chetana put her arm around Meena and kissed her forehead. "He was an old man with one foot in the grave. Your argument didn't put him there."

"But next time, don't go about yelling and arguing with old people," Renuka said. "We die easily."

There wasn't anyone to really mourn Narayan Garu and his body was cremated quietly. His children didn't show up to bury him but Narayan Garu had left provisions with Kokila in the form of his wife's jewelry to pay for his funeral. He had said that any money left should go toward the keeping of Tella Meda.

There were a set of six thick gold bangles, two gold and ruby rings, and one pair of diamond earrings. Except for the diamond earrings, everything else was actually silver-plated with gold and not worth much. The stones in the rings were not rubies but red coral. Kokila found out the truth when she took the jewelry to the jeweler wanting to sell them to pay for Narayan Garu's funeral. The diamond earrings brought in some money but the diamonds were small, less than half a carat each, and the money was all used up to pay for the funeral.

A Brahmin was hired to light the fire to Narayan Garu's pyre as his own sons didn't bother to do so.

Meena and Padma, feeling guilty about his death, cleaned up Narayan Garu's room. There wasn't much to clean. His clothes were given away to the poor and his books, those which Meena and Padma didn't claim, were sold as waste paper. In all the years he lived in Tella Meda he had accumulated little and at the end there had been no one even to mourn or miss him.

Puttamma suggested that Balaji stay in Narayan Garu's room and take care of the garden. He was twenty years old now and had recently married a young girl from Puttamma's village, Karuna. If he and his wife could live in Tella Meda and take care of the garden and the housework, that could constitute rent. Balaji also had a job at a small printing press, which would suffice for their other expenses.

Kokila talked to Charvi about it and it was decided that Balaji and Karuna would take up residence in Narayan Garu's room. Just a week after Narayan Garu died, his room was occupied again. This time with a woman's touch.

Karuna took over all of Puttamma's responsibilities and also offered to wash the dishes. Puttamma would still come to Tella Meda every day, mostly to gossip with the women there and check on her son.

"At my age I shouldn't have to work," Puttamma said to Kokila. "But I still have to clean houses and wash dishes. You save up for old age, okay? Being old and poor is just not good."

"Being poor is just not good, no matter what your age," Kokila said.

"Did you hear they are doing interrogations, even here, for the Rajiv Gandhi killing?" Puttamma said. "There were these two Tamils who came to stay with some friend or something in the *basti* and the police arrested them. They were from Sri Lanka, some refugee camp. No one has heard from them. People in my *basti* are scared, it used to be a safe area, now . . . "

Kokila sighed. "God knows why people go about killing each other."

Puttamma shrugged. "Balaji was telling me how what Rajiv Gandhi did in Sri Lanka when he was the PM was very bad. The Indian army's soldiers killed men, raped women . . . not good what the army did."

"They did that? Really? Are you sure?" Kokila asked.

Puttamma nodded. "The owner of the press where Balaji works, he is good friends with lots of important Tamils in Madras. He tells Balaji how things are in Sri Lanka. What do we know? We stay here and we don't know anything."

Kokila wasn't sure if she should believe Puttamma and Balaji. On the other hand, she didn't really care who did what in Sri Lanka. These days she was busy getting Karthik ready to start school in September. There were two schools in Bheemunipatnam and Kokila wanted Karthik to join the good one. It was a little expensive, but she would just hand over that thousand *rupees* Bangaru sent every month to the school if necessary. She wanted the best for Karthik and he was such a bright boy too. He had passed the good school's entrance exam and had top marks.

Chetana thought the world was going to hell if four-year-olds were being asked to take exams.

The police and the Central Bureau of Investigation were determined to find the killers of Rajiv Gandhi. People with ties to the LTTE and supporters of the Tamil Eelam were being questioned routinely. Those who had carried out the assassination were still at large and a massive manhunt was on for a man named One-eyed Jack Shivrasan and a woman named Shubha who had been a backup human bomb.

Their pictures were plastered all over newspapers and transmitted on television.

"We're keeping our eyes open," Meena announced. "If they come to Bheemunipatnam, we know the direct phone number to the chief inspector's office."

Chetana sighed. "Why will they come all the way to this pit?"

"It could be quite a safe place," Padma said seriously. "Not too many people live here and it's far away from the city."

"If I was running away I would hide in a big city," Chetana said. Her younger daughter was influenced largely by Padma and Chetana couldn't really complain. Meena's marks in school were right next to Padma's and they were always first and second in class, always competing with each other. They were constantly together, studying, and were the closest of friends. They reminded Chetana of how she and Kokila had run around Tella Meda.

"Somehow, I remember having a lot more fun than these two," Chetana told Kokila while she watched her daughter and Meena argue over how to solve a mathematics problem. "These two are always studying. Do you see them do anything but study or talk like they know so much more than everyone else?"

Kokila smiled. "We should've also gotten a good education. Who knows how our lives would have turned out."

"Bhanu's turned out fine and she isn't even metric pass. Didn't want to go to college after tenth class and I didn't press her," Chetana said, and then nodded. "I know, I know. Can you imagine my daughter being a doctor? A prostitute's granddaughter will become a doctor? Unimaginable!"

"There's more to who she is than Ambika's granddaughter," Kokila said.

It was then that a hubbub could be heard coming from the temple room and front verandah. Kokila rushed to investigate when she heard Charvi call out for her.

"This inspector here says that Balaji is a terrorist," Charvi told Kokila. "They want to arrest him. Do you know where he is?"

Kokila shrugged. "He usually goes to the printing press in the day. He should be back at four o'clock or so. But you must be mistaken, Inspector Garu. Balaji is a nice young man, not a terrorist."

Padma and Meena peeked from the temple room and followed the proceedings carefully.

"We could be harboring a terrorist," Padma whispered to Meena.

"I always thought Balaji was suspicious," Meena agreed.

Charvi didn't subscribe to Padma and Meena's point of view and she let the inspector know it.

"Just because he sometimes says that he supports the Eelam doesn't mean he's a terrorist," Charvi said. "The boy is a good boy and this is a free country, isn't it?"

"These are heightened circumstances, Amma Charvi," the inspector said politely. "Are you sure he isn't here? Because the printing press is shut down and the owner, Murugan Murthy, is also missing."

Kokila looked around helplessly. "We can go look for him if you like but—"

"Do you mind if my men and I have a look inside?" the inspector asked, and started to gesture at the two khaki-clad men who were accompanying him. "If you could show us his room . . . Amma Charvi, I mean no disrespect but you have to understand, a political leader was assassinated. We have to take all measures to catch the culprits."

Kokila was followed by the three policemen as she walked toward Balaji and Karuna's room.

Karuna opened the door when Kokila knocked. Her eyes were red, as if she had been crying and her hair was slightly mussed.

"Is he in?" The inspector pushed Kokila aside and faced Karuna.

Karuna shook her head like a nervous deer but even Kokila could see Balaji hiding under the bed from where she stood.

They handcuffed Balaji and all but dragged him out of Tella Meda while he screamed that he was innocent and had done nothing.

"What will happen to him, Charvi Amma?" Karuna asked as she wept uncontrollably.

Charvi leaned on the walking stick she had recently purchased to help with the arthritis that plagued her aching knees. "I'll make some phone calls. Vishnu Mohan is a good friend of the police inspector; he will let us know what is going on. Don't worry. It's just a mistake and it will all get sorted out."

But there was no news for almost two weeks. Karuna went to the police station every day with Puttamma and Kokila and every day they were told that Balaji had been transferred to a prison in Visakhapatnam and he was still being questioned regarding his affiliation with the LTTE.

Dr. Vishnu Mohan couldn't prevail upon his friendship with the police inspector because the matter was of grave importance and no favors were being granted. A new crack special investigation team had been established to find the killers of Rajiv Gandhi and the leader of the team was a man named D. R. Kartekeyan from the CBI, who was leaning very heavily on local police to find LTTE supporters and obtain information regarding the assassination.

"What does that poor boy know? Why would they take my boy away?" Puttamma cried almost all day, not eating or sleeping properly. She was staying with Karuna in Tella Meda and was afraid that the police had killed her only child.

Every time Kokila listened to Puttamma cry she held on to Karthik tighter. She could understand Puttamma's pain and she wished she could do something to assuage it.

"People die in police custody all the time," Puttamma lamented. "Oh, Kokila Amma, do you think they killed my boy?"

All the women at Tella Meda tried to console Puttamma but they all knew her fears were legitimate and that until Balaji came back home no one would know what happened to him. And there was also a chance that he would never come home. People routinely disappeared all the time and the police were so powerful, they could do anything.

Two weeks after they arrested Balaji, Dr. Vishnu Mohan and his wife, Saraswati, came to Tella Meda with bad news.

"They have found the press owner, Murugan Murthy, and he is up to his neck in this LTTE business," Dr. Vishnu Mohan said. "They have confirmed his association."

"What about Balaji? He's just a little boy," Puttamma said.

Dr. Vishnu Mohan shrugged. "I don't know where he is; no one tells me. What I know is that Murugan Murthy is a staunch LTTE supporter and has donated money to them and also prints LTTE pamphlets in his printing press. Balaji could be involved, the police think."

"He wouldn't kill anyone, my little boy," Puttamma said. "He's a gentle boy. Why would they think he killed Rajiv Gandhi? That woman, she killed him by wearing a bomb."

Dr. Vishnu Mohan sighed. "But a lot of people planned it and they think that Balaji and Murugan Murthy could be those who helped the people who planned it."

Puttamma shook her head violently. "If my son knew what they were going to do, he'd come and tell me and I would have told the police. He tells me everything. He's a good boy, Doctor Garu. You talk to the police and see if they'll let my boy come home."

A few days later, in some small town near Bangalore, those who had plotted to kill Rajiv Gandhi were found. They had killed themselves by swallowing cyanide, knowing that capture was imminent. It had been less than two months since the assassination and the country applauded the efforts of the CBI and the local police in Bangalore.

Puttamma's son was still missing and the police still wouldn't say where he was. Just because the killers were caught didn't mean that the police were going to slacken their stance on the LTTE. Supporters of the organization were considered enemies of India and Indians and they were to be weeded out and thrown in jail or killed.

"Poor Puttamma," Kokila said when more than a month had passed since Balaji's arrest. Puttamma slept with great difficulty, crying all day and eating nothing. Kokila tried to care for her but no one could console Puttamma. Even Karuna, Balaji's young wife, seemed to be dealing with the loss better than her mother-in-law.

"If they took my child away I'd go mad too," Chetana said. "You keep thinking you're safe and then they come and arrest you and that's it."

"Maybe he's guilty," Meena suggested as she helped Chetana string jasmine flowers into a garland for the temple room.

"Yes, maybe Balaji was as involved as Murugan Murthy," Padma said.

"Shut up, both of you," Chetana said angrily. "Better not say this in front of Puttamma. And you both need to learn to not give your opinion about everything. Girls should know when to keep quiet. Talkative little girls like you are not very attractive. No one will marry you if you don't learn to behave yourselves."

"But we don't want to get married," Meena announced. "We're going to both become doctors and open a big clinic and make a lot of money."

Chetana smacked her hand against her forehead. "This is my *karma*. One daughter marries too early and my second daughter doesn't want to marry. Nice. Don't marry, just be smart-mouthed, but be so someplace else, not in front of me."

"My mother says that we should speak our mind. That's the only way our country can progress: if women stand shoulder to shoulder to men and say what's in their hearts," Padma said stoically.

"Then get on inside the kitchen and irritate Sushila," Chetana suggested, and Meena and Padma left in a huff.

"Is Chetana Auntie angry?" Karthik asked, looking up from the toy cars he was chasing around the courtyard.

"Yes," Chetana said, and grabbed him in a big hug. She kissed him all over his face while he tried to wiggle away. "I'm very, very angry and you watch out. I'll tickle you if I get any angrier."

Karthik squealed with laughter and escaped to hide behind Kokila. "Where is Karthik?" he said, and Chetana rose quietly to grab him as he burst into fresh peals of laughter at being caught and tickled.

From the other end of the courtyard, near Balaji's room, Kokila saw Puttamma watching them with tear-filled eyes.

Balaji came home the next day, all by himself. He had lost weight and was about half the size he used to be. His clothes were filthy, as if he had lived in them for a whole month. There were bruises around his eyes and on his hands. He was dehydrated and starved.

Charvi gasped when she saw him as he stumbled into the temple room during her morning *puja*.

"Oh my God, what have they done to you?" she cried, and then called for help.

Balaji didn't talk much about his arrest or about where he had been taken. He just said that they had interrogated him and then had let him go because Murugan Murthy had cleared him of any association with LTTE. Murugan Murthy himself had managed to get released with the help of some politician friends of his.

Balaji had always been a quiet boy but he had seemed content with his life. But a month in jail had killed the contentment within him. It was as if all the joy had been sucked out from him and there was nothing left inside that could feel happiness. He remained like that for months. His wife tried Ayurvedic herbal medicines, homeopathy, and even witchcraft, hoping to bring her husband back from his silence and lack of animation, but nothing worked.

Dr. Vishnu Mohan found out that Balaji had been tortured for information regarding the LTTE while in custody. The Bheemunipatnam police inspector wasn't even apologetic that Balaji had been unjustly tortured and put in prison for a month. Sometimes innocent bystanders got hurt, he told Dr. Vishnu Mohan when the doctor complained about the situation. He wasn't sorry because if he had to do it again with the proof he had, he wouldn't change anything.

Three months after Balaji returned from prison, Bhanu had a baby boy. Just two days after she delivered, Balaji committed suicide by jumping off one of the many cliffs in Bheemunipatnam. Karuna, widowed at the age of nineteen, continued to stay in Tella Meda. Puttamma, heartbroken, left Bheemunipatnam and went back to her village near Kavali. No one at Tella Meda ever heard from her again.

12 March 1992. A devastating wave of car-bomb explosions killed an estimated three hundred people and injured hundreds more in the large western Indian port city of Bombay. The first blast ripped through the city's stock exchange building, and minutes later a dozen slightly less powerful explosions rocked the bustling city center.

8 December 1992. Today, amid worldwide protest against the demolition of the Babri Masjid, a mosque in Ayodhya, Lal Kishenchand Advani, Musli Monohar Joshi, Ashok Singhal, and other Bharatiya Janata Party figures were arrested for leading the mob that destroyed the mosque on December 3, 1992. In response to the Ayodhya demolition, several temples were burned in Pakistan and Britain by Muslims.

Catastrophe Is Coming

Charvi woke up on the morning of her fiftieth birthday with bitterness coating her mouth. She had been waiting for this morning, it seemed for years, and dreading it.

Fifty years, she thought, shocked as she looked at herself in the mirror. Her hair was now completely white, and had been for a while; her skin was loose around her mouth, wrinkled around her eyes, and blotched with light brown marks. Her eyes, the eyes she had always been proud of, light brown eyes, different from others, had lost their luster as well. Her skin wasn't milky white anymore, it had darkened. The process had been gradual, so gradual that she hadn't noticed it until now.

It wasn't like she woke up this morning and saw youth far behind her, but it was a difficult morning because Tella Meda was going to celebrate its *guru*'s fiftieth birthday and Charvi knew there was nothing to celebrate.

What had she achieved in fifty years?

Until a day ago she had been able to fool herself that she had Tella Meda; if nothing else, she had made a home for the discarded women of the world and children who had nowhere to go. She had devotees and friends, people who looked after her and respected her. Now she had to tell them that they might have to leave Tella Meda, that they all would have to find a new home.

The letter had looked innocuous and Charvi didn't pay much attention as she read through the initial pleasantries. It had been so long since Srikant Somayajula or anyone from his family had contacted anyone at Tella Meda that Charvi had all but forgotten that the house with the white roof that glittered as though studded with diamonds in moonlight didn't belong to her. The letter was plain enough, written by Srikant Somayajula's eldest son, Kedarnath. He informed Charvi that his father had passed away, peacefully in his sleep, two weeks ago. Kedarnath and his two younger brothers had decided to sell Tella Meda as many development companies had approached them about the land and the house. The idea was to tear down Tella Meda and construct luxury flats with a view over the Bay of Bengal.

He was candid in the letter, saying that he respected his father's desire to leave the house as it was so that it could be used as an *ashram*, but he and his brothers wanted to sell. The house and land, in today's market, would sell for three *lakhs* of *rupees*. Charvi had six months to vacate the property. They were sorry that they were asking this of Charvi but they hoped Charvi would understand their situation and appreciate that she and her flock had been allowed to live free of rent in Tella Meda for almost thirty-five years now, since 1957. As an afterthought, Kedarnath added that he would try and help them find a new house but also mentioned that since he knew no one in the Bheemunipatnam area, he wasn't sure how much help he could be.

Charvi had not talked about the letter to anyone. She was shell-shocked.

Tella Meda was home and now they would have to leave it. Where would they go? She knew she had to talk to Kokila so that they could find other accommodations. She flirted with the idea of asking some wealthy devotee for the three *lakhs* of *rupees* that would help them buy the house but she didn't know how to ask for money. That was always something Kokila did.

And it wasn't as though devotees were flocking to her door as they used to some years ago. Her luster had faded and the numbers of those who came to Tella Meda every Sunday had thinned. Some Sundays in the past few years no one would come, except for the beggars and the homeless looking for a free meal.

It was an insult, cause for alarm, and Charvi had felt both. But she had curbed the emotions and hidden them under apathy. She was a *guru,* she thought. If no one needed her, that wasn't her fault.

And she would have continued as before, pretending to be a *guru* even though she doubted her godliness and spirituality every day, if that letter had never arrived. Now she had to confront her future and the futures of all those who lived in Tella Meda. Where would Kokila go? What about Chetana and Meena? What about Karuna, Sushila, and Padma? What about Shanthi? What about all those who came once a year for solace? Could any other house match the opulence and character of Tella Meda?

It was imperative to talk with Kokila. They had to either find a new home, find three *lakhs* of *rupees,* or convince Kedarnath to continue to let them stay in Tella Meda as his father had. Charvi wished she didn't have to deal with such materialistic things; she wished she didn't have to worry about finances and the like. She wished she hadn't received the letter. She wished Kokila had and then she wouldn't have to think about what to do.

Charvi looked at her reflection in the mirror and closed her eyes, appalled at the old woman staring back at her. How had the years flown by? And why had they gone by without even a whisper?

When she opened her eyes again her reflection was replaced by an image of a large tidal wave, a tsunami, rising high and crashing onto Tella Meda. The vision lasted for short seconds but Charvi almost fell off the chair in front of her dressing table. Catastrophe was coming, she thought in fear. A tsunami would crash down on Tella Meda and destroy all that was within. Panic rose within her and she gasped for breath, afraid of her own reflection, the world and her vision that swirled around her. She clutched at her face, wanting to scratch her eyes out, and then she started to cry. Catastrophe was coming. Big catastrophe, she realized, and she knew she had to tell everyone so that they could be saved.

Charvi meditated for a few minutes, hoping to gain control. By the time she finished her bath and was ready for the morning *puja* where everyone was waiting to wish her a happy and prosperous birthday, she was her usual calm and stoic self.

Not for the first time since she'd left, Charvi missed Subhadra. She got letters regularly from her erstwhile cook and caretaker and it was obvious that Subhadra and Chandra were enjoying Chandra's children's hospitality. They spent their time in devotions to Lord Venkateshwara Swami and cooking elaborate meals for Chandra's children and grandchildren.

Usually on Charvi's birthday, Subhadra would give her a bath in the morning, wash her hair with *rita,* and put a decorative *bindi* on her forehead. Since Subhadra had left no one else volunteered and Charvi decided she wouldn't be comfortable with someone else's attentions either. Tella Meda seemed to be slipping away through her fingers. Kokila was running it now. No one asked Charvi how things should be done; everyone went to Kokila. It was Kokila who decided that new toilet bowls were required, not Charvi. It was Kokila who had the west wall repaired because rainwater was seeping in and no one asked Charvi if it should be done or not. After Balaji committed suicide, Kokila decided that it would be best to lay down stones in the garden to reduce garden work. Charvi had been consulted but even then Charvi knew that Kokila was telling her what would be done, not asking for her permission. The new gardener, some man from the *basti,* had not been introduced to her.

Since Puttamma had left, Karuna had taken over cleaning the rooms and the bathrooms and sweeping the courtyard. She washed the dishes after every meal and even spent some time in the evenings pressing Charvi's legs, which hurt more and more since the onset of arthritis some years ago.

A table and a chair had been introduced in the verandah, next to the knee-high dining table, so that Charvi wouldn't have to sit on the floor during meals.

Besides Karuna, Charvi felt none of the residents of Tella Meda saw her the way her devotees who had flocked around her every Sunday did, the way Subhadra used to. They were not like the guests who arrived and left all the time, full of devotion, convinced that Charvi was a *guru,* an incarnation of a goddess. Maybe it wouldn't matter that Tella Meda would have to be closed down. They would find a new place to stay and this time Charvi knew she would be careful about who was allowed to stay, only those who truly believed in her. Of course, people like Chetana and Kokila couldn't be kicked out, but maybe they wouldn't want to stay. Maybe she could find women and devotees like Karuna, prepared to do anything for her.

She was fifty years old, Charvi thought with some indignation. It was time everyone started giving her the respect she was due.

They had to believe in her and those who didn't could leave. *Yes,* she told herself as she closed her eyes while singing the morning devotional songs. And as soon as she closed her eyes she could see it again, a huge tidal wave smashing against Tella Meda, destroying everything in Bheemunipatnam in its wake. All that was left was the temple on top of the hill, gleaming white against the darkness of the sea water that claimed Tella Meda and the rest of the town.

"*Pralayam,*" Charvi said suddenly, and everyone, holding their hands together in prayer with their eyes closed, opened their eyes and frowned. "*Pralayam,*" Charvi repeated again. She had seen the future and it was her duty to let everyone know what was coming.

"*Pralayam?*" Sushila asked.

Charvi nodded. "The end of the world is here," she said carefully. "A wave will rise from the sea and claim everything in its wake."

"What?" Chetana said.

"When?" Shanthi asked.

Charvi closed her eyes again. "It will happen on the night of the full moon. Tell everyone you know to come up to the temple that night because with the moonrise, the water will rise and will swallow everything."

"What?" Chetana said again.

Renuka clapped a hand against her forehead. "I knew this was coming. It's the sinners who have made this happen."

Chetana stared at Renuka in bewilderment and then shifted her glance to Charvi.

"Are you sure?" Sushila asked. She wasn't superstitious but she was also not brave enough to discard predictions of imminent danger from a *guru*. Her belief in Charvi might not have been as strong as Subhadra's had been, but she still trusted Charvi and felt that a goddess's soul could have taken residence in Charvi's body.

Charvi nodded. "We will have to go to the temple before the moonrise. And we will have to pray to God the entire night. Kokila, could you talk to the temple priest and arrange this?"

Kokila wasn't sure what to say. On the one hand, she didn't really believe what Charvi said; on the other, she knew others did and she didn't want to cause panic among the people of Bheemunipatnam. If she told the priest what Charvi told her, the news would spread like wildfire, and most of the town would turn up at the temple with their belongings.

In the thirty-five years Charvi had lived in Bheemunipatnam, she had developed almost celebrity status in the town. Even though the number of devotees visiting Tella Meda had decreased, locally Charvi was still a well-known person and Tella Meda a sometimes famous and sometime infamous house. The people of Bheemunipatnam might look down upon the residents of Tella Meda for being without home and family, but they looked up to the *guru* of Tella Meda. They came to her with their problems and trusted her words. Those who didn't believe in her didn't voice their opinions too loudly and in general she was regarded as an important member of the Bheemunipatnam community. Besides the fact that people would panic, Kokila was worried that when the tidal wave didn't engulf Bheemunipatnam, as she was certain it wouldn't, it would leave Charvi's reputation scarred and she would be treated as a joke.

"Why don't we talk about this first?" Kokila suggested.

Charvi's eyes flashed fire. "Do you doubt this vision I have had? Do you?"

Kokila looked out of the doorway at the bay uncomfortably.

"I can see into the future and I can see this. *Pralayam* is coming. Doomsday will arrive at our doorstep," Charvi said in a clear voice. "After all that we have put Mother Earth through, didn't you expect this?"

"I don't think *pralayam* is a real concept," Meena said suddenly. "It's a myth—"

"Hush." Chetana nudged her daughter and glared at Padma before she could speak. Both girls had become increasingly precocious, asking questions and imparting their opinions. They couldn't understand why people thought a goddess lived inside Charvi. Science didn't prove the existence of gods and goddesses, hence how could it be true?

"Talk to Pujari Garu," Charvi said. "I need some time alone to think."

"But several people are coming to visit you today," Shanthi said, licking her lips. They had dried up when Charvi made her prophecy. After Subhadra, Shanthi had taken over the job of lining up the devotees and arranging for their visits on Sundays and holy days, which included Charvi's birthday. She hadn't believed in Charvi when she first arrived at Tella Meda, but in the past decade and a half of her stay, the close contact with Charvi and her devotees had engendered a deep sense of respect for Charvi in Shanthi.

She was an indomitable woman and Shanthi believed that Charvi never lied. If she thought she could see the future, it was because she could. Shanthi wasn't like Subhadra, who insisted everyone believe in Charvi. She trusted the *guru* of the *ashram* and didn't hold a grudge against those who didn't.

"What am I supposed to tell Pujari Garu?" Kokila asked Chetana as they rode in a bicycle rickshaw to the temple. Shanthi was caring for Karthik, though in reality, everyone at Tella Meda cared for all the children who lived there. It was a blessing and a bane. Because everyone took care of all the children, everyone thought it was perfectly acceptable to give Kokila parenting advice and raise Karthik in the way they thought fit.

"Tell him that Charvi is going through menopause and is losing her mind," Chetana suggested.

Kokila sighed. "Do you think that is it?"

"It's her time for change. She complains about the heat and her moods are swinging . . . and now this," Chetana said. "I have no doubt. Her eggs are drying up."

"And how long does it take to adjust?" Kokila asked.

Chetana shrugged and Kokila sighed again. "I didn't even know she had menses. Have you ever seen her sit out? Her menses has always been a big mystery to me. She never sits in the menses room, she always comes for *puja* . . . which means she never has menses, right?"

"Maybe there are different rules for *gurus*," Chetana said, and then grinned. "And maybe she just never told anyone about her menses to avoid having people think she's less than a goddess."

"You think real goddesses don't have menses?" Kokila asked, and Chetana shrugged again. "Pujari Garu is going to laugh at me," Kokila said wearily.

"Well, I'll be there too, so he will laugh at both of us. And he doesn't like me anyway; he always told me that it was my job to set Ravi straight," Chetana said. "I can't believe that old man is still alive. When he got us married he was an old man and now Ravi is dead, I'm a grandmother, and this man is still the *pujari* of the temple. That young assistant of his is not even young anymore. He must be waiting for the old coot to die so that he can take over."

"Maybe we can talk to the assistant *pujari*," Kokila said thoughtfully. "Maybe we can explain to him that Charvi is going through this change—"

"And malign her reputation?" Chetana interrupted.

Kokila nodded. "This is horrible. I'm supposed to tell Pujari Garu to have an all-night *puja* on a full-moon night. Do they even do stupid things like this in films?"

Pujari Garu surprised Kokila and Chetana by readily agreeing to the all-night *puja*. He said he would tell those who came to the temple for the next eight days about it, so that everyone could find safety in the temple.

"Amma Charvi is a great woman who has had a great vision," he said, and both Kokila and Chetana wondered if he was going through some change as well that left his brain soft. "Scriptures say that on a full-moon night when sin has spread rampantly around the world, the water will rise and submerge all who don't cleanse themselves. Those who come to the temple and pray will cleanse themselves and survive," Pujari Garu continued. "And those who don't will die a pitiful and painful death. I will make sure everyone knows about Amma Charvi's prophecy. We are indeed lucky to have her. The rest of the world will collapse but we will survive."

Kokila cleared her throat to stop him from going on anymore. "She didn't say anything about the whole world, just about Bheemunipatnam."

"The whole world to us is our world," Pujari Garu said with a smile, and called the assistant *pujari* and explained the matter to him.

Kokila felt sympathy for the assistant *pujari* because, unlike his mentor, he couldn't quite see how (or why) anyone would believe this baseless story about a huge tidal wave.

The news spread rapidly across Bheemunipatnam after that. A small coastal town could be influenced easily without much effort, and especially if religion was involved.

Devotees came to Tella Meda every day now wanting reassurance from Charvi that in the next eight days before the full moon, if they prayed hard enough and touched her feet long enough, they and theirs would be saved from the *pralayam*.

Karuna went about her business in fear, trying to remember what her sins were. She knew her biggest sin was losing her husband to suicide the previous year and hoped that she had done enough since Balaji died to atone for his sins as well as her own. Shanthi, who was usually quite sensible, was also caught up in the fear and wondered if leaving her husband would be considered a sin by God. Even Sushila was concerned and stayed up nights trying to remember every sin she thought she had committed.

Besides Kokila and Chetana, only Padma and Meena watched the entire drama with scorn and a little bewilderment.

"There isn't going to be a tidal wave," Meena said to Chetana while sandbags were placed around Tella Meda to protect it.

"I expected better from Doctor Garu," Chetana said, and sighed as

Dr. Vishnu Mohan organized the packing of the sandbags. "Saraswati has already taken half the things in their house in that new car of theirs to her sister's house in Visakhapatnam. What is going to happen to us when there is no disaster? The people of Bheemunipatnam will kick us out of the town."

Padma sighed. "Amma is also packing up all the jewelry and books in a metal trunk so that it will be safe from the water. She wants to take that with us to the temple. I don't know whether I should believe Charvi or not. Amma does, but I don't know . . ."

"I'm not going to the temple," Meena said. "Do I have to have go, Amma? I think it's stupid."

Chetana shrugged. "Do what you want to do. What will you do, Kokila? She's going to expect us to be at the temple."

Kokila buried her face in her hands. "Karthik was asking me as well. What should I tell him? He's so scared and he's just a little boy. I'm so angry with her for scaring everyone like this."

"What if there is a tidal wave?" Padma questioned primly, and then quickly added, "As a coincidence."

"There hasn't been a tsunami in the Bay of Bengal, ever," Meena countered. "It's something that takes place in areas like Japan where they have many earthquakes in the ocean."

"Sometimes things can just happen without any scientific reason, you know," Padma said, obviously influenced by her mother.

"Well then, this is your way of saying you will be going to the temple," Meena said, and flipped her braid from one shoulder to another. "How very narrow-minded of you!"

While the two teenagers argued, Chetana and Kokila wondered what they would do after the full-moon night and what its repercussions would be.

"You have to talk to her," Chetana said. "She can't go about announcing *pralayam*. She thinks she's a goddess and so does everyone else but when they find out she isn't, they will rip her apart."

"Maybe she's doing this so that they will," Kokila said, and then shook her head. No, Charvi prized her status as *guru* too much to jeopardize it.

That night after *bhajan,* Kokila decided to speak with Charvi in her room. Charvi was in the bathroom when Kokila came into the living area of her quarters and stood by Charvi's desk, waiting for her to step out of her bathroom, constructed especially for her in the late seventies.

She looked at the pile of letters on Charvi's desk and sighed. So many devotees, all telling her she was wonderful, a goddess—no wonder she believed it.

One letter was set aside and Kokila could read some of the words even though they were turned away from her. The words "sell Tella Meda" caught her attention and without thinking she picked up the letter and read it. Charvi stepped out of the bathroom just as Kokila was finishing.

"What is this?" Kokila demanded, and Charvi's face transformed into a guilty pout.

"What business do you have reading my private letters?" Charvi demanded.

"This is not private," Kokila said, furious because the postmark said the letter had arrived a week ago. "If we're to lose our home, we need to know."

"You have a home because of me," Charvi said indignantly. "How dare you read my letters? Who do you think you are?"

Kokila had always respected Charvi for her calm bearing, even in the middle of chaos. Charvi never raised her voice, was never rude, and was never this aggressive and confrontational.

"We have six months to find a new place . . . *you* have six months to find us a new place," Kokila said, putting the letter back on the table. "Maybe we could write to this man and ask him to allow us to stay in the house longer. Have you written to him?"

Charvi shook her head. "I didn't know what to say. I didn't want to beg."

She was scared, Kokila realized, of losing her home, her followers, her family.

"Do you want me to write to him?" Kokila asked.

Charvi nodded sheepishly and then looked away from Kokila.

"Okay," Kokila said. "I don't think you should worry about this too much. He will come around. This is an *ashram* and no one wants to kick out a *guru* and her flock from her home."

Charvi nodded again, still not looking at Kokila, but just before Kokila left the room, she cried out loudly.

Kokila stopped in her tracks and turned around. Charvi's calm face was red, as if ready to burst with anger.

"I hate you," Charvi said, and the words were choked out of her. "I hate you."

Kokila was taken aback. "Why?" she asked, more out of surprise than hurt.

"I hate you," Charvi repeated instead of explaining. "Get out," she said next, and then went back inside the bathroom and locked the door.

Kokila wondered if she should stay. Charvi never spoke like this. It was as if . . . as if she were someone else, a child. Yes, Kokila realized, her behavior was childish.

Kokila worried about Charvi, wondering if she should speak with Doctor Garu and see if he had some suggestions about how to make Charvi less volatile. But it seemed like the wrong time to discuss Charvi's mental health. Doctor Garu was getting ready for the *pralayam* Charvi had predicted.

Kokila didn't tell anyone about Srikant Somayajula's son's letter. Most people at Tella Meda, especially those who had recently arrived, didn't even know who Srikant Somayajula was. They didn't question who Tella Meda belonged to. The basic structure, the building, was considered irrelevant, considering the deity who lived there. And those who lived in Tella Meda had become so much a part of it, just like the fading whitewash on the walls, the rotting windows in some of the rooms, and the creaking fans, that they didn't question their right to live in the formerly opulent house.

And Kokila didn't want to worry everyone unnecessarily. She hoped that Srikant Somayajula's son would have his father's benevolence and generous heart, along with the wealth, because only a wealthy man could ignore the three *lakhs* of *rupees* that could come from selling Tella Meda.

Kokila worried about how to write the letter and what to say in it.

While everyone went about getting ready for the arrival of the *pralayam,* she wondered how to avert this more real catastrophe waiting to be unleashed upon those who lived in Tella Meda.

Kokila wondered if it was the letter that had pushed Charvi over-the edge. Charvi had never predicted nonsense like this before. She pretended to cure people and somehow some of them did get cured but this was a new facet to Charvi, an exhibition of a new self-proclaimed power. And Kokila worried that it was a ruinous one. People would never forgive Charvi for not being correct about the tidal wave that was supposed to engulf the town of Bheemunipatnam.

The activity in the temple room soared in the next few days. It was just a few days to doomsday and no one was taking chances. And since Charvi had said the only way to be saved was through prayer, people from all over the town came to Tella Meda to pay their respects to Charvi and join in the singing of devotional songs with her.

"I'm so tired of cooking and making tea all day long," Sushila complained, flushed from standing in front of the stove for hours. "I don't think I have seen so many people in Tella Meda before."

"And all of these people are going to throw stones at us when nothing happens," Chetana warned. "*Array,* Meena, what does the weather report say?"

"Sunny and bright . . . a little cold, only seventeen degrees on Saturday and Sunday," Meena said.

"We can't rely on weather predictions all the time," Padma said. The girls usually agreed with each other, but this time Padma was taking her mother's side, while Meena was taking Chetana's.

"Babu is going crazy talking about the *pralayam,*" Bhanu complained as she moved her suckling ten-month-old son from one breast to the other. "Says we should leave, go stay with his mother in Visakhapatnam. That woman lives with her useless brother and mother in a small flat. We should also go and live with them? I say that's when we'll have *pralayam,* when I lose my mind living with that old lady."

"If it's just for a few days, you should go," Sushila advised. "If we had anyplace to go, I'd take Padma and leave."

"So you don't believe in Charvi?" Chetana asked.

"Of course I do. That's why I want to leave," Sushila said.

Chetana shrugged condescendingly. "If you believe in her ability to predict the big wave that will eat us up, you should also believe in her ability to save us. That's what I think."

While Chetana and Meena debated the possibility of Charvi having lost her mind, Kokila wrote a letter to Kedarnath explaining why it was important to let Charvi continue to live in Tella Meda. She suggested that Kedarnath could decide on rent if he liked, though Kokila wasn't sure how they would all survive if they had to pay rent, especially after people found out that Charvi was just menopausal and couldn't really see disasters in the future.

Karthik was full of questions about Charvi. He never really saw Charvi as the *guru* of the *ashram,* just as this old lady everyone deferred to. Now he was old enough to understand that she was someone different and was curious if she was really able to see the future.

"Do you think she can tell if I'll get good marks in my science exam?" he asked Kokila.

"I don't think so," Kokila said.

"If she can't even see that, how can she see the destruction of a whole town?" Karthik wanted to know.

Kokila didn't want to disparage Charvi in front of her son. No matter how she looked at it, they all lived in Tella Meda because of Charvi. And Charvi was an old lady. Kokila didn't want Karthik to think poorly of Charvi for being unable to control her emotions due to surging hormones.

"Maybe she only sees important things," Kokila said. "And there's no guarantee that a tidal wave will consume our town. Okay?"

Karthik wasn't sure and wandered around the house listening in on conversations about the upcoming *pralayam* and dropping by Kokila to give her the details of what everyone was saying and how he had more questions because he was listening to them.

Finally, the day before the *pralayam,* Kokila finished the letter to Kedarnath and dropped it in the postbox. She said a small prayer to Lord Venkateshwara Swami by the postbox and put her faith in the goodness of a strange man and the miracle of God.

Back in Tella Meda, Charvi was delighted at how much attention she was getting from everyone. The letter asking her to leave Tella Meda in six months was all but forgotten. She had given that problem to Kokila, she decided, and therefore she didn't have to worry about it anymore. The sun was bright and the sky was blue but Charvi wasn't daunted; she knew what she had seen and she could feel the force of knowledge, of power, within her.

Having heard of her sister's pronouncement, Manikyam had arrived in Tella Meda as well to show her support for her estranged sister. Charvi still refused to speak with Manikyam and her husband, no matter how many people tried to convince her otherwise. Manikyam's husband didn't really bother much with trying to convince Charvi to accept him again but Manikyam did. She sincerely believed that Charvi was a true incarnation of a goddess and being disliked by her was a catastrophe in itself. As she was getting older, Manikyam was turning more and more to religion and piety and it was becoming very important to her that Charvi accept her and forgive her for her past behavior.

Manikyam came frequently to Tella Meda, wanting to spend time with Meena and Bhanu, whom she openly called her granddaughters now. She showered Shashank, her great-grandson, with clothes and jewelry when he was born. She knew this was the only future for her family, as Prasad's wife had passed away a few years ago and everyone had thought it was a blessing for her. Prasad was dying slowly; at least that's what her husband told her. Due to heavy drinking, Prasad had serious liver problems and spent as much time in hospitals as he did in bars.

Bhanu accepted Manikyam with a polite and pleasant demeanor but Meena didn't bother with her at all. Chetana seemed to encourage Meena's behavior and never failed to remind Manikyam that if only she had been able to convince her husband to accept them in the beginning, they all could have been a family, a happy one, living in Manikyam's big and now empty house in Visakhapatnam.

Charvi's other sister, Lavanya, also heard of Charvi's forecast of imminent disaster and wrote her a scathing letter that would not reach Charvi until long after the day of *pralayam* passed.

There were critics, but mostly people believed Charvi and she was flattered, humbled, and delighted. More and more people came to Tella Meda every day, bringing her offerings, and Charvi was torn between weeping and laughing most of the time.

"See," she wanted to tell Kokila, "look at how people believe in me. Not like you—you have never believed."

Charvi was *guru* again, in charge of Tella Meda. Kokila could make the small domestic decisions, Charvi decided, but she wasn't going to take over the *ashram*. She was just a servant, while Charvi was the mistress of the house. Just because she wasn't bothered with the small details of running the household didn't mean she was less important than the servant.

On the morning of the day of the full moon night people started to fill the temple from dawn. Devotional songs were played on loudspeakers and there was a festive atmosphere at the temple. People brought along their precious belongings and took refuge in the temple, praying to God, hoping to avert the upcoming disaster with their faith and prayer.

"There isn't a cloud in sight," Chetana remarked, looking at the perfectly blue sky. "They're going to lynch her in that temple."

Sushila had convinced Chetana to come to the temple and she now sat with Kokila, who sat next to an excited Karthik.

"So, if this happens, there will be no school tomorrow, right?" Karthik asked.

"There will be school tomorrow," Kokila said.

"But all my friends said that there will be no school tomorrow . . . no school building, so no school," he said.

"Well then, we'll just have to find you a new school to go to," Kokila said.

Karthik thought about it for a moment and smiled. "But that will take some time and I will get a free holiday."

"And what will you do? We won't even have a home. If the school building is eaten up by the big wave, so will Tella Meda," Kokila pointed out.

Karthik nodded gravely. "That is a problem. Let me think about it."

A local Visakhapatnam television news crew, a cameraman and a man with a microphone, had also made their way to the temple. They were filming the people and had done interviews with Charvi, the *pujari,* and some of the people at the temple.

"Do you believe in *pralayam*?" the man with the microphone asked Kokila and Chetana as they were sitting together.

For an instant they didn't answer and then Kokila said, "We are here, aren't we?"

The man moved on, hoping for more detailed answers.

"We should have told him the truth," Chetana said.

"And achieved what?"

"I don't know. I'm just so angry to be here. This is foolish," she said right before Charvi, who was seated on a podium by the idols of the temple gods, started to speak.

Devotees were sitting next to her, tuning musical instruments, getting ready to sing and celebrate the power of God.

And even though the celebration was about preventing a *pralayam* and showing respect for God, people were still trying to make money out of it. The man who ran the canteen by the toddy shops in Bheemunipatnam had set up a food stall with the permission of Pujari Garu. He had promised the temple 25 percent of all his earnings from the night. Plates of food were priced exorbitantly.

"They're making money off people's misery," Chetana said.

"You don't have to buy that food. I have brought food for all of us," Sushila said, and opened three tiffin carriers full of rice, *sambhar,* curds, pickles, fried potato, and green bean curry.

As the day slid into afternoon, the sky remained clear, but as the afternoon became evening, the skies started to change, to become dark.

"The weather forecast didn't say anything about this," Meena said.

"I told you that you can't always rely on the weather forecast," Padma said smugly.

The people in the temple started to sing songs for Lord Venkateshwara Swami with greater gusto and Charvi's voice was the loudest as she sat in front of the microphone.

"It's happening," people cried out.

"Amma, Charvi, save us," some others cried out.

"This is nonsense," Chetana muttered.

But now even she wasn't so sure. Rain started to fall in big large drops, and the wind blew hard. The bright day dissolved under ominous-looking clouds and the air smelled of a storm.

Charvi, who'd never had any doubts, was not surprised. She had known that this would happen, that a storm would come and a wave would rise.

"So, what do you think?" Chetana asked Kokila, who just raised her eyebrows in amusement.

"Looks like Charvi might be able to predict storms," Kokila said.

"See, I told you, you can't rely on the weather forecast. Amma is right—Charvi does have the power to see into the future," Padma said to Meena, pleased with herself.

"It's just a coincidence," Meena said defiantly.

As coincidences went, Kokila had to give high marks to Charvi in the luck department. The two hundred people gathered in the temple were talking excitedly while Charvi read scriptures from the *Bhagavad-Gita* and Upanishads on the microphone.

"Usually she gets tired if she has to sit and eat with all of us. Today, look at her sing and preach," Chetana remarked.

It was as if Charvi had received a new shot of energy. As the rain slapped onto the earth and waves clamored to reach the sandy shore of the Bay of Bengal, her strength rose. Charvi was in full goddess mode, sure of her ability to predict the future.

Since the rain had begun, more people had come to the temple, skeptics mostly, who had never thought Charvi could be right.

The dark evening was cold and people huddled together, now truly frightened of what lay ahead.

"Amma, are bad things going to happen?" Karthik asked, looking around him with his big black eyes.

"No," Kokila said firmly. "While I'm here with you, nothing bad is ever going to happen."

"Are you sure?" Karthik asked, and huddled into Kokila's lap as lightning scarred the skies and was then followed by the rumble of thunder.

Charvi was filling people with more fear, warning them that the thunder and lightning were Lord Venkateshwara Swami's message to everyone that he was unhappy. The pace of the prayers increased and the volume of the people who were singing rose a few notches each time there was lightning and thunder.

The prayers continued through the night and people fell asleep on top of each other, leaning against walls, sagging on the floor. It was a long night and even Charvi fell asleep, sitting on the podium, leaning against soft cushions.

The storm ran out of steam sometime in the middle of the night and dawn broke at five in the morning, showing a wet landscape but not one marred by the washout of a large tsunami.

"We have been saved," someone cried out. "Charvi Amma saved us with prayer."

Kokila and Chetana's fears that if Charvi was wrong it would prove calamitous were unfounded. People were pleased that the storm had passed without leaving behind any damage. And Charvi was bright and alive, looking years younger than she had just a few days ago. She had turned fifty, people said, and she had acquired a new power, the power to look into the future.

The local TV news in Visakhapatnam had a clip about Charvi and her prediction. All of a sudden, Charvi's fame spread beyond the bounds of Bheemunipatnam.

Kedarnath Somayajula's wife, a devout and pious woman, read about Charvi and her *ashram* in Tella Meda in the *Deccan Chronicle*, where there was a small news item with a photograph of Charvi and Tella Meda. She put two and two together and convinced her husband to let the holy woman stay on with her flock. Her husband and his brothers reluctantly agreed, especially after hearing how Charvi had stopped a tidal wave from engulfing all of Bheemunipatnam with just prayer. It was obvious that the woman was powerful and not to be trifled with.

"I just got a letter from Kedarnath Somayajula," Kokila told Charvi excitedly.

"He's letting us stay, isn't he?" she asked, and when Kokila nodded, Charvi took a deep breath. "I predicted it. I knew we would not be turned out of Tella Meda," she said. "We could find another place, certainly, but I like it here. Now I have to go for my walk."

As Kokila turned to leave Charvi's sitting room, she saw a letter on her desk with a familiar postmark. She picked it up after ensuring that Charvi had indeed left. The contents of the letter made Kokila smile. It was a letter from Kedarnath Somayajula's wife sent a day earlier than the letter her husband had mailed to Kokila. It told Charvi that her husband would let them stay in Tella Meda, with no rent, just as her father-in-law had, and she also said that she would like to come and visit Charvi and stay in the beautiful house.

So much for Charvi's prediction, Kokila thought with a smile as she put the letter back on the desk.

12 May 1995. India refused to sign the nuclear nonproliferation treaty because of what it called its discriminatory form.

24 October 1995. A total solar eclipse was seen over Rajasthan, Uttar Pradesh, Bihar, and West Bengal, while a partial eclipse was seen in the rest of the country.

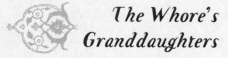

The Whore's Granddaughters

Sushila didn't sleep at all the night she waited for the Engineering and Medical College Entrance Test (EAMCET) results to be announced. Both Padma and Meena had taken the test after studying almost every waking hour for the past two years.

They, like other sixteen- and seventeen-year-olds all over Andhra Pradesh, were waiting to find out what rank they had received and if the rank would qualify them to enter a medical and/or engineering college. Sushila knew Padma had to get a rank under six hundred because that was the only way she could get into Andhra University in Visakhapatnam, a good medical college. But even then it would be a financial stretch.

"I hope Meena's rank is not too high," Chetana confessed to Kokila while the girls waited to get the newspaper where their ranks would be displayed next to their examination roll numbers.

"Why would you hope that?" Kokila said, surprised.

"How will I pay for medical college? How will I pay dormitory fees? Sushila is planning to take a bank loan. As if anyone will give her one. But she at least has some pension. I have nothing," Chetana said. "And since Srinivas got married to that cousin of his, I don't even get free balcony tickets at the cinema anymore. How will I pay for her education?"

Kokila tilted her head and made a sound.

"I'm not going to ask Manikyam," Chetana said, interpreting Kokila's sound accurately.

"It's her future and if her rank is good, why not? And Manikyam has already offered to help," Kokila reminded her.

"No," Chetana said emphatically. "Don't try to convince me otherwise."

"Okay," Kokila said just as the newspaper arrived and the commotion on the front verandah began.

"Eighty-three," Meena screamed as she came running into the courtyard where Kokila and Chetana were drinking their morning tea. "My rank is under one hundred. Can you believe it, Amma? Can you?"

Chetana set her tea aside and hugged Meena tight. "I'm so proud of you. Under one hundred . . . oh my God . . . oh my God. You are a genius, aren't you?"

Meena started to cry then. "I can't believe it. Maybe I should look again, maybe I read it wrong."

Chetana cast an eye at a somber Sushila and a weeping Padma coming into the courtyard and thought that if Meena had read her number wrong, Sushila would let them know.

"Congratulations, Meena," Sushila said with a tight smile.

"What's your rank?" Meena asked Padma, wiping her tears.

Padma sobbed even more loudly then and ran to the room she shared with Sushila.

"Two thousand and three," Sushila said quietly. "No medical college; she'll have to do her degree somewhere . . . I don't know."

"She can take the EAMCET again next year," Kokila said. "Many students try again and get a good rank."

"But how can that be?" Meena asked, genuinely shocked. "We

studied together and I know everything she knows. Are you sure? Give me the paper, let me look."

But it was quite clear that Meena had gotten a much better rank and Padma was not going to get into any medical college in Andhra Pradesh. It was an honor and a matter of great pride, Meena knew, to be ranked so high. Over forty thousand students took EAMCET in 1995 and she was in the top one hundred. She wished Padma had done well because now she couldn't shout with joy as she wanted to; she had to be careful so as to not hurt Padma's feelings. But inside she was so excited she couldn't stop smiling.

"Now what am I going to do?" Chetana said to Kokila that night. "I'm so glad. I mean, a rank of less than one hundred . . . oh my God, not even in my wildest dreams did I think she would get such a good rank. And I'm so happy her rank is good because I look at Padma and I don't know if I could stand it if Meena was that sad. But now she can go to medical college, any one she wants. What am I going to do? How am I going to pay for this?"

"I have something to tell you. Don't start screaming right away," Kokila warned. She went into her room and came back. "Here," she said, and handed over the bank passbook Dr. Nageshwar Rao had given her after Ravi passed away.

Chetana went through the passbook and her expression didn't change as she scanned through the pages. "How long have you had this?" she demanded, her anger just below the calm surface of her question.

"Since Ravi died. I gave Bhanu hers after she got married," Kokila said, waiting for the storm to break. Chetana would not forgive her for this.

"This will be enough for medical college," Chetana said, vibrating now with a silent anger. "How dare you take money for my children? Why did you take it?"

"Because we all need money and this wasn't money for you but for Meena and Bhanu's future," Kokila said. "I know how you feel about Ravi's parents and I understand if you're angry with me but I couldn't let you sacrifice Bhanu and Meena's future because of your anger."

"I *am* angry," Chetana said as tears filled her eyes and a half-hysterical laugh escaped her. "But I can't even throw this passbook back at that bastard, can I? This is Meena's future. She worked so hard to get that rank."

"Sometimes how you feel is not important. You have to kill your pride and do what is right," Kokila said.

"I'm surprised Bhanu hasn't told me," Chetana said.

"She didn't want Babu to know. She's saving the money for a rainy day," Kokila said. "Do you hate me for this?"

Chetana slowly shook her head. "I'd do the same for Karthik."

Meena's stellar performance in the EAMCET made her a celebrity in the small town for a few days. The local Bheemunipatnam newspaper did an article about where Meena had gone for EAMCET tutoring and how she had made the town proud. Chetana cut the article out of the paper and had it framed along with the newspaper clipping where Meena's rank was highlighted next to her roll number.

Since the *pralayam* incident the traffic to and from Tella Meda had increased immensely. Earlier Kokila had had to work hard at managing the Tella Meda finances, but now there was always some money left in the safe at the end of the month. Charvi was proud that she was being treated like a *guru* again and offered to help Meena financially if she needed it. After all, Meena was her grandniece, almost like her own granddaughter, since she'd known her from the day she was born.

Padma refused even to come out of her room. It was a betrayal of immense proportions that Meena should have gotten such a good rank. Padma's twelfth-class marks were quite good and she knew she could get into a good college in Visakhapatnam, where she could pursue a bachelor's degree in science, specializing in genetics. It was a three-year course and after that, Padma thought, she would do a master's in genetics as well. She would be able to get a job with a master's degree, she was sure, or she could go to America. She would make something out of her life, she promised herself, even though she didn't get a good rank in EAMCET.

But Sushila was so disappointed that she said Padma would just have to go to the local college in Bheemunipatnam. How did it matter where she did her degree now? She would never be a doctor and that was all Sushila had ever wanted for Padma.

Sushila went about her business at Tella Meda rigidly, ignoring talk about Meena's rank and how she could choose the medical college she wanted to go to. Sushila's heart was broken and she knew it wasn't Meena's fault but she couldn't keep jealousy out of her voice when she spoke with Meena and Chetana. It was devastating that Padma, who was the one who had inspired Meena to study hard, would not become a doctor, while Meena, daughter of a woman like Chetana, would be donning the white coat and wearing a stethoscope around her neck.

Manikyam heard the news of Meena's EAMCET rank and arrived at Tella Meda with her checkbook, immensely proud of her granddaughter.

"If Ravi hadn't fallen into bad ways, he would've been just like his daughter," she said to anyone who would listen.

"Old lady, if your son hadn't fallen into bad ways, he wouldn't have died young, that's all," Chetana said angrily. "You still think he was worth something? I was his wife and I'm telling you he was a useless human being, good for nothing. Meena is the way she is *because* she got nothing from that loser son of yours."

Manikyam didn't listen, she was too euphoric. Even Dr. Nageshwar Rao, who had spent a lifetime denying that Chetana was a real wife to his son and therefore denying that her children were legitimate, came to Tella Meda to make amends. Both his sons had amounted to nothing. Now that he was growing old and his clinic had grown in size and stature, he needed an heir. He didn't want to give away his hard-earned clinic to his partner's son, the only other doctor available. He wanted his blood to enjoy the fruits of his labor and continue his work into yet another generation.

"Meena has proven she is my granddaughter," he said to Chetana, who raised her eyebrows and laughed in his face as if he were telling a joke.

"Chetana, please, you have to look at the practical side of things," Manikyam said.

"Where is she going to college? Not Gandhi in Hyderabad. It's popular but she should go to Andhra University," Dr. Nageshwar Rao said, choosing to ignore Chetana's sarcastic laugh.

"Yes, yes," Manikyam agreed with her husband. "And she can stay in our house while she goes to college. She'll get homemade food and someone to take care of her."

"And that lecher of a son of yours will be there," Chetana said. "She can stay in a dormitory."

"Prasad is her uncle. He will also take care of her," Manikyam said.

"Just the way he suggested taking care of his brother's widow?" Chetana demanded. "Your Prasad is a loser and another useless human being, just like Ravi. I'm not going to let my daughter stay in your house. She'll stay in the dormitory. But if you like you can pay her bills, and she's free to visit you whenever she can . . . if she wants to, that is."

Dr. Nageshwar Rao and Manikyam agreed to that immediately. Secretly they were relieved that Chetana was allowing them any contact with Meena.

Meena, on the other hand, didn't really care who was paying her college tuition and hostel expenses, as long as someone was. She couldn't wait for August, when she could leave Tella Meda and start college.

Her friendship with Padma had been ruined completely. Even Sushila, who had always been nice to her, didn't speak with her. They were behaving as if it were her fault that Padma got a low EAMCET rank. Their conduct made her think that maybe she wouldn't even come back during summer holidays. What would the point be? It saddened her and angered her that Padma was swallowed by jealousy.

Bhanu was delighted with her sister's success. She didn't care so much about education and EAMCET ranks but was pleased that Meena was also getting out of Tella Meda.

"Life is better out of that house," she told her sister. They had never been friends but they had managed to forge a decent relationship after Bhanu married. Meena visited Bhanu in her home and even took care of her niece and nephew, now one and four years old.

"I can't wait to start college. Manikyam has brought all these *salwar kameezes* for me, you should see. There is this *pattu*-silk green and yellow one that's just beautiful. She bought a ten-thousand-*rupee sari* and asked Shanthi to make the *salwar kameez* out of it," Meena said excitedly. "And she gave me these as well." She held up her wrists and Bhanu whistled softly.

A few years ago she would have been envious of the gold bangles, but now Babu took such good care of her that she couldn't work up jealousy. His business was thriving and they had built a nice house away from the studio, a Maruti car, and a full-time servant at home. She didn't begrudge her sister the bangles or the expensive clothes.

"Who would've thought Ambika's granddaughter is going to become a doctor," Bhanu said with an easy smile.

"You know, Amma managed to do okay by the both of us, even living in Tella Meda," Meena said, and waited for Bhanu to contradict her.

"She did," Bhanu said, surprising Meena. "What? I'm not some chit of a girl now, hating her. I still don't understand why she didn't love me as much as she loved you. But I had Renuka Atha and that wasn't so bad. Amma's here all the time now, trying to help out with Sunita and Shashank. But you know Amma— she can't handle babies."

Meena laughed. "She handles them fine until they start crying."

Bhanu nodded. "I'm thinking of asking Renuka to come and live with me if she wants. Babu says it is okay but I don't know. She's so old now and . . ."

"She'll hate it here," Meena said, and Bhanu nodded.

"That's what I thought. At Tella Meda she has company, people around her all the time to gossip and spend time with. Here, there's just me. She'll get bored. If she falls too sick, then I'll ask her to come and stay with me," Bhanu said.

"You want to repay her for taking care of you when you were a baby," Meena said, nodding in understanding.

"I do. But you be careful out there and take good care of yourself," Bhanu said seriously to Meena. "Don't ever sleep with any of the boys, okay? You sleep with them and it's over. You keep your head and don't fall in love, don't sleep around, just focus on studies. And then if you see someone who you feel is the right one for you, then come to me and we'll lay out a plan to land him."

"I'm not interested in boys," Meena said frankly. "I've been so busy trying to get this rank that I don't care about anything but becoming a doctor."

"Don't take the bus from Visakhapatnam to here when you come home. Babu goes there all the time. Just telephone me and I'll make sure he brings you with him in the car, okay?" Bhanu said.

"I'm going to leave Tella Meda," Meena said gleefully. "Can you believe it?"

Bhanu laughed then. Yes, it was joyous that even though Chetana hadn't been able to get out, both her daughters were successful.

Meena thought hard about where to go to medical college. The options were enormous and her mother had assured her that with the money Dr. Nageshwar Rao had put in the bank for her and the fact that he was still rolling in *rupees,* expenses would not be a problem.

Dr. Nageshwar Rao tried to convince Meena to go to Andhra University where he could keep an eye on her, where he had gone to medical college himself. But Meena wasn't sure. If she was leaving Tella Meda, shouldn't she leave completely?

Chetana wanted to protest when Meena came out of her medical college interview at Andhra University saying that she had decided to go to Gandhi Medical College in Hyderabad. But Meena had already signed up and nothing could be done about it anymore.

All the way back in Babu's car, Chetana admonished Meena for choosing to go so far away.

"Why Hyderabad? Do you know how many Muslims live there? Always riots and curfews and whatnot," Chetana said.

"Amma, Gandhi Medical College is not in a bad area and these riots and stuff happen only in the Charminar area where the Muslims are," Meena said even though she had no idea where the riots really took place. She just hadn't heard of students being killed and it must be safe in Hyderabad, she deduced, since GMC was the most sought-after medical college in all of Andhra Pradesh.

In Bheemunipatnam the animosity that had been simmering for the past several years between Hindus and Muslims was almost unknown, but Chetana was aware that in Hyderabad dreadful things happened during riots. Just a few years ago when those Hindu politicians broke down the mosque in Ayodhya thousands of people had been killed in Hyderabad.

And every year at the anniversary of the breaking of the mosque more people were killed. If that wasn't bad enough, Chetana heard about curfews being imposed on Hyderabadis. It was a big city—how would Meena survive in a big city? She had lived her entire life in Bheemunipatnam. Chetana was afraid for her, but she knew she would be afraid for Meena no matter where she went. Tella Meda and Bheemunipatnam meant security. The rest of the world was unknown and therefore mired with problems she couldn't envisage and protect Meena from.

Bhanu couldn't understand why Chetana would have any objection. "She got a very good rank. Why should you interfere with her success?" she demanded.

"It's not like there's anything I can do now," Chetana said angrily. "She already made the decision, the *maharani,* without telling anyone, just as you did when you wanted to marry Babu."

"Can we keep my marriage and life out of this?" Bhanu cried, and the conversation between Chetana and Bhanu deteriorated into an argument that no one could really win.

Finally, Chetana stopped being angry about Meena making the decision to go to Hyderabad and hoped for the best for her daughter.

"Just stay away from trouble," Chetana warned Meena almost every day in the weeks before she left for Hyderabad. "Dormitories are not supposed to be the best places for girls to live. But we don't know anyone there, so you will have to live in a dormitory."

Meena was thrilled to be living in a dormitory with other girls. In the brochure she received from Gandhi Medical College, there were pictures of the rooms showing two students sharing one room. There was a canteen in the dormitory where breakfast, lunch, tiffin, and dinner were served and the food was covered in the dormitory fee itself. The college was walking distance from the dormitory and most students found it convenient to live in the dormitory because they had more time for studies.

Dr. Nageshwar Rao insisted on accompanying Meena to Hyderabad. Chetana wanted to protest that he did not need to do so but decided that he could take care of the administrative tasks better than she. And he had booked AC car seats for Meena and himself in the train from Visakhapatnam to Hyderabad. They would stay at some rich doctor friend's house in Hyderabad. The doctor friend had assured Dr. Nageshwar Rao that he would keep an eye on Meena and help her out whenever she was in need.

A brand-new black Maruti arrived to take Meena to Visakhapatnam, where she would stay with Dr. Nageshwar Rao and Manikyam for a day before leaving for Hyderabad the next day.

Chetana thought of the irony of the situation. Ravi's father had never allowed her to enter his house because she was the daughter of a prostitute, but now he was allowing the granddaughter of a prostitute and the daughter of a drunk and womanizer into his home. How desperate the times had become for Dr. Nageshwar Rao and his wife, she thought, that he was allowing this travesty. Both his sons had amounted to nothing and his only hope for a bright future for the family was Meena and to some extent Bhanu and her children. It pleased Chetana immensely that her archenemy and the man who ruined her life and Ravi's had had to come to her on bended knee to ask if he could help her daughter.

Everyone at Tella Meda bade Meena farewell with a mixture of sadness and joy and wished her the best, but it saddened Meena that both Sushila and Padma were curt with her.

"I'm sorry that I'm going and you are not," she told Padma, who pretended not to be too bothered that Meena was leaving while she was still at Tella Meda.

"Amma is looking for a U.S. boy for me," Padma said instead. "I'll do what I want to do there after my degree here. And I will live in America."

Many girls were marrying the numerous Telugu boys working and living in America. Everyone was gushing about computer science and almost all engineering students seemed to be on their way to one place or the other in America. They would do their master's in the United States, get jobs, and then come back to India to find themselves a wife.

Sushila had already listed Padma with her photograph in numerous matchmaking agencies. Her requirements were quite simple: the boy had to be a Brahmin, living and working as an engineer in America, and under twenty-seven years of age. Padma was a beautiful, fair-skinned Brahmin girl and Sushila was certain that there would be someone out there who would be interested in her daughter. Every time Padma went to Madras to see relatives someone or another always suggested that she should become a model or a movie actress, not that Sushila would ever consider those kinds of lowly professions for her daughter. But her daughter's good looks, to a certain extent, guaranteed a good match.

"Maybe you can go to medical college in America," Meena suggested brightly.

"Who wants to study for years and years and years and get nowhere?" Padma said coldly. "Have you heard that there are too many doctors in India and not enough jobs? I think I'm lucky to have not gotten into medical college. I'll just finish my degree and go to America."

"Well, I hope everything works out for you," Meena said, aware that years of friendship were being washed away by EAMCET ranks.

"Why shouldn't everything work out for me?" Padma demanded angrily. "Just because you got some fancy rank doesn't mean things will work out for you. You could . . . well, you could fail your exams and things could go badly for you too. Maybe you just got lucky with your EAMCET rank. Medical college is very hard, you know."

Meena nodded. "And it will be harder because you won't be there to study with me."

Meena never saw the tears in Padma's eyes as she left. She hoped that in the coming years she and Padma would be able to renew their friendship, or at least get past the bitterness that lay between them, but she wasn't too optimistic.

5 June 1999. The Indian Army released documents seized from three Pakistani soldiers to substantiate its claim that Pakistani forces were involved in the clash between India and Pakistan at Kargil in Kashmir province, claimed by both countries.

30 June 1999. India reiterated that any peace talks with Pakistan would resume only after Pakistan's unconditional withdrawal from Kargil. Meanwhile, the Indian Army continued to attack the Tiger Hill area and captured two positions in close proximity to Jubar.

A Suitable Boy

If Charvi had been against television, she was dead set against the newfangled contraption standing erect on several roofs: dish antennas. She had heard enough bad things about the foreign programs that came through the satellite to be certain that at Tella Meda there would be no kissing, groping, or half-naked women dancing on television.

In the past few years small satellite television businesses had sprouted like mushrooms after monsoon. They purchased dish antennas along with licenses to distribute programming to a certain number of homes. Then cables would be run from the dish antennas to homes all around the neighborhood so that everyone could receive programming from all over the world. People watched CNN, BBC, MTV, Star TV, Zee TV, and everything else in between.

Karthik was the Tella Meda advocate for satellite television, which all his friends in school had. They talked about watching NBA basketball, NFL football, and MTV, and he wanted to watch that too. He also wanted to see the shows with all the kissing and groping and the half-naked women gyrating their hips in an obscene fashion but he knew not to mention that, so he only talked of the sports. If they had satellite TV, Karthik argued, he could watch all the cricket matches, instead of just the few shown on Doordarshan, the government-run television station. Last year Doordarshan had not shown several matches from the India-Australia series. All his classmates had been able to talk about the games, while Karthik had had to listen on the radio, which was just not the same thing.

"It's not like it's all just naked women. There is a lot of cricket," Karthik protested to Sushila and Kokila, who had joined Charvi in saying that they didn't want that nasty satellite TV in Tella Meda. "And once Padma goes to America, this is the TV she will watch. Don't you want her to get used to it before she goes?"

"She will have a husband who will help her adjust to America, don't you worry about her," Sushila said as she peeled potatoes for lunch.

Kokila, who was chopping the bottlegourd for bottlegourd *pappu* for lunch, had already said her ears were closed to the topic. Tella Meda had been prospering the past few years and they could definitely afford satellite TV, which wasn't too expensive, but this was not about money. It was about morals and Kokila had heard enough bad things about all that foreign programming that she didn't want it to be a part of Karthik's everyday life. She couldn't stop what he saw in his friends' houses but she definitely would control what he saw at Tella Meda with her.

"All my friends have satellite TV," Karthik said, his twelve-year-old face glum.

"Well, all your friends don't have me for a mother," Kokila replied.

"Lucky them," Karthik muttered as he went out of the kitchen.

"Sometimes I'm scared I'm spoiling him completely and other times I'm scared I'm too strict and he's going to start wondering if he would've been better off with his real parents instead of me," Kokila said with a sigh.

"Parenting is never easy," Sushila told her. "And Karthik is a smart boy. He knows he's adopted but he understands you love him like a real mother. Does he ask a lot of questions about his real parents?"

Kokila shook her head. "Just that one time last year. I told him his mother was dead and that I knew nothing about the father. I didn't mention Bangaru Reddy to him. Maybe when he's older and he asks again, I'll tell him. Now he's too young and I'm scared he'll hate me for not being his real mother."

"You *are* his real mother in all the ways that count," Sushila said firmly. "Don't ever forget that."

"Are you going to miss Padma when she leaves?" Kokila asked, changing the subject.

It had taken Sushila two years, but she had found a U.S. boy for her Padma. There had been numerous bride-seeing ceremonies, and many grooms rejected Padma because she lived in Tella Meda. One marriage broker even warned Sushila that she should find another residence. People didn't want their future daughter-in-law to have grown up in a place like Tella Meda with people like Chetana, who everyone knew was a prostitute's daughter.

Sushila would have left if she could, just to be able to find Padma a good marriage match, but she didn't have the resources to leave Tella Meda. So she had doggedly kept on looking for a match, hiring every marriage broker from Visakhapatnam to Bheemunipatnam.

And finally, when she least expected it, the right marriage offer had fallen into their laps like a ripe mango from a tree.

Sushila laughed softly. "All my life I have wanted that girl to leave my side and make a better life. And now I'm scared she's going to make a better life and she'll never thank me, never know how much I did for her. Children forget their parents' sacrifices for them. Padma is already busy with her fiancé. She doesn't have time for me. She only has demands: 'I want this and that for the marriage and for America.' Once she's gone . . . I wonder if she'll even write."

"She's still angry that Meena went to medical college and she's still here," Kokila said.

"I know. Maybe I should've let her take the EAMCET exam again but I wanted to protect her from that hurt. And myself too. I love

Meena just like she were my own, but I was so angry that she got such a good rank and Padma was left behind," Sushila confessed. "Now when Meena comes for summer holiday I don't know what to say to her. She wrote to Chetana that she's coming for Padma's wedding. Maybe they will patch things up and become friends again. What do you think?"

Kokila cut a big chunk of bottlegourd into small pieces. "Chetana and I didn't speak for several years after Bhanu was born. We just drifted apart and lost our friendship. And then it came back. Maybe Padma and Meena can be friends again too."

"Chetana said the same thing. I told her I was so sorry for my behavior. She was angry, saying that it wasn't Meena's fault that Padma didn't get a good rank. But she said that she didn't have any hard feelings, and that Meena probably didn't as well," Sushila said sadly. "I wanted Padma to become a doctor. I wanted it so much."

"And now she's going to go to America," Kokila reminded her. "Her fiancé seems like a good boy. He phones every Sunday and sends her presents and sweets. She'll be happy with him."

"Yes," Sushila said, and her face lit up suddenly. "My daughter is marrying a good boy from a good family. Ah, so his mother is not a Brahmin, but we can't have everything. His last name is a good Brahmin name and my girl is going to have her own car in America. And she will have children, and who knows, I might go to America too, stay with Padma, take care of her children."

If Padma had heard her mother's dreams for herself, she would have been appalled. She couldn't wait to leave Tella Meda and her mother. Padma wasn't sure if she hated Sushila but she didn't love her, she knew that much. Sushila had been very harsh after Padma's bad EAMCET rank. She had called her a good-for-nothing girl who must be married off. Padma could have gotten a good seat in a degree college in Visakhapatnam but Sushila had said she would rather save the money and spend it on her wedding than send her to some silly degree college. A degree college was where losers like Padma got their bachelor's degrees. Smart people with good EAMCET ranks went to engineering and medical colleges. Padma had hated going to the degree college in Bheemunipatnam. She had wanted to go to a good one in Visakhapatnam but Sushila wouldn't hear of it. The college in Bheemunipatnam was small and the students all seemed stupid. The girls were only interested in marriage. She hated it that Sushila had made her like them as well.

But she couldn't deny that she was excited about getting married. Agreed, Manoj, her husband-to-be, was no catch. When they first showed her his picture, Padma had wanted to run, but her mother warned her that this could be her only chance of going to America. Manoj Chintalapaty came from a decent Brahmin family. His father was an officer at the railway department and his mother was . . . well, his mother was not a Brahmin. She had worked in the same railway department until a few years ago. Manoj's parents had had a love marriage, which Sushila didn't condone, but the boy was an engineer from the Indian Institue of Technology in Madras, had a master's degree from a nice American university, and now worked for a big software company in California. So he was a little dark, maybe a little too dark, and his bout with chicken pox as a child had left a few marks on his face. But he wasn't fat or losing his hair or anything.

Padma had had objections, but Manoj, after seeing just one picture of Padma, had said yes. But why wouldn't he? Padma was fair and beautiful, like a marble statue. Everyone said she looked a little like the actress Madhuri Dixit, and Sushila knew that was, alas, her daughter's only asset. A fatherless girl with no money in the family was hard to get rid of these days, especially if she didn't have a medical or engineering degree. In addition, there weren't many decent families that would want a daughter-in-law from Tella Meda. The fact that Manoj's family was saying yes was because they had their own problems finding a good Brahmin girl for their son. No good Brahmin family would want their daughter to marry a boy whose mother was not a Brahmin.

Manoj sent some new photographs to Padma as the marriage talks progressed. In one of the photographs, Manoj stood next to his brand-new black BMW wearing dark sunglasses, looking like a movie hero. In another he was standing in front of a big building, which was his office. And in yet another, a big red bridge was behind him. Padma didn't know why they called it the Golden Gate Bridge when it was red but she was impressed. The car was nice and big and Manoj was already talking about buying a car for his new bride. Not a BMW, his parents told Padma, because they were so expensive, but maybe a Toyota or a Honda.

It would be years before Meena could own a car, Padma thought, and asked Sushila to agree to the match. Once the *tamboolam* was exchanged, the engagement was finalized. Padma's future in-laws were good people, Padma learned, who loved their only son and wanted the best for him. Her mother-in-law had indicated without malice that they had hoped for a doctor or an engineer but Manoj had seen Padma's photo and decided that he wanted to marry her and they didn't want to crush the boy's dreams. If he liked Padma, they liked her as well.

The wedding was to take place in Tella Meda. Manoj's parents didn't want any dowry or an extra-lavish wedding. They just wanted a decent wedding where they wouldn't be embarrassed in front of family and friends. A reception was arranged by Manoj's parents in Visakhapatnam. They hoped that everything could be arranged smoothly by June, when Manoj would come to India. He only had two weeks' holiday so the wedding would have to take place in the first week, after which the new couple would go for a honeymoon to Ooty or somewhere close to Madras. Padma could get the necessary H-4 visa required for her to go to America in Madras as well. Manoj said he would pay for his wife's plane ticket and Sushila was very happy to hear that this particular expense would not have to come from her meager savings.

Padma didn't care about the expenses. She told her mother she wanted a fabulous wedding. Since she had forgone a good education to get married, she demanded that she not be disappointed.

"I didn't get a good EAMCET rank but thanks to my looks I got a great groom. Now *you* give me a good wedding," she told Sushila.

Padma and Manoj talked every Sunday on the new telephone that had been installed in Tella Meda two years ago. The phone had first been placed in Charvi's room and then when she complained about the noise, the phone was moved to the temple room. The phone was moved back to Charvi's room on Sundays to avoid misuse by devotees who came on that day to pay their respects to Charvi.

Padma would settle down at Charvi's desk and talk with Manoj for a good hour while everyone else in Tella Meda was busy with the influx of devotees.

She told him about Meena and how she hoped that Meena would come for the wedding. Then she could show Meena how much better she was doing than her. So what if Meena was going to become a doctor? Padma was going to get married and go to America. And her husband would buy her a Honda car. Manoj warned her that the car might be slightly used but promised it would be safe and in good condition.

As the wedding drew closer, the hubbub at Tella Meda increased. Chetana bitched and moaned that no one had been this involved in her daughter's wedding and she had lived in Tella Meda all her life, but she still helped with stitching falls on *saris* and helped Shanthi cut blouse pieces for new blouses for Padma and Sushila.

Sushila had saved *saris* for years for this day and she brought them all out, one after the other, from a trunk. She bought new *saris* for the ceremony for Padma and herself, and she bought *saris,* as required by tradition, for Padma's mother-in-law and Manoj's cousins, who would be acting as his sisters for the wedding ceremony.

Karuna's new husband, Puttaswamy, was arranging the *shamiana* tent and the marriage musicians. With the blistering July heat in full swing during the wedding, it was absolutely necessary to have a good *shamiana* to provide shade for the guests.

The three guest rooms (including the TV room) in Tella Meda were being set up as the bridegroom's home, while the other rooms were occupied by the bride's side. Dr. Vishnu Mohan's home was also being used to house some of the people from the bridegroom's party. Dr. Vishnu Mohan's wife, Saraswati, had not wanted to help but when Charvi personally asked her to open her doors for Padma's wedding, Saraswati agreed.

Meena had written offhandedly to Chetana that she would maybe attend the wedding. She wasn't planning on coming back this last summer of her college days. She had plans to go to Bombay and Goa with friends and that seemed a lot more appealing than attending Padma's wedding. Meena had moved on since she left Tella Meda, making new friends in college.

"Why is everyone in this great hurry to go to America?" she wrote to Chetana. "Even here at Gandhi, there are some girls who want to finish their medical degree and marry some engineer in the United States and go there to do postgraduate work. I just don't understand why we can't stay in India and make India as wonderful as the United States is supposed to be. All of my friends intend to stay in India. A good friend of mine, Asif, and I have decided to finish our postgraduate studies and work in India. I hope Thatha Garu will offer Asif a job in his clinic. He's a very good friend and if I do come for Padma's wedding, I'll probably bring him along. I really get bored during the summer at Tella Meda. I can spend time with Bhanu and you, but really, I don't feel I have anything in common with anyone there anymore."

That was the nature of Meena's visits in general. On her way to Tella Meda, she stayed in Visakhapatnam for a few days with Dr. Nageshwar Rao, who had truly now become Thatha Garu to Meena. Manikyam, who was addressed as Bamma, would shower her with gifts and express great gratitude that she was amounting to something.

Prasad's health had deteriorated and he was coughing all the time, drinking himself to death, living mainly in his room. Manikyam looked at Meena and saw the future, leaving her only living son to his own devices.

And Meena knew her future was rosy. She had a job already lined up in Dr. Nageshwar Rao's clinic, to begin right after postgraduate studies. Her only concern was her growing relationship with Asif. Even though Chetana might overlook the fact that Asif was a Muslim, her grandparents probably would not. Already Manikyam was suggesting this one's son or that one's brother as a potential husband for Meena. Meena was only interested in Asif and smartly decided not to tell anyone at home about him. For now it was enough that Chetana knew he was her friend.

Asif was her classmate and Meena had felt an immediate attraction to him. A very bright and intelligent boy, he felt the same for her and within the first month of college they became good friends. Before the first semester was over they were lovers. It had been four years since they started seeing each other, and they planned to marry right after they graduated, hoping to do their postgraduate studies in the same place. After that Meena wanted them to work together in Dr. Nageshwar Rao's clinic.

Asif had warned Meena that she might have to change her religion to marry him because even though his parents weren't conservative, his grandparents were and he didn't want to upset his entire family if it was too important to them that his wife be a Muslim. Meena didn't think much of it. She didn't feel much like a Hindu and she didn't think of Asif as a Muslim. How would it matter what her religion technically was? But she understood that this subject would have to be broached with caution in front of her mother and grandparents. And she could only imagine what Charvi would say about Asif and how she would react to Meena becoming and marrying a Muslim.

The matter was moot right now as Asif wasn't entirely sure she would have to change her religion to appease his family and the wedding was still a whole year away.

But anti-Muslim sentiment was high in India. It hadn't been easy for Asif and Meena to be a couple. Some of the Hindu students had threatened them, and some Muslim students who had strong ties with the conservative Muslim community had done the same. It was difficult to be a mixed-religion couple, even in a metropolitan city such as Hyderabad. Since the whole Babri Masjid incident in 1992 things had only gotten worse. And with the Bharatiya Janata Party in power in India, the Hindi-Muslim rift was only deepening.

Both Meena and Asif saw themselves as a symbol of peace between the Hindu and Muslim communities. If there were enough couples like them who had mixed-religion children, this war between the religions would disappear. And their close friends agreed with them. Growing up in Bheemunipatnam, Meena had never met a Muslim before and Asif had at first seemed like an alien creature. She used to believe the stories and the rumors about Muslims: they married four women, they didn't take baths, they only ate beef, all Muslim men were lechers, all their women were subjugated and wore *burkhas* all the time. It was a revelation to meet Asif and find out that his family was actually quite normal, more normal than Meena's.

Falling in love with Asif had been easy, but Meena knew that keeping that love alive through threats, gossip, and hatred would be the difficult part. At least she wasn't in her mother's position, she thought happily. If her grandfather refused to accept Asif as his grandson-in-law, both Asif and she had a solid education that they could fall back on. They wouldn't have to live their lives in Tella Meda, wasting away.

Karthik couldn't understand why everyone was making such a big fuss about satellite TV. *Everyone* had it these days, so what was the big deal? He was sick and tired of having to go to someone else's house to watch television when they had a nice color one in Tella Meda. It was a little old and didn't have a remote control, so what? It worked and could receive satellite TV.

This seemed like the most insurmountable thing he had ever faced in his life. Kokila was intractable and Charvi . . . well, she wouldn't even listen. Usually Charvi heard him out and then told him why she thought he should listen to his mother, even if she disagreed with Kokila. This time, she had just put her hands to her ears and shook her head.

"No, Karthik. This is a religious house. We won't have that kind of nonsense here," Charvi said, and then smiled because she had a soft spot for the handsome Karthik. "Why don't you buy yourself a tape recorder? Then you can hear whatever music you want. I'll give you money for the tape recorder, okay?"

Karthik didn't have the heart to explain to Charvi that tape recorders were passé and what he really wanted and couldn't afford was a CD player. These were the times he wished he had a father just like his friends did. Fathers earned money and ensured that mothers and their sons didn't live in *ashrams*.

He was adopted. He knew his mother had died and Kokila had taken him in. He had no complaints, really, except that Amma could be so stubborn about certain things, such as satellite TV. If he had real parents, he was sure, they would have succumbed to his pleas by now. And they would have bought a new color TV with those fancy remote controls as well. He would also have gotten a CD player and loads of other stuff people seem to have. Not all his friends were fortunate enough to have well-earning fathers but they had homes, real homes, not a strange home with so many people in it and people who randomly came and went. Whenever Karthik thought of the guest rooms in the front, he had the image of faces rushing past him like faces framed in the windows of a fast train. He remembered no one and he didn't care all that much for living in Tella Meda.

He was bored. Summer was here, there was no school, and Tella Meda was mind-numbing. In addition, everyone was so busy with Padma's wedding. Like he cared. And the boy she was marrying looked like a total geek.

Karthik didn't mind geeks. He himself could be called one because he was very good at math, but still, Padma's future husband looked weird. And what a show-off, sending pictures of himself standing next to cars and whatnot.

Karthik didn't admit it to anyone but he wanted to go to America as well. He followed Meena's example and talked about nationality and staying in India because he wanted a good EAMCET rank like her. Besides, he also wanted to become a pilot. He was planning to take the National Defense Academy exam after his twelfth class so that he could join the Indian Defense Services as an officer. He wanted to be an air force pilot and wear those cool dark glasses along with the gray bomber jackets. He had watched *Top Gun* several times on video, as one of his friends had the tape, and he thought that flying was very cool. Even cooler was the motorbike in that movie. But it was such an old movie and a girlie movie at that, so he didn't admit to anyone that he liked it.

When he thought about the movies he watched, the books he read, and the games he played, he knew Kokila would understand none of that. She didn't even speak English and understood very little of the language. Why, she didn't even speak Hindi, even though she understood it. His life was more than his mother's had ever been, even in small-town Bheemunipatnam. And because Kokila didn't understand the things he understood and took for granted, Karthik felt his mother didn't really understand him or his needs. It wasn't just satellite TV, it was everything. Kokila didn't understand his need to spend more time with his friends or go to Visakhapatnam with them and eat pizza in the new pizza restaurant there. She didn't understand that he knew what a McDonald's was and all his friends had been to Visakhapatnam and had actually eaten a chicken burger, while he had only seen one and could only imagine how good it tasted.

At Tella Meda there was only vegetarian food and the only times Karthik had eaten meat and omelets had been at his friend Rajan's house. Rajan's father worked in the bank at Bheemunipatnam. They were not Brahmins but Kammas, and their caste permitted them to eat meat. Rajan's mother made goat curry and she put omelets and bread in Rajan's lunch box.

When Karthik once suggested to Kokila that maybe they should try to eat some nonvegetarian food, she had been appalled.

"Why? Why would you want to kill and eat some poor animal? Our food is not good enough? It's good food. Why would you want to eat that disgusting meat? Tell me? Why?"

Kokila had been so upset that Karthik never brought up the subject again. He didn't know why he liked meat, he just liked it and he wanted to eat it more often. Even Rajan's mother didn't cook meat that often because of how expensive it was, but whenever she did, Rajan would sneak away some juicy morsels for Karthik. Rajan was Karthik's very best friend and they both made plans to become pilots and fly jet planes.

Rajan lived in the next street, where new houses had been built a few years ago. Earlier there was no street, just barren land behind Tella Meda, but now streets had developed and paved roads had emerged from the muddy and empty land. Houses were being built constantly, and more and more businesses were opening in Bheemunipatnam. It still wasn't as nice as Visakhapatnam, but things were happening in the sleepy coastal town. There was a vacation resort being constructed on the beach some thirty kilometers away from Tella Meda where rich people were buying space in summer cottages. The resort promised to have tourists from all over the world. The plan was to make Bheemunipatnam the "Goa of the east."

Even though so many things were happening in Bheemunipatnam, Karthik felt that everything was at a standstill in Tella Meda. People were going about their lives in the very same fashion as they had for decades. Everyone talked about how important caste was and they discussed religion all the time. They didn't eat any meat and refused to have satellite TV. Sometimes, Karthik hated, hated, hated, hated Tella Meda and wished his real parents were alive so that he could go live with them. Of course, he'd take Kokila along because he loved her so much, but he wouldn't live in Tella Meda. Not if he could help it.

The argument for satellite TV reached new heights when Sushila rented a VCR from the video store along with videotapes that Padma said would appeal to Manoj and his friends who were coming for the wedding from America.

"Why for them and never for me?" Karthik demanded as the VCR was placed on a small settee next to the television and the video store boy hooked it up.

"Because they are the bridegroom's people and this is a temporary thing," Sushila informed him. "When you're old enough to get married, I'm sure your wife's family will also get for you whatever you want."

"Amma, why can't we just get satellite TV? Star TV is great and I'm sure that Padma's Manoj will like it," Karthik suggested.

Kokila shook her head. "You have to sign a contract for one whole year and I don't want to commit for that long. Now that the VCR is here, you can also get some tapes and watch, if you like. Can he, Sushila?"

Sushila cleared her throat and smiled uncomfortably. "I'd like to leave it free from tomorrow onward when Manoj and his family arrive. This is for them. Karthik can rent the VCR some other time."

Karthik glared at Kokila and Sushila. "I live here," he yelled at Kokila. "Do you even care about me?"

Kokila sighed. "Karthik," she called, but he ran out of the TV room, into the temple room, and then straight out of Tella Meda.

"I'm sorry but this is for the bridegroom's family and—" Sushila began, but Kokila shook her head.

"It's okay. He's just being so difficult these days. Nothing is good enough . . . It was so much easier when he was smaller," Kokila said.

"It's the age and he's a boy. Boys have more tantrums than girls," Sushila said. "He'll come around, don't worry."

But Kokila worried and her worry increased when Karthik didn't come home that night. She went to Rajan's house to see if he was there, but Rajan was missing as well.

The boys, it seemed, had run away together.

"Oh, it's my wedding in two days and he has to run away now?" Padma demanded angrily. "Does anyone care about me? Now I have to worry about him when I should be happy about getting married. How can he do this to me?"

Sushila agreed that Karthik's timing could have been better. "We'll just focus on what we have to do. The boys will come back, don't worry about that. Where will they go?"

They could go anywhere, Kokila thought, anywhere at all. There were five hundred *rupees* missing from Rajan's home. On that money, two boys could go anywhere.

She couldn't sleep the night the boys went missing. No one had seen them and no one had heard anything. Other friends of Rajan and Karthik didn't know where they were. Some thought they might have gone to Visakhapatnam because that was where they always wanted to go, while others were sure that they had drowned while playing in the water. Some others thought that UFOs were involved. Rajan's mother confided in Kokila that she feared the boys might indeed be in

Visakhapatnam to watch the India-versus-Australia one-day interna-tional cricket match being played there. The police had been informed but they had no leads. Kokila felt like she was in the past again, run-ning around as she had done so many years ago when Vidura ran away.

"Remember Vidura?" Kokila asked as she and Chetana sat on the terrace, Kokila standing where Ramanandam Sastri had years ago, waiting for his son to come home.

Chetana smiled and nodded. "Ramanandam had beaten him a few days before he ran away," she said as if remembering an old, old story.

"Really?" Kokila was surprised. "You never told."

"I didn't?" Chetana shrugged. "Ramanandam came to me and said that I should not tell anyone about it as it had nothing to do with Vidura running away. He made me promise and he was crying, so I forgot about it. I thought I told you; I guess I didn't."

"Is that why he ran away, you think?" Kokila asked.

"Who knows why he ran away. I have seen enough of the world to know that people do strange things for strange reasons." Chetana sighed. "But don't compare Vidura with Karthik. Karthik is coming back home when that money runs out. Vidura had other demons chasing him."

"Like what?" Kokila asked.

"Like he hated Charvi and he hated his father. Vidura was thirteen but he had already had sex . . . did you know that? He would kiss me and touch me and . . . Oh, I had almost forgotten about Vidura," Chetana said with a laugh. "I thought I was the queen around here and obviously better than you because Vidura did more kissing with me than with you."

"He kissed me once, did I tell you?" Kokila said. "We went for a walk on the beach."

Chetana laughed out loud. "I know, I saw you go with him. That's where he always took me and kissed me, right behind the big rock there. Looks like he wanted to take advantage of both of us and we'd have let him too. Stupid, we were."

"What happened to him, you think?" Kokila asked.

"Anything could have happened," Chetana said. "The world out there is dangerous . . . but don't think about that. Karthik is fine. He will come home and you will scold him for running away. In a few years you will laugh about this."

She would never laugh about this, Kokila thought, she would never be able to laugh about feeling like this.

Kokila looked at the empty road in front of Tella Meda and felt panic clench her. The house below was full of people and this was a festive time but she could not stop the terror within her from rising. Karthik had run away and what if she never saw him again? Just imagining that was crippling and she strained her eyes to see farther so that she could catch a glimpse of Karthik coming back home with Rajan.

"Do you think Karthik will disappear and never return like Vidura?" Kokila asked, tears filling her eyes.

"Vidura had no one to love him here. Karthik has you. He'll come back. He just wanted to have some fun and that's all. He isn't like Vidura," Chetana said.

"Why did Ramanandam beat Vidura?" Kokila asked.

"I don't know. Something about something Vidura had seen or said. Vidura wasn't very clear when he talked to me. Then two days later, he ran away. I talked to Ramanandam and he then asked me not to tell anyone about the beating. Those days I thought Ramanandam was second to none and what did I know? I was a little girl," Chetana said.

"Ramanandam never told me," Kokila said, suddenly feeling betrayed by a man who had been dead for over two decades. "He never said anything to me about Vidura. I was crazy about Vidura. I stayed in Tella Meda and didn't go with that boy I was married to because of him. I was scared you'd steal him away if I left."

Chetana smiled. "And I would have too if he hadn't run away."

"I can't bear it, Chetana, if Karthik doesn't come back. I will die," Kokila said bleakly.

Chetana put an arm around Kokila. "He'll come back. He's just out there blowing off five hundred *rupees*. He'll be home by . . . I say, tomorrow night. That's how long that money will last them and then they'll come running home, too scared to face the world alone."

"He's angry that we won't get satellite TV at Tella Meda," Kokila said as she sniffled, pushing the tears off her face with her hands.

"If it wasn't satellite TV it would be something else. With children there's always something missing that they want or something that we can't or won't give. That's life," Chetana said, and wiped Kokila's face with the *pallu* of her *sari*.

Downstairs in Tella Meda there was festivity brimming. Telugu movie music (much to Charvi's chagrin) was playing loudly and people were milling around the courtyard and verandah. Relatives and friends who hadn't seen each other since the last wedding were chatting and catching up, while Sushila and Karuna served tea and snacks.

Padma was sitting in one corner talking to Manoj while Manoj's parents and some others stared openly at them, talking about how good the couple looked together.

Padma sat shyly, slightly turned toward Manoj, who looked much less spectacular in person without the image of his car behind him. He wore a gold chain and a shiny gold bracelet on his wrist. His face had a matching shiny texture and he wore a black T-shirt with faded blue jeans. He smelled of cologne and he talked with a slight American accent.

He is terrible to look at, no matter his smell and his accent, thought Meena with a slight smile. She had arrived with Asif the day before, just before Karthik's disappearance.

"What do you think of Tella Meda?" she asked Asif, who was sitting by her, watching the proceedings with unabashed curiosity. It wasn't every day he, a Muslim, was invited or allowed to participate so intimately in a Telugu Brahmin wedding.

When Meena introduced him to everyone at Tella Meda, there was such silence that Meena started to laugh a little out of nervousness. It wasn't as though Asif had "Muslim" stamped on his forehead. He was a nice-looking boy with fair skin. He was quite tall, almost six feet, and definitely didn't look like a Telugu boy. *And thank God for that,* Meena thought. As soon as people heard his name, they became uncomfortable. Chetana had been the least concerned—at least that was the way it appeared to Meena.

"He's just a friend, right?" Chetana asked Meena to her face, and Meena lied without compunction.

"Good," Chetana said, "Because I won't tolerate you marrying some Muslim. Do you know that you have to become a Muslim to marry one?"

"That isn't how it always works," Meena had argued. "I don't really think Asif's parents are that type of people. They're not very conservative."

"But that isn't really important to us, now, is it?" Chetana asked slyly. "Since you're only friends with this Muslim boy, right?"

"Right," Meena said, knowing she had been caught.

Now as she sat beside Asif, watching Padma talk and laugh shyly with her husband-to-be, Meena smiled. Her life, she knew, was much better than Padma's would ever be. Padma was marrying some stranger off the road. Tomorrow, after the wedding ceremony, she would have to have sex with this man. She would have to take her clothes off and be naked in front of this stranger. She had talked to him on the phone for a few months now but it still seemed extremely rushed, unnatural.

Meena and Asif had fallen in love before they had taken their clothes off in front of each other. They had been intimate with each other *after* they had known each other, not before. She had kissed Asif, felt her heart race, months before they had made love. Padma would have to forgo all that excitement and foreplay and just jump in and have sex. And since this Manoj chap was probably a twenty-eight-year-old virgin, Meena could only imagine the disaster that awaited poor Padma the next night. Meena knew that Padma had always woven dreams around the first night and her husband, who would, of course, be handsome.

Meena felt some satisfaction that she sat next to the good-looking Asif, while Padma was being saddled with Mr. Black-as-Coal. Padma had treated Meena shabbily, unforgivably, because Meena had done well in EAMCET. Padma showed off about going to America, getting married, and Meena could only frown at that. What was the big deal about America? Already people were talking about how the information technology business in the United States was not doing very well and Indians were being laid off and sent back to India.

And why would an engineer want to go to America when there were so many good jobs available in India now? All the big IT companies were in India now, opening offices in Bangalore and Hyderabad. What was the big show-off element about going to America?

"Did you tell your mother?" Asif asked Meena as she watched Padma. "And stop staring at the poor girl. You'll poke a hole into her."

Meena made a face. "No, I didn't tell my mother. I think I'll wait till I'm not around her to tell her. And I'm staring because that fellow is ugly."

"And she's quite a beauty," Asif said. He grinned when Meena looked at him angrily. "Just wanted to get your attention. She isn't better-looking than you."

"Do you find her attractive?" Meena asked.

Asif shrugged. "I think she's beautiful. She is, Meena, even a blind man can see that. But do I find her attractive? Now, how could I find anyone attractive when I have you with me?"

Meena smiled at that and playfully jabbed him in the shoulder. "You're smooth, aren't you?"

"I took classes," Asif said with a laugh.

Just as Asif laughed, Chetana saw them from the terrace and frowned.

"She's lying," she told Kokila.

"About the Muslim boy?"

"Hmm. He's not *just* a friend. She's sleeping with him. I can tell," Chetana said, and sighed.

"How do you know?"

"A mother knows," Chetana said.

Kokila raised her eyebrows in disbelief.

"I went through her suitcase," Chetana admitted. "She had birth control pills. And just look at them! Of course they're doing it. At least she's being careful. But I must say I can't stand the idea of her marrying this Muslim."

"He's very nice to look at," Kokila said. "And Manikyam also hated the idea of Ravi marrying you. Do you think it's wise to make the same mistakes Manikyam and her husband made?"

Kokila couldn't imagine being upset about whomever Karthik wanted to marry. She would welcome any daughter-in-law into her home, she thought, benevolent now because she would even say yes to satellite TV if it would get Karthik home. And once he was home, she would lock him up. School and home, that was it, nowhere else— no friends, no nothing.

"At least I wasn't a Muslim," Chetana said, watching the intimacy between Meena and Asif. "Renuka was telling me that Meena would have to become a Muslim and they would change her name to some Turku name. Meena thinks she's in love with him. And that boy, look at how he looks at my daughter. Like he knows what she looks like without her clothes on. And he probably does. These Muslim boys seducing nice Hindu girls . . ."

"You can't fight this, you know," Kokila said softly. "They're both going to be doctors in one year. They will be independent. They don't need you or anyone's money."

Chetana nodded. "That's why I won't say anything until she does. You think she'll tell me the truth before she leaves?"

Kokila shook her head. "She'll wait till she's back in Hyderabad and then she'll phone you."

"That's what I thought," Chetana said. "Well, at least he's not a lecher like Babu."

"Bhanu is very happy with Babu," Kokila reminded her. "He takes very good care of her, loves her very much."

"I still wish she'd married someone who looked better, felt better, and was better," Chetana said before correcting herself slightly. "But she's happy and has money. I couldn't have done better for her if I'd gone looking for a boy for her."

"And look at Padma's bridegroom," Kokila said and they both winced.

"He is not very nice to look at to start with, and seeing him next to Padma . . . oh, Sushila's heart must be breaking to marry her beautiful daughter off to that boy," Chetana said with a sly smile. "Not that

it was ever a contest, but Meena will be a doctor and will marry a doctor."

"A Muslim doctor," Kokila said, and Chetana sighed.

"Don't keep saying Muslim. He's a fair, good-looking boy. I'll try
not to think too much about his religion. Oh, Kokila, will they really
change Meena's name?"

As Chetana had predicted, Karthik came home the very next night.
He and Rajan had spent all the money they had stolen and came back,
their heads hung and their hands and faces grimy. They had ridden
home from Visakhapatnam in a truck transporting chickens and they
smelled like chicken shit.

"We didn't have bus money," Karthik said to Kokila as she poured
water over him and scrubbed him with soap, complaining about how
dirty he was and how bad he smelled.

"Amma, are you angry with me?" he asked when Kokila started to
dry him.

"What do you think?"

"I think you're very angry with me."

"Then you're thinking right," Kokila said. "Now go get dressed.
Rajan and his parents are going to be here soon."

The boys confessed that they had gone to watch the India-versus-
Australia one-day match in Visakhapatnam. To both Rajan and
Karthik, Saurav Ganguly, the Indian cricket team captain, was a hero
and they had wanted very badly to see him play. Unfortunately they
tried to buy tickets on the black market and were swindled out of a
major portion of their money. The man selling the tickets had given
them fake tickets and they were not allowed to enter the stadium. By
the time they figured that going home was the only option left, they
had run out of money and were too embarrassed to phone their parents and ask for help.

Kokila was relieved that Karthik had come home unharmed, and
unlike Vidura, had not disappeared for life. Now when she thought of
Vidura, Kokila couldn't even remember his face. How could she have
forgotten the face of the boy who had made her throw her life away?

On the other hand, she couldn't remember the face of the boy she had been married to for a few short years either.

After so many years it didn't hurt at all that Vidura had run away and that she had no idea what happened to him. It didn't hurt that Ramanandam had beaten him a few days before he ran away and Kokila would probably never know why. Something had been wrong between father and son and also between father and daughter, but then all of Ramanandam's relationships were tainted with some malignance. After almost twenty years, Kokila couldn't even remember Ramanandam's face very clearly unless she looked at one of the pictures of his in the house. But Kokila had forgotten the love she had felt for him. She now only felt a measure of regret when she remembered her relationship with that old man.

Rajan's father watched his son sternly when they arrived at Tella Meda. Rajan's mother, however, seemed only happy that Rajan had come back home, not unlike Kokila.

"There is the matter of the stolen money," Rajan's father said. "Kokila Amma, Rajan here says that it was Karthik's idea to take the money. Now, five hundred *rupees* is a lot of money. You do understand, I can't let the amount just slide by."

Chetana, who had been sitting in the temple room, where Rajan and his parents had seated themselves by the musical instruments, cleared her throat.

"I don't mean to interfere, but didn't your son spend that money along with Karthik?" Chetana asked, and looked away sheepishly when Kokila glared at her. "Come on, Kokila, they *both* spent that money or rather lost the money to a swindler."

"Karthik, who stole the money?" Kokila asked, ignoring Chetana. Karthik shook his head.

"What does that mean?"

"We both stole it."

"No, you stole it alone," Rajan's father said. "Right, Rajan? Karthik stole the money, didn't he?"

Rajan nodded, unable to look Karthik in the eye.

"Well, speak up," Rajan's father said, and Rajan's face crumpled into tears as his mother pulled him into her embrace.

"We both stole it," Karthik repeated, and looked at Kokila. "I'm sorry. You can have all the money in my piggy bank."

"Well, I'll need all five hundred back," Rajan's father said. "Now stop crying, Rajan. You did what you wanted to do and now you cry? Stupid bastard. And this running away was also Karthik's idea. But what else can we expect from a boy growing up in *this* house? He's always in our home, eating and watching TV. He knows where we keep the money and . . ."

Kokila's face flushed with embarrassment. This man made it sound as though Karthik had no home, no food, and no TV.

"I'll make sure he never goes to your house again," Kokila said. "About the money, I don't believe Karthik stole it. He has no reason to steal from your house when he can easily steal from Tella Meda if he wants to." Kokila pointed to the safe keys hanging at her waist. "Since your son spent half the money, I think it's fair that only half the money is returned to you. Chetana, if you could keep an eye on our guests, I will be right back."

Kokila went into Charvi's room, where the safe was, where she kept her money as well as Tella Meda's, and brought back two hundred and fifty *rupees* to the temple room.

She handed the money to Rajan's father, who took it hastily. "I still think your boy stole the money and you're encouraging him to become a thief by not paying me the entire amount," he said.

"See, Karthik, this is the kind of friend you have," Kokila said, speaking to her son but wanting Rajan and his family to hear her. "He implicates only you in a theft while you maintain that both of you are guilty. His father says that you eat their food and watch their TV and they don't want you there, while you keep saying that their house is so much nicer and Rajan is so much happier because he has satellite TV. Now what do you think?"

Karthik was close to tears and his voice was shaky when he spoke. "I think Rajan is not my friend," he said, and then ran into the courtyard away from Rajan.

"Now, you may leave," Kokila said to Rajan and his parents. "By encouraging your son to lie, you have taught him not to take responsibility for his actions because he can always blame someone else. He ran away too and he spent the money too. Maybe you should worry about that and not who stole the money and whose idea this was."

Kokila didn't wait for an answer and marched into the courtyard to find her son and mete out the punishment he deserved.

Karthik thought he got off easily. Kokila put him on garden duty, where he was to help Karuna with the weeds and the watering of plants for the next three months. In addition, he was not allowed to watch any television or visit any of his friends for a month. He was never to be friends with Rajan again and his piggy bank, which held almost a hundred *rupees,* was emptied.

"Is she still angry with you?" Padma asked Karthik as the woman from the Cinderella Beauty Salon put henna on Padma's hands. She was making intricate designs of flowers and leaves. Padma's feet had already been decorated with a similar design. The *muhurat* for the marriage was at 11:22 in the morning, which meant that the wedding ceremony would begin early. At the time of the *muhurat,* Manoj would put a mixture of cumin and jaggery on Padma's head and she would do the same to him. The *shenai* would be played loudly and everyone would throw uncooked turmeric rice at them. And right after that, Manoj would tie the *mangalsutra* around Padma's neck and they would be husband and wife.

"Amma is very angry," Karthik said, and then changed the subject. "Are you excited about getting married?"

Padma nodded and smiled.

"Your henna is the best work I have done in years," Saroja, the owner of the beauty salon, said. "What do you think, Karthik?"

Karthik had no idea what was good work and what wasn't, so he just nodded. "I bet you can't wait to go to America."

Padma laughed, her voice tinged with excitement. "He has a very nice car and it has air-conditioning inside it. Even our flat will have air-conditioning so when it gets hot, we can just turn it on and it will be nice and cool."

"Like in that big supermarket in Visakhapatnam," Karthik said, now eager to share his adventure.

"Is that where you went?" Padma asked. "He ran away to Visakhapatnam for two days," she informed Saroja, who grinned and called Karthik a naughty boy.

"We had pizza and we ate lots of ice cream. We went to this music store and they had so many CDs there, and cool CD players. Hey, Padma, you'll send me a CD player from America, won't you?" Karthik asked.

Padma nodded. He might have run away at the wrong time but still, he was like a younger brother to her. "As soon as I know how much it costs and how much money I can spend. First thing I'll buy is a hair dryer for myself, and *then* a CD player for you. I hate having to dry my hair with a towel. In all those TV shows, everyone has a hair dryer. And Manoj said that there are so many Indian hotels and shops where he lives that we can have *dosas* every morning at a hotel if we like. He makes a lot of money. Eighty-five thousand dollars every year. That is—"

"Almost thirty-eight *lakhs* of *rupees*," Karthik said, calculating the exchange rate quickly. Everyone knew that one dollar was equal to forty-five *rupees*.

"So, you're getting a rich husband," Saroja said as she set her henna tube aside and blew gently on Padma's hands. "And you are going to America. Girl, your beauty has brought you great luck. Look at that Meena, studying and studying and studying, while you, ah, you're getting married and going away."

"Have you seen the boy she's come with?" Padma's voice dropped to a conspiratory whisper.

"Asif is cool," Karthik said with a grin. "He told me that even he ran away once when he was my age. He came back the same night because he was too scared."

"Asif is a Muslim," Padma said, not wanting Karthik to like anything about Meena, not even her friends. If she was the one who would send him a CD player, then he should be on her side.

"So what?" Karthik said. "I'm a Hindu, big deal. Didn't they teach you in school, 'All Indians are my brothers and sisters'? I don't think he's any different from us because he's a Muslim."

"They eat meat," Padma said.

Karthik nodded. "And so have I. I love chicken. Does that make me a bad person?"

"Does anyone here know?" Padma demanded, shocked.

Karthik sighed. "Don't tell Amma. She'll feel bad and get angry. I don't need her to get any angrier with me right now."

Padma sighed and watched Saroja pack her things. "If Meena marries this Muslim, she'll have to become Muslim too. Would that be no big deal too?"

"If she wants to change her religion, it's up to her," Karthik said.

"I'll be back tomorrow morning to do your makeup and hair," Saroja said. "Now you sleep nicely. We don't want bags under your eyes in all your wedding photos. And keep sprinkling lime water on your hands to make the henna color dark."

Saroja left behind a small spray bottle filled with lime water. Karthik sprayed a little and made the drying henna wet again after Saroja was gone.

"Are you and Meena still fighting?" Karthik asked. Everyone knew that they used to be good friends and then they had stopped being friends.

"No, we don't even fight anymore," Padma said.

"You used to be so close, you must miss her," Karthik said. "I miss Rajan. He was my best friend."

"I have other friends now," Padma said. "Why would I miss her?"

"I'm going to miss Rajan for a while. I mean, I know he's not a nice guy, what with putting all the blame on me and accusing me of stealing money, but still, he was my best friend. Now I don't have one," Karthik said.

"I missed her in the beginning. Now we're almost strangers," Padma said, suddenly sad. She realized she had no friend with whom to share the joys and fears of marriage. Her college friends were okay, but she had never told them how she really felt, the way she used to with Meena.

"Meena is cool," Karthik said. "You're cool too," he added with a smile. "I'll miss you when you're gone."

"But I'll write and send you a CD player," Padma said.

"As long as you send the CD player," Karthik said.

Meena sat alone on the balustrade up in the terrace watching the sun go down. The red ball of fire mingled with the waters of the bay, making the water pink and red before slowly dipping below the surface and disappearing. Black glossy water was left behind and a gentle warm summer breeze ruffled the surface.

It was hot. It was so hot that even in the evening the cool air from the bay was warm and only marginally helped to assuage the heat. Padma would have to wear loads of jewelry and thick silk *saris* the next day, Meena thought, and then she and her husband would have to sit in front of a fire and make promises they would have to keep as husband and wife. Padma would fry in her clothes in this heat.

In the past four years, Meena had cut her ties with Tella Meda. Now when she came back she felt and was treated like a guest.

Asif had gone for a walk and for the first time since she came to Tella Meda two days ago, Meena stood all alone, aware that this was not her home anymore. And she could hardly call her dormitory room home. So for now, until Asif and she married and rented a house, she was homeless, while Padma was going from a home in Tella Meda straight to her husband's home in America. There would be no struggles for Padma. Her husband was already established financially and he would take care of her, while Meena and Asif would have to struggle as new doctors.

A spark of jealousy blossomed within Meena at her ex-friend's good fortune. Even though Manoj was not nice to look at, he was going to make life so easy for Padma. Meena loved Asif but the fact was that they both were students right now and they would be students for a while longer.

Maybe Padma was better off having gotten a bad EAMCET rank. Maybe this was the easy and better route. What had Meena achieved in the past four years? She had studied and studied and studied. She had studied while Padma had three easy college years and was now going to have an easy married life. Everyone was happy about Padma's match. Meena's marriage to Asif would only cause trouble.

A sound alerted Meena and she turned. Padma had come up to the terrace to find some solace as well.

Each looked at the other uncomfortably. They hadn't spoken alone since Meena left Tella Meda four years ago.

"Nice night," Meena said, her eyes darting around the road, looking for Asif.

"Yes," Padma said, and came to stand by Meena, looking out at the dark bay in front. She was holding her palms up and her *sari* was hiked up as well to prevent smudging the henna before it stained her skin properly.

"Well, I'll go down and—"

"I'm leaving India," Padma said quietly. "I don't know when we'll see each other again."

Meena sighed. "Are you happy?"

Padma nodded with a small smile. "And you?"

Meena watched as Asif finally appeared, opening the gate, entering Tella Meda, and she nodded as well.

"He's very good-looking," Padma said. "Very handsome and fair. And very tall."

"He's also a Muslim," Meena said.

"So what?" Padma said, and laughed. "I know it's too late to say I'm sorry and I don't know what I'd be saying I'm sorry for. But I wanted you to know that I'm glad you came for my wedding."

"I didn't get a good EAMCET rank on purpose," Meena said, tears filling her eyes suddenly. It was so terribly sad that two good friends had been driven apart by competition.

"I hated you for it because it made me feel like a complete failure," Padma confessed. "Now I'm getting married and I feel like I'm not too much of a failure."

"And now I'm a little jealous," Meena admitted.

"Why?"

"Well, you're going to America and you don't have any struggles ahead of you. Asif and I have to finish medical school and then do our postgraduate studies and then find work. That is at least three, four years away," Meena said.

"But you'll be a doctor and I will be just a wife," Padma said. "I'm so scared of what will happen. What if . . . what if Manoj is not really a nice boy? What then?"

"What do you mean? Amma said you've been talking to him for months now. You'd know if he wasn't nice," Meena said.

Padma looked around to make sure no one was coming upstairs and would hear them. "I read this article in some magazine about how girls get married to boys in America and there the boys beat them and ill-treat them. And because they're in a foreign country they are unable to do anything. I got so scared, but Amma found this match with great difficulty and she always wanted me to go to America. I know Manoj . . . at least I think I do, but I'm still scared."

"In America they have very good police, not like in India. There you can trust them," Meena said. "There is this show on Star TV called *Cops*. You have to dial some number for police . . . like here you have 100, there they have 911, I think. Call them and tell them if he beats you and they'll arrest him."

"I don't want my husband to be thrown in jail," Padma said.

Meena raised her eyebrows. "You'd rather he hit you?"

Padma sighed. "Okay, so what was that number I can call?"

"911," Meena said, and Padma repeated it. "But check to make sure that is the number."

"Okay," Padma said. "One more thing—now that you're going to be a doctor and all, you can tell me what to do about birth control. Amma says that medicines are bad and I should not take anything. What else is there? I know about condoms but magazines say they don't work and men don't like using them. I don't want children right away. We don't even know each other. I thought we'll wait a little, get to know each other for a few years, and then have children."

"There's nothing wrong with pills," Meena said. "They're actually good for you. They make your menses more regular and if you don't want to have menses a month here and there you don't even have to with the pill. I'll give you a packet before I go and when you're there go to a doctor and get more. If you're not comfortable with pills, make him wear a condom. Before I started taking birth control pills, Asif used to wear them and he—" Meena stopped as she realized what she had revealed. It had never been her intention to tell anyone that she and Asif were having sex.

"You've had sex?" Padma asked in a scandalized whisper.

"Don't tell anyone," Meena said, panicked.

"So," Padma said, a smile wreathing her face, "tell me about it."

Meena looked around, mortified, and then grinned.

And as Meena shyly described what it meant to be intimate with a man, the past four years fell away.

5 December 1999. India's glamour scene was jubilant after Ms. India, Yukta Mookhey, was crowned Miss World.

24 December 1999. Indian Airlines Flight 814, which was enroute from Kathmandu, Nepal to Delhi, India was hijacked and taken to Kandahar, Afghanistan.

31 December 1999. Five hijackers, who had been holding 155 hostages on an Indian Airlines plane, left the plane with two Islamic clerics they demanded be freed.

The Heart-Broken Goddess

*T*he world was excited.

The old millennium was coming to an end; a new millennium was about to begin. There were posters everywhere about parties being organized to welcome the new year and millennium, and in the newspapers there were several millennium specials. What were the most pivotal moments of the millennium? Who was the man (or woman) of the millennium? Would India win the World Cup in cricket again in the next millennium?

Bheemunipatnam got a computer center to mark the special year. Somehow Karthik seemed to know a lot about computers and spent most of his free time either playing cricket or in the computer center. He was so good with computers that Jeevan, the owner of the computer center, offered him a job maintaining the computers and helping newcomers learn how to operate them. When something went wrong with the dial-up connection, Jeevan called upon Karthik. When something went wrong with the printer, Jeevan relied on Karthik to fix the problem.

For Karthik, who was just thirteen years old, earning money was a great kick. He gave his first paycheck to Kokila, who gave the money back to him and asked him to buy the new sneakers he had been wanting.

As he was growing up, Kokila could feel the pinch of money increase. Bangaru's thousand *rupees* were starting to mean less and less every month as costs rose. Kokila made some money working with Shanthi and Chetana in their new tailor shop but it was hardly enough.

Shanthi and Chetana had opened a tailor shop in the town with Babu's help. Since Meena had left Andhra Pradesh to do her postgraduate studies with Asif (to whom she was now openly engaged) in Bombay, Bhanu and Chetana had drawn closer. Chetana took care of Bhanu's growing son and daughter while Bhanu pursued a degree at the Bheemunipatnam degree college. After watching Meena get a worthy education, Bhanu was inspired to get a B.A. She convinced Babu and took her metric and intermediate exams. Everyone including Bhanu was surprised at her tenacity.

Babu, whose photo shop had grown into a large business, still loved his wife and took care of her as he had when he first married her. There were several servants in the house and Bhanu was driven to and from college by a driver in a brand-new Daewoo car (bought in Bhanu's name) while Babu drove the old Maruti.

He had offered a job to Kokila keeping some accounts but it was charity for a family member and Kokila knew it. She could not accept it. She made some money working for Shanthi and Chetana, but at fifty years of age, she was starting to worry about her future and Karthik's. He was set on becoming an air force pilot and was already studying hard for the NDA entrance exams. He had become friends with a retired army colonel who had moved with his family to

Bheemunipatnam. The colonel was a staunch devotee of Charvi and encouraged Karthik in his air force ambitions. They had bought a house close to Dr. Vishnu Mohan's, which had been rented out after Dr. Vishnu Mohan passed away the previous winter. His widow, Saraswati, had left to live with her daughter in London.

Everything, it seemed, had changed in Bheemunipatnam and even the world. Yet Kokila thought that Tella Meda was eerily still the same. It was the start of a new millennium and it seemed as if in the fifty years of her life, Kokila had achieved little. She still managed money at Tella Meda but her relationship with Charvi continued to be uneven. Most of the time, Kokila was sure that Charvi hated her, even now, for her relationship with Ramanandam. Other times, it seemed as if Charvi was grateful that Kokila was still at Tella Meda, a link to the past.

Charvi was just fifty-eight years old but she looked much older and her body was starting to stall.

"It's betraying me," she would tell Chetana, who still sat with her during morning *puja* sewing jasmine flowers into garlands. "This body won't take me very far."

"You'll outlive us all," Chetana would say, and she believed it. Chetana could feel the pinch of age as well. Her back had started to hurt a few years ago and getting up from bed in the morning was a chore. Once she had even had to ask Kokila to help her up. Meena said that it was the bed and promised to buy her a new one as soon as she took over Dr. Nageshwar Rao's practice.

"Is Meena coming for the winter holidays?" Charvi asked as she turned away, the *puja* finished. She needed to wear her glasses all the time now. She was the small old lady who hunched a little. Her hair had turned completely white and she didn't tie it anymore as it was quite thin. It hung around her face and shoulders loosely and mingled with the whiteness of her white cotton *saris*.

"No, she and Asif are going to his parents' house," Chetana said. "At least they've agreed to a marriage without her changing her religion. That is more than I had hoped for. And you have to admit Manikyam and her husband took it well."

"Is Manikyam still pestering you to ask me to talk to her?" Charvi asked astutely.

"She's dying, Charvi. Pancreatic cancer. She won't live for more than maybe a year. Don't you think it's time you forgave her? I have, and her crimes were committed against me," Chetana said. "I thought if I married Ravi, I'd leave Tella Meda and find my own life. I was so scared to be like Ambika that I rushed into marriage with a boy who was not a fit human being. I was young and foolish."

Charvi smiled. "I remember how vivacious you were. You still are. I used to worry about you, that you would grow up without love because Ambika gave you none."

"God knows what happened to her," Chetana said, now unable to remember her mother's face or anything else about her mother too clearly. "I saw her all those years ago, before I married Ravi. And then she was gone. I know Subhadra got letters for a while, but even Subhadra stopped keeping in touch with her."

"Poor Subhadra," Charvi said. "Everyone seems to be getting closer to death, don't you think?"

"Subhadra is almost eighty," Chetana said in amusement. "And she's had diabetes for almost eight years now. She should've known better."

A few months ago they had found out that Subhadra had to have her leg amputated. She had gone into diabetic shock and gangrene developed in her right leg, which then had to be cut off at midthigh. The diabetic shock was the result of eating too many sweets during Ganesh Chaturthi. She and Chandra had come to visit Charvi early in the year for the Telugu New Year, and they both had seemed healthy, happy, and well taken care of by Chandra's son and daughter-in-law. But within a few months everything had changed.

"Without a leg, God knows how long she'll last," Charvi said, and then sighed. "I wonder when it will be my turn."

"Why do you talk of death so much?" Chetana asked.

"Because my time is getting closer," Charvi said. "I'm not scared, just aware of it."

"How long do you think I'll live?" Chetana asked then, and Charvi turned her palms up in the air. "Lord Venkateshwara Swami only knows."

A week before the year 1999 became 2000, Charvi had a stroke.

It happened while she was performing morning *puja*. Kokila was up that morning, along with Chetana, and just as Charvi closed the *Bhagavad-Gita,* her reading glasses slipped down her nose and she collapsed.

Babu rushed Charvi to the hospital in his car, but by the time they reached the hospital, Charvi had lost all ability to move her right hand and right leg. Even the right side of her face was frozen, paralyzed.

The Bheemunipatnam hospital used to be a small, dingy little place with few beds and fewer doctors, but with the influx of people in the small town, the hospital had become bigger and there were more doctors as well.

However, it was suggested that Charvi be taken to King George Hospital in Visakhapatnam. Dr. Nageshwar Rao, who was consulted, suggested that Charvi would be better off in a private hospital than in a government one. Kokila was worried about money, but Manikyam said her husband said they would foot the bill. If Charvi was going to die, Manikyam hoped that she would forgive Manikyam for her ill-treatment of Chetana and Ravi all those years ago. So Charvi went to an exclusive private hospital.

Shanthi took over the responsibilities at Tella Meda, while Kokila and Chetana lived with Manikyam and her husband as they took care of Charvi.

"Ironic, isn't it?" Chetana said as she looked at the opulent house from the inside for the first time in her life. "I wanted to come inside this house so much all those years ago and now that I am here, I feel nothing."

Kokila looked around the house and raised her eyebrows. "It's a rich man's house."

"What rich? One son died of toddy poisoning and the other son is lying in a hospital waiting to die because his liver has been eaten by alcohol," Chetana said. "I look at my children and I'm happy because they're leading productive lives."

"Do you think Charvi is going to die?" Kokila asked.

"I hope so," Chetana said pragmatically. "If she lives, she will be our responsibility and with half her body paralyzed, God knows how much work that will mean. And what's left to live for? I can say I want to see my grandchildren grow up and you can say you want to see Karthik grow up. What can Charvi look forward to?"

As she lay in the white hospital room, Charvi contemplated the same thing. She had no sensation in her right leg, her right hand, and the right side of her face. There were tubes everywhere.

She had had a stroke, they said, and Charvi wasn't sure what that really meant. She knew what a heart attack was but she didn't know what this stroke thing meant. The doctor said something about blood not reaching her brain and part of her brain dying. That was why half her body was paralyzed.

The embarrassment of it was crushing Charvi. She wanted to be in Tella Meda. She wanted to die there, not here with tubes all over and inside her. A small machine was keeping track of her heartbeat and as it beeped, Charvi wished it would all be over. There was really nothing to live for now.

As she lay half eaten by a disease she wondered if the goddess inside her was also half-paralyzed. Had there ever been divinity inside her? Charvi had seriously believed for many years that she could cure people but when her own arthritis started to cause her considerable pain, she came to the conclusion she couldn't cure anyone, especially herself. But she argued with herself, saying that no one could fight age. Her body was growing old and old bodies started to decay. That didn't mean she wasn't a goddess.

She thought back to her father, and his first recognition of the goddess within her. Had he been right? She'd had her doubts from the start.

Manikyam sat by her side, her expression vacant, her skin old and decaying, her hair as white as Charvi's. She was dying too, Charvi thought. But then she was almost ten years older than Charvi.

If Ramanandam had not annunciated Charvi as a goddess, would she have had a life like Manikyam's? Would she have married, loved, had children and grandchildren?

She wanted to talk to Manikyam, wanted to tell her that all was forgiven. But something within her stopped her. If she forgave

Manikyam, it would be because she thought and believed she was dying and all of a sudden, Charvi didn't want to die. She wanted to live. There was a spark within her that wanted to claim all of her and even though she understood the futility of her life, she couldn't accept the darkness of death, not quite yet. And because she couldn't, she didn't call out to the staring Manikyam who was waiting to be forgiven.

Shanthi telephoned Kokila every night and told her that everything at Tella Meda was fine, especially Karthik, who was busier than ever. He and his friends were having a millennium new year's party. The party was to be held at the computer center and there was going to be loud music and whatever it was young boys these days were interested in.

Kokila didn't even remember how they had passed into the new year when they were young, but both Chetana and she agreed there had not been much noise. No party, no nothing. They always celebrated Ugadi, the Telugu New Year, but no one paid much attention to the calendar new year. That had obviously changed. The young people seemed to be learning all sorts of Western things from TV and the Internet. Kokila wasn't sure if that was a bad thing or a good thing. Chetana believed it was for the better. People were starting to have more fun in their lives, and that could never be a bad thing.

Charvi's condition deteriorated and the doctors declared that she would not get back the use of her right side. She was probably not going to live through the year either. Charvi refused to accept that and clung to the hope that her health would improve and she would be able to go back to Tella Meda.

Lavanya was informed of Charvi's declining health and she came to visit. In the past years, her beauty had faded and she had come to realize she had more in common with her "goddess" sister than she would admit. She didn't have a family or a husband and she was living with a friend in a small town in coastal Tamil Nadu. The bitterness had left her and she didn't blame Charvi for all the ills in the world anymore. Lavanya didn't stay long at the hospital, but the sisters made up before Lavanya left.

Charvi lay in bed, staring at the ceiling, talking to Kokila and Chetana about things that didn't matter and spending many hours in drug-induced sleep. With half her face paralyzed her words came out slurred and sometimes she was barely coherent. She was slipping away, the doctors said, as parts of her body started to shut down one after the other.

"I was in love once," Charvi said to no one in particular. Kokila was in the hospital room with her, reading a magazine, and her head shot up immediately.

"He was an American," Charvi continued, a half-smile on her face, and it looked as if she was in a different time and place. "Mark Talbot. Remember, Kokila, he sent me that picture in black and white? I looked so beautiful. He never wrote, never came to visit, and I waited, every day. In the beginning I waited with a huge fountain of hope inside my heart and after some years I knew he wouldn't come. I thought he was in love with me. Maybe he wasn't."

Kokila didn't know what to say. These were the ramblings of a dying woman.

"I remember him. He was a photographer for some foreign magazine," Kokila said. "Chetana and I had a big crush on him. He was very good-looking. I think he was attracted to you."

"You do?" Charvi said, and her voice held the excitement of a young girl finding out that the boy she likes wants her too. "I think so too. He had the bluest eyes and he talked to me. He just had to talk to me and I'd melt. Sometimes hearing his voice would make my knees weaken like they were filled with water. And he kissed me once. Just once, on the cheek."

Her hand drifted to her left cheek and she brushed herself gently. "Like the flutter of a butterfly, Kokila. He kissed me and I can still feel the heat of his breath. Oh, I could've married him, had children. Do you think that could have happened?"

"Yes," Kokila said, and put a hand on Charvi's forehead, stroking gently, hoping to console her. "It could have happened."

"It didn't happen for you either," Charvi said. "You should've gone with that boy you were married to. I tried to get rid of you, tried to send you away, but you were so stubborn."

Kokila smiled, remembering. "I was young. Who knows? I might've had a worse life with him than I did at Tella Meda."

"I hate you," Charvi whispered hoarsely, her eyes closed, her body rocking gently. "You took my father away and I hate you."

Kokila stopped stroking Charvi's forehead for a moment and then continued. She had always known that Charvi held a grudge about Kokila's relationship with Ramanandam; it was only a small surprise, to hear it so bluntly.

"He lusted after you. We all knew, we all could see," Charvi said. "Vidura could also see. He had a fight with him, a big fight, and Nanna beat him. He slapped him and hit him. Vidura said that Nanna kept you in Tella Meda for himself. And he did, didn't he? The first chance he got, he was spreading your legs."

Kokila's throat burned as emotions rode through her. Charvi's words were ugly. What she was insinuating was deviant and Kokila was sure that Ramanandam had not been the man Charvi was describing. He hadn't made her stay at Tella Meda and Vidura had run away for reasons that had nothing to do with her. Charvi was old and sick and confused. She was rambling, she was delirious.

"*I* wanted to stay. No one made me stay," Kokila said tightly. "I didn't want to leave Tella Meda."

"And he let you," Charvi said, then sighed. "Did you love him the way I love Mark Talbot?"

Kokila didn't answer.

"No, you couldn't. I saw you one day, sneaking out of his room, holding your *sari* to your body. You had slept with him, had sex with him. I hated him then too," Charvi said. "And Vidura . . . Vidura was so sad that his father had an eye on a girl he liked. On you."

"No, he didn't. Ramanandam didn't notice me that way until many years later," Kokila said, now certain that this was Charvi's delirium speaking. Truth or not, Kokila had the rest of her life to live and she wouldn't live it believing Charvi's words. How could she trust this woman who had called herself a goddess all her life yet had hated Kokila for so many years because Kokila had been young and gullible enough to sleep with an older man? Charvi felt no sympathy for Kokila, just hatred.

No, Kokila thought, and stared at Charvi's face as it convulsed with grief. She would not let Charvi taint her past with innuendo and suppositions.

"And Vidura ran away," Charvi cried out softly. "I never saw him again. Never. I promised my dying mother I'd care for him and I didn't. I don't even know if he's dead or alive." She started crying then, tears streaming down her face. Kokila wiped the tears off her wrinkled cheeks.

"It wasn't my fault, was it, Kokila?" Charvi asked. "Did he run away because of me? He hated me, didn't he? He told you he hated me."

"No, he loved you," Kokila said, and it wasn't a lie. It was so long ago now that she couldn't remember what Vidura had told her and what he had meant.

"He had a fight with Nanna. I think it was about me," Charvi said, and started to sob loudly. "And then he ran away. He is the only regret I have. No, that's not true, there are a hundred others as well. So many regrets that I'm not sure where one starts and one ends. Don't have regrets, Kokila, they weigh heavily and make you want to live even when life isn't worth living."

She mumbled on some more but Kokila couldn't understand her. She stood by Charvi, one hand on her forehead and the other holding her hand.

"Go to sleep now, Charvi, rest a little," Kokila whispered, and despite herself she felt a strong affection for this woman who was an indelible part of her life, a woman who had given her a home, a purpose. Charvi was friend, sister, guardian, and nemesis, all wrapped into one.

Charvi fell asleep then. Kokila, Chetana, and Manikyam took turns keeping vigil by her bedside over the next few days. Charvi slept for longer and longer periods.

And the day before the new millennium arrived, Charvi quietly passed away in her sleep.

Charvi's body was taken back to Tella Meda and it was debated where her *samadhi* would be built. When saints passed away, they were known to reach a higher plane of existence and they went into *samadhi.* Their bodies were not cremated but buried and a building, a *samadhi,* was built there in their honor.

News of Charvi's death traveled among her devotees and many of them arrived to pay their last respects. Among the devotees were Kedarnath Somayajula and his wife, the legitimate part-owners of Tella Meda. With Charvi dead, they were now ready to sell Tella Meda to the construction company that had wanted to demolish the big, old house with a white roof and build an apartment complex.

It was not a surprise—Kokila had been expecting this—but now she didn't know where the *samadhi* should be built. It couldn't be built in Tella Meda, as Tella Meda would cease to exist in a few months.

The old *pujari* at the temple suggested that the *samadhi* be built there, but there wasn't enough room on the temple grounds. Finally, Subhadra suggested that maybe the *samadhi* should be built by the bay on the beach. After all, Charvi had gone for a walk there every day and it would be public enough that people would be able to pay their respects to her.

Money was raised from devotees for the building of the *samadhi* by the roadside on the beach, right in front of Tella Meda. The Municipal Committee of Bheemunipatnam wholeheartedly supported the idea, as they believed that Charvi had been an integral part of life in Bheemunipatnam and therefore a proper monument to her death had to be built.

The *samadhi* was made quickly and the contractor who made it did it for free.

Being dead is like being within a rainbow, Charvi thought as she lay under splendid colors that shimmered brightly over her. She had transcended her body. She could feel weightlessness race through her. She didn't have a corporeal form, no face, no eyes, no flesh.

She swam past the people thronged around the verandah and in the temple room, who were waiting to catch a glimpse of her body in the courtyard, covered in white, lying on a straw gurney.

Subhadra was sitting next to Charvi's body, crying, as she swatted mosquitoes off Charvi's face with one hand and fanned with the other. Meena and Asif were sitting in a corner, looking bored. Meena had never believed in her, Charvi thought, and smiled because it didn't matter anymore. All sins had been forgiven, hers and others'. And God knew she had sinned just as others had.

Kokila, as always, was coordinating everything. She was in a heated discussion with a contractor, arranging for the *samadhi* to be built. Charvi liked the idea of her *samadhi* being close to the water.

Charvi went up to all those present and felt regret that she had never made up with Manikyam. Lavanya was not there, but Charvi had already said good-bye to her in the hospital.

The walls of Tella Meda seemed alive as she slipped through them and floated around the old house for one last time. She had lived here for over four decades. This was her home and soon it would be gone. It seemed befitting that as she died, Tella Meda would also die.

She stood outside Tella Meda for a while, watching her *samadhi* being built on the beach with big electric lights shining around the construction area. The full moon was rising and Charvi smiled as she saw the old house with the white roof shimmer in the brilliant moonlight.

Charvi saw herself standing on the terrace on another moonlit night years ago, looking down to see a man taking her photograph. The image was strong for an instant and then it dissolved, lightening her heart.

The house moved with its own energy, in synchronized rhythm with the waves of the bay and Charvi's spirit, and then the house enfolded Charvi into its bosom.

In the years to come, the words on the marble remained clear:

Here lies Goddess Charvi. May her light shine over all of us.

But people forgot who she was and once Tella Meda was gone, it was even harder to remember the house, the goddess, the magic. A new era claimed Bheemunipatnam as computers and big airplanes made the world smaller, as the slums shrank in size, and people started to live better.

19 March 2000. Bill Clinton, the president of the United States, arrived to a warm welcome in India. His was the first United States presidential visit in two decades.

7 April 2000. The Delhi police unearthed a multimillion-*rupee* cricket-betting and match-fixing racket involving five South African cricketers, including the South African cricket team captain, Hansie Cronje.

Tella Meda, the House with the White Roof

*T*he last time Kokila stepped out of Tella Meda was in the beginning of the new millennium.

When she looked back at the house she still saw the most beautiful house she had ever lived in. But now she could see the marks of the years, and she could, she thought, see that the soul of the house was not innocent and untouched anymore. The house had been built in 1955 and now was being broken down in 2000. It was a short life for a house but Kokila thought with a smile that it was not the number of years but the quality of those years that were important.

Tella Meda would be demolished the next day. A big ball of iron would be rammed through its center and then workers with hammers and chisels would come and chip away the rest. And in a few days, they would take all the remains away and there would be nothing left.

The house's foundation would be dug up and a new foundation would be laid in. A new house would emerge—a house bigger than Tella Meda, a house with more rooms, a house that would stand higher, a house in which more people would live than had ever lived in Tella Meda.

"But some of us will remain," Kokila whispered to Tella Meda as she stood in its verandah.

It was really Babu who had come up with the idea. He'd found out that since Kokila and Chetana and the others had lived in Tella Meda for over twenty years for no rent, according to the law, the house was actually theirs and they could fight for it in court. Neither Kokila nor Kedarnath wanted that, so a deal was struck. Of the thirty apartments to be built on the plot of land where Tella Meda stood, one each would be given to Kokila and Chetana since they had lived in Tella Meda the longest and had the most right to the house.

When Kokila looked back and remembered the people who had come and gone, there were so many who hadn't had any impact on her; yet there were those who had broken her heart and there were those who had eased her sorrow.

This house, she thought, *has had an interesting life.* It had been named by a goddess and had embraced her presence within its walls for four decades. And she had been fortunate as well, Kokila knew, for she had lived with brave women such as Charvi, Chetana, Subhadra, Shanthi, and Renuka. She had watched the birth of the future, Meena, Bhanu, and Karthik, and the death of the past, Ramanandam and Narayan Garu.

Yes, Kokila decided, hers had been an interesting life too, and with her son poised to realize his dreams, she felt her life had been a fruitful one as well.

She walked through the garden, now unkempt since no one had bothered with it after the sale of the house had been announced. When she reached the metal gate and opened it, she felt a pinch in her heart.

This house, this home of hers, would be gone tomorrow.

Next year she would come back here, to live in an apartment that one could see the Bay of Bengal from, but she knew that it would never be the same again. There would be no coconut trees to make dolls with, there would be no courtyard to sit around, no big kitchen to cook in and bicker with the others about chores.

And maybe that was okay too. She sighed and closed the rickety gate as she stepped away from the house. Maybe it was okay that Tella Meda would go, as Charvi had gone. Maybe it was right as well because Tella Meda had been Charvi's regardless of who the legal owner of the house was.

At least one person was glad the house was being demolished, Kokila thought with a laugh as she walked away from Tella Meda toward Bhanu's house, where she was going to live with Chetana until the apartments were built. Chetana had clapped her hands when Kokila told her Tella Meda would be torn down. And Chetana thought it was ironic that after all her attempts at trying to get away, she would live the rest of her life in an apartment on the same land where the house with the white roof had stood.

It was dusk and the lilting notes of a cuckoo bird's song filtered through the air. Kokila looked back at Tella Meda one last time.

She stood and watched the house as the sun set into the shimmering waters of the bay, and when the house became just a silhouette, she turned around and walked away.

*Song of the
Cuckoo Bird*

AMULYA
MALLADI

A READER'S GUIDE

A Conversation with Amulya Malladi

Amulya's mother, Lakshmi Malladi, helped her write *Song of the Cuckoo Bird*. Not just by saying all the encouraging things mothers say, but by telling her the stories that found their way into this book. Amulya feels that this book is as much her mother's as it is hers.

Amulya Malladi: So, how did you think the book turned out? I took a lot of the stories you told me to write this book. I made them my own stories, but still . . . they started from your descriptions.

Lakshmi Malladi: You wrote the stories differently, but I felt that they were still real, still very down-to-earth, not contrived at all. I liked the book. I liked the characters very much, maybe because they seemed so real to me.

AM: A friend of mine, Jody Pryor, who always helps me with my books while they are being written, felt that the book was quite an experience for her. She thought everything was new and fresh. I think she might have even felt that parts of the book were unbelievable.

LM: No, no, I was not surprised by any of the stories of the characters. I have seen it all . . . nothing was unrealistic or unbelievable. But tell me, which character did you feel had the unhappiest life in the book? Let's see if we agree on that.

AM: I think that would be Charvi. She got pushed into a life she never really had a chance to reject and in the end she was all alone. She lived the life that others expected her to live. She was this *Guru*, this goddess and she never had a husband, a lover, children . . . she was lonely in the end.

LM: I agree that she was the saddest person in the book, but not for the same reason. I think that her life was the most painful because she was never sure if she was a goddess. She doubted herself all the time and probably lived with guilt that she was cheating all these people by taking their money. To not be sure of who you are, especially if you feel you are being dishonest . . . that is probably the hardest way to live. What do you think?

AM: I agree. I never thought about it that way, but you are right. That is a hard way to live. So, who did you think had the fullest life?

LM: That has to be Chetana. I don't like her as a character, she is self-centered, thankless . . . I just didn't like her. But she managed to have a full life. She got married, had children who did well, and she was the only one who did whatever she wanted. Her husband died and she wanted to have a boyfriend, so she went and got one. Her daughters took care of her in her old age. She was the luckiest of them all.

AM: I think Chetana was the happiest, and she is also my favorite character in the book. She is so spirited and she was a lot of fun to write. She is very selfish and yet, there is something redeemable about her because she is Kokila's friend and Kokila is the best person in that entire story. She is the one with the big heart and good soul, the one who wants to help others, save others.

LM: Yes, Kokila is the person with the big heart, but her life was so tragic. You know, all the others who lived at Tella Meda were people who had lost something before they came there. Kokila came there and lost her life. She lost her parents, yes, but it was after she came to Tella Meda that she lost the chance for having a life . . . you know, to be a wife and mother.

AM: But she got to become a mother; she adopted Karthik.

LM: Yes, yes, but it isn't the same thing. She had no man, no husband, and even the men she *had* been with . . . What good would even the sex have been with that old man, Ramanandam? Why did she go with him?

AM: I think she was in love with him. I think Kokila is the kind of woman who needs to be needed. She loved Ramanandam because he needed her, which is never a good basis for a relationship.

LM: And it was the same with the professor whose daughter committed suicide.

AM: Yes, Manjunath. He was also a sad man who needed someone to hold on to him, so she volunteered.

LM: Manjunath I can understand, he sounded like a good-looking man, but Ramanandam?

AM: Love is blind!

LM: What I can't understand is why Charvi didn't do something to stop the relationship. She seems very possessive about her father, so why didn't she?

AM: First, I think she did try, in her way. She spoke with her father and then she also spoke to Kokila, she—

LM: She didn't speak to Kokila about it; she just told her that she knew she was sleeping with Ramanandam.

AM: I think that was her way of trying. Charvi, I think, has a strong moral code and she feels she must not interfere in anyone's life. She would never forcefully try to make anyone do anything. But no one else in the *ashram* said anything either. Subhadra actually tells Kokila that she thinks it is a good thing that she is having a relationship with

Ramanandam and Kokila is furious. She has always thought of Subhadra as a mother but a mother would never be happy about her
daughter sleeping with a man twice her age, a man she could not
marry or have children with.

LM: Still, it is a shame that no one did anything to help Kokila. She
was just a child, what did she know? Do you think Ramanandam did
not encourage her to go with her husband because he liked her?

AM: No, I don't think he had designs on her from then. I hope not;
that would be even more disgusting. I think he truly believed that children needed to do what they wanted to do without interference from
elders.

LM: That girl needed some elders in her life, people who would have
told her that staying at Tella Meda was going to ruin her life.

AM: Okay, I have a specific question. Some women writers, especially
from South Asia, are accused of always portraying men in a bad light.
Were all the men in my book bad?

LM: No, no, not at all. You had Shankar, who was a very good man.
Narayan Garu who lives at Tella Meda, he is also a good man. But Ramanandam was not a good man, and that professor . . . Manjunath, he
was somewhere in between. And you also had women who were not
very nice. There are good people and bad people; it is not specific to
being a man or a woman. And then there was that American man,
Mark. Do you think he was interested in Charvi?

AM: No, I don't think so. I think he was interested, even fascinated
about this side of India, but he was not really interested in Charvi. He
had a crush on her, but that was about it.

LM: He seems not to believe in her, so why did he come to Tella
Meda?

AM: He came looking for something new, but he didn't come back. And he respected Charvi, I think. He thought she was a smart single woman making the best of the hand she was dealt.

LM: When Mark asks her why she takes money and gifts from people, Charvi says that if they want to give something, who is she to say no. Which is really nonsense! Still, it must not have been easy for Charvi to accept that money and those gifts when she was in doubt of her godliness.

AM: But don't you think she felt she deserved the money and the attention because she was making so many sacrifices by being a goddess?

LM: I don't like Charvi much. But then again I have to like her as well because she helped so many people by giving them a roof over their heads.

AM: I agree. Tella Meda is part *ashram*, part women's shelter, part orphanage, and part home for the elderly.

LM: But she also never helped anyone get out of there. She never encouraged Kokila or Chetana to have better lives, to leave Tella Meda and become productive members of society. And they didn't make much of an effort either.

AM: People get used to something and then they are afraid of making changes. Chetana and Kokila were used to living in Tella Meda and they were afraid of going out and facing the real world.

LM: It is like a goat that is tied up; it gets used to eating the grass around it and does not want to wander away from the pasture where it is tied up. Who knows what is there beyond the pasture? Here it gets food and it is safe, god only knows what the goat will find outside. I feel that is why they stay.

AM: That is a fine way of putting it.

LM: And also, they are a family at Tella Meda. They are not related by blood but there is a sister figure, there are sort of children, a father figure, a surrogate mother . . . all in all, with all these broken pieces, these broken people, they get together and become a family in Tella Meda. And there is security with family!

AM: Yes, there is. They fought over things and didn't get along all the time, but all through they remain a family.

LM: What was your favorite part of the book?

AM: Several things, but my favorite chapter was the one where Tella Meda gets a television. I had to send a lot of e-mails to Daddy to find out how much televisions cost in 1984, how many televisions a small company would make . . . it was a good chapter to write. I had fun writing it.

LM: I like the last pages the best. After Charvi dies, you write about how Kokila looks at the house and feels that after having tried for so many years to leave Tella Meda she and Chetana would live in apartments built over the same land. I thought it was very fitting. It was a good ending.

AM: The ending used to be different. I wrote the Prologue and Epilogue from the point of view of the house first, but my smart editor, Allison Dickens, told me that it took away from the book, and she was right. But it means a lot to me that you liked the book. So . . . do you think it'll be a bestseller?

LM: Of course, the book is very good; I liked it very much, but . . .

AM: Did you like the book because I wrote it or would you have liked it off the rack at a bookstore?

LM: I think I would always like this book because it is so real to me. And that is why I worry, that maybe people who read it will say, "Oh that doesn't sound real." These situations are real; I have seen things like this happen all my life, and I don't want people to think that this is completely made up. These things happen, have happened several times, will continue to happen . . .

AM: I think with this interview we will convince them that the book is as close to reality as it can get without being nonfiction.

LM: I hope so.

AM: Thanks, Mama.

LM: I hope I asked all the right questions. If I didn't, just change it to something better, okay?

AM: I don't think I will need to. (And I didn't!)

1. Perhaps the most pivotal moment of this novel occurs at the beginning when Kokila decides to leave her marriage and stay at Tella Meda. Did you agree with her decision? Would you have made the same choice at her age in her situation? Would you make the same choice knowing how her life turned out?

2. Do you think Kokila was satisfied with her life and, at the end of the novel, felt she had lived a productive and worthwhile life? Do you feel she lived a productive and worthwhile life?

3. In *Song of the Cuckoo Bird,* the women of Tella Meda frequently discuss their need for a husband and children, and the placement those things will guarantee them in society. How important is marriage and having a family to a woman's identity today where you live? How much is it a part of your own identity?

4. Which of the women at Tella Meda did you identify with the most closely? Did you have trouble connecting to any of the women and if so, why do you think you found her difficult to understand?

5. Both in the novel and in the conversation between Amulya Malladi and her mother in this reader's guide, there is much discussion of whether Charvi is a good person, particularly in terms of her acceptance of money. Did you feel she was a good person? What inconsistencies of character did you spot in Charvi? Can a person be both good and bad?

6. Are there any purely good or purely evil characters in *Song of the Cuckoo Bird*?

7. How did you feel the men in the novel were portrayed? Fairly or unfairly? Realistically or unrealistically?

8. Did you find the news headlines at the start of each chapter helpful or were they unimportant to your understanding of the characters and setting?

9. Would Tella Meda be a good place to grow up, whether it was located in your hometown or in India, or during different time periods?

10. What do you think happened to Vidura?

PHOTO: © SOREN RASMUSSEN

Amulya Malladi lives in Copenhagen in Denmark
with her husband and two sons. You can contact her at
www.amulyamalladi.com.

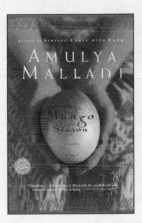
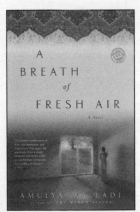
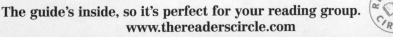